HALO®

GLASSLANDS

DON'T MISS THESE OTHER THRILLING STORIES IN THE WORLDS OF

HALO

GLASSLANDS

BOOK ONE OF THE KILO-FIVE TRILOGY

KAREN TRAVISS

BASED ON THE BESTSELLING VIDEO GAME FOR XBOX®

GALLERY BOOKS

New York | London | Toronto | Sydney | New Delhi

G

Gallery Books
An Imprint of Simon & Schuster, Inc.
1230 Avenue of the Americas
New York, NY 10020

This Gallery Books trade paperback edition April 2019

GALLERY BOOKS and colophon are registered trademarks of Simon & Schuster, Inc.

The Simon & Schuster Speakers Bureau can bring authors to your live event. For more information or to book an event contact the Simon & Schuster Speakers Bureau at 1-866-248-3049 or visit our website at www.simonspeakers.com.

Manufactured in the United States of America

10   9

Library of Congress Cataloging-in-Publication Data is available.

ISBN 978-1-9821-1183-0
ISBN 978-1-9821-1184-7 (ebook)

For my mother, who never found out how it ended

GLASSLANDS

PROLOGUE

November 2552, location undefined.
Last verified realspace location:
the core of the planet Onyx.

It's a beautiful sunny day. The oak branches are swaying gently in the breeze and the air's scented with unseen blossom.

And we're trapped.

Did you ever run and hide as a kid? Ever slam the closet door behind you, giggling because you were sure you'd never be found, and then realize you'd locked yourself in? Did you panic or breathe a sigh of relief? I suppose it all depends on what you were hiding *from*.

We're hiding from the end of the world.

For all we know, it's already happened. If there's anyone left out there, they don't even know we're here. We may be the last sentient life left in the galaxy—me, Chief Mendez, and a detachment of Spartans. Correction: three of my Spartans—Fred, Kelly, and Linda—and five others who are something else entirely, five I didn't even know existed until this week, and if there's one thing I can't stand, it's *not knowing.*

You'll explain yourself to me, Chief. I've got all the time in the world now. I've got more time than I know what to do with.

Mendez takes something out of his pants pocket and gazes wistfully at it like a pilgrim with a holy relic before putting it back.

"You can read Forerunner, Dr. Halsey," he says, impassive. We're still ignoring the elephant looming over us at the moment, neither of us saying what's really on our minds. He has his secrets, and I have mine. "Do you know the symbol for *pantry?* That would be handy right about now."

He's staring up at a sun that can't possibly be there, set in an artificial sky that runs from summer blue at one horizon to starless midnight at the other. We're not on Onyx any longer—not in this dimension, anyway.

"Chief, this is the most advanced doomsday bunker ever built." I'm not sure who I'm trying to reassure, him or me. "A civilization sufficiently advanced to build a bomb shelter the size of Earth's orbit wouldn't forget to address the food supply. Would they?"

It's a permanently lovely day inside this Dyson sphere, and beyond its walls is . . . actually, I don't know any longer. It *was* Onyx. Now it's somewhere in slipspace. Every time I think I have the measure of the Forerunners' technology, something else pops up and confounds me. They must have shared our sense of beauty or bequeathed us theirs, because they made this environment idyllically rural; trees, grass, rivers, almost landscaped perfection.

Mendez pats his pocket as if checking something is still in

there. "Better hope they evolved beyond the usual procurement charlie-foxtrot too, then. Or we'll have to live off the land."

"We've got unlimited water, Chief. That's something."

Mendez has known me a damned long time. Over the years he's perfected that hoary old CPO's carefully blank expression that looks almost like deference. *Almost.* It's actually disgust. I know that now. I can see it.

But you're in no position to lecture me on ethics, are you, Chief? I know what you've done. The proof's right in front of me here. I'm looking at them.

Mendez walks away in the direction of the two recon teams waiting under the oak trees. The Spartans—my protégés and Ackerson's little project, these Spartan-IIIs—look impatient to get on with something useful. They don't handle idleness well. We made warfare the sole focus of their lives.

Now we don't know if there's still a war outside to fight, or even a galaxy left to fight it in.

But that's fine by me. My Spartans are safe here. That's all that matters. Safe if the Halo Array fires, anyway. I don't know if this is the haven it appears. Perhaps it's already got tenants. We'll find out the Navy way, Mendez says.

"Okay, Spartans, the camp's secured, so let's shake out and see what's in the neighborhood." Mendez unslings his rifle and looks at Fred. "Conserve rations until we know if there's anything on the menu here. Right, sir?"

"Right, Chief. Radio check, people." Fred, Spartan-104, has been made a lieutenant at the ripe old age of forty-one. "Priorities, in this order—secure the area, locate a food supply, and find a way to revive Team Katana and the others."

How many Spartan-IIIs did Ackerson create? Five are already in suspension here, with three other men we can't identify, but we have no idea yet how to open their Forerunner slipspace pods. They'll have an interesting story to tell when we do.

Fred gestures to take in the terrain. "Treat this as an acquaint. Spartan-Twos familiarize themselves with Spartan-Threes so that when we get out of here, we're ready to fight effectively. Kelly, Dr. Halsey, Tom, Olivia—you're with Chief Mendez. Linda, Lucy, Mark, Ash—with me. Move out."

Just as Fred turns to walk away, I catch his eye. He was never much good at burying his feelings, but he can't hide them from me anyway. I know all my Spartans better than their mothers ever did. He shuts his eyes tightly as if he's blocking out an unbearable world, just a fraction of a second, and then it's gone. We've buried our dead here. Two of those Spartan-IIIs, just into their teens, just *children* . . . and Kurt never made it into the sphere.

I thought you were dead already, Kurt. Now I've lost you twice.

Fred pats Lucy on the shoulder. "You okay, Spartan?"

She gives him a distracted nod. She's a disturbing little scrap of a thing, too traumatized to speak. Mendez trained these kids. He *knew*. He knew what Ackerson was doing with my research. He was part of this all along.

And I won't forget that, Chief.

Kelly slows and drops back to walk beside me. I'm not twenty-one anymore and I certainly don't have the stride of a two-meter Spartan, or even these . . . new ones. My God, they're *too small*. How can they be Spartans?

"You've fallen on your feet again, Dr. Halsey," Kelly says. "Some rabbit hole. Did you know it was here?"

"I should stop trying to look as if I know everything, shouldn't I?"

"You think we're going to lose this war. I know we're not."

"I extrapolate from known facts. But I don't mind being wrong sometimes."

How far would I go to save my Spartans? *This* far. I lured them to Onyx, the safest location I could think of, because I knew they'd never abandon their posts any other way. I lied to them to save them.

And they're all that stands between me and damnation. I've done terrible things—monstrous things, criminal things—that were necessary, but I did it *to them*. Kidnapped them as children. Experimented on them. Altered them terribly. Killed half of them. Made them into soldiers with no life outside the UNSC.

It had to be done, but now I have to do *this*.

There's no god waiting to judge us when we die. This is our heaven or hell, the here and now, the pain or the fond memories we leave behind with the living. But I don't want the forgiveness of society, or Mendez, or even to forgive myself.

I just want to do what's right for these men and women, whose lives I *used*. Theirs is the only forgiveness that can absolve me.

Kelly—tall, confident, nothing like the victim I feel I've made her—points into the distance. I'm starting to forget we're trapped in a sphere in the folds of another dimension, because my brain's getting used to telling me benign lies. I stare across a sea of trees at two elegant honey-gold structures protruding above the canopy some kilometers away.

"That's impressive, Doctor," she says. "Hey, Chief, what do you think they are?"

"Better be the chow hall." Mendez keeps scanning the trees as if he's still expecting to run into trouble. "Or a way out of here. Don't forget there'll still be a hell of a mess to clear up when we get out."

He's right. Won or lost, wars never end cleanly. I think we've lost already. If the Covenant doesn't overrun the galaxy then this life-form they call the Flood will, or the Halo Array will fire and wipe out all sentient life. But if we win—

Even if we win, the galaxy will still be a dangerous, desperate place.

I wonder where John is now. And Cortana. And . . . Miranda.

See, Miranda? I didn't forget you. Did I?

CHAPTER 1

A GOD WHO CREATES TOOLS IS STILL A GOD. IT IS NOT
FOR US TO IMPOSE QUALIFICATIONS UPON THE DIVINE OR
PRESUME TO GUESS ITS INTENTIONS.

(Former field master Avu Med 'Telcam of the Sangheili
Neru Pe 'Odosima—Servants of the Abiding Truth—
on revelations about the nature of the Forerunners)

Former colony of New Llanelli,
Brunel system: January 2553.

It was an ugly bastard, and the temptation to kill it where it
stood was almost more than Serin Osman could handle.

It was also pretty upset. Its arms flailed as if it was on
some passionate Sangheili rant about politics or religion or whatever they played instead of football, its cloverleaf jaws snapping
open and shut like a demented gin-trap. Osman watched from the
shuttle cargo bay with her rifle resting on the control panel. Matters could get out of hand with a two-and-a-half-meter alien before

you knew it. She was ready to drop the thing before it crushed Phillips.

He could actually speak their language, even if some of the sounds defied simple human jaws. She wondered what he sounded like to them. He was making mirroring gestures back at the Sangheili, and although she couldn't hear the conversation it seemed to be working. The alien did that odd trick with its split mandibles, pressing the two sides together to mimic a human jaw and trying to force out more articulate sounds.

So the hinge-head was mirroring too. It was a good sign. *A good sign in a bad deal.* No, not a bad deal: a dirty one. Osman stepped down from the bay, careful to keep her rifle close to her leg so she looked prepared but not threatening. Phillips glanced over his shoulder at her, seeming oblivious of the risk.

I'd never take my eyes off that thing. God, what do they teach these academics about personal safety?

She leaned against the hatch frame and waited, glancing at her watch to check Sydney time. Around her, the ruins of New Llanelli felt like a rebuke. The dead tapped her on the shoulder, appalled: *And you're talking to these bastards now? On our graves?*

A shaft of sunlight struck through a break in the clouds and threw up a bright reflection from a lake in the distance. *No . . . that's not a lake.* Her brain had joined up the dots and made the wrong assumption. She eased her datapad out of her jacket pocket one-handed and checked. There was no body of water for a hundred kilometers on the map in the CAA Factbook. The reflective surface was vitrified sandy soil, mirror-smooth, square hectares of it where there had once been rye and potatoes.

When the Covenant glassed a planet, they really did just that.

Phillips gestured to get her attention and distracted her from the uncomfortable thought that the planet was making a point to her. He walked over to the shuttle, looking pleased with himself.

"The Bishop wants a word," he said. "I told him you were the boss woman. His English is pretty good, so play it straight. And don't call him an Elite. Use the proper name. It matters to them."

Osman pushed herself away from the bulkhead with her hip. "What, like *bishop*?"

"Ignore that." Phillips—Professor Evan Phillips, another respectable academic who'd been sucked down into ONI's drain—put on his serious face again. "They told me he was devout, but I didn't realize *how* devout."

"Is that going to be a problem?"

"Might be a bonus."

"Yes, they do tend to stick to a plan."

"I meant that he's a fundamentalist. The Abiding Truth. Very, *very* old tradition of faith."

"Prompt me. I'm not an anthropologist."

"They're said to have squirreled away original Forerunner relics from the time of their first contact. Their equivalent of saints' fingers."

"It must be my birthday." Osman wasn't sure when that really was. Today seemed as good a day as any. "Maybe they've got some schematics in a dusty drawer or something."

"Come on, don't keep him waiting."

"How is he with women? I don't think I've ever seen a female Sangheili. Do they keep them in purdah or something?"

"It's not that simple." Phillips beckoned to her to follow. "The ladies wield a hell of a lot of political power in the bloodline stakes. When you've got a few hours to kill, I'll explain it."

She didn't, and it could wait. She walked up to the Sangheili, steeling herself not to call him an Elite or a murdering hinge-head bastard.

Osman was taller than the average man, and at one-ninety she wasn't used to having to look up at anybody. But the Bishop towered half a meter above her like a monument in gold armor. For a moment she found herself looking into a disturbingly featureless face before she settled on the black eyes and small, flaring nostrils just below them. The Bishop was sniffing her scent. Unsettling didn't even begin to cover it.

"Captain Osman," Phillips said cautiously, looking back and forth between her and the Sangheili. "Let me introduce you to Avu Med 'Telcam, speaker for the Servants of Abiding Truth. He used to be a field master but he's . . . renounced the ways of the infidels and cleansed his name, because they've brought shame and misery on the Sangheili . . . and they deserve to hang from spikes." He seemed to be quoting very carefully, glancing at the Sangheili as if for confirmation. He gave her a don't-say-anything-daft look. "He means the Arbiter."

'Telcam sniffed again. Osman could smell him too. It was a faintly leathery scent, like the seats of a new car. It wasn't unpleasant.

"I'm Captain Osman. I'm a shipmaster." 'Telcam would get the point. "So I keep my word. May we talk?" She gave Phillips her get-lost look. This wasn't for his ears, and that was as much for his own good as Earth's. "Can you give us ten minutes, Professor?"

Phillips nodded and turned to walk away. This was why Osman didn't like using co-opted specialists. If he'd known what she was about to do, he would probably have gone all ethical on her.

I might be underestimating him, of course. But his job's done. It's not his problem now.

'Telcam tilted his head to one side. Osman had to strain to make out the words, but it was no harder than concentrating on a bad radio signal. The creature really could speak pretty good English.

"Shipmaster, my people have been punished because they had no *faith*," he said. A fine mist of saliva cooled on her face every time he hit a sibilant or an *F*. It didn't look easy to articulate those four-way jaws. "The traitor Thel 'Vadam and his ilk now say the gods are deceivers, and so they shall die. We have been in thrall to mongrel races long enough. We have let the false prophets of the San'Shyuum corrupt our pure connection to the divine. Now we shall do our penance and bring the Sangheili back to the true path. So what can you possibly want with us? Do you want to agree to a truce?"

"How were you planning on killing 'Vadam and the other . . . traitors?"

"We have few ships left now. Few weapons too. But we have our devotion. We will find a way."

Osman noted the energy sword on his belt. *We've got a right one here. A god-bothering, heavily armed maniac. Lovely. I can do business with that.* She tried to find genuine common ground in case he could smell fear or deceit on her. A small dash of truth in a soup of lies worked wonders.

"What if *we* supplied you with some weapons?"

He jerked his head back. "And why would you do that? The traitor sides with humans against his own."

"Humans gamble. I'm betting that your side will win. Dead friends aren't much use."

"Ah." 'Telcam made a little sound like a horse puffing through its lips. A fine spray rained on her again and she tried not to recoil. She picked up a whiff of something far too much like dog food. "*Kingmaker.* This is your policy. You help us take control so that you know your enemy and think you can then control *us.*"

"Look, we're never going to be friends, Field Master. But we can agree to stay out of one another's way and lead separate existences. Too many lives have been lost. It has to stop."

'Telcam leaned closer again as if he was doing a uniform inspection. "You have colonies here. This is part of the war. This is the cause of our enmity."

"Some of our colonies don't like us very much either. Humans kill humans too."

"How tangled your lives are."

"My, you *do* speak good English."

"I was a translator once. I interpreted your communications for my old shipmaster. I speak several human languages."

Well, that explained a hell of a lot. Phillips obviously didn't know, or at least he hadn't said, but Osman decided to cut him some slack because he'd only been tasked to do one thing: to get her an audience with dissident Sangheili who were likely to disrupt any peace deals. He was lucky to get that far without having his head ripped off.

"Well, Field Master, I think we can help one another keep our troublesome factions in line." Osman turned slightly to keep Phillips in her peripheral vision, just in case he wandered back and heard too much. "It might require some discretion, because we can't be seen to ally with you. But an unstable Sangheili empire doesn't help us, and an unstable human one is a threat to you. Yes?"

"And some of my brethren might not understand my willingness to talk to infidels. So we do favors, you and I."

"Indeed. For the greater good." Osman paused a beat and made sure she didn't blink. Sangheili had a military sense of honor, and the truth she was about to drop into the deceit went some way toward satisfying her own. "If I thought 'Vadam would survive as leader, I would be doing deals with him instead."

She wasn't sure if Sangheili ever smiled. If they did, she had no idea what it looked like, not with that four-way jaw. But 'Telcam's expression shifted a little. The muscles in his dog-reptile face relaxed for a moment.

"I have a condition," he said.

"I thought you might."

"You blaspheme about the gods. You spread vile lies about them. This must stop."

"We just showed you what the Halo was." *Oh shit. Come on, think. There's a way through this.* "We didn't set out to insult your beliefs."

"So the Halos are machines of destruction. So you say the gods themselves were killed by them." 'Telcam leaned over her, almost nose to nose. He was so close that she couldn't focus on those dog-like teeth. They were just cream blurs in a purplish haze of gum. "*Your* god chose to die for you and that is precisely why you revere him, yes? And why you say he also *lives.* This so-called proof about the Halos means nothing. Not even to *you.*"

And he uses the plural. Halos.

Osman suspected that he wanted her to agree with him, to reassure him that gods could be both dead and eternal at the same time like some divine Schrödinger's cat, to put some certainty back in his life. She knew that feeling. But the last thing she wanted was a theological argument with a heavily armed alien four or five times her weight. She bit back a comment that her name was Osman and that he was thinking of someone else's religion.

"We've had scientists who claim they've disproved the existence of God, and others who argue you can't prove anything," she said carefully. "But it hasn't made any difference to any of our religions. Faith is quite separate."

"Then you understand." 'Telcam drew back. "If you arm us . . .

if you stay away from our worlds . . . then when we take power and restore the rightful ways, we will leave you alone."

"Deal," she said. She almost held out her hand to shake on the agreement but thought better of it. "I'll be in touch very soon."

The Sangheili just turned and loped away to his ship without another word. It was too easy to look at them and see only an ungainly animal with strangely bovine legs, and not a superior force that had almost brought Earth to its knees. Phillips walked up to her but didn't ask what had happened. His expression said he was bursting to find out.

"Are we done?"

Osman nodded. "That's one enemy we don't have to fight for a while." She gave him a thumbs-up. "Well done. I never thought we'd get one of them to talk to us, let alone reach an agreement. We owe you."

"I admit it's satisfying to be able to put the theory into practice. And wonderful to have unique access to Sangheili space with all expenses paid, of course. Good old ONI. My taxes, well spent."

Osman headed back to the shuttle, suddenly aware of small fragments of glass crunching under her boots. *Damn, that's not broken bottles. It's vitrification.* "You don't feel your academic cred's been stained by mixing with us grubby little spooks, then."

"God, no. I'm not that naive. I know what you're up to. Just don't tell me, that's all. I have to be able to deny it with a straight face."

So he certainly wasn't stupid, and ONI wasn't doing anything that countless governments hadn't done over the centuries to look after their interests. She should have expected him to work it out. "And we're doing what, exactly?"

"Oh, I thought I was helping you establish diplomatic channels with the hard-to-reach Sangheili demographic. . . ."

"You told me not to tell you."

"Yes, so I did." He winked at her. "Well, you've slapped a saddle on that tiger. Now you better make damn sure you don't fall off."

They settled into their seats and she ran the preflight checks before handing over to the AI. Phillips was whistling tunelessly under his breath, as if he was glad to be leaving. Osman had expected him to be reluctant to go home but he obviously had what he wanted—some dazzling scientific paper, some award-worthy research, maybe even a lucrative book—that nobody else in his field had, and that seemed to be enough.

He wouldn't be coming back here. He probably realized that. ONI regarded him as a single-use sharp.

"Just remember that my enemy's enemy isn't my friend, Professor," she said, opening a secure comms channel. "He's my enemy who's just taking a sidebar."

Phillips burst out laughing. "You sweet, innocent little flower. You've never worked in academia, have you? Red in tooth and claw. Feuds, plots, vengeance. The works."

"I can imagine." The secure channel indicator flashed and Osman lowered her voice. "Osman here, ma'am. Professor Phillips and I are on our way back."

"Thank you for letting me know, Captain." Admiral Margaret Parangosky, head of the Office of Naval Intelligence, never raised her voice and never needed to. "I assume things went well."

Osman could translate Parangosky-isms easily enough. *Have you set up the Sangheili insurrection?* That was what she meant. Few outside the Navy and the senior ranks of government knew who Parangosky was, let alone knew to fear her. Osman suspected she was the only person in the Admiral's circle who would always be forgiven even if she failed. But she wasn't in a hurry to test it.

"Everything's fine, ma'am," she said.

"Thank Professor Phillips for me. Safe flight."

Osman signed off and the AI took over. The shuttle shuddered on its dampers as its engines reached peak power. In a few hours, they'd rendezvous with *Battle of Minden* and head back to Earth, where the mission would be over for Phillips but only just beginning for her.

So far, so good.

"Do I get a gold star?" he asked.

"Maybe an extra cookie."

"Where's the best Turkish restaurant in Sydney?"

"I don't know."

"Oh. Really? Sorry."

It always caught her short. She'd never actually *said* she had Turkish roots, and—odd, for a woman so used to lying for a living—she couldn't bring herself to construct a cover story for herself. She simply allowed everyone to make assumptions based on her name and her Mediterranean coloring. Her real name hadn't been Osman, not as far as she knew, and she had no plans to use her access to ONI classified files to find out who she really was. She could only be who she was now.

Phillips would have treated her very differently if she'd had *Spartan-019* on her ID badge. It was better if nobody knew what she was, and what she was *not*.

"Yes, I've been away too long," she said, relenting. "But I can smell a good *imam bayildi* ten klicks away."

Anyone could. It wasn't really a lie. Phillips rubbed his hands together, miming delight at the thought of food that didn't come out of a ration pack. The shuttle lifted clear of New Llanelli, and Osman caught one last glimpse on the monitor of that lake of vitrified sand.

That's why I'm entitled to break the rules. To make sure it never happens again.

Osman was sure she'd heard that argument before, more than thirty years ago, but she couldn't remember if it was before or after she met Dr. Catherine Halsey.

"Academia," she said. "Yes, it's a savage old world, isn't it?"

**Mark Donaldson Way, Sydney, Australia:
Australia Day, two months after the
Battle of Earth, January 26, 2553.**

There was just one flagpole left intact on the shattered Sydney Harbour waterfront, and a workman in a hard hat and orange overalls was clambering up a maintenance gantry to reach it.

It was a damn long way to fall.

Corporal Vaz Beloi wandered out onto a stump of a girder that had once been part of a pedestrian overpass, trying to get a better view. A piece of dark blue fabric dangled from the workman's back pocket. Vaz couldn't see a safety harness, but then there wasn't much left of the crumbling building to secure it to.

And they say ODSTs are crazy.

He watched the man with renewed curiosity. Mal Geffen caught up with him and leaned on what was left of the overpass safety rail. It creaked as he put his weight on it.

"Come on, we've only got an hour." Mal gestured irritably with his wrist, brandishing his watch, then frowned at something on his sleeve. "Sod it, I'm covered in crap already. We can't rock up in our number threes looking like this. It's the *Admiral*."

"It'll brush off," Vaz said, distracted by the reckless workman again. He held up a warning finger. "Wait. I have to see what this guy does."

He knew Mal wasn't being disrespectful. He was just nervous about being summoned to ONI without explanation, and Vaz understood that, but they had another mission to complete. A visit to Sydney was rare.

And we made a promise. Admiral or no Admiral.

A small crowd watched from the shore, a mix of construction workers, firefighters, and sappers who were still digging bodies out of the rubble two months after the bombing. The workman, now teetering on the end of the gantry, lunged at the flagpole and managed to haul in the halyard. He clipped the flag to it and wobbled for a moment before tugging on the line to reveal the white stars of the Southern Cross on a deep blue ground, with a single gold Commonwealth star on green ground in the canton.

Everyone cheered. A fleet tender in the harbor sounded its klaxon.

Mal seemed to be working something out, lips moving as if he was counting. "Well done, Oz. Seven hundred and sixty-five not out." He nudged Vaz in the back and strode off. "Come on, we've got to find the bar. If we don't do it now, we won't get another chance for years."

Vaz watched the workman edge back down the gantry to relative safety before he felt able to turn away and catch up with Mal.

"Okay, why seven hundred and sixty-five?" he asked.

"Seven hundred and sixty-five years since the first migrants landed here. It's Australia Day." They walked across a temporary walkway that spanned a crater the full width of the road. It vibrated under their boots like a sprung floor. "You understand *not out,* don't you? Don't make me explain cricket to you again."

"I understand cricket just fine." Vaz bristled. "What's your problem?"

"Sorry, mate. Parangoskyitis."

Both of them had done more than a hundred drops behind enemy lines and accepted they might not survive the next one, but the prospect of being hauled before a very elderly woman with a stoop and a lot of gold braid had kept them awake every night for the past week. Even ODSTs were wary of Margaret Parangosky.

"She's over ninety," Vaz said. "None of those stories about her can be true. She just spreads them for effect. Like my grandmother used to."

"Look, we said we wouldn't play guessing games about this. We'll know soon enough."

"You started it."

"Well, she's not invited us for tea and medals, has she? It'll be a bollocking."

"You want ODSTs to do a job for you, you ask for a fire team. Or a company. A battalion, even."

"You know how paranoid ONI is. Top-secret-eat-before-reading." Mal picked more specks off his sleeve, frowning. "Ah, come on. It's just a bloody meeting. It's not like we're storming a beachhead."

But why us? Vaz checked the tourist map again. "This thing's useless. I can't see any landmarks."

Mal fumbled in his pocket and took out the ancient button compass that he always carried. "Fieldcraft, Vaz. Back to basics. If we can't find a bar, we're not worthy of the uniform."

There wasn't a living soul in sight, not even a cop or a construction worker to ask for directions. The hum of activity— bulldozers, trip hammers, drills—was receding a street at a time. The bank that should have been standing on the next corner was a tangle of metal joists and collapsed masonry.

There was no sign of the plaza full of pavement cafés, either, and the shopping center that was supposed to be on Vaz's left looked like a slab of honeycomb with the wax layer ripped off. All he could see was a procession of composite block walls, now just a few courses high. Red-and-white cordon tape fluttered between steel poles. The smell of raw sewage hit him.

"You lads look lost."

A civil defense warden popped up like a range target behind a barrier fifty meters away, and Vaz almost reached for a rifle he wasn't carrying. It was hard adjusting to a place where there were no threats.

"Yeah, I think we are," Vaz said.

"You trying to find Bravo-Six?" The warden meant the UNSC headquarters. "Wrong direction, son."

"No, a bar," Mal said. "The Parthenon."

"It's gone." The warden glanced at his watch as if he thought it was a bit early for a drink, then studied Mal's uniform, peering at the death's-head insignia with a baffled frown. Maybe the Corps had taken the low-profile special forces thing a bit too far. "What are you, then, marines?"

"ODSTs." Mal paused. The guy didn't seem to be catching on. "Orbital Drop Shock Troopers. Yeah, marines."

"Oh. Them."

"So how do we get to the Parthenon Bar?" Vaz asked.

"I told you. It's just rubble now. They're clearing the site."

"We don't want a drink. We've got something else we need to do."

The warden gave Vaz a sideways look. Maybe the man thought his English wasn't so hot because of his heavy accent. "Just keep going that way," he said, indicating forty-five degrees and slowing his speech down a bit for the hard of understanding. "You'll see the bus station. It's two streets north of there."

Vaz was starting to sweat as he walked away. It was midsummer and his formal uniform was frying him, not that he had the option of showing up in shirtsleeves. Mal somehow still looked pristine despite the concrete dust on his elbows and boots.

"What are we going to use for a drink?" Mal asked.

"I don't know. Maybe we just say what we have to say and leave it at that."

They'd promised Emanuel that if they ever passed through Sydney, something Vaz had thought highly unlikely, then they'd find the man's favorite bar and raise a toast to his memory. It had been a very matter-of-fact conversation. ODSTs didn't think of getting killed as an *if*. It was more like a *when*.

Doesn't make it any easier though. Doesn't mean we miss him any the less.

"Ah," said Mal. As soon as they turned the corner and looked up the road, they could see the bulldozers at work. "Ripe for development."

Some of the clearance crew stopped to watch them walking along the center line of the road. Vaz counted the stumps of internal walls and decided that 21 Strathclyde Street had stood where there was now a ragged crater fringed by the remains of four bright turquoise Doric columns. Mal looked them over, uncharacteristically grim.

"Manny never did have much taste in bars," he said quietly. "Poor bugger."

One of the construction workers took off his hide gloves and picked his way over the rubble toward them, head down and eyes shielded by the peak of his hard hat. It was only when "he" looked up that Vaz realized it was actually a woman, a nice-looking redhead. Vaz sometimes tried to imagine how alien he must have looked to a civilian these days, but he could guess from the slight frowns he'd been getting this morning that he didn't come across as the nice friendly boy next door. He decided to let Mal do the talking and stood back to look down into the crater. A pool of stagnant water lay at the bottom like a mirror, busy with mosquitoes.

"What can we do for you, mate?" the redhead asked.

Mal pointed at the complete absence of a bar. "Was that the Parthenon?"

"Yeah. Better stay clear of the edge. You can see it's not Happy Hour."

"We've got a promise to keep to a mate who didn't make it back."

The redhead cocked her head on one side. "We're supposed to keep people out of this road. Safety regs. You know what the council's like. But what they don't know won't hurt 'em."

Vaz pitched in. They had half an hour to do this and then make themselves presentable to report to Bravo-6. "We just want to raise a glass to him, ma'am. Then we'll go."

The redhead stood with her hands on her hips, inspecting Vaz. "Did you bring a bottle?"

It was a good question. They'd expected the bar to be open, not demolished, and they'd run out of time to find a *bottle shop,* as the locals called it. Mal shrugged, doing his I'm-just-a-lovable-rogue look that usually worked on women. The redhead gave him a sad smile and turned to her crew with her hand held out like she was asking for a tool. One of the men picked up a lunchbox from the seat of a dump truck and tossed her a plastic bottle. She handed it over to Mal with due reverence.

"Best we can do, Marine," she said. "Go ahead, but don't fall in and break your neck."

After some of the jumps Vaz had done, that would have been an embarrassing way to go. Mal read the label and smiled.

"Fruit juice. He'd see the funny side of that. Thanks, sweetheart."

The clearance crew moved back a little but they were still watching. Vaz squirmed. It felt like taking a leak in public. So what did they do now? All the vague plans to get hammered and reminisce about Emanuel had gone out the window, and Parangosky would be waiting.

Mal unscrewed the cap and handed it to Vaz. He took a swig—passion fruit or something, warm and fizzy—and handed it back. Mal took a pull and held up the bottle like a glass of vintage champagne.

"Emanuel Barakat," he said. "Helljumper. Brother. One of the best. We miss you, Manny."

Vaz forgot the audience of hard hats. All he could see was the water trickling from a broken main into the pool at the bottom of the crater. "Yeah, Manny. Rest in peace."

Mal handed the bottle back to the redhead. "Thanks again. We'll get out of your hair now."

"No worries. I'm sorry about your mate." She paused. "Is it all over, then? Is the war really over?"

"I don't know." Mal turned and started to walk away, Vaz following. "But it's pretty quiet out there for the first time I can remember."

They were a few paces down the road before the clapping started. It was the strangest thing. Vaz turned around, and there they were, a dozen men and women in high-viz tabards and rigger's boots, just clapping and looking at them. And it wasn't a general reaction to Mal's comment on the war either. The workers were applauding *them*.

Nobody said a word. Vaz couldn't have managed one even if he'd known what to say. They'd reached the end of the road before Mal spoke.

"That was decent of them."

Vaz wasn't sure if he meant the fruit juice or the applause. But maybe the war *was* finally over. Everywhere they'd stopped off in the last few days, at every shop and transit point, the atmosphere was a strange blend of dread, bewilderment, and elation. Civvies were still getting used to the idea. He'd expected it to be like the newsreels from the end of the Great Patriotic War, with people dancing in the streets and climbing lampposts to hoist flags, but that war had only lasted six years, however bloody the battles. People in 1945—and 2090, 2103, and 2162—could recall what peace felt like and knew what they'd missed.

But now there were two generations that couldn't remember a time when Earth wasn't at war with the Covenant. Nobody had signed any surrender or cease-fire yet though. Vaz wasn't taking anything for granted.

Mal quickened his pace and Vaz matched it, deciding not to tell him he had a splash of mud drying on his pants leg. He'd sort it out later. They headed back to the nearest intact main road to hail a cab. Even in a city smashed to rubble, there was still a decent living to be made from ferrying UNSC personnel around, and one of the few places that remained untouched by the attack was the massive underground complex of Bravo-6. The driver who picked them up just glanced at them in the rearview mirror and said nothing for a while. When he caught Vaz's eye, he looked away.

"Were you here when the Covenant attacked?" Vaz asked, trying to be sociable.

"Yeah." The driver nodded. "Hid in the sewers. Didn't even know where I was when I came out." He licked his lips. "Is it all over, like the news keeps saying? I mean, you'd know better than anybody, wouldn't you?"

"I don't know," Vaz said. "But the Covenant looks like it's fallen apart. Maybe that's the same thing."

It wasn't, and he knew it. It just meant the certainties of Us and Them would be replaced by a ragbag of trouble from unpredictable quarters, just as it always had on Earth. Aliens were a lot more like humans than anyone liked to admit.

But, like humans, they could all be dropped with the right ordnance too. That wasn't going to change. Vaz was glad there were still some things he could rely on.

"Come on," Mal said as they showed their ID to the duty sergeant. "Practice your nice big smile for She Who Must Be Obeyed. Whatever she wants—it's only pain."

Forerunner Dyson sphere—last definitive position, Onyx: three hours into reconnaissance patrol.

Catherine Halsey jerked her head around and stared into the bushes.

She realized she was the last person to react to the rustling in the leaves. Mendez, Tom, and Olivia already had their rifles trained on the same spot and Kelly had sighted up and was edging toward it. Something small and green shot up the trunk of the nearest tree to cling to the bark and stare at them.

"Not much meat on that, I'm afraid." Kelly lowered her weapon. It was a lizard with a narrow, almost birdlike face and a frilled crest. For a moment it paused, crest raised and absolutely still, then zipped down the tree again to vanish back into the bushes. "Still, it confirms we have a food chain here."

"Just as long as we're at the top of it," Olivia murmured.

Halsey wished she still had her sidearm. While she respected the Forerunners' vastly superior technology, they hadn't been around to mind the shop for a very long time, and there was no telling what might have evolved since they'd left this place ticking over. There were plants here that definitely weren't from Earth. If the fauna here was drawn from all the worlds the Forerunners had visited, then anything was possible.

She didn't need to point that out. All unknown territory was presumed to be potentially hostile.

Mendez came to a halt and fumbled one-handed in his pockets. "Why?"

"Why what?" Tom asked.

"Why did the Forerunners put trees and animals here? Just to make the place nicer while they sat out the holocaust, or is it some kind of zoo?" Mendez tapped his radio and Halsey suddenly heard the crackle and hiss from the receiving end. "Lieutenant? Mendez here. We're seeing some wildlife now. Lizards. Anything your end?"

Fred's patrol was now on a parallel path a kilometer away. "Not yet, Chief. But we've got blossom on some of the trees, so I'm guessing there'll be pollinators around."

"Insects, birds . . . small mammals."

Halsey couldn't bear assumptions. "Or they're self-pollinating."

"Some of the plants *look* like Earth species, but so far we haven't . . . seen anything confirmed as edible." Fred sounded as if he was climbing something, pausing for breath. "Keep looking."

They were spread out in patrol formation with Mendez on point and Kelly walking tail. Halsey was suddenly conscious of being the misfit rather than the boss here, the theoretician who'd created a generation of Spartans but had never actually served, and all the small soldierly things that the Spartans seemed to do automatically—constantly scanning the branches of the trees, turning to take a few paces backward and check behind every so often—leapt out at her. She simply didn't move that way, and not just because she was lugging a bag that seemed to get heavier by the minute and burdened with a skirt. It just wasn't part of her unconscious fabric as it was with them.

It unsettled her. Nobody expected her to behave like a Spartan, even if she'd trained a generation of them. She wasn't sure why that troubled her.

"Bird?" Tom said to nobody in particular, pointing. He sighted up. "I can't tell, even with the scope."

Halsey followed his gesture to see a few tiny black dots making lazy passes high above them. Something about the movement wasn't birdlike. It reminded her of a bat's flight, but much slower.

"If it is, it doesn't fly like any avian species I know," Kelly said. "We're going to have one hell of a nature table."

They were moving through knee-high grass now, rolling downs dotted with stands of trees, some of which were made up of the terrestrial oaks that seemed to be everywhere. Others had bloated gray trunks and tiny, deep red, frondlike crowns that Halsey didn't recognize at all. It still didn't answer the Chief's question as to whether this was ornamental or part of a conservation project.

So how many did they expect to shelter here? The whole Fore-runner population? Or just the great and the good? And for how long?

The quiet was as unfamiliar as the vegetation, layer upon layer of small, wild sounds that merged into the white noise of a countryside that sounded utterly alien. Humans had their own template of normal ambient noise, Halsey decided, and it remained unnoticed until they didn't hear it. She noticed the absence of hers now; no familiar birdsong, no distant rumble of traffic, no aircraft overhead. It kept her on edge. Every sound seemed suddenly magnified. The Spartans' armor clicked as their weapons shifted slightly with each pace. Mendez reached behind him and took something out of his belt pouch, making the material rasp against his webbing.

Then something touched Halsey's shoulder. She yelped and spun around.

"Sorry, ma'am." It was Olivia, one of the Spartan-IIIs. She held out something between her thumb and forefinger. "This was crawling up your back. Might be harmless, but I'm erring on the side of caution here."

Halsey's heart was hammering. She hadn't even realized the girl was behind her. "For God's sake, don't creep up on me like that."

She felt like a fool as soon as she said it. Olivia didn't react. But when Halsey looked around, embarrassed, she caught Mendez giving her a long, unblinking stare. She could see what he was holding now—his one weakness, a Sweet William cigar, or at least the last few centimeters of one. He rolled it between thumb and forefinger for a few slow moments like a rosary before stowing it in his belt pouch again.

"Let's you and me walk awhile, Doctor," he said, ambling back down the line toward Olivia. "Up you go, O. Take point."

"O" must have been Olivia's nickname. Halsey found herself the outsider again, not the matriarch. The girl lifted off her helmet one-handed to take a closer look at the creature that was squirming between her fingers, a beetlelike thing about ten centimeters long with bright orange stripes and a long tapering spike of a tail. Olivia couldn't have been more than sixteen or seventeen. She had poreless coffee-brown skin and delicate features that made Halsey think her origins were in the Horn of Africa.

"Just a tail. Not a sting." Olivia let the insect go and replaced her helmet. "But you never know."

Halsey glanced around. Kelly had now fallen back a distance

and Tom had moved well to the right. Halsey realized the Spartans had instantly given her and Mendez some fight space, apparently without a single gesture or word passing between them. That was a testament to good shared situational awareness.

"Is there anything you want to say to me, Doctor?" Mendez said quietly. He took out his cigar butt again and parked it in the side of his mouth without lighting it. "Because we've been awfully *civil* so far."

You knew. You damn well knew. "Is that your last one?" Halsey asked.

"I've got three left. I'm rationing myself for the good of the mission."

"Spoken like a smoker."

"Don't worry. I won't light up anywhere near you."

"Always the gentleman."

Mendez was a hard man to read but it was safe to assume that the less emotion he showed, which wasn't much at the best of times, the more he was keeping his reaction battened down. He just gave her that dead-eyed look. It was probably the last thing that a lot of Covenant troops ever saw.

"Okay, ma'am, if you won't open the batting, I will. You are, I know, ticked off that there's a whole batch of Spartans you didn't bless or know about." Mendez took the cigar out of his mouth and pocketed it again. "Now, while I'm happy to discuss all that, I'm asking you to do one thing. Treat the Spartan-Threes the way you treat the others. If you've got a problem with the program, Doctor, direct it at me. Not them. They're Navy. They've earned respect."

It stung in the way that polite rebukes always did, with a little extra smack in the mouth for disrespecting men and women in uniform. *Am I really that rude? Yes, I suppose I am.* Halsey bit back the indignation that had been fermenting since she'd first seen complete strangers on Reach daring to wear the Spartans' Mjolnir armor.

It had all fallen into place. Parangosky putting Onyx off-limits, Mendez dropping out of sight all those years ago, Ackerson raiding her data around the same time . . . all she'd needed was the video logs and the information from Cortana to add the Halo Array and the Flood into the equation, and then she had a fairly reliable set of signposts. Parangosky must have had a good idea of what might be on Onyx even if she didn't know the full nature of the threat and couldn't access any of it.

It was why Halsey had picked Onyx. It was about more than realizing there were Spartans there, Spartans she had to save. It was a gamble on the Forerunners' meticulous survival precautions.

I'm lucky. But we make our own luck.

"I don't have a problem with them, Chief, or I wouldn't have come here to save them, would I?" she said. Maybe that sounded too messianic. She watched his eyes harden a little more. "But it's not easy finding that someone you've worked with for years kept something of this magnitude from you."

"It's called need-to-know, ma'am, and I don't decide who needs to. I just follow lawful orders." He gave her that look again, heavy-lidded, as if he was shaping up to spit on her. "But you knew more about Onyx than you're telling me."

"Just putting two and two together. Following the crumbs."

"And I'm sure you're too professional to withhold any information from us that we need to stay alive."

Ouch. "My only aim is to save the Spartans. I think you can count on that."

Mendez looked away in silence and kept walking. Halsey realized she was matching his pace, struggling to keep up with him. *I really wish I'd worn pants. And I wish I was fitter. We're the same age, for goodness' sake.* She was following his lead, one of those little psychological tells. He was the dominant individual now because this was his natural environment—the concrete, the physically dangerous—and not hers. She didn't like that at all.

"Who told you not to mention the Spartan-Three program to me?" she asked. There was a chance it would never matter, but she had to know. Colonel Ackerson had hacked her confidential data, but that didn't mean that his was the only score she'd have to settle. "Ackerson? Parangosky? Or both?"

"I was only told who I *could* tell. But I wouldn't have told you anyway." No, this wasn't quite the Chief she was used to, the one who looked away and kept his counsel: rounding on Olivia had definitely provoked him. "You'd have spent all your time arguing that we didn't have good enough candidates and trying to get it shelved. And I'd have told you that attitude trumps genetics every time."

"I know that. I—"

Halsey didn't have a personal radio, but everyone else did. Mendez turned away from her instantly and responded to a call she couldn't hear.

"Go ahead, sir." It had to be Fred. "Where?"

Where. The word made Halsey spin around, left then right. It was pure instinct. But when she caught sight of Kelly, the Spartan was looking *up.*

"Damn, he's right," she said, and aimed.

Halsey could see now. There was a black dot in the picture-perfect blue sky, getting bigger by the second. Something was swooping down on them.

Tom was nearest to her. "Ma'am, *down!*"

It was a fluke. If anyone had the lightning reflexes and sheer speed to reach her, it was Kelly. But Tom cannoned into Halsey and pinned her down just as a charcoal gray cylinder the size of a wine bottle whisked by so close that she felt the rush of air on her face. For a moment she couldn't see where it had gone. She was looking up at the lower edge of Tom's visor, wondering for a moment why she could still breathe.

That SPI armor was light, cheap stuff. *Thank God.* Three hundred kilos of Mjolnir armor would have killed her. But Tom was kneeling over her on all fours, shielding her from whatever had decided to target them. He'd just pushed her down.

"It's okay. It's *okay.*" That was Kelly. Halsey heard her rifle click. "I've got it. It's not doing anything."

Tom got to his feet and helped Halsey up. Kelly had her rifle trained on the cylinder, frozen at a silent hover two meters off the ground.

"Is that some kind of mini Sentinel?" Mendez asked. "Because if it is, we've already seen the big ones. And you know what happens when those bastards link up."

For a moment, Halsey was totally distracted by the matte gray device and completely forgot her moment of ignominy in the grass. It wasn't a defensive machine like the deadly Sentinels they'd encountered on the surface. It gave the impression that it was waiting for something, although it had dived on them like a fighter. Halsey edged closer despite Kelly waving her away, and looked at the underside. A cluster of lights—no, illuminated symbols she couldn't read—was visible, two blue and one a greenish white. The blue ones were blinking.

It could have been counting down to detonate, of course. The Forerunners would have gone to a lot of trouble to ensure no unwanted life-forms contaminated this sanctuary. Halsey still had no evidence that the sphere's apparent tolerance of human intrusion was anything more than luck.

"No telling what'll happen if I shoot it," Kelly said. "And size doesn't mean something isn't lethal. Right, O?"

Olivia suddenly appeared from nowhere. Halsey really never heard her coming. Maybe old age was creeping on.

"Shall we—well, catch it?" Olivia asked. "We're supposed to be acquiring technology here."

Kelly reached out, slow and cautious for once. She was a finger-length from the cylinder when it shot up in a perfect vertical and vanished before she could target it.

"Damn, I've finally been outrun," she said. "Oh, the shame of it."

Mendez watched from a distance, lips moving. He was talking to Fred's squad on the radio. Halsey's stomach growled, reminding her of the top priority.

"It'll be back," she said. "And I'd like to take it alive." She turned to Tom, who'd taken off his helmet and was scratching his scalp. He was just as luminously young as the other Spartan-IIIs, with dark hair and a bruise on his chin that was already turning yellow at the margins. "Is that from when Kurt knocked you out?"

"Yes." Tom stared at a point between his boots and blinked a few times. "I'd never have left him to hold off the Elites on his own."

"It's okay, I know you wouldn't." Halsey wasn't sure if she was trying harder because Mendez had snarled at her or if she really did feel a pang of regret. "Saving someone is a reflex. Nobody who's wired that way thinks about it. Do they?"

Tom just shrugged. "No point taking chances, ma'am. You're the only one here who can read a Forerunner menu, aren't you?"

"Thanks, Spartan," she said. *Do I mean that? Yes, I think I do.* "I'll try to find you a steak."

CHAPTER 2

HUMANITY CAN NOW BREATHE AGAIN.

THE COVENANT HAS FINALLY BEEN DRIVEN BACK. THE COST IN LIVES—OUR TROOPS AND OUR CITIZENS—HAS BEEN ENORMOUS.

BUT FREEDOM NEVER COMES CHEAPLY, AND NOW, WE REBUILD.

I PROMISE THIS TO EVERY MAN, WOMAN, AND CHILD ON EARTH AND IN ITS COLONIES. WHILE WE WILL CONTINUE TO STRIVE FOR A PEACEFUL COEXISTENCE WITH OTHER SPECIES, HUMANITY WILL NEVER AGAIN ALLOW ITSELF TO BE THE VICTIM OF AGGRESSION. THIS IS THE MOMENT WE START TO RECLAIM OUR RIGHTFUL PLACE IN THE UNIVERSE.

(Inaugural speech of Dr. Ruth Charet, new president of the Unified Earth Government: January 2553)

Core 5, Office of Naval Intelligence, Bravo-6 facility: January 26, 2553.

Don't mind me. BB settled down to watch and learn. *I'm no trouble at all. I'll stay out of your way. I'm just observing.*

And he was observing a man who seemed to think his time had come, the idiot. Didn't he realize the war was anything but over? David Agnoli, Minister for the Colonies, sat on the low oak bookcase with his back to Parangosky's office. He still didn't seem to have the measure of UNSC yet.

"Do you think the old bat's *ever* going to die, Captain?" Agnoli reached down between his legs to pull out a volume at random, but BB was pretty sure he was keeping an eye on the office door via the reflection in the glass panel opposite. "Or will she transmogrify into her true basilisk form, and vanish in a puff of sulfur? I'd pay good money to see that."

He started leafing through the book, a faded and ancient copy of *The Admiralty Manual of Seamanship Vol. II*. Captain Osman glanced at him with faint contempt.

"The Admiral speaks very highly of you too, David," she said sourly. "I think the word was *weasel*. Well, it began with a *W*, anyway."

"Come on, you're the anointed one. You can get me in to see her, can't you?"

"If she'd known you were coming, I'm sure she would have made time for you. But she's got a lot of souls to digest." She gave him a look of faint disgust as he riffled through the yellowing pages. "Look, do you know how many *centuries* old that book is? Admiral Hood gave it to me. Don't get greasy fingerprints all over it."

Agnoli turned to look over his shoulder as Parangosky's door opened. Her flag lieutenant, Dorsey, hovered with his hands braced on the door frame as if he didn't dare cross the threshold.

"The Admiral will see you now, Captain." Dorsey made a polite show of noticing Agnoli. "Oh, hello, Minister. Will we be seeing you at Dr. Charet's reception later?"

"Possibly." Agnoli closed the ancient book with exaggerated care and stood up to put it back on the shelf. He nodded at Osman as Dorsey vanished. "I'll show myself out, then. Perhaps the lieutenant can make an appointment for me."

Osman watched him until he was out of sight—but not out of BB's—then reached out to pick up some files from her desk. BB decided it was time to introduce himself. He projected his three-dimensional holographic image into the doorway and waited for her to react.

How else was an AI supposed to shake hands?

Osman stopped in her tracks and stared at him. "And whose little pet are you?" She cocked her head a fraction as if she suddenly wasn't quite sure what he was. "You *are* fully sentient, aren't you?"

"I'm Black-Box," he said. "I thought I'd introduce myself before we see the Admiral."

Osman looked him over with no change in her expression whatsoever. BB's holographic avatar was a cube, a featureless box picked out in blue light, because he saw no point in masquerading as something other than what he was—pure intellect, his intricate thought processes a closed book to organic life. He couldn't bear the theatrics of manifesting as flesh and blood.

Faces are for wannabes. I'm not a surrogate human.

"You didn't answer my question, Black-Box," Osman said, waiting until he moved aside. "Whose AI are you?"

He followed her for a few meters as she walked down the corridor, as far as he could project himself using her desk terminal. "I report to the Admiral. And she calls me BB. You might like to as well."

Osman looked over her shoulder to say something, but he'd run out of range and had to switch to another terminal. It took him a fraction of a second to reroute himself through the fire alarm system and the mainframe to project from Parangosky's terminal and pop up again in front of Osman. She was in the process of turning around again to look for him. Judging by the way she flinched, he'd actually managed to startle her.

"Apologies, Captain," he said. "As I was saying, I work for Parangosky."

"Doing what, exactly?"

"Whatever she wants," BB said.

Look after Osman. Trust her. I've kept her under wraps for years, hidden her even from Halsey. She has a job to do. The Admiral thought the sun shone out of Osman's backside, and even a dolt like Agnoli could see that she'd take over when Parangosky decided to call it a day, even if he didn't know why.

And if it was good enough for Parangosky, then it was good enough for BB.

Ah . . . Hogarth. An alert rippled through BB, detected by extensions of his program that he'd distributed throughout the communications and security systems in key government buildings. *There he goes. He's on the prowl.* Even if Captain Hogarth hadn't put a private appointment with the UEG in his diary, his comms handset made his movements trackable, and each secure door that he passed through betrayed his identity. He was moving around the president's suite of offices. *So you're off to do some lobbying, are you? You really do fancy your chances as head of ONI. Shame that you've backed the wrong horse. What possible deal could the civilian government offer you?*

In the time it took BB to run all his monitoring systems and check intelligence reports from fifty ships, Osman had only just begun her instant reply.

"I never knew she had an AI," Osman said, walking straight through BB's hologram into Parangosky's office. Humans didn't usually do that to AIs. They'd walk *around* them. He wasn't sure how to take it. "Well, nice to meet you, BB."

Parangosky gave him a wink as he moved in behind Osman. "I see you two are getting to know each other," she said, gesturing

Osman to a seat. "That's good. Don't worry, Captain, you can trust BB with your life. Not a phrase I use lightly. Or figuratively."

"And am I going to need to, ma'am?" Osman asked.

"Very possibly." Parangosky leaned forward, slowly and painfully, to check the status panel on her desk. The office was secure, door seals shut and soundproofing activated. BB had his own defenses to keep unfriendly AIs out of the Admiral's systems, but the benign dumb ones needed dissuasion too. He exploited them to spy and expected other AIs to do the same. "Which is why I decided that you needed your own AI. And why this conversation is strictly between you, me, and him."

Osman looked BB over, chewing her lip. He couldn't tell if she was pleased with the appointment or not, but she certainly seemed a little uneasy. Everything he could observe told him so. He could infiltrate any electronic system and ride its vectors, seeing, hearing, and sensing far more than a limited human—even a Spartan—ever could. From the minute feedback adjustments in the environmental controls, he could detect how much CO_2 Osman was exhaling. The security cameras enabled him to see her in any wavelength, including infrared. She looked rather flushed in that spectrum, which mirrored her increased respiration.

Anxious, Captain?

"Are we talking about Kilo-Five or something else?" Osman asked.

"Something else." Parangosky twisted a little in her seat as if she was trying to ease her arthritic hip. "I'll come on to the squad later. But this is about Catherine Halsey."

"You've found a body."

"Oh, she's still alive. I can feel it in my water. But, more to the point, *Glamorgan*'s ELINT has picked up something *much* more concrete." Parangosky indicated the screen. "BB, do the honors, please."

BB pulled up the files he'd collected from the ONI corvette. The holographic display unfolded itself just over the desk between the two women, showing a chart of the system that once contained Onyx before the artificial planet had deconstructed itself. Slightly irregular concentric rings radiated out from the Onyx coordinates. One forlorn blue light was set within the red lines, a pinprick that marked a signal from a Spartan armor transponder, the only KIA that had been confirmed—Lieutenant Ambrose.

BB had left a fragment of himself in *Glamorgan*'s system to alert him as soon as anything else was found. The corvette's nav AI didn't seem to mind the intrusion.

"Sifting for debris out there is a slow process." Parangosky reached into the display and enlarged the detail. "You know what it's like. Hard to spot anything smaller than a family car. It'll take the rest of the year to complete a visual search, but *Glamorgan*'s picking up massive electromagnetic anomalies. Something's still there, but we can't see it. And unless every single sensor's malfunctioning, it's enormous, the size of a solar system. We knew there were areas underground that we couldn't access, but now we know that Onyx was wholly artificial, it's starting to support the theory that it was built as a citadel. A last-chance saloon."

Osman was staring at the chart with a slightly openmouthed expression that told BB she was forming a theory. "That's not any slipspace signature I'd recognize, but it looks a hell of a lot like it. Makes me wish I hadn't sent a wreath."

"You didn't. You may yet get the chance though."

"Well, it was only a matter of time before she found enough pieces to put together. You can't keep that much information completely quiet for that long. But are you sure?"

"Oh, I never assume *anything* where Halsey's concerned, and she might well actually be dead, of course, planning or no planning. But there's a logical progression." Parangosky counted out on thin fingers, joints swollen despite her doctor's best efforts. "We have the Onyx battle reports from *Dusk*. We know she kidnapped Spartan-Zero-Eight-Seven. We know she persuaded Hood to deploy Spartans to Onyx. And we know damn well just how many Forerunner artifacts there were on that planet and what they might be. So she had her Spartans, and she had access to Forerunner technology. Now—your turn."

"So she jumped ship," Osman said. "She's used something the Forerunners left behind."

BB felt free to chip in with his own theories. "And after reading her journal, I think she's cleansing her conscience by hiding her Spartans."

"That's big of her. Hiding them from us?"

"Who knows?" BB said. "The woman rewrites her own reality as she goes along."

Parangosky sucked in a breath. "Osman, she's effectively abducted some very scarce special forces personnel as well as Chief Mendez. She can steal all the paper clips she likes, but she does *not* get to stroll off with billions of dollars' worth of UNSC resources in the middle of a battle. If she had a military rank, she'd have faced the death penalty for that. She still might."

BB noted Osman nod involuntarily. There was no love lost there, and it wasn't just because Osman had taken on her mentor's loathing of Halsey.

"When did you last have contact with her, Captain?" BB asked.

"You already know that," Osman said stiffly. "But if you don't, then you ought to. When she discarded me as *breakage* from her program. *That's* when."

"Just testing for potency of venom, Captain. . . ."

"Savored cold and all that, BB. The best way."

Parangosky turned to BB and gave him her don't-be-a-naughty-boy look, a rueful half smile. He suspected that Parangosky had been the kind of little girl who kept pet scorpions and doted on them the way other children cooed over puppies.

"We don't do pointless vengeance in ONI, BB," Parangosky said gently. "We do vengeance with a pragmatic outcome in mind. Revenge might give you a warm feeling, but unless it delivers some lasting results you might as well have a nice cup of mocha instead."

"So you want me to take Kilo-Five to Onyx," Osman said, obviously in a hurry to move on from the personal stuff. "Or the gap where Onyx used to be. So who's going to handle the Sangheili mission?"

"That's still our top priority. We've got Elites to neutralize and the rest of the Halos to locate. Just stand by to divert to *Glamorgan* if and when we find something. Mendez and some of the Spartan-Threes could still be alive too, but don't forget you're going to have Spartan-Zero-One-Zero in your squad, and she thinks that Halsey walks on water. They all do. Hence my preference for this private briefing."

"If you can't trust a Spartan, then who can you trust?"

"I'm not saying they can't be trusted. I just don't want to put that loyalty to the test if we find Halsey, that's all. I'm not briefing the ODSTs about it either. Just so that we don't have any slipups. We stick with our story. Halsey died a long way from Onyx, all suitably sacrificial and heroic. But that's for the UNSC's benefit, not hers."

"You could have made her vanish a long time ago, ma'am," Osman said. "There has to come a point where the irritant factor outweighs her usefulness."

"She's reached it now she's compromised our ability to fight." Parangosky turned her head slowly and glanced at the virtual window. The image it projected from above ground was a bright, sunny summer day. She looked almost wistful, as if she wanted to be outside for a change. *Tomorrow's a bonus, BB.* She said that quite a lot these days. "So I *want* to find her alive. It's keeping me going, believe me."

BB had access to every record in the ONI archives, and in the six months since his creation Parangosky had answered every question he'd put to her. Even so, it was hard for an AI to extract as much data from a human as he needed, even from an articulate and succinct one like Parangosky. Flesh and blood was so very, *very* slow. The question that most fascinated him had still to be fully answered.

What made you dislike Halsey so much, Admiral? ONI has plenty of unpalatable, unlikable, dangerous people in its ranks, but you tolerate them. What did she do?

She *had* answered, in a way. Halsey had lied to her, she said.

But ONI was all about lies. They were now about to tell some more.

"So, on to today's business." Parangosky shut down the holo-image. "BB, are they all here now?"

"Yes, ma'am." BB checked on the monitors in each separate waiting room, where the candidates sat isolated by specialty. "Staff Sergeant Malcolm Geffen, Corporal Vasily Beloi, Sergeant Lian Devereaux, Naomi-Zero-One-Zero, and Dr. Evan Phillips."

Osman didn't say a word for a moment. Sometimes Parangosky didn't tell her everything. But then Phillips had been a last-minute change of mind on Parangosky's part, and BB still wasn't convinced that the professor understood what he'd agreed to in a matter of seconds. *Phillips craves knowledge, like an AI. Can't exist without it. Gorges on more and more every day. I think we'll get on just fine.* Phillips had rushed to Bravo-6 so fast that he was still repacking his holdall in the waiting room.

"I didn't know he was coming," Osman said at last.

Parangosky looked almost apologetic. She always took care not to offend Osman, but BB knew there were things she didn't tell her for her own good. The time was approaching, though, when she would need to be told everything, and when the name *Infinity* would finally mean something to her.

"He's a gamble I took two hours ago," Parangosky said. "You might need his expertise, even with BB around. I'll worry later about how I get him to keep his mouth shut."

She eased herself up from the chair and reached for her cane. She needed it for the walk to the elevator down into the core of the HIGHCOM complex, but somehow she made it look like a weapon she had every intention of using.

"Time to put Kilo-Five together, then," she said. "BB, you're formally assigned to Captain Osman as of now. Lead on, Captain."

Private quarters of former shipmaster Jul 'Mdama, Bekan Keep, Mdama, Sanghelios: January 26, 2553 in the human calendar.

Nothing had changed since the Covenant had fallen, just the deceptive surface of events, but Jul 'Mdama despaired of making the Arbiter listen.

"They'll be back," he said, running a polishing cloth over his armor for the tenth time that morning. "They're like the Flood. They expand to fill every available space. They devour everything in their path. Except they can plan and wait, and persuade our more gullible brothers with clever argument, which makes them even more dangerous."

Raia didn't say anything. She was still looking out of the window, jaws moving slightly as if she was talking to herself, and passing a stylus from hand to hand. The sound of youngsters squabbling in the courtyard below rose on the breeze as Great-Uncle Naxan waded in to restore order, yelling about discipline and dignity.

"And even *you* don't listen to me," Jul said. He stopped short of seizing Raia's shoulder to make her look at him. Within the family keep, her word was law. "Am I the only one who can see that the humans are just catching their breath? They won't forget, and they won't forgive. They certainly won't stop their colonization."

"Jul, we face far more immediate problems than humans," Raia said. "I want you to look at something."

She stepped back from the window and gestured to him with the kind of weary patience she reserved for small children. Jul humored her. From the third-story window, he had a good view of the landscaping that surrounded the keep. To the east, the hills were stepped with terraces of fruit vines, designed to catch the sun. Looking west, he could see fields in a neat mosaic of green and gray-blue on either side of the lake. Set against the gold mid-morning sky, it looked exactly like every image he'd ever seen of this landscape; it hadn't changed for centuries, and generations of his clan had worked hard to make sure it didn't. He had every expectation that it would look that way to his sons' children and their grandchildren too.

The Sangheili might have been betrayed and defeated—temporarily—and their faith upended, but Mdama never changed.

"I don't have time for this," Jul said. "I have to go to the kaidon's assembly. The Arbiter's going to be here soon."

"Then you *make* time," Raia snapped. "A world needs more

than warriors to survive. The San'Shyuum knew how to make their servant races weak—they confined us to one skill." Nobody called them the Prophets now. It was too painful, but it was also a hard habit to break. "And, of course, we lap that up, vain fools that we are. We all want to be warriors, nothing else. Now we have no engineers, no traders, and no scientists. How will we feed ourselves?"

"I leave the estate management to you and Naxan." Jul hadn't noticed any food shortages. It had only been half a season since the Arbiter had killed the last treacherous Prophet of the High Council and every certainty in life had evaporated, but there was still food on the table. "I know better than to interfere with my wife's business."

Raia drew back her arms, head thrust forward a little in that don't-you-dare posture. He hadn't seen her this angry for a long time. "That's the problem!" She hissed. "Thousands of years doing the San'Shyuum's bidding, each species made as dependent as children, and we never asked ourselves what would happen if it all fell apart. The San'Shyuum made us reliant on *savages*. Now we have to relearn their skills just to restore basic communications. We built *starships*, Jul. We were a spacefaring culture long before the San'Shyuum arrived and turned us into their personal army."

Jul could still hear the youngsters in the courtyard. Sticks crashed against sticks. *"No, not like that!"* Naxan, Raia's grandbrother, roared his head off, probably putting on the angry theatrics. *"Control yourself! If that had been a blade, you would have taken your own arm off!"*

Jul heard a loud *thwack*—followed by absolute silence—as if Naxan had rapped one of the children with his dummy weapon. There was no yelping or sniveling. It might even have been one of the girls; Naxan taught them all basic combat skills, the young females of the keep as well as the males. Daughters would probably never serve in the front line, but they had to be able to defend the keep if the worst happened.

Raia was right, as usual. Every Sangheili judged himself solely by his combat skills. Jul definitely couldn't remember any of his brothers or cousins saying they wanted to be an administrator or a cook. The shame would have been unbearable, and yet keeps and assemblies had to be run and food had to be provided. Sangheili had stopped thinking about how the Covenant kept itself running a long time ago.

"It's only been half a season," Jul said. "The world hasn't ground to a halt yet. We can import food if the crops fail. We can hire engineers."

"No, we *can't*," Raia said. "We might find Kig-Yar traders willing to do business, but do you really think Jiralhanae can maintain our technology now the Huragok have fled? And even if you don't give a damn about the domestic side of things, at least worry about your fleet. What happens when our ships and weapons need replacing? Think of that before you choose to carry on fighting the war."

"We'll discuss this later," he said, picking his moment to escape. "I have to see the Arbiter."

He heard her hiss irritably again as he made his way down the passage. It was a simple problem to fix. There were still a few loyal Unggoy and Jiralhanae around, weren't there? They could easily learn to be farmers or factory workers. *Or engineers.* It was simply a matter of giving them clear instructions and making sure they didn't drug themselves into a stupor or start too many fights.

But it was far easier to vaporize every living thing on a planet than reform an entire culture from scratch.

The humans don't have this problem. Clever little vermin. Backward, small, and not the best at anything. But good enough at everything. Survivors.

That was all the more reason to make the Arbiter see sense and crush them before they started recolonizing.

Jul looked down over the windowsill on the stairwell to make sure that it wasn't Dural or Asum who'd received the smack around the ear from Naxan for careless swordsmanship. *No. It's Gmal. Not my boys. They're better than that.* It was hard not to show his sons favor, but that would have told them who their father was, and no Sangheili male was allowed to know that. Jul's sons had to make their own way in the world, judged solely on their merits and without any assumptions based on their bloodline.

But I still wish I'd known who my father was. I think we all do.

Sangheili mothers might not have been frontline fighters, but they certainly held the real power, the knowledge and selection of bloodlines. Being a Sangheili male could sometimes be lonely and uncertain.

Jul had to pass through the courtyard to get to his transport. The youngsters were still doing weapons drill, taking the wooden sticks very seriously as Naxan stalked up and down in front of them, tapping his baton against his palm as he watched the parries and thrusts. He gave Jul a nod and didn't break his stride. None of the children looked Jul's way either. *Focus.* It had to be taught and reinforced from the crib.

Jul was almost at the gate when Naxan called out to him. "Tell the Arbiter to watch his back."

Jul found that funny. He looked over his shoulder. "I don't think he needs me to remind him of that."

Jul's young aide, Gusay, had been reduced to his personal driver now. Ships were in short supply and there were more crew than positions to be filled—and no tangible war to fight anyway. It was the first time in living memory that any Sangheili had to face the prospect of being idle and purposeless. Even the vehicles at the keep's disposal were a painful reminder of the disarray and confusion the entire world seemed to find itself in. Gusay collected Jul in a Revenant that still had hastily repaired shell damage all over it, with a particularly spectacular gouge a hand-width deep running from the nose to the driver's seat.

Jul wondered if the occupants had survived the attack that caused it. The plasma mortar was intact. He leaned over the open cockpit and stared at the seats, trying not to show his dismay.

"Did you raid the scrapyard? Making a virtue of frugality, are we?"

"Sorry, Shipmaster, but there are a great many Revenants around, and very little else." Gusay always did his best. Jul tried to keep that in mind. "Better that you arrive to greet the Arbiter in a vehicle that's seen action, though, yes?"

"Is the mortar operational?"

"I didn't think it was going to be *that* sort of a gathering, my lord."

Jul could never tell whether Gusay was being literal or trying to be funny. He decided to take the comment at face value. "I'm sure we'll all listen reverently to what the Arbiter has to say."

The Revenant swept north across land that was a lie in itself. Much of the landscape outside the cities looked like the neat agricultural terrain of an ancient Sanghelios long gone. Even the keeps—the regional assembly houses and the clan settlements—tried hard to at least nod to the old architecture. Jul had always thought of it as a splendid regard for tradition and lineage, but not now. *We still pretend to be farmers, like we deluded ourselves that we were still warriors, when we were only cannon fodder for the*

San'Shyuum. Keeping up appearances wasn't going to change anything. Sangheili needed to remember who they were long before the San'Shyuum came. They needed to reclaim their honor and independence.

Very well, Raia. You have a point.

"So we find ourselves like the humans," Gusay said. "Licking our wounds and learning lessons."

"We're nothing like them," Jul snapped. "Don't let me hear you say that again."

Gusay didn't breathe another word for the rest of the journey. Jul settled back as best he could in his seat—the metal frame was buckled, he was certain—and inhaled the scents on the breeze, eyes shut. The smell of the ocean mingled with the sharp scent of roadside herbs bruised by the Revenant's thrust. It was a fragrant and familiar mixture that he'd missed during his years at the front.

"The Arbiter's drawn a good crowd, my lord." Gusay slowed the Revenant to a halt and Jul opened his eyes. "I believe the humans would call that a *full house.*"

Every elder entitled to bear the 'Mdama title seemed to be here already. An assortment of transports sat along the sweeping road up to the kaidon's keep, mostly Revenants and Ghosts, but also a human vehicle, a hydrogen-powered thing of which he'd seen far too many: a Warthog. So somebody had brought home a battle-field trophy for his clan. Well, there was no edict against tasteless eccentricity. It might even have belonged to Kaidon Levu 'Mdama himself. Whatever his reputation in combat, old Levu had such vulgar tendencies that it made Jul wonder if his mother had consorted with a Kig-Yar.

"Wait here," Jul said, climbing out of the Revenant. "I doubt this will take long."

Levu was a traditionalist, so Jul forgave him his undignified taste. The kaidon still had a huge tiered chamber at the heart of his keep, the kind that ancient Sangheili warlords had once held court in, albeit with the latest comforts and technologies provided by the San'Shyuum. The walls were an electric blue, almost painfully intense, and shiny with lacquer. Jul nodded at the clan elders he knew well and caught the eye of those he didn't, then took his seat. The purplish-black upholstery was just as glossy and awful as the walls. He wondered if Levu was trying to emulate the leather cushions and lapis paneling of Old Rolam.

Someone leaned forward from the tier above and behind him to tap his shoulder. "So what are we going to do for a High Council now we've kicked out the San'Shyuum, Jul? An assembly of kaidons? We don't even have a global capital to meet in. The keeps will argue about *that* until I grow a damn beak."

It was Forze, another shipmaster without a ship. "Do we even need a council?" Jul asked. "All we need to worry about is holding an army and a fleet together. We can manage that."

"Of course we need a council. The only reason we didn't have one was because the San'Shyuum told us what to do, the—"

He was interrupted by a growing rumble of murmurs as the doors on the lower level opened. Jul looked down from his second-tier seat to see Levu usher in the Arbiter, Thel 'Vadam.

I wonder if he's missing his pet humans. Why does he think any of them are worth sparing?

'Vadam wasn't quite as tall as Jul had imagined. Somehow Jul had expected someone iconic, unreal, as befitted a fleet commander, but 'Vadam simply held himself as if he were much bigger. He seemed to have slipped automatically into the role of pulling Sanghelios together whether it wanted him to or not.

"Brothers, it's time to listen to what Thel 'Vadam has to say to us," Levu said. "So let's be gracious while he speaks."

"Has the human *Admiral* given you permission to talk to us, then?" someone jeered. "How generous of him."

The Arbiter ignored the jibe, looking around the chamber as if he was settling on a target, but Levu brought his fist down on the balustrade with a crack. "*Courtesy,* brothers. Hear the Arbiter out. He has the floor."

'Vadam took a few circling, slow strides, picking his moment. "*Arbiter* is a title I would prefer to forget," he said. "I'm simply a kaidon again. As such, I've come to appeal for unity. I know there are . . . *misgivings* about my recent cooperation with humankind, and strong opinions on both sides. But this is not the time for another civil war. We have to rediscover what unites us. And we have to repair the fabric that the San'Shyuum have left in tatters. We must learn to be an independent people again for the first time in millennia."

It was hard to object to any of that. 'Vadam was talking like a politician, bland and conciliatory, switching back and forth between the formal language of authority and a comradely, I'm-one-of-you informality. Jul waited. He was itching to make his challenge, but he also wanted to see if the elders from the larger, more powerful keeps would reveal their positions first.

A voice drifted down from one of the upper tiers. "Now, Kaidon 'Vadam, tell us something we *don't* know."

"We think we've lost the gods, but we haven't," 'Vadam said. "We've lost *ourselves.* Millions of our finest, our young males, have been killed—not fighting humans, but in the Great Schism. Are we insane? Our bloodlines have been weakened and our ships have been lost in a civil war, all because we were deceived into loyalty to the San'Shyuum. Brothers, we *must* consolidate what we have, whether flesh and blood or machine, before we can decide on a common purpose. But it will be *our* purpose. Not another empire's."

"Perhaps our purpose is just to survive without being exploited by false prophets," Levu said.

The Arbiter made sense. There had been a time when the San'Shyuum had made sense too. Jul wondered if he could actually speak up now, but the words formed and suddenly he could hear his own voice filling the chamber.

"What do you plan to do about the humans?" he asked. "Gods or no gods, they'll return to their colonies and rebuild them, and they won't forget what we did to them and how much they loathe us."

"We'll consider that if and when it happens."

"Instead of finishing them off before they regain strength?" There. It was out in the open now. "We should regroup now, while their guard's down, and exterminate the threat once and for all. Unless you're too fond of them as pets, that is."

The chamber was horribly silent now. Jul could suddenly hear the slow shuffling of boots as elders squirmed. He expected Thel 'Vadam to round on him, but the Arbiter just snapped his jaws together a couple of times in amusement as if there was something he should have told Jul but chose not to.

"The humans say that a fool does the same thing twice and expects things to turn out differently." 'Vadam lowered his voice. "It might have escaped your notice that we never managed to defeat them, and we're in worse shape now than we were a year ago." Then his expression changed, as if he was steeling himself to break bad news. "We've stopped fighting. We *need* to stop because we can't rebuild without stability. Therefore I plan to reach a peace agreement with the humans, to formalize what has already taken place. Both sides have finally run out of blood to shed, brother."

"But you can't do deals with humans. Have you forgotten

already?" Jul was appalled. Not pressing home Sangheili superior-
ity was one thing, but willingly giving in? That was close to trea-
son. "They're liars and thieves. All of them."

'Vadam walked over to the balustrade that separated the floor
of the chamber from the first tier of seats to look up at Jul. It
wasn't a threatening gesture. It seemed more like curiosity to see
what this upstart, this young elder of a small keep, looked like at
closer quarters.

"There *are* honorable humans," 'Vadam said, resting his hands
on the balustrade. "I've fought alongside them. None of us would
be alive now if there weren't. But I plan to agree to a treaty, not
because I have any fondness for humans but because I love Sanghelios." He pushed away from the balustrade and walked back
into the center of the chamber, suddenly the charismatic leader
again, the hero of the fleet. "The law is clear. If anyone disagrees,
you have a remedy. You may attempt to assassinate me. That is
your legal right."

Jul sat there for some minutes after the address ended. The rest
of the elders filed out and he found himself staring at the empty
chamber floor with just Forze behind him. He could hear him fidgeting with his holster.

"I think we're going to live to regret that," Forze said.

We? Jul had felt like the lone voice of reason. "Challenging
him? He seemed amused."

"No. We'll regret letting the humans off the hook."

"So . . . are you with me, then?"

As soon as Jul said it, he realized he wasn't even sure what *with
me* meant. He just knew that whatever dismissive things he'd said
about his enemy, humans were *not* all the same, Thel 'Vadam's
honorable pets were the exception, and the rest would go back
to doing what they'd always done as soon as they recovered their

breath. Jul had to galvanize the Sangheili into stopping human-kind while they still could.

"Yes, I'm with you," said Forze. "What now?"

Jul got up and wondered how he would explain this to Raia.

"I'll think of something," he said.

Threat Analysis wing, Bravo-6, Sydney: January 26, 2553.

Mal Geffen had never liked corridors, especially dimly lit ones.

It was a weird phobia for a man who was happy to freefall into the pitch-black unknown or drop from low orbit behind enemy lines in a glorified coffin. He'd given up trying to fathom it out. He just knew that he didn't like what he could see, or *couldn't* see in this case. The double doors at the end of the passage were picked out by emergency lighting, the kind you had to follow in the event of a fire.

"You still with me, Vaz?"

Vaz's parade boots clicked behind him on the tiles. "I warned you that it'd make you go deaf. . . ."

"It's the Wendy House."

"What is?"

"This is where the fleet brass used to war-game and run ta-bletop exercises." Mal's voice echoed. He dropped to a whisper as they came to a halt in front of the doors. "Wendy House. You know. Where kids play at being grown-ups."

They stared at the security panel. Vaz shrugged, still miserable as sin. It was going to take Mal some time to make him forget that useless tart who dumped him. He'd keep trying. The kid needed to get out more.

"Cheer up, it might be a stripper in a cake," Mal said. He still had no idea why they were here. It wasn't going to be a celebration, that was for sure. "Surprise party for the conquering heroes."

Vaz put his palm on the entry panel, unmoved. "Yes. I tripped over all the rose petals on the red carpet."

The security doors opened and Mal took a pace inside. The smell of cleaning fluid and musty carpet hit him. The room looked like it hadn't been used in years, its walls lined with old chart display panels showing trouble spots that hadn't been active for decades: Earth colonies in a dozen systems, human-on-human violence. War had been a lot simpler then, or so his grandad had told him. He walked around tables pushed together into a rectangle, wiping his finger across the unconvincing oak-effect surface but finding no dust at all.

"Are you here for the free sandwiches? 'Cause there aren't any."

It was a woman's voice. Mal guessed Canada, northeast. She emerged from behind one of the tote boards where make-believe generals had once tallied imaginary KIAs in counterinsurgency battles that never happened; about thirty, Asian, and wearing a flight suit with a pilot's brevet and sergeant's stripes.

And an ODST 10th Battalion badge. One of us. Well, that's something.

Her name tab said DEVEREAUX L. Either she hadn't been told this was a number-threes occasion or she'd come straight from a sortie.

"You're not a stripper," Mal said.

"No. Are you? Because if you are, I want my money back."

"We better keep our clothes on, then." Mal held out his hand for shaking, seeing as formalities had fallen by the wayside. "Mal Geffen. And this is Vaz. Vasily Beloi. He isn't a stripper either. Any idea why we're here, Sergeant?"

"Lian Devereaux." She looked Vaz over. Mal hoped she was just checking him out, because Mal was always ready to dive in and ask what the hell was so interesting. Civvies stared at scars. ODSTs knew better, and Vaz didn't need reminding that he didn't look as good as he used to. "No," she said. "Not a clue."

Mal stood there in silence for a moment, just looking around and evaluating the environment. *It's some psych test, isn't it? Some study into how damaged we are and how they can save money putting us right.* It didn't take long for the bean counters to crawl out of their holes once the shooting was over.

Devereaux tilted her head on one side and gave Vaz a mock-wary look. Maybe she hadn't even noticed the scar. "Weren't you the guys who hijacked a Spirit to exfil from Imber?"

"The hinge-heads left the keys in the ignition," Vaz said. "So we took it for a burn."

"But where is it now?"

Mal winked. "That's for us to know and the Corps to find out."

The doors opened and cut short any more bragging about the Covenant dropship. That was the problem with most of the meeting rooms and offices in Bravo-6. They were soundproofed, and nobody could hear anyone coming until it was too late. The tallest, scariest woman Mal had ever seen stalked into the room.

Even without Mjolnir armor, it was obvious what she was. Mal had never seen a Spartan in the flesh before. She looked more unreal in her UNSCN uniform than she would have in armor, he decided. He cast an eye over her sleeve.

"Morning, Petty Officer." He outranked her but he still had to tilt his head back to look her in the eye. Christ, she had to be over two meters tall, easy. "Good to see the Navy's managed to drag itself out of its bunk before lunch."

Mal expected to get a bit of abusive but friendly banter back from her. That was the way of interservice diplomacy, the custom of centuries. But the Spartan just looked down at him, unmoved. He couldn't work out if she was very blond or completely gray.

"Naomi-Zero-One-Zero, Staff," she said. "I believe we're waiting for Admiral Parangosky."

"That's the idea." Mal couldn't read her at all. *She's a bloody Valkyrie. She really is.* "Yeah, we are."

Mal edged away to the tote boards and feigned intense interest in the list of unit acronyms scribbled beside actions on the incident timeline. Vaz and Devereaux sidled up to him. The three of them had already closed ranks without even thinking about it.

"Here we go," Mal murmured. "They're going to inject us full of crap and put bolts through our necks. Frankentroopers."

"Ah, that's just stories," Devereaux said. She didn't sound convinced though. "But if it's not, I'm sure as hell not volunteering."

Naomi the Valkyrie interrupted. "Officer on deck."

Mal turned and snapped to attention, the reflex of fifteen years, slipping instantly behind the facade of the stony-faced, unreadable ODST. He decided his guess about a psych test was right.

So this was Parangosky.

Admirals never retired, technically speaking, but Mal was sure nobody really expected the old salts to front up and earn it for real once they were past seventy. Parangosky walked in slowly with a cane for support, somehow managing to be both frail and terrifying at the same time, the crazy old woman who scared all the kids in the neighborhood. But she obviously wasn't crazy. Mal met her eyes for a disturbing second and fully believed the rumors that she could erase anyone stupid enough to cross her.

"Stand easy," she said. "My apologies for the location, but *Strength through Paranoia* is my motto. Meet Captain Osman and Professor Phillips. They already know all about you. Take a seat."

Phillips was a bearded bloke in his thirties who had civvie

hired help written all over him. Osman was tall, not Spartan tall, but conspicuous just the same. Parangosky settled down at the far corner of the tables and gestured to them to sit. The old girl handed six datapads to Osman, who passed them around. Mal didn't get a chance to look to Vaz for a reaction before his screen flashed into life and told him the captain was Serin Osman, ONI, and Phillips was a Sangheili expert from Wheatley University.

Debrief, then. About what? The bloody Spirit? What was so special about that?

"I'll get to the point," Parangosky said. "You're under no obligation to undertake this mission."

That sealed the deal for Mal. ODSTs didn't turn down tasking, *any* tasking. They'd automatically volunteered for everything and anything, now and forever, world-without-end-amen, on the day they'd turned up for the selection board. Being RTU'd— Returned to Unit, sent back to their original regiment or ship or squadron in whatever country because they didn't make the grade as a Helljumper—was the worst thing that could happen to them. Death was a minor embarrassment by comparison.

Parangosky fixed Vaz with a watery but intimidating gaze. "Corporal, when's the best time to kick a man?"

"When he's down, ma'am," Vaz said quietly. "And preferably in the nuts. Hard as you can."

Mal could have sworn that Parangosky smiled. It was more like a twitch of the lips, but he was pretty sure Vaz had hit the target.

"A man after my own heart," she said. "Very well, I'm asking you all to go and kick the Sangheili in their collective nuts in ways that might seem foreign to you. I want you to sow discontent and strife. They're already infighting and I want to keep that going until we're ready to finish the job. Anyone not keen on that?

There's no shame in refusing. I've seen your service records and you've all more than earned the right to say no."

Yeah, Mal was pretty sure she knew every last thing about them, right down to how many sugars they took in their coffee. So she had to know the answer she'd get. It was still a decent gesture though. Nobody said a word. Osman seemed to be keeping an eye on the Spartan, and the Spartan kept giving her a furtive glance as if something was bothering her. They were both roughly the same age, so maybe there was some weird alpha female power struggle going on. Mal made mental note to stay well clear.

"I'm up for it, ma'am," Devereaux said. "But how *foreign* is this going to get? Because we're fine with assassination and sabotage."

"I know. I'm talking about arming Sangheili dissidents. Misinformation. All deniable." Parangosky squinted at her datapad for a moment. "You're going to have to think on your feet. Intel's very patchy now and we're not sure exactly where the fault lines are forming between the various factions, so you'll be gathering information as you go. I wish I could prepare you more thoroughly."

Mal knew that ONI were a law unto themselves, and the one question he'd learned never to ask was *why*. It was always *how* and *when*. He certainly didn't plan to ask if every member of the UNSC security committee was on board with Parangosky's op.

Devereaux didn't seem to worry about all that. "We'll manage, ma'am. So no peace treaty, then?"

"Admiral Hood believes it's possible to reach a formal deal with the Arbiter," Parangosky said. "But he's going to be busy dealing with the colonies now that we need to bring our wayward sheep back into the fold."

Mal thought she'd avoided the question until the answer sank in. *Oh God. She's even sidelining Hood now. Never mind. That's so far above my pay grade that I'd need a telescope to see it.* Had he been given a lawful order? Well, he hadn't been given an *unlawful* one yet.

Phillips was still sitting there with the expression of a rabbit about to be hit by a truck that it just hadn't seen coming. He hadn't said a word yet. Vaz glanced at him.

"So what's the professor's status, ma'am?" Vaz asked. "We're looking after him, yes?"

"No, he'll be armed and he'll take his chances, just like you." Parangosky hovered on the edge of looking concerned. "You'll have to forget the chain of command and make your own decisions out there. Our comms are a shambles, we've got relays down, our people out there are struggling to get word to us, and the colonies—well, where they've gone silent, we don't know whether they're a smoking heap of charcoal or if they've just decided to sever links with us."

Mal wanted to ask why she'd picked them. He could understand the professor, the spook, and the Spartan, but there were still plenty of ODSTs around, and any of them could have done the job. It obviously wasn't a lottery or else Vaz wouldn't have been here too.

He'd find out sooner or later. It didn't make any difference anyway. He was going.

"We're shipping out in the morning," Osman said. "If you want to do any drinking tonight, do it within the complex. Your personal effects are being brought over from the barracks. We'll transfer to the ship at Midpoint—it's *Port Stanley.* She's got the latest Forerunner enhancements to her drives, so we can cover a lot of space fast. A corvette's a big vessel for six, but we'll have an AI to handle her."

Parangosky laid her pad down like a winning hand of cards. "Come on, BB. Don't be coy. Introduce yourself."

Mal had never worked with smart AIs. A ship would drop him and his mates, and if they were lucky it would show up again and extract them when the job was done, but he didn't get to play with any of the technology that ONI took for granted. He waited for the hologram to appear. When a blue cube materialized in the center of the tables, it was a bit of an anticlimax. He'd expected something a little more exotic. He'd heard all the hairy stories about the weird forms that AI avatars took.

"That'd be me," the blue cube said in a news anchor's tenor voice. "The taxi driver. Black-Box. Airport runs my specialty."

Mal leaned back in his seat and caught Vaz's eye for a second. He looked carefully blank, like he always did.

We don't do psyop. We've never worked with Spartans before. And we're definitely not trained for this spook stuff. But how hard can it be?

They were ODSTs. They could do anything. It was all about the right attitude—a commando's state of mind.

"Hi, BB," Mal said. "Take us to Hinge-head World, then."

CHAPTER 3

IT'S BEEN ANNOUNCED TODAY THAT ADMIRAL LORD HOOD, CHIEF OF NAVAL OPERATIONS, IS TO HEAD A DIPLOMATIC MISSION TO THE SURVIVING EARTH COLONIES TO DISCUSS RECONSTRUCTION. UEG SOURCES SAY THAT SOME COLONIES HAVE REBUFFED THE OFFER AND WON'T NEGOTIATE WITH THE ADMINISTRATION THEY FEEL ABANDONED THEM. IN OTHER NEWS, UEG PRESIDENT CHARET HAS UNVEILED HER NEW CABINET. AMONG THE CASUALTIES IS COLONIES MINISTER DAVID AGNOLI, WHO'S BEEN REPLACED BY AKEYO ODUYA.

(Waypoint Nine news update, January 2553)

**Forerunner Dyson sphere, Onyx:
four hours into reconnaissance patrol.**

Mendez did the calculations in his head again as he waded through long grass that left burrs on his pants. Three thousand times three, divided by five hundred, equaled eighteen. They could eke out their emergency rations for eighteen days if they scraped by on a rock-bottom five hundred calories a day.

Eighteen days eating that crap. It's going to seem like a hell of a lot longer. How bad can lizard be? I ate a lot worse in escape-and-evasion training.

As far as he knew, Halsey didn't carry an escape belt, which meant she didn't have a survival pack that included three bars of the most foul-tasting but nutritionally dense substance known to man. Anyone who'd had to survive on special forces emergency bars found regular MREs to be a damn five-star restaurant experience by comparison. It was just as well the escape belt included an animal snare plus a hook and line. Mendez was up for cooking anything that moved.

But he and the Spartans would have to pool their supplies to feed Halsey if push came to shove. He wasn't sure if he resented that or not.

Okay, stay hydrated, and hope the Forerunners thought of everything.

The two structures looked more like old-fashioned cooling towers the closer he got to them. Their walls seemed to be either tiled or decorated with ashlars. It was hard to tell with Forerunner structures because they had a habit of shifting and changing moment to moment, but he could definitely see a grid of indented lines at regular intervals. The grass gave way to scattered trees. Mendez kept a wary eye above him, expecting more flying cylinders to buzz them.

Tom caught up with him as if he was going to ask a question but he didn't say anything. They walked side by side in silence for a while, picking their way through the trees, dividing their attention between scanning for possible threats in the branches and checking the ground beneath for anything edible. Mendez couldn't see Tom's expression. He knew him well enough by now to pick up on his mood though.

"You okay, son?" Mendez asked.

"Yes, Chief."

"You know you did all you could."

"Yeah. It's just the first time someone's sacrificed their life for me. Deliberately, I mean."

Mendez knew that was hard and that it would only get harder until Tom made peace with himself about it. But it was way too soon. Kurt, William, Dante, and Holly weren't cold in their graves yet, and everyone—himself included—was still at that stage where the deaths hadn't become an integral part of the new reality. Mendez found himself thinking and acting as if nothing much had happened, and then suddenly remembering who he'd lost. He hadn't forgotten about it; it was just that grief was set aside out of habit because that was the only way to cope, and every so often it would come crashing back on him, triggered by a dumb thought like needing to tell Kurt something and then remembering that he was dead.

They didn't have a war to fight any longer. Terrible as it was, combat could be a blessing. It didn't give you time to think until much later. Now they all had plenty of quiet time on their hands to brood about the people they'd lost.

"We don't *know* he's dead," Tom said. "Only that he didn't make it into the sphere."

Mendez just looked at him. He didn't believe in humoring anyone. It didn't spare them the reality that would eventually hit them all the harder.

"Even a Spartan can't hold off a Covenant army," he said. *And even Spartans lose one buddy too many and start to crack.* He thought of Lucy. "No matter how much gung-ho BS we spin the public."

Tom did a quick reluctant nod that seemed almost apologetic, as if he was embarrassed to be caught clutching at straws. Mendez turned slowly and took a few paces backward to check behind, but he was more interested in keeping an eye on Halsey. *You wouldn't stop at anything, would you, Doc?* Kelly ambled along beside her, looking more like close protection. She didn't seem remotely troubled by the fact that Halsey had abducted her for this jaunt.

Not for the first time either. Goddamn. The things we treat as normal. The things we accept. I used to be a regular guy, and now look at the crap I get up to.

Halsey glanced at him for a second, all suspicion. Yeah, so Ackerson took her research and Mendez had cooperated with him. *So what?* She'd already given up on the Spartan program because she didn't think her next tranche of candidates was good enough. What did she think this was, some private hobby, that all those lives lost and all that pain could just be flushed because it didn't meet her personal standards? If she'd called it a day because her conscience had kicked in, that would have been different. But it hadn't. And Ackerson, unlovable dick or not, at least made sure that lives spent on the program hadn't been wasted.

Wonder where he is now?

Listen to yourself, Mendez. Denial. You're still in goddamn denial. The UNSC used child soldiers. Under-tens. Tin-pot dictators who did that ended up charged with war crimes. What does that make you?

Mendez forced himself to concentrate on the crisis right in front of him. Being cooped up with Halsey and the fruits of their guilty labor was only going to get harder. He brought the patrol to a halt fifty meters from the towers to assess the entrance and the safest way to approach, looking up at the concave walls for anything that resembled doors. He couldn't see any, but that didn't necessarily mean there was no entrance.

He opened the radio attached to his collar. "Lieutenant? We've reached the foot of the tower. We don't see you."

"We took a detour, Chief." Fred sounded upbeat. "Got something to show you. We're heading for your position."

The trees and grass ended fifteen meters from the tower. A paved perimeter surrounded the whole structure, like a service road made of completely regular flagstones. Mendez walked a few meters along the wall, peering at the pale gold stone blocks in the hope of seeing a hairline split that would indicate an opening. He didn't plan to touch it until the other squad caught up with him, just in case he triggered an unknown mechanism that swallowed them up in another protective sphere. Halsey wandered along behind him. She didn't touch the wall either.

"If this place is a survival bunker, then there has to be more here than supplies and accommodation for sitting this out," Mendez said. "There'll be whatever the Forerunners needed to start rebuilding after it was safe to come out. Weapons. Comms. And transport. How did they get ships in here?"

Kelly took off her helmet to scratch her scalp. "Let's hope they were as smart about expiration dates as they were with dimensional physics."

"But how would they know when it was safe outside?" Olivia asked. "Okay, they'd have a good idea *in theory* of how long the Halos would take to wipe out the Flood, but if all that was left of their entire civilization was holed up here, they'd want to make absolutely sure."

"Now there's a good question." Halsey rummaged in her bag and took out a water bottle. Mendez wondered if she'd hidden another sidearm in there. He wasn't planning to give her weapon back to her until he was sure she wasn't going to pull another stunt like the hijack. "This might not have been their only bunker, of course. It's a big galaxy. But they'd still want to be able to check outside before they opened the door. Perhaps even communicate with other shield worlds."

"But who put the Katana and the other guys in the cryo pods?" Mendez asked. He wondered why he hadn't worried about that detail sooner. "Doesn't that bother anyone?"

"Perhaps we should be asking why they decided to get into them instead," Halsey said.

"Sounds like an assumption, Doctor."

Mendez knew she hated that. She took a pull from the bottle and put it back in her bag, ignoring the bait. He stared hard at the leather, looking for an outline of a weapon, but the bulges just looked like women's stuff and square-edged books or data-pads.

"So let's see what we find, Chief," she said carefully.

Mendez checked his watch, wondering just how much out of sync with real time the Dyson sphere would be. Halsey gave the impression of being able to work out that kind of stuff on a nap-kin. He hoped she could. Could any of them really know if time was suspended in here, like it seemed to be in those cryo pods? What did that *feel* like?

The crunch of boots on gravel and then on paving heralded Fred's arrival with Lucy, Linda, Mark, and Ash. Fred had some-thing in his hand. Mendez's reflex reaction was to wonder what the hell he was doing with tennis balls, but then he realized Fred was clutching three spherical yellow fruits one-handed. He held them out to Mendez.

"We ought to run tests on these first," Fred said. "I've logged the location. Anyone got an assay pack?"

Mendez sniffed one of the fruits cautiously, picking up a faint smell of cedar wood. Its texture was like sticky suede, almost quince-like, but it wasn't a quince. He hadn't had to do this bush-craft stuff for years.

"Over to you, Doctor." He handed the fruits to Halsey, who

put them in her bag. "I've got some test strips for cyanogenic glycosides and alkaloids somewhere in my kit."

"I'll take a look at them later," Halsey said. "Let's find a way to get into this tower."

Fred motioned for everyone to move. "Okay, people, spread out and take a section of wall each. This tower first, then we'll try the other one. If anything opens, nobody steps in. Just call it. I don't want anyone stuck on the wrong side of a door we can't open."

The scale and lateral curve of the tower only sank in when Mendez began inching his way along his section of ashlars. He realized that he couldn't see Mark to one side of him or Linda to the other unless he took a few paces back from the wall. He ran his hands over the stone, not sure what he was feeling for but expecting some kind of mechanism to detect him and either open a hatch or at least display some controls. All the Forerunner technology he'd encountered so far did that kind of thing. But the wall remained steadfastly unresponsive.

"If you build a bomb shelter, you make it easy to find and get inside." Halsey walked past him. She wasn't searching the wall but pacing slowly along the paved perimeter with her eyes on the flagstones. "Imagine it. Things have gone badly wrong, the Flood is overrunning the galaxy, and all the Forerunners in the sector pile in here as fast as they can. No matter how advanced they were, they'd have needed to orientate themselves."

"Then why not put the signs near the front door?" Mendez asked. "What if they never finished this place? Because they're not around anymore, are they?"

Halsey said nothing but walked on, head down, the soles of her black loafers tapping on the flagstones. It was too easy to see the Forerunners as not simply advanced but godlike, just like the

Covenant did. But Mendez knew all too well that brilliant technology didn't guarantee infallibility. Even humans hadn't always
thought of their own gods as being perfect, honest, or even competent.

"Ah well . . ." He promised himself a few comforting drags on
his cigar in two hours. The gold wall felt oddly warm and smooth
under his fingers, like living skin. "Maybe we need to go back and
check the portal area."

Click . . . click . . . click.

"Jackpot," Halsey called. "Look."

Mendez turned and jogged after her. All the Spartans con-
verged on the same spot. Halsey was standing with her weight on
one foot, the other held a little off the ground as if she'd been
frozen in the middle of playing a kids' game of hopscotch. She'd
looped the strap of her bag around both shoulders like a satchel,
adding to the impression of a middle-aged schoolgirl.

"So *this* is what happens if you tread on the cracks," she said.

Mendez stared at the flagstones. They'd come alive with pulsing illuminated symbols. A straight line of Forerunner glyphs,
picked out in a soft blue light, led along the paving and curved
up the wall to waist height. Halsey walked along the line. For all
Mendez knew, it could have been a warning to keep clear. They'd
find out the hard way.

"Can you read that?" he asked.

"It's a sequence of numbers," Halsey said. "But beyond
that—no idea."

She reached out and touched the top symbol. Nothing happened for a few moments, but then Linda and Fred swung around
ready to open fire as if they'd heard something that Mendez hadn't.
He looked back at Halsey just as the wall above him split along
a neat vertical line and parted all the way down to the ground.

Nothing actually moved; the stone blocks just suddenly vanished. In his world, doors that suddenly flew open tended to spew small-arms fire.

The Spartans split instantly into two groups without a word and stacked either side of the opening, rifles ready. Halsey froze. Mendez reminded himself to give her his pistol.

"Steady . . ." Fred said. "Check first. Shoot later."

Mendez moved around to face the opening head-on. He could see movement in his optics and his finger began tightening on the trigger. Then the movement resolved into gliding gray cylinders like the one that had swooped on them earlier. There were six this time. They moved out of the opening and arranged them-selves along the wall at head height. Mendez wasn't sure if they could detect weapons, but they didn't seem to be making any de-fensive moves.

"So what *are* you?" Halsey murmured. One cylinder separated from the rest and came to a halt just in front of her face. To her credit, she didn't even blink. "What are you monitoring? That's what you're doing, isn't it?"

The cylinder moved from Halsey to Mendez, hovering so close that he felt it was staring into his eyes even though he couldn't see a single damned detail on it. He held his breath until it moved away, smooth and silent, to hover in front of Kelly's visor. She stood motionless with her rifle in one hand. Then she grabbed it, as fast as a chameleon ambushing a fly. It was so quick that Men-dez didn't even have time to flinch.

"Gotcha," she said, peering at it.

The cylinder didn't seem to be struggling. The other cylinders drifted away into the trees as if they had better things to do than hang around amusing humans.

"It feels like it's not here. It doesn't weigh anything." Kelly flexed her gloved fingers around it. "Wow. This is the strangest thing I've ever felt."

Halsey held her hand out and took the cylinder cautiously. She drew her chin in, frowning. "I see what you mean. That's . . . well, extraordinary. Better hope I'm right and that it's just some kind of recon drone."

Mendez resisted the urge to touch it and see what all the fuss was about. "We're still making a lot of assumptions, Doctor."

"Forerunner technology can recognize humans. So I'd call it an educated guess."

Lucy peered around the opening in the wall and Mendez gestured to her to cover him while he checked inside. He couldn't see anything. Then the whole damn interior lit up like Christmas, flooding the walls with lights and symbols from waist height to about five meters, reminding him of the control room of a power station. But it was completely, eerily, *silent*.

Lucy, just as silent, explored the chamber. It was about thirty meters wide but Mendez couldn't see a ceiling in the gloom above. When he glanced back over his shoulder, Fred and Kelly were in the doorway, silhouetted against the daylight.

"There's no way we can jam this open if it decides to shut," Fred said.

Mendez felt they didn't have much choice but to explore the place. "We'll have to take our chances."

Then Lucy grabbed his forearm so hard that it hurt. He spun around. She made a shut-up gesture, finger to lower third of her visor, and pointed into the shadows on the left. The poor kid hadn't spoken a word for eight years. But he knew how to listen to her. He held up a hand to stop everyone and edged forward.

Maybe she'd picked up something in her infrared filter. He still couldn't see anything. But then he *heard* it.

Something was moving away from them. It wasn't a cylinder. It sounded like wet leather slapping against stone followed by the clatter of metal, getting fainter and almost echoing. Something was moving down a passage. The sound died away into silence again.

Mendez nodded at Lucy. Halsey crept up to him, ignoring the order to stay put, still clutching the cylinder.

"What is it?" she asked.

"No idea. But that didn't sound like the central heating boiler to me."

"But we were the first in here. We activated the core room."

"No, we just found a way in." Mendez checked his ammo clip and headed into the shadows, stomach knotted tight. "But some- one else found it first."

Osman tried the CO's seat on the bridge and felt small and alone. She hadn't expected that. It certainly didn't give her a thrill.

I've always been a spy in a blue suit.

She'd never felt like a real naval officer. ONI had taken custody of her as a fourteen-year-old, educated her, put her through the ONI commanders' program, and reinvented her. She'd deployed in ONI's fleet before, but she'd never had day-to-day command of a ship. Now she was going to find out the hard way if she could cut it.

Well, Parangosky thinks I can. . . .

"In case you're interested," BB said, "I'm doing the final launch checks. Would you like me to spell them out?"

Osman couldn't see him. She stared straight ahead at the disc of Mars, a small rusty smudge framed in light-speckled blackness in the forward viewscreen. "I trust you, BB." He could have left it all to the dumb AI, of course. "Where is everybody? Secure for launch."

"The ODSTs are in the wardroom. They're *very* excited about having their own cabins. I can tell from their bio signs. Poor little waifs."

"Don't stalk them, BB. It's creepy."

"Just monitoring, Captain. And Phillips is checking out the crates in the cargo bay. I think reality has dawned on him. Are you happy having him embarked?"

"Not really. Opsec worries."

"All comms go through me, Captain."

"I meant when we get back."

"Oh, I'll guarantee his silence. One way or another."

"I'll bet."

Osman suddenly needed something to focus on. She turned around in her seat because BB's voice felt as if it was coming from behind her. He was, of course, everywhere at once; he was in every part of the ship's systems, observing via every monitor and camera, controlling every aspect of its operation, in touch with Earth and able to hear and respond to any callsign in the galaxy, omniscient and omnipotent—for the few years he had to live, anyway. An AI was a short-lived god. When she turned back to face forward, BB materialized a meter in front of the bulkhead.

"And where's Naomi?" she asked.

"Heading this way," BB said. "You might as well tell her."

The Spartan had been giving Osman odd looks all the way out here in the shuttle. Naomi seemed to realize she knew her but couldn't place the face. Osman thought she'd changed a lot since her early teens, but some features didn't alter with age.

"Yes, we've already got enough secrets to keep from one another." Osman got up and stood facing the doorway onto the bridge, resting her backside on the comms console. "I'll tell the others too. If we're running arms for Sangheili psychos, I suppose my status pales into insignificance. No reason why I can't, is there?"

BB moved around to settle in her line of sight. "The Admiral gave you carte blanche. Weapons free, repel all boarders, no prisoners, et cetera et cetera. Do whatever you need to get the job done . . . just don't get caught, there's a dear."

BB had a rather arch way with him. Osman found herself smiling. *Dear.* Things were going to get very informal. She could hear Naomi coming now, the steady thud of her boots on the deck as she strode along the passage in that massively heavy armor she didn't actually need at the moment. Spartans had their comfort blankets too.

How would I have coped with the Mjolnir? Would I feel naked without it? Would I know where I ended and it began?

Naomi loomed in the doorway. She had that faint frown that said a memory was still eluding her. "Ready to slip, ma'am?"

"Five minutes." Osman realized BB had disappeared, or at least his avatar had. "Anything you want to ask me, Naomi?"

Using her name rather than addressing her as *Spartan* got a slight reaction. Osman noted a couple of rapid blinks.

"Yes, ma'am," Naomi said at last. "I think I know you, but I don't know where from."

"It's been a long time. And my name wasn't Osman back then. Like you, I didn't even *have* a surname."

Osman had rarely come face-to-face with Spartans from her batch. On the handful of occasions when she had, she found they were pretty good at forgetting because they'd been made to forget so much. She concentrated on Naomi's pale gray eyes, searching for the moment the penny dropped. The Spartan had now stopped blinking completely.

Naomi struggled with the name. "Sarah?"

"*Serin.* Serin-Zero-One-Nine. Remember me now?"

As Osman watched the revelation build on Naomi's face, she felt the tension drain from her own shoulders. The relief was both unexpected and incredible. She hadn't realized she'd been that worried about it.

But it's out. Thank God for that. Someone other than me and the select few in ONI knows who I am.

Nearly half of the seventy-five children who'd been taken for the program didn't make it past augmentation treatment at fourteen. The few who didn't die were left disabled. Osman didn't know what Halsey had actually told her successes about the fate that had befallen her failures.

"We thought you'd died," Naomi said.

Well, that answered Osman's question. "I did, near as damn it. ONI put me back together again, so now you know. And don't tell me how *normal* I look. I still have some enhancements, but nothing skeletal."

All Osman had needed was to see the look on Naomi's face. It was a kind of validation. She'd been wiped out of existence twice, first as a kidnapped kid taken to Reach, then erased from the Spartan program, but now nobody could erase her again.

I exist. I'm here. And I'm going to head up ONI.

Naomi settled at one of the comms stations and secured the seat belt as if nothing had happened. "We'd better get going, ma'am."

Osman wasn't sure if the subject was closed or not. If it wasn't, it would have to wait. She was about to summon the ODSTs when they arrived on the bridge with Phillips and BB. All three of them—even Devereaux—stood at ease looking like everyone's worst nightmare; unsmiling, unblinking, and silent. Mal and Vaz had do-not-spill-my-beer written all over them. It was partly the buzz-cut hair and complete absence of expression, but also . . . damn, Osman couldn't quite pin it down. Whatever it was, she was sure she could pick an ODST out of a lineup every time, male or female. It was that earnest hardness, that sense that they would do absolutely anything they were tasked to do, however insane or impossible, and that once they were let off the leash only shooting them would stop them.

"Cabins okay?" she asked.

Mal thawed a little. His file said he was thirty-three but he looked younger, with a fuzz of dark hair and just a few lines around the eyes that suggested he actually spent a lot of time laughing. Vaz—who managed to look both time-worn and twenty-something at the same time—had one of those lean, high-cheekboned Slavic faces and a spectacular scar the full width of his jaw. He didn't seem the laughing kind at all.

"Brammers, ma'am," Mal said, deadpan. Osman assumed from his tone that it was high praise. "We never normally get a pit to ourselves. Vaz is delirious about it. Honest."

"I'll take your word for it." The only problem with drawing ODST recruits from all nations and all three services was that many of them were completely unintelligible even in English. It was part of their curious charm. "There's a set of upgraded recon armor for each of you too."

"Thank you, ma'am. Luxury."

"Okay. Secure for launch. BB, you have the ship."

Phillips never said a word as he buckled in. Osman caught his eye. If anything, he looked amused, as if she hadn't fooled him at all about what ONI was actually up to.

BB appeared settled on the console in front of her. "Thirty seconds . . . receiving final updates . . . you *could* have sedation, you know."

Osman couldn't hide a thing from him. She knew she'd kissed good-bye to privacy before she was even old enough to understand what it was, but an AI could know more about someone than their own mother. Protective or not, it rattled her. BB had access to every cockpit recording and medical report, and he could probably pick up her pulse rate, too, the intrusive little bastard.

She heard one of the ODSTs trying to stifle a yawn. Nothing fazed them. *Port Stanley*'s drives rose from a faint whine to what she could only describe as an intense nonsound that made her brain feel like it was being sucked down her Eustachian tubes.

It was too late to stop. The drives were spooled up and committed to jump now. "I can deal with it," she said.

"Late databurst incoming . . . never mind, that'll have to wait . . . five seconds." BB executed a smart one-eighty-degree spin. "Place your bets on where and when we emerge, ladies and gentlemen . . . and *jump*."

Osman never looked at the external view. She couldn't. Her gut plummeted and went on falling. Her brain told her she was tumbling head over heels down an unending tunnel, even though she could see her own fingers digging into the padded black armrests of her chair. Her eyes flickered uncontrollably as they tried to make sense of the misleading impulses from her brain. She was falling, completely out of control, and that was all there was to it. The sickening sensation behind her eyes crept down her neck and made her hunch her shoulders.

Then she hit a brick wall. For a moment she was swaying horizontally on a storm-tossed deck, and then everything slowed to a stop. Throwing up wasn't a very captainly thing to do. She gritted her teeth and waited for it to pass.

She must have sat there longer than she realized. One of the ODSTs leaned over her.

"You okay, ma'am?" Devereaux asked.

Osman made an effort to stand up and look vaguely in command. "Jumps don't agree with me."

"Like Nelson. Never did his reputation any harm though."

"Nelson had a translight drive, did he? Well, that explains Trafalgar."

"No, ma'am, but he always puked his ring when he went to sea. . . ."

Osman smiled despite herself. She was grateful not to see her breakfast in her lap. "Could be worse, then."

The view from the forward bulkhead projection was a dense, featureless void far blacker than normal space. But it wasn't just *Port Stanley* that had slipped into a different dimension. Osman found herself in a new reality as well. This wasn't ONI. Nobody here was calculating the best moment to make a play for her job or sending their AI to hack her systems. The people around her were just doing a job and watching their buddy's back, not looking for the best place to insert a knife in it. Osman suddenly found herself disarmed by something that wasn't exactly innocence—they *were* ODSTs, after all—but that pressed the same button in her.

Uncomplicated. Straightforward. Transparent. Loyal. No threat. Well, not to me, anyway.

"Okay, people, I make it forty-eight hours to Brunel, so familiarize yourselves with the ship," Osman said. "BB, what was in that databurst?"

The AI flashed an image onto the bulkhead display. It was a video transmission showing the pennant code ident of UNSC

Ariadne. Osman wasn't an engineer, but she could recognize an accelerator-shielding bulkhead when she saw one. *Ariadne*'s engineers were sending back images of a technical problem and asking for advice from Earth. There was no way of finding out what had happened until *Port Stanley* was back in normal space and comms were restored.

"Where is she?" Osman asked.

"She had to drop out of slip near Venezia," BB said. "The CO made contact with the colony to ask to land nonessential personnel because of the safety risks, but they refused."

"Since when did a human colony get to say no to a UNSC request for assistance? Even Venezia?" Osman realized *Ariadne* was only a small patrol ship, but she was still armed. Osman would have landed shuttles and argued the toss later, cannoned up if need be. Venezia had gone quiet during the Covenant War, but everyone remembered what it had done during the colonial insurrection. "Who the hell's driving that tub?"

"Commander Pasquale."

The name didn't ring a bell. She started to check her datapad for the UNSCN list, but decided to leave it for later. "As soon as we're out of slip, check whether anyone else has responded or if they're still in trouble."

"You're not planning to divert, are you?"

"I know my orders, BB. I just want to know what Venezia's playing at."

Osman had mentally filed most of the hundreds of human colony worlds with one-word labels: glassed, silent, hiding, resentful, struggling, loyal, outlaw. Venezia had dropped off the plot more than ten years ago, when it was a known safe haven for terrorists. It could have been dusting off old grievances now that it thought the Covenant was gone.

Vaz stared at the image of the backside of a hazmat-suited engineer squeezing into a small machinery space. He didn't look amused.

"Can't help hoping the hinge-heads pay Venezia another visit," he muttered. "But I suppose you can make that happen, can't you, ma'am?"

Vaz seemed to catch on fast. *Good choice, that one. The Psych Eval deadbeats have their uses.* Ethics were never simple in ONI, because planetary politics weren't simple either, but Osman could see that lines would get much more blurred before too long.

"Yes, I can," she said.

Parangosky's words came back to her. *Never settle a score until it's tactically useful and you're certain you can finish the job. Then make sure they know you did it. That's how you keep them all in line.* Osman had all her mentor's words of wisdom filed mentally too, just like the disposition of colony worlds.

She went back to her cabin and splashed her face with cold water to stop the throbbing in her temples. When she straightened up from the basin and scrutinized herself in the mirror, she still looked drained of blood. That wasn't going to inspire confidence in anyone. She reached into the small cabinet behind the mirror to find a shot of analgesic, but her fingers brushed against something smooth and sharp-edged that crackled.

It was a glistening, transparent bag of crystallized ginger, scrunched into a pouch and tied with a gold bow. A tiny handwritten tag dangled from it. Osman read it, chuckling to herself.

You'll find this works pretty well for nausea. MP.

Yes, Parangosky had hidden facets. If you crossed her, she could make sure you ended up very, very dead. But if she liked you—if she trusted you, if she respected you, if she felt you deserved better than the hand you'd been dealt—then she'd be your guardian angel.

It didn't happen often.

Osman popped a cube of ginger in her mouth and savored the burn all the way down to the hangar bay.

Mdama, Sanghelios.

Jul 'Mdama realized that the old ways weren't working any longer, but he had nothing to take their place.

He stood at the kaidon's door and waited for the old man to acknowledge him. Courtesy cost nothing, after all, and Levu had always been a sensible leader. Jul was ready to tear down society but he drew the line at personal disrespect.

"You don't look happy, Jul." Levu, seated at his huge wooden table, beckoned him into his office. The table had been carved from a single piece of jet-wood, legs and top together, no joints or separate pieces at all, and a thousand years of constant use had polished it to a satin blackness. "What can I do for you?"

"I have to know where you stand on the Arbiter," Jul said.

"On the truce with the humans?"

"That's our most immediate problem. Whatever my wife says."

"I haven't opposed him, if that's what you mean. But I don't plan to sanction an assassination either."

"Well, I have my answer, then. A mistaken answer, but an answer nonetheless."

Jul had no idea why he stood there a moment longer. He'd been given his answer and Levu wasn't going to change his mind. Helplessness overwhelmed him for a moment, a frustration akin to seeing flames licking at a building and being unable to make its occupants heed his calls to run and save themselves. But it was his world that would burn if nobody listened. He was sure of that.

"Do *you* think we can make peace with humans, Kaidon?"

Levu put his hands flat on the table in front of him. It was a gesture of resignation. He'd always been a pragmatist. "I think they're devious creatures that can be held in place with the right degree of mutual threat," he said. "And I think that we're in no shape to mount the kind of attack that could wipe them out cleanly. But that's not to say I *want* to make peace with them. We do what we must."

The only items on Levu's desk were his computer from the San'Shyuum system that had linked the Sangheili city-states to their Prophet masters, and an *arum*—part puzzle, part ornament, a wooden ball of nested concentric spheres carved from a single piece of wood much as the ancient desk had been. It sat on a carved base. Hidden in its core was a small gem crystal of some kind that could only be shaken free when the player worked out the complex alignment of spheres.

The object seemed impossible to anyone except the craftsman who made it. Youngsters learned patience from it. Apart from providing diversion and strengthening character, it was said to represent what made the Sangheili strong; a perfectly engineered, orderly system that presented a smooth, impenetrable face to the outside world, and each had his appointed place in it. Jul suddenly saw it another way.

He reached out for it and waited for Levu to give him a nod to pick it up.

"Have you ever released a crystal?" Levu asked.

"Once. Then never again." Jul held the *arum* in his right hand, one thumb on the anchor piece, and pushed his nail into one of the holes to move one of the inner spheres. He put it back on its base. "But this is indeed what we are. Good day, Kaidon."

"Good day, Jul. Have patience."

Jul bowed his head politely and left. There was no point arguing with Levu because there was nothing to argue against. The kaidon made perfect sense, just as the Arbiter had also made perfect sense when he said the Sangheili had surrendered their selves and their ability to run their own affairs.

And the *arum* summed up the problem. To reach the core, each sphere had to be operated in turn to activate the next. No sphere could act without the next one in a hierarchy that was impossible to reorder. It mirrored the Sangheili social structure and Jul wondered if that was the unspoken rule the *arum* actually taught children and reinforced in adults—that the keep system had to be obeyed and that flouting it was impossible. The family keeps all needed the approval of their township keep to act, and the township keeps answered to their city keep in its turn, spheres within spheres.

Above that, though, there was nothing now that the San'Shyuum had been ousted. A world of eight billion needed more than a mass of uncoordinated fiefdoms to deal with the humans.

And those Jiralhanae who've turned on us. We have many enemies now. As the humans say—the lid has come off.

Jul found himself at the end of the colonnade that connected Levu's keep to the marketplace without remembering the walk at all. It was a bad sign. And he still didn't have a plan.

Do I dispute Levu's decision and exercise my right to assassinate him?

His grievance wasn't with Levu, and there was no point acting alone anyway.

There's Forze . . .

But he needed more than a friend to back him up. He needed to find an army of like-minded patriots. Honor was all very well for settling clan disputes, but it was pitifully inadequate for fighting a war.

He walked all the way back to Bekan. It took him hours, but he needed the time to think. As he walked along the highway, he saw serfs working in the fields, but still very few Unggoy. Perhaps it was for the best. Sanghelios should never have allowed itself to rely on alien races, either as masters or servants.

He stopped on the aqueduct to gaze out over the valley. In the center of the Relon clan's farmland, a fifty-span area of grass had been left untouched around the remnants of a Forerunner monument, an elegant but crumbling three-sided spire that had snapped off five meters above the soil. It was sacred ground, the handiwork of the gods, and not to be touched. As a child Jul had never dared say he thought it strange that gods should need to build ordinary things, and that many of those things would crumble in time just like any mortal's work, but now he knew he'd been right.

Even now that the Prophets had been exposed as liars, though, nobody had attempted to cross the boundary and plow up the grass.

Does it matter? I think not.

By the time Jul got back to his keep, it was long past the mid-afternoon mealtime. Children raced past him, hissing and squabbling. He grabbed one of the boys by his collar and yanked him to a halt.

"Discipline, Kimal," he said. He noted that his sons weren't in the unruly mob. *Good.* "You're not infants, any of you. I expect better."

"Sorry, my lord."

Kimal slunk away. The sober mood spread through the others in a heartbeat. Jul climbed the steps to his own keep and went looking for Raia. He found her in her private chamber, doing the accounts for all the Bekan clan keeps, a time-consuming job that fell to the wife of the elder. It never improved her mood.

"Where have *you* been?" she demanded. "Forze called. He wants to talk to you. And you missed the meal. Is this what it's going to be like now you're back from the front? Wandering around wasting your time?"

"I went to see Kaidon 'Mdama. He's going to support the Arbiter." Jul waited for an acid comment but none came. "Did Forze say what he wanted?"

"He said that old man Relon's going to blow up the holy spire. Seeing as the gods are dead, he didn't think they'd mind him plowing the land to grow tubers."

Jul found it odd to hear her talking so disrespectfully about the Forerunners. She'd always been the devout one in the marriage. Perhaps, like others, she was punishing the gods for letting liars and parasites deceive them and exploit them for so long.

"Aren't you offended by that?" he asked.

Raia considered the question, eyes fixed on the accounts folio, all her jaws clenched.

"It'll ruin a pretty view," she said at last.

Jul decided to leave well alone and went to find some leftovers in the kitchens, braving the disapproving snaps and hisses of the older wives who were trying to clean up before the next meal. Raia was right. He was in danger of looking for something to fill his time, just like every other Sangheili warrior who suddenly had no war to fight.

How do I wake my people? How do I galvanize them? The war isn't over.

He grabbed a couple of slices of roast meat on the way out, stopped to take an *arum* from one of the children in the courtyard, and went off to seek some clarity in the quiet at the top of the old watchtower. From the battlements, he could see right across the valley on a clear day. He lost himself in the *arum* for a while, utterly absorbed in trying every permutation of movement until a distant explosion jerked him out of the puzzle.

He stood up just as a second rumbling boom carried on the afternoon air, leaning on the edge of the stonework to look north. Smoke was rising into the air farther up the valley. When it cleared, Jul realized that the sacred spire was gone.

Relon had been as good as his word. Jul suspected it was another expression of the sense of betrayal, blaming the gods for three millennia of deceit. Gods, after all, should have been able to step in and bring the San'Shyuum to heel. They didn't: so they were either neglectful gods not worth worshiping, or they didn't exist at all. It was sobering to be alone in the universe.

Raia didn't pass comment on it at supper. Jul wondered whether to point it out to her but decided against it. He suspected there would be a rash of this destruction and then the novelty would wear off, and everyone would get on with their lives.

After breakfast the next morning, he went to the armory to see what personal resources he had left. It was all small arms. He couldn't seize a ship, not even if he added Forze's armaments and brothers to the raiding party. He would need to assemble a small army to commandeer a frigate from a crew loyal to the Arbiter, and assassinations—perfectly legal challenges to authority, an orderly and honorable way to resolve disputes—required personal weapons. Anything beyond that was dishonorable. It was also designed to stop feuds escalating into civil war.

So how do I find like-minded Sangheili? How do these old laws apply to the situation we find ourselves in now?

He was wondering whether to enlist his keep brothers in the plot when the ground beneath him shook a little. Then he heard three muffled *whumps* more like artillery fire than tree clearance. But the Forerunner spire had already been destroyed; what was Relon doing, pulverizing the rubble? There were quieter ways to do that. Annoyed at the thoughtlessness of his neighbor, Jul stormed outside and activated his comms to call Relon's keep. The channel was dead. *The old fool.* He'd have to drive over to the keep and ask him to stop this nonsense.

Jul called Gusay to bring the Revenant. "Gusay, where are you?" Jul was in the outer courtyard now, wondering why he could hear the familiar sound of a Spirit dropship in the distance. "Gusay, I need to pay a visit to Relon."

The comm channel was silent for a moment.

"My lord, Relon's keep is on fire. It's been attacked."

For an insane moment, Jul's first thought was that the gods had finally chosen to make an appearance. The destruction of the spire had enraged them. *No. That's superstition to keep you in your place. You know that now.* He was about to reply when the sound of the Spirit's drives grew a lot louder and the dropship suddenly roared over the keep, heading south. By the time Jul got outside, the Spirit had dwindled to a speck in the distance and a pall of smoke hung in the sky. Relon's keep had probably been burning for some time, judging by the density and spread. The Revenant whined to a halt at the end of the path and Gusay beckoned him from the open cockpit, looking agitated.

Raia shouted after them from an open window. "What's happening? Is it Jiralhanae? Humans? How did they get past our defenses?"

"It's *Sangheili,* my lady," Gusay called back. "It's our own."

Jul sprang into the passenger section. "What do you mean, *our own?*"

"The keep's been hit by plasma cannon."

"Impossible."

"Why? Who would do *that*?"

"No idea, my lord."

Jul tried to make sense of it as Gusay steered along the line of the highway between the keeps. Other keeps in the area had already responded to the explosions. The Revenant joined a small fleet of vessels and vehicles trying to get close to the burning buildings, and the kaidon's transports seemed to be everywhere. Nobody could accuse Levu 'Mdama of not coming to the aid of his client keeps.

Jul stared as Gusay brought the Revenant to a halt. The main keep was just a stump of rubble shrouded in smoke. He knew only too well what a plasma cannon strike looked like. He jumped down from the vehicle and went to walk through the gates, wondering why all the activity seemed to be in the courtyard and not the keep itself. The fire was cracking and hissing, but he could hear no roars of anger or panic. It was only when he turned a corner, gulping in a lungful of acrid smoke as the heat hit his face, that he understood why there was such *silence.*

He didn't take in the group of warriors, wives, and children clustered in the yard. He saw only what they were staring at. A scaffold of sorts had been made from a joist that jutted from the wall, and from it hung two objects that Jul took a few moments to recognize.

It was Relon and his brother, Jalam, both very old warriors, and both dead. Beneath their dangling bodies—what was left of them—were pools and splashes of purple blood. They were so mutilated that it was hard even for a shipmaster like Jul, used to combat and the ugly scenes it left in its wake, to work out exactly what he was looking at, but he couldn't drag his eyes from the horror even though he was desperate to look away. It took him some moments to realize Levu 'Mdama was standing next to him, staring in silence too.

A handwritten board hung from cords around Relon's neck made the situation very clear. The script was stylized and ancient, more like the scrolls of the priests from before the time of the war with the San'Shyuum. But Jul could read it easily enough.

We do not allow blasphemers to live
The gods demand a return to piety
Truth abides

"I thought they were all talk," Levu said quietly. "It seems that they've woken up again. They were everywhere when I was a boy."

"Who?" Jul couldn't work out why nobody was ushering the family away from the terrible scene. "How did they manage to do this in a keep? What are they?"

"The *Neru Pe 'Odosima*," Levu said. It was an ancient name in a form of Sangheili that was no longer spoken. "Fanatics. Fools."

Jul recalled the name. "The Servants of the Abiding Truth? But they were *monks*."

"Well, we let them become warriors, and now they're danger-ous, savage *fools*. And they seem to have stockpiled arms." The kaidon gestured to his aide to do something about the bodies. "Thun? *Thun!* Get those bodies down from there. Cover them. It's not decent."

Jul looked away from the slaughter and that brief lapse of attention let a stray thought cross his mind. He wished it hadn't, because the sane, responsible elder in him said this was all utterly wrong, cowardly—*dishonorable.* These were just old warriors who'd served Sanghelios and the gods all their lives. But the thought wouldn't go away.

And there was no better idea to take its place.

If these *Neru Pe 'Odosima* would butcher venerable old men for blowing up a meaningless ruin, they would surely take on the Arbiter for turning all Sangheili from the gods.

Abiding Truth was an existing network that Jul could draw on. Its followers were clearly willing to break every moral convention on disputes. Jul just had to work out how to organize and discipline them, and then he could bypass the kaidon and anyone else to bring down the Arbiter—and unite Sanghelios against the real threat that would inevitably return.

He would have to do deals with monsters for the greater good. The rules of war had changed.

CHAPTER 4

WHY DO WE BOTHER TO FORCE UNHAPPY COLONY WORLDS
TO STAY IN THE UN FOLD? BECAUSE UNSC BUDGETS AND
UNSC HEAVY LIFT ENABLED THOSE COLONIES TO EXIST.
BECAUSE THE UNSC NEEDS AS MANY SUPPLY BASES
IN DEEP SPACE AS IT CAN GET. AND BECAUSE THEY'RE
HUMAN—THEY'RE US. IN A GALAXY OF HOSTILE ALIENS,
YOU'RE EITHER FOR US, OR YOU'RE THE ENEMY.

(Admiral Margaret O. Parangosky, CINCONI,
to Captain Serin Osman)

Forerunner Dyson sphere, Onyx, four hours into reconnaissance patrol: local date November 2552.

The passage ahead of Lucy wasn't the tunnel it first appeared to be.

It could have changed shape in the second that she'd looked away, or maybe her helmet optics were on the fritz, but the opening was at least six meters high, a black, featureless maw that didn't appear to have interior walls.

Why make a door that big?

She took a few steps inside, rifle raised, and flicked on the tactical lamp. Her visor flared for a moment. *Nothing.* The cavern swallowed the light and kicked her armor's reactive coating into mottled black. She glanced down at her boots—now matte black, barely there—and realized she couldn't see a floor underneath them. It triggered a brief, primal panic. For a moment she was falling. It took a conscious effort to look up and make herself believe that she was on solid ground. She struggled to trust what she could feel rather than what she could see.

"Lucy? Hang on." It was Tom on the radio. "*Lucy!* Wait, will you?"

Two sets of boots thudded behind her. She hadn't realized how far into the opening she'd gone. Her helmet's head-up display showed that Chief Mendez and Tom were following her, the only two icons at close range. Tom's bio readout showed his pulse was raised. She decided to risk taking her eyes off the passage and turned around.

"What have we got, Lucy?" Tom caught up with her and put his hand on her shoulder. "You okay?"

Why did he think she wouldn't be? She waved him away. Something had come down this passage and she couldn't turn back until she'd found and identified it, and—if necessary—neutralized it. She checked her display for EM or thermal signatures ahead, but there was nothing. The ground was definitely flat and smooth like terrazzo. Now she'd started to trust her proprioception rather than her eyes, she picked up speed and started walking at a pace she thought of as cautious-normal.

"I'm going to fetch Halsey in here to evaluate this," Mendez said. Lucy kept moving. "Hold it here, Lucy. We'll secure a perimeter in case whatever it is decides to come back. You hear me, Petty Officer? *Hold it here.*"

Lucy halted. She couldn't shake the feeling that if she didn't hunt down whatever had fled, it would come back for them all. *Get it before it gets us.* She stood staring into the black void, wondering what kind of material could absorb light so completely.

The trouble with staring at a featureless surface was that it soon stopped being featureless. She could now see pinprick flashes of light and brightly colored moving shapes like mingling currents of dye. It was just her optic nerve trying to make sense of the absence of light, but she couldn't stop her brain from pouncing on the phantoms and reshaping them. Suddenly it was a twisting path with a tantalizing hint of lights ahead, and movement, and people.

Then the colored lights became the afterimage of a white-hot explosion.

Lucy had been here before. Part of her knew it wasn't happening, but it couldn't stop the animal core of her reacting to it. She was in a maze of pipes, in a Covenant refinery, and she could even see the coolant leaking and bubbling on the floor ahead of her. Tom was to her right. They were the last two Spartans left alive from Beta Company and now they were going to die as well. She was twelve years old; scared, running on autopilot, trying to gulp in a breath that never reached her lungs because the pounding pulse in her throat was choking her.

Then hands grabbed her shoulders and spun her around.

She raised her fist with no idea why, no thought involved. Only the crack of a visor against her own faceplate stopped her. She could still see the coolant pipes in her peripheral vision, fading and drifting, and then they were gone.

"Come on, Luce, get a grip." Tom still had hold of her shoulders. He knocked his helmet against hers a couple more times. "It's okay."

It felt like long minutes and Lucy was certain she'd moved a few meters. But it was seconds and she was still rooted to the same spot, just facing in the opposite direction. Her bio readouts must have spiked and scared the hell out of everyone.

"It's okay. I get it too," Tom stepped back as if he was satisfied she wasn't going to lose it. "Just take it easy. Breathe. It's not real. Any of it."

There were times when Lucy wished she could answer him, but there were no words left inside her now. After seven silent years, she didn't talk and she didn't scribble notes. Her head was full of things that nobody else would understand or want to hear. At first she'd had nothing to say in the hours after she'd escaped from the sabotaged refinery with Tom, and then she'd had things she'd wanted to say that were too painful. The heavy silence settled like silt in her chest, a little more each day, and each time she tried to work up to talking it was harder to find words that conveyed the images in her head, and then even her inner voice faded away.

She couldn't imagine speaking now. She didn't know where to start. It was just as well that Tom could work out what was going on in her head.

"Hey, Lucy." She was suddenly aware of Olivia striding toward her with Mark and Ash at her heels. They'd have seen her bio signs spiking too. "Couldn't you find the light switch?"

Ash tapped his knuckles against her armor and Olivia gave her a rough hug. When Lucy looked past her, Halsey was framed in the dim scatter of lights at the far end of the passage. For a moment she looked like she was standing in front of a decorated Christmas tree. It was a sharp little echo of buried memories, and then it was gone.

"Environmental controls," Halsey called. Her voice didn't echo. Lucy could hear her even with her helmet on. "Come here. Look."

Lucy hung back as the others headed for the entrance and

stood a meter inside the passage, just in case whatever it was she'd heard decided to return.

It's got to get past me.

It won't.

Halsey was running one hand over the illuminated Forerunner symbols on the walls. After a few moments of frowning at the lights as if they were being willfully stubborn, she held out the cylinder to Kelly.

"Here, hang on to this for me." She took out her datapad and unfolded it like a piece of origami into a laptop format. That didn't appear to satisfy her and she folded it up again into a datapad. Then she carried on running her hand along the symbols. "Okay, perhaps it's not environmental. I've found a symbol for humidity. This might be controlling storage conditions, so one of these could activate lights or orientate us."

"How do you know that?" Mendez asked, all suspicion.

Halsey flipped the screen and held it toward the wall. "I just do. Let's see what my database makes of this."

"And you wouldn't dream of keeping anything else from us."

"Chief, I won't lecture you on the wisdom of stones and glass houses, so just accept that I don't know *how* I know yet. I'm not hiding anything."

Lucy expected a scientist like Halsey to be more disturbed about random hunches. She backed away into the passage and set her helmet to record, just in case she picked up something.

"Luce . . ."

Tom's voice in her helmet was a quiet warning. She gave him an I'm-okay gesture, diver-style, and carried on. He could still see her bio readout so that would keep him happy until she came back. *Normal pulse and respiration. See? I'm fine. I can handle this. I'm not crazy. Just low blood sugar. Fatigue. I ought to eat something.*

"Luce, wait up. I'm coming. Damn it, you know better than that."

She moved across to the wall and held her rifle one-handed, skimming her left hand across the surface to orient herself, and suddenly she felt much better. The ground beneath her boots was smooth and level. Even if she couldn't see it she had a better idea of where she was.

I have to find where this leads. Something's in here. Something's waiting for us. If we found our way in—so might the Elites.

And Lucy had a lifetime of scores to settle. She didn't think there was anything wrong with her judgment at all.

When she stopped and looked over her shoulder, the faint light from the entrance had gone. She turned back, almost giddy because there was nothing to orient her. But the squad's bio signs were all visible on her HUD, so she hadn't lost comms signals, and she wasn't alone.

"One-Zero-Four to Bravo-Zero-Nine-One." It was Fred on the radio now. "Lucy, where the hell are you?"

He should have known he wouldn't get an answer, but if she could see his bio readout, he could see hers. He'd know she was fine. If the others wanted to faff around and look for the light switch, fine, but someone had to secure this passage. She was about to flash back a status signal when she collided with something that bounced her back a couple of steps.

Damn, she'd walked into a wall. That was what came of not concentrating on the task in hand.

"What is it, Lucy?"

Her heart rate must have blipped. She transmitted status-OK, then put her hand out ahead of her to feel her way around the obstruction. When her fingers touched it, it felt exactly like the side wall she'd been using for orientation, but then it yielded and her hand went through something soft. It was almost as if she'd put her hand into a closet and found a pile of towels.

Except . . . except her *whole body* passed through it. The wall brushed past her. It was the only way she could describe it.

As the wall engulfed her, the squad bio readouts in her HUD winked out. She tried to turn back. Too late: sudden pressure popped her ears, the ground dissolved under her, and she fell, pitching forward. Her helmet bounced away. It cracked loudly against something but she couldn't see where it had rolled.

And then the lights came on.

She couldn't yell a warning. She couldn't transmit a status report.

But she still had her rifle, and now she could see where to aim.

Hangar deck, UNSC *PORT STANLEY:*
approximately ten hours from New Llanelli.

"History's not my subject." Vaz bent over a crate of Covenant rifles and wondered whether ONI had paid for them or looted them. The hangar deck was a warehouse of crates stacked either side of a small dropship that looked like a civilian patrol vessel, although its matte gray stealth coating said otherwise. "But I recall that things like this often end very badly."

Naomi loomed over him. "So you *do* speak."

That was rich coming from her. She hadn't said more than a few words since the meeting with Parangosky. Vaz had already chalked that up to Spartans believing too much of their own PR, because everybody knew that they were winning the war single-handed. It was official. The UNSC media people had decided it was great for morale to tell the civvies all about the Spartans and what a superhuman job they were doing of saving Earth.

That didn't go down well with ODSTs. Vaz suspected it didn't go down well with all the other average, unglamorous grunts who were doing their fighting and dying behind the scenes either.

"Yes, I talk," Vaz said at last. "If I have something to say."

He couldn't read her expression at all. Even Mal hadn't tried to flirt with her, and that was a first. Naomi was just *odd*. Vaz had expected Spartans to be like the heroic PR image presented to the media, fearless and godlike, gazing nobly into the distance with one boot on a pile of dead hinge-heads. They weren't supposed to be *awkward*.

Her looks didn't set him at ease either. It wasn't so much the sharp features as her pale, translucent skin and platinum hair. They reminded him of nightmarish folk tales his grandmother told him as a kid, where female demons who looked like ice princesses dined on the giblets of unwary children. There wasn't much happily-ever-after in Russian fairy tales.

Come on, I'm ODST. I'm a big boy now. This is insane. Stop it.

Naomi tucked a strand of hair behind her ear. "You have to know how much gas to pour on a fire," she said, not even looking at him.

It sounded a bit zen. But they were up to their elbows in a crate of identity-tagged Sangheili rifles, so he decided they were back on the topic of the wisdom of arming hinge-heads.

"How come they're short of arms?" he asked. "I don't recall that being a problem when they were blowing our heads off."

"The Covenant civil war. The Great Schism. It cost them a lot of ships and equipment. And once they drove out the Prophets, they lost their supply chain. And their command and control." Naomi was suddenly transformed into something like a regular woman. This was obviously her pet subject. Her pack-ice eyes lit up. "So most of the rank and file don't have access to serious hardware now, and they're too disorganized to use it effectively anyway."

"So are they still fighting the Brutes?"

"Some. As far as we know." She seemed to be working up a sweat, puffing a bit as she heaved crates around. Without that power-assisted Mjolnir armor she had to rely on raw muscle, just like him, but he still didn't think he'd beat her at arm wrestling. She was genetically enhanced and it showed. "That'll spread them thinner than the butter on a Navy sandwich."

As soon as she said that, as soon as she even brushed close to griping, Vaz felt her change from the terrifying Baba Yaga into one of his own. Everyone in uniform griped about everything all the time. It was one of those fundamental things that bonded ships and armies. When the griping stopped, officers worried. Vaz relaxed a little.

"That's one feud we won't need to stir up." All the weapons were invisibly tagged to make them trackable, the transponder material worked into the metal itself. Vaz examined one of the energy swords to see if he could detect it on a casual inspection. "Will the hinge-heads fall for the tracking?"

"They've lost their Prophets and Engineers so they're not so technically hot now. But even if they spot it, I doubt they'll care. They'll think they can pick us off later."

Naomi suddenly jerked her head up, frowning. Vaz strained to listen and caught the sound of two Elites chattering on the radio. It had to be a recording of voice traffic intercepted before they entered slipspace, but it still had the power to make his flesh crawl. He wasn't going to shake it that easily. Nobody who'd fought those things at close quarters ever would.

He followed the sound, squeezing between the stowed drop pods, and ended up outside a small fire-control compartment aft of the dropship. The hatch was open. When he stuck his head inside, he found Phillips with his boots up on the console, fingers meshed behind his head, and eyes shut. His datapad sat in his lap. Its screen was flickering with rapidly scrolling lines of text.

Vaz waited for him to notice someone was there. It took a full minute. Phillips just opened his eyes and didn't even look startled.

"Dialect variation," he said. "Good stuff, this ONI eavesdropping kit."

Vaz had never actually heard Elites just talking before. He'd only heard them roaring what he assumed were terms of abuse as they came at him, or gurgling out their last curses or pleas as he finished them off the hard way. It was strange to imagine them having a chat. "You understand all that?"

Phillips tapped his jaw with his index fingers. "I *understand* it, and I can read it, but I don't have enough jaws to speak it like a native. There's a whole tonal layer I can't reproduce."

He cocked his head at the sound. There were two distinct voices, then a third cut in. The rumbling tones didn't mean a thing to Vaz but he was suddenly aware of a lot of clicks and gulps within the words.

He still didn't know what to make of Phillips.

They'd met less than two days ago and now they had to trust each other with their lives. Phillips was about Mal's age, with reddish brown scrubby hair and a matching beard. He looked a little fitter than the average civvie in a set of unbadged UNSC fatigues. Vaz suspected he'd probably wanted a bit of adventure in his life but hadn't had the balls to enlist. He wondered how Phillips was going to shape up when an Elite took a potshot at him.

"Do you *like* them?" Vaz asked.

"I've had direct contact with them. They're fascinating."

Vaz had had pretty direct contact with them too, and

fascinating wasn't the word that sprang to mind. "But you don't mind shafting them like this. Because that's what we're doing."

"Come on, it's not as if I'm falsifying research." Phillips made that sound like the worst possible thing a man could do. "I'd rather stay alive than die academically pure. Look, I know the Sangheili. They despise us. There's no forgive and forget, not after nearly thirty years of killing each other. The only reason they split from the Covenant and allied with us was because the Prophets were trying to exterminate them. Hardly the basis for a lasting marriage, is it?"

"We're not good at forgetting either," Vaz said. "Glad to know you haven't grown fond of them."

The conversation ended abruptly when BB appeared and hovered in the gap next to Vaz. ONI might have taken AIs for granted, but Vaz didn't, and judging by the way he jumped, neither did Phillips.

"Come along, gentlemen," BB said. "Chop-chop. Places to go, mayhem to cause." He rotated and headed for the ladder, not that he even needed to. "Final briefing at eighteen hundred. Captain on deck."

Phillips swung his feet off the console and stood up as BB vanished through the bulkhead. *Port Stanley* was so crammed with systems and holoprojectors that an AI could cover almost every centimeter of the ship. Vaz decided BB was just jerking a few chains for his own amusement.

"This is why I didn't do theology," Phillips whispered, as if he thought BB wouldn't hear him. "He isn't actually in any one place, is he? *Omnipresent.* That really messes with my mind."

It was a frank admission for a smart guy. "He's spread through-out the whole ship," Vaz said. "He's in every system. Right now, he *is* the ship."

"That occurred to me when I was taking a leak. It's not a happy thought."

Phillips didn't seem used to the indignities of communal living like service personnel. Vaz stifled a smile. "Don't you have AIs at the university?"

"Not like *that*. They're either dumb or they're terminal-restricted. And they're not that *human*."

"I think that's why UNSC ones have avatars, so we don't get too paranoid. I don't think the AIs actually need them."

"But he's not where his avatar is. That's what I'm struggling with."

"No." Vaz had learned the art of not fretting about unsettling things that he couldn't control. He just worked on the basis that BB, like the Corps, saw every move and heard every cough and spit he made. "Assume the worst. It makes life simpler."

He could hear Osman's boots on the gantry. As he picked his way between the crates around the dropship, Devereaux looked busy in the cockpit, head down and shoulders moving as if she was running her hands across the instrument panel. When he stepped up into the crew bay it was instantly clear that it wasn't a regular security vessel. The ONI engineers had gutted it. Now every centimeter of bulkhead was lined with surveillance equipment and screens.

Mal was stacking small crates. "Luxury, eh?" he said. "Can't remember the last time I landed on a planet without smashing into the ground."

Devereaux's voice came over the bulkhead speaker. "Can't recall the last time I did either."

"Okay, that's it. I'm changing my airline."

Both of them roared with laughter. Devereaux squeezed through the hatch into the crew bay and gave Vaz a friendly thump in the chest with her fist. "You know we haven't got a plan, don't you?"

"We never do." Vaz checked over his shoulder to see where Phillips was. He'd vanished. "They just drop us into the sewer and we work out how to clear it."

"Have you been charming our Spartan?"

"Just talking."

"Keep at it, Vaz," Mal said, winking. "Older birds are more grateful. Did she say why she keeps giving Osman the hairy eyeball?"

"No. I didn't ask."

"Trust me, there's definitely something going on there."

Vaz put his finger to his lips. They really weren't used to having fully sentient AIs around. Then it occurred to him that he was standing in a snake's wedding of cables and surveillance feeds accessible to BB, so even a shut-it gesture wasn't private.

Devereaux gave Vaz a very discreet wink. She nudged Mal with her elbow to get him moving kit again. "Come on, Mal. Put your back into it." She stuck her head out of the crew bay. "Phillips? You too. Come and shift this."

Vaz didn't have to wait long for proof that BB saw all and heard all. Osman appeared at the bay door with Phillips at her heels. He looked as if she'd smacked him for being a bad boy.

"How's it going?" she asked.

Mal straightened up. "Fine, ma'am. What's the plan?"

"I *do* have one."

Mal didn't even blink. "Ah. Permission to feel reassured."

"Granted. The Sangheili effectively have no top-level command and control left so the best we can do is hand them the weapons and see where the fault lines form." She didn't seem irritated, whatever BB had relayed to her. If anything, she seemed a little apologetic. "We're at the mercy of very patchy short-range comms, so there'll be a lot of surveillance to carry out."

"We can do patient too, ma'am," Mal said. Naomi appeared in the door and stood with one boot on the step, half-turned toward them. "We don't just jump out of orbit and shoot bad guys."

"Don't worry, Staff, you'll see some action." Osman paused a beat as if she was working up to something, then glanced at Naomi. "And you might as well know this now," she said, carefully matter-of-fact. "I was in the Spartan-Two program until I was fourteen. Naomi and I knew one another. But I'm not a Spartan now. Everybody okay with that? We're going to be living in each other's pockets for quite some time, so I don't want there to be any more secrets than are operationally necessary."

That was an unnatural thing for an ONI officer to say. Secrets were meat and drink to them. But it wasn't half as unnatural as the word *fourteen*. Osman just stood there as if she was inviting comments. Vaz assumed it was calculated, because ONI officers were never lost for words and patted down every syllable for incriminating evidence before it was allowed to leave their mouths.

Mal filled the gap. "You said *fourteen,* ma'am. Eighteen's the minimum age for enlistment."

"Correct. We started the program aged six." Osman gave Naomi a slow look and turned back to Vaz. "They couldn't complete the full augmentations until we were fourteen."

Mal went quiet, probably doing the same calculations and gap-filling that Vaz was right then. But Phillips just dived in, unafraid of the braid as only a civvie could be.

"This was a military academy, I assume," he said.

"Not exactly." Osman seemed to be on a gutspill. Vaz couldn't imagine any ONI officer doing that without a calculated reason. "Boot camp. Live rounds."

She looked as if she was going to say more but stopped dead. Vaz caught Naomi looking at Osman. Her thin-lipped expression said one thing: *traitor.* Vaz didn't know why the captain had decided to share it with them, and he definitely didn't know why it had pissed off Naomi so much, but Spartans obviously disapproved of talking outside the tent. Naomi just stood there, grim and silent.

Osman scratched the nape of her neck as if her neural interface was bothering her, then glanced at her watch. "Well, that's obviously broken more ice than I expected. Okay, BB, prepare to drop out in two hours and carry out a full comms sweep of the sector."

She jumped down from the crew bay and walked away. Naomi peeled off in the opposite direction. Nobody spoke until the click of Osman's boots changed to a metallic clang as she climbed the ladder to the upper gantry.

"Wonder why they didn't share *that* little gem with us," Mal said. "And why she *did.*"

Phillips looked from face to face as if the ODSTs knew more than he did. He really didn't understand the military yet. "Was she serious? That means they started the Spartan program before the Covenant war."

"Correct," said a disembodied voice. BB took a couple of seconds to appear, and Vaz noted that nobody flinched this time. "It's a long and complex story. A rather *messy* one."

"Thanks for not engaging our interest, BB," Devereaux said, sliding back through the cockpit hatch. "We're not remotely curious. Really."

Mal wasn't amused at all though. Vaz saw his jaw muscles working. "BB, are you going to trot off to her with every bloody thing we say?"

"You were concerned about the obvious tension," BB said

calmly. "I thought it was worth getting the captain to address it, seeing as we're living *en famille,* so to speak."

There was no answer to that. BB turned to Vaz. For a cube that wasn't really there and didn't actually need to turn to look at anything, his ability to convey which way he was looking fascinated Vaz. He seemed to have a faint dappling of light on one face of his cube.

"And you're right, Vasily," BB said. "An avatar *is* for the benefit of humans. Not for the AI. Well, in my case, anyway. Some of my kind have *issues* about identity."

The question escaped before Vaz even thought about it. "So why not look human?"

"That," BB said, drifting away through the door, "would just be too *needy.*"

Brunel system: two hours later.

Mal savored the novelty of being on the bridge when *Port Stanley* dropped out of slipspace.

It was better than the movies. He'd never take a moment for granted. At this stage of a mission, he was usually already sealed into his drop pod in the launch bay of a frigate, blinded by the instrument panel and too preoccupied with final checks to think about the physics. Now he was sitting in front of a full-height viewscreen—the real deal, not some projection from an exterior cam—and about to watch creation return to existence.

BB sat on the chart table like a ghostly box of donuts. "Five . . . four . . ."

Osman just grunted. Mal watched her press back into her seat's headrest as if she was steeling herself not to throw up. Beyond the viewscreen was absolute, unbroken nothing. Mal let the slight giddiness of reentry roll over him.

"Three . . . two . . . and we're *back*."

And then there was light.

Stars, rank upon rank of stars, red and yellow and blue-white, were somehow not there one second and there the next. Even the black of space was a different black. He fought down an urge to grin like a kid. After more than five centuries of space exploration, there was still only a relative handful of people who got the chance to do this on a regular basis. He turned to look at Vaz and Devereaux; no reaction. How could they be that jaded? Naomi and Phillips weren't in his eyeline.

"So how did we do, BB?" Osman got to her feet and moved to the chart table. She couldn't predict exactly where and when the ship would drop back into realspace, even with the combined processing power of BB and the corvette's own dumb navigation AI. "How far off target?"

"Oh ye of little faith," said BB. "Current position is approximately one hundred and forty-nine million kilometers from Brunel, so we're about five hours from New Llanelli, and well within our time window. That's not too shabby. Making OPSNORMAL and starting comms scan now." It couldn't have taken him more than a second. The speed those things worked at was frightening. "Messages waiting—sitrep for you from the Admiral, Captain. She's also passing on personal messages from Ten-ODST Five-Five Flight and Fifteen-ODST Lima Company. *Awww. Bless.*"

Cocky little bugger. But as soon as the thought formed, Mal realized that he'd accepted BB as an oppo, a brother in arms— body or no body. *And good old Parangosky. How about that?* Any admiral who understood that ODSTs worried about their mates disappearing was okay in his book.

"Any update on John, BB?" Naomi asked quietly.

BB paused for a second, which must have been a long time

for an AI. "We haven't given up, but it's not looking hopeful." He sounded genuinely sorry. "The Master Chief's gone."

Naomi just blinked a couple of times. "And Dr. Halsey?"

"She died on Reach," Osman said flatly. "They're still recovering bodies."

Mal felt for Naomi. Spartans had mates just like everybody else. He had no idea who Halsey was, but everyone knew about the Master Chief.

"Okay, Prof, this is where you earn your keep," Osman said, changing mood. She gestured Phillips to the communications console and Naomi moved in beside him. "You're our ears."

Phillips seemed to be an old hand at this kind of thing. He took a molded earpiece from his top pocket and pressed it into his ear canal two-handed like a woman putting on a fiddly earring, then sat back in the seat, staring in defocus at the display in front of him while he listened for Elite comms frequencies.

Devereaux went over to the chart table. "Give me another look at New Llanelli, BB."

Twenty centimeters above the surface of the table, an image of the colony world rotated as a sphere and then peeled itself like an orange, flipping out into a grid of colored lines to show the planet's topography. Mal and Vaz had nothing better to do right then than to take a look and work out the least likely place to get ambushed.

"Is New Llanelli the colony itself or the whole planet?" Vaz asked.

Osman stood over Phillips, watching something on the screen in front of him. "*Was* both. There were only three townships there anyway. BB, found any contacts out there?"

"I've got a live connection to Kilo-Three-Nine," BB said. "No response, but he's receiving. I'll loop it until he picks it up."

"Where is he, ma'am?" Mal leaned on the chart table, bracing

for an ONI need-to-know rap across the knuckles. "If you're allowed to say."

Osman didn't turn a hair. "There's a listening station on
Reynes. He's been camped out in the glasslands running a string
of Jackal informers. He knows Sangheili dialects even better than
Dr. Phillips. But he's not ONI, and he thinks this is all part of
brokering peace with the hinge-heads so that Hood can waltz in
and shake hands with the Arbiter."

Phillips took the news that he was the understudy pretty well.
He didn't even flinch. "Hope I get to debrief him one day."

"He'd talk your ears off. He's not had much human conversation for some years."

Mal was aware that agents had been working undercover for
years in Covenant space, but it suddenly struck him as a lonely
and miserable job. He'd never given it much thought before. When
he was plummeting through a planet's atmosphere in a drop pod
smaller than a car, trailing flame and heading for an uncertain
landing behind enemy lines, he could only think of himself and
his mates. Sometimes he didn't even have the time to think at all.
The pod would crash into the ground—upright if things went to
plan, flat on its side if they didn't—and the front hatch would burst
open, coughing him out into a hail of fire. The job was clear-cut
and immediate. All he had to do was kill everything in front of him
before it could kill him. Even the slower tasks like training militias
or doing long, patient recons had finite objectives most of the time.
But to live in hiding on your own for years at a time, just listening
and always in danger of being betrayed by informers . . . no, he really didn't fancy that at all. He preferred to hunt his enemy down,
look him right in his dog-ugly face, and then slot the bastard.

"Captain, I've got Kilo-Three-Nine," BB said. "Do you want
him on the speaker?"

"Let's hear him," Osman said. "Hey, Spenser. How are you doing?"

"Good to hear you, Oz." Spenser sounded like a grumpy uncle who smoked fifty a day. "You came all this way to check on me?"

"What have you got?"

"It's going to rats out here. You want me to cut to the chase? I'll upload all the comms codes and detail to your AI, but the headline is headless chicken mode. Most of their C-Two's gone. They were reliant on the Prophets for the big command picture. Plus there's a real split in the ranks about the Arbiter allying with us. One interesting development for you—a religious sect just killed a couple of keep elders for blasphemy."

Osman's voice didn't change at all. "What did they do?"

"According to the chatter, these old hinge-heads wrecked a Forerunner relic and ended up disemboweled by the Abiding Truth. I sent Big Maggie a file on them a while ago. Anyway, the mad monks hit the keep with an air strike. They're cannoned up."

This was what the mission was all about: to get the hinge-heads to focus on killing each other. Mal searched for a hint of satisfaction on Osman's face, but she just looked totally unmoved.

"You're still on Reynes, then," she said.

"It's kind of nice this time of year. I have a Grunt who comes in once a week to clean."

"I'm going to pull you out, Spenser. We'll take over local surveillance now. It's getting too dangerous."

"It's been pretty damn dangerous for the last two years."

"You said it yourself. It's falling apart. Can you exfil to an RV point on your own?"

"I haven't had orders to pull out."

"You have now. We'll extract you after we've done a recon. Stay in touch with BB and keep your head down."

"Okay, Oz. Hang on to your entrails. Three-Nine out."

Mal found himself staring at the bulkhead, wondering what it was like to live alone on a dead colony world. Spenser obviously knew Osman well enough to call her by a nickname. It was hard to think of her as Oz. But it was even harder to think of Margaret Parangosky as *Big Maggie*.

"How long has he been there, ma'am?" Vaz asked.

"Two years, this time around." Osman moved along the bank of monitors and readouts, eyes darting from screen to screen. *Port Stanley*'s bridge looked more like a TV studio crossed with a reactor control room than a warship. "I don't want him restabilizing what we destabilize. BB, patch me in to 'Telcam and let's get this done."

Nobody asked for confirmation that Hood was out of the loop on this, but Mal could work that out for himself. It was one of those gray areas that he hated. *But Osman's the boss now. What goes on above her is between Parangosky and Hood.* He turned his head very casually, just to get Vaz's reaction without BB noticing, and Vaz held his gaze for an extra second that said it all.

Ours not to reason why. Right, Vaz.

They waited. Only the faint sigh and hum of the ship's systems broke the silence for a long five minutes, and then there was a burst of static.

"It's the Bishop for you, Captain," BB said. "I've taken the liberty of piggybacking on his comms just to check who else he's talking to. I'll route that audio separately to Dr. Phillips." Phillips jerked in his seat as if BB had plugged him straight into the main power supply. "Oops, volume problem there . . . sorry."

Osman wandered over to the viewscreen and stared out as she tapped her earpiece, then turned back to the surveillance screens. " 'Telcam, this is Captain Osman. Are you ready to take delivery of the consignment?"

"Your arrival is timely, Shipmaster." Mal hadn't expected the thing to speak such good English. "More of the faithful turn to us every day, and they need arming."

"So we rendezvous on New Llanelli." Osman gestured to Naomi and pointed to the radar screens. Mal could see several small returns on one of them. "How soon can you get there?"

"By your time—five hours, maybe six. Where are you? I detect no ships."

Osman gave Naomi a thumbs-up. "I'm hiding, 'Telcam. Most of the Jiralhanae aren't on your side and they aren't on ours either. Very well, same coordinates as last time. Six hours from now."

The comms line went dead. Naomi stood in front of the radar screen with her arms folded.

"He's got three ships," she said. "What are they, BB?"

"One boarding craft and two old Tarasque fighters. He's been rummaging through the scrapyards."

Phillips swiveled his seat to face Osman. "Anyone want a quick summary of the comms chatter? They don't trust us and they can't work out why they can't locate us or the source of the signal. They just don't have access to the technology they've been used to, and it's thrown them."

"That's what I like to hear," Osman said. "Blind, deaf, and needy."

"And one of the pilots wants permission to attack us on the surface once we do the handover. Someone told him to shut up and remember that they need us to keep bringing the goods until the sect's strong enough to seize the Arbiter's fleet."

"Yes, but remember we can't touch them either," Osman said. "We need to find some willing Jiralhanae. Nothing like a few angry Brutes to keep things interesting for them."

"So much for all that Elite warrior honor," Devereaux said. "They're just as bad as us."

"Then we need to dirty up our game." Osman looked like she was starting to enjoy herself. Mal couldn't work out if that was good or bad. "I'd hate to see ONI lose the title of Most Devious Bastards in the Galaxy to a bunch of hinge-heads."

"Go, Team Devious," Phillips muttered, one hand to his earpiece. "No moral depth left unplumbed."

Mal had always tried to avoid contact with ONI. Any sane fighting man did. They were organized crime in uniform. A visit from them was everyone's worst nightmare. And now he was happy to do their dodgy bidding, pumped up for a fight on their behalf, all in the space of a few days.

Am I a bad bloke?

He didn't feel any better or worse than anyone else. But he looked around the bridge, and he didn't see a weird Spartan, one of ONI's most senior spooks, a creepy AI with way too much mouth, and a bloke with a Ph.D. in hinge-heads.

He just saw his CO and his mates. Not ODSTs, admittedly, but people whose backs he'd watch, just like Vaz and Devereaux.

And he'd expect them to watch his.

CHAPTER 5

IF YOU'RE GOING TO PRACTICE DIVIDE AND RULE TO MAIN-
TAIN SOME SORT OF EQUILIBRIUM IN ONI, IT'S NOT ENOUGH
JUST TO SET PEOPLE AGAINST ONE ANOTHER. THE TRICK IS
TO MAKE SURE THAT YOU GET SOME USEFUL WORK OUT OF
THEM AS WELL. OTHERWISE JUST DISPOSE OF THEM AND
SAVE YOURSELF SOME TIME.

(Admiral Margaret O. Parangosky, CINCONI,
to Captain Serin Osman)

**Forerunner Dyson sphere, Onyx:
local date November 2552.**

Where the hell *was* she now?

Lucy struggled to her feet by pressing her back to the wall and sliding up it, rifle leveled. The ferocious blue-white light that flooded the chamber left her a sitting duck. She had no cover and she couldn't see a damn thing. It took her a second or two to work out that there was a column to her right, a five-meter dash that she decided was worth the risk. She ran for it.

The light dimmed to daylight levels as she dropped behind the column and got her bearings. To her left, she could see her helmet in the middle of a patch of pale gray tiles. She turned her head to the right as far as she could, still flat against the column, wondering if she was going crazy. The wall seemed to extend a lot farther than she'd expected, as if the room was bigger than it appeared from the outside. But it was hard to tell. She'd stumbled in here in pitch blackness.

She sucked in a breath and held it for a moment, listening for movement. The place smelled oddly like a hospital and had the muffled deadness of a room full of heavy drapes. But that wasn't what she could feel under her boots. She put her left hand on the ground to confirm it, and felt perfectly smooth, cool stone, a kind of terrazzo just like the entrance.

Either there's a lot of bodies in here or it's soundproofing. Let's take a look.

Lucy detached the scope from her rifle and angled the lens to see the reflection of what was behind her. It didn't help much. It was a segment of a curved surface, maybe white or pale gray, and it could have been anything from another Dyson sphere to a piece of Forerunner art.

Whatever it was, she couldn't stay here.

She snapped the optics back on her rifle and decided to make a grab for her helmet before she worried about anything else. It wasn't just protection. It was her comms and sensors, too, for whatever good they'd do in here. She eased herself into a squat, ready to dart out but not sure yet where she'd find cover on the other side.

Okay—three, two, go.

She sprang out and ran for the helmet. She found herself in a warehouse full of machinery, none of it instantly recognizable, and scooped the helmet under one arm before sprinting full tilt for the nearest cover, a bizarre statue that made her think of an ancient Babylonian frieze.

Winged bull. No, not a bull. A lion? A horse?

Whatever it was, she skidded under one of its pillar-sized legs—not vertical, raked back at an angle—and flattened herself against it before putting her helmet on one-handed. The head-up display scrolled through a menu of red status icons: no bio signs from the rest of the squad, no radio signals, and no global positioning. Well, at least its optics worked. And it would save her from a headshot.

She looked up at the underbelly of the bull-lion-horse, much less animal in form now that she was up close to it. It was a dark gray, boat-shaped vessel with four landing struts and a headlike bow section. The organic curves didn't look aerodynamic at all and she couldn't see anything that resembled a human ship, but the openings at the stern had to be afterburners or something. She just knew it. She might simply have been jumping to the wrong conclusion, misled by familiar shapes, but it was a guess she felt confident about.

Maybe this is the Forerunners' parking garage. Makes sense. All part of rebuilding their civilization if the worst happened, just like the Chief said.

As she looked along the hull above to find a hatch, she picked up a sound. Her hearing was hypersensitive at the best of times. But the helmet's audio amplified a noise exactly like someone sliding a pair of pants off the back of the chair, dragging a leather belt over wood. It was so slowly done, so careful, that all Lucy could think was *ambush*.

I can't just wait for it to get me.

It's coming from . . .

Lucy leveled her rifle and swung around in the direction of

the noise. Her eye caught movement and short-lived shadow, but whoever it was had taken cover between the vehicles. She started stalking it.

Okay . . . let's see your legs.

The vessels or whatever were all different shapes and sizes, some ten or fifteen meters high, some much smaller. But the terrazzo floor was perfectly smooth and flat. Lucy darted under the nearest vehicle and lay cheek to the ground, looking for boots moving between the stands and struts. Over the sound of her own rapid breathing—pumping adrenaline, fiercely focused—she could still hear the slithering leather, and what she thought was a gasp of effort.

Actually, it sounded more like a fart. It was a weird, unfunny moment. She was trying to get the jump on someone who was more likely to blow her head off than shake her hand, and here she was listening to a damned *fart.* But she still couldn't see any legs. Elites just couldn't move that quietly. And a Brute would have smashed through everything in the garage to get at her.

But she saw a shadow moving slowly right to left about four vessels ahead of her. She crawled under the ships on elbows and knees, rifle cradled in the crook of her arms, keeping her eyes on that shadow. It paused for a moment.

Is there a gantry above me? Is that what I can see? Someone on a gantry?

Lucy couldn't look up to check. She kept going. She didn't think she was making much noise, but it was hard to be completely silent. She was trying to tiptoe on joints. It was slow going.

And then she was under the curved hull of another dark gray ship, one that gave her a glimpse of much more familiar undercarriage gear, and within two meters of the shadow.

Okay. Still no legs. You're standing on something above me.

Maybe some walkway between the vessels. So I'm coming up underneath you. That'll be a lovely surprise, won't it?

Lucy left it to the last moment to flip over onto her back. It wasn't easy with a backpack, but she did it, balancing herself on it and putting one boot against a strut. If she pushed off hard enough, she'd skid out like a skate and come up under the bastard, whoever it was. She clutched her rifle to her chest, right index finger on the trigger, left hand cupped around the muzzle, then tested her boot against the strut and braced her quads.

Deep breath. Three . . . two . . .

She drove off from the strut and shot out into the gap between the vessels. Right above her, a dark shape blotted out the light. In the fraction of a second between seeing it and squeezing the trigger, her brain told her *tentacles, Engineer, could be rigged to explode, do it.*

She squeezed off a burst, straight up. Liquid splashed her visor. A terrible squealing noise like a balloon venting air told her she'd hit it. She tried to roll clear, but it crashed down on her, tentacles flailing.

It didn't blow up. And neither did she.

Oh God. I shot an Engineer. I shot a poor damn Engineer.

Lucy couldn't move for a moment. Engineers—Huragok—were lightweights, less than sixty kilos, but it was still hard to move with a dead weight like that on her chest. She squirmed out from under it. It was still alive, making terrible wheezing, sucking noises now, looking like a beached squid with a face. The creatures had gas sacs that enabled them to float and that was what she'd hit. But the sacs were their lungs as well. It was suffocating.

Lucy couldn't even tell it she was sorry. She couldn't explain that she'd seen too many Engineers with booby traps strapped to them by the Covenant, and that she was trained not to take chances.

She couldn't explain that she overreacted to threats and sometimes got it wrong either.

She tried to lift its head and comfort it. Its face reminded her of an armadillo, long and narrow. She took off her helmet and tried to look into its eyes, three on each side of its head, and make some sort of contact with it, but it was hard to work out where to focus. The poor thing was dying. It was like shooting an autistic child. Huragok were harmless, obsessed with repairing technology and tinkering with machinery. They didn't fight or take sides; they were only dangerous when the Covenant strapped explosives to them.

That had always disgusted Lucy. She had a faint recollection of a pet cat before the Covenant killed her family and glassed her colony.

Savages. Monsters.

But humans did that too. We did it with dogs and dolphins and all kinds of helpless creatures. We made them into bombs. And now I've killed an Engineer.

It might not have troubled most Spartans, but it troubled her. All she could do was hold it. The sucking noises were getting weaker. There was nothing in her medical pack that could save it. She didn't even know where to start.

And I've killed the only sentient being that could help us find a way out of this place. Or get me out of here.

The Engineer seemed to get heavier as she tried to prop up its head, then it stopped wheezing and its tentacles went limp.

God, I'm sorry. Did you realize I didn't mean to do it?

Lucy sat back on her heels and wondered what the hell to do next. Now she knew there was no real threat, she had to work out how to contact the squad and let them know where she was and what she'd found. If she could locate the point where she'd entered the chamber, maybe she could tap a Morse message on the stone.

Amid all this incredible alien technology, the one thing she could rely on was a simple, seven-hundred-year-old system of on-off signals that almost everybody else had forgotten.

She stood and looked down at the Engineer for a few moments. She'd never killed anyone she hadn't wanted and intended to. She was wondering what to do with the body when she heard that leather belt sound again.

Several leather belts, in fact. Shadows flickered in her peripheral vision.

Engineers were harmless—weren't they?

Hangar bay, UNSC *PORT STANLEY:* fifteen thousand kilometers off New Llanelli, Brunel system.

"Aren't you going to help Naomi into her Mjolnir?" Mal said, stuffing a magazine of armor-piercing rounds into his belt. "You two were getting on so well."

Vaz looked over his shoulder with some difficulty as he eased himself into his new armor. It didn't smell familiar. Maybe that was just as well. He swung his arms to get a feel for the extra range of movement in his shoulders and wondered if it was worth the trade-off against shoulder plates.

"She's too old and too scary," he said. "And she needs a technician for that."

"If you're still pining for Chrissie, I'll thump you. She didn't stand by you, mate."

"And you think that being crushed by a Spartan with bigger biceps than me is going to make me feel better."

"No, but I almost made you smile, didn't I?"

BB popped up in front of them. "Oh, you're matchmaking. How adorable. Are we ready to move, gentlemen?"

"We?" Vaz asked. "I thought you were staying here with Naomi."

"I'll split off some of my dumb processes." BB projected a second box, a small, battered, peeling thing. Vaz was starting to understand AI humor. "I can't afford to fall into enemy hands. And don't get Phillips killed. Too much paperwork."

"I'm *here,* you know," Phillips said. He stuck his head out of the dropship's door. "ONI said I'd get some weapons training."

"They lied, Prof," Mal said. "It's what they do. Don't worry, we'll show you how it's done."

Vaz secured his helmet, looking at BB through a filter of boot-up icons and status displays. He tapped Mal on the back. "Helmet check." A few moments later, the view from Mal's helmet cam, inset on one side of the HUD, blinked from idle to a head-on close-up of Vaz's mirrored visor with Mal's faceplate reflected in it.

"Well, I'm fabulous," Mal said, brushing off imaginary dust from his shoulder. "Let's go wow the hinge-heads."

Devereaux's helmet cam feed flickered, then became a tilted view of the cockpit and Osman's leg in regular infantry armor as she reached out to press a control. "Got you, Staff. Starting drives."

The dropship was packed to the deckhead. Between the Warthog, a small forklift, and the trailer full of crates, there was barely enough room for Vaz to find a space to lean his backside against, let alone sit down. The airtight bulkhead sealed behind them and the ship maneuvered toward the ramp, then slipped through the parting doors into the black silence.

Osman's voice crackled over the comms speaker. "BB, keep the intercepted channels patched through to Phillips. Naomi, where are they now?"

"One Tarasque still in low orbit, one's landed approximately five kilometers from the RV point, and the boarding craft's where you expect to be."

"Okay. Devereaux, set us down behind that ridge." Osman sounded as if she was looking at a chart on the nav display. She didn't have a helmet on, so Vaz couldn't see her viewpoint. "As soon as we're done, we're going to extract Spenser and transfer him."

"You still need someone to man the listening station on Reynes?" Phillips asked.

"If you're volunteering," Osman said, "the answer's no. You're not trained for undercover work, let alone anything remote."

"But you could catch up on lots of reading," Mal said. "Never mind."

Phillips, wedged in a gap between two coolant housings, looked disappointed. At least he didn't lack guts. Vaz leaned forward and tightened the strap on his body armor for him. The guy was still getting the hang of unfamiliar kit.

"Don't leave any gaps," Vaz said. If the Elites turned an energy weapon on Phillips, then a few pieces of upper body armor wouldn't do him much good. But they had projectile weapons as well, including looted MA5Bs. "You'd be amazed where rounds can penetrate."

Phillips gave him a thumbs-up, right hand pressed to his ear as he listened in on the hinge-head frequencies.

"Wonder what happened to *Ariadne*?" Mal asked.

"Can BB hear us?"

"Of course I can," said the voice in Vaz's audio. "*Ariadne* is still undergoing emergency repairs. *Monte Cassino*'s been diverted to take off her nonessential crew. Sounds like they might have to abandon her."

"And no help from Venezia."

"No. They won't be getting a Christmas card from the Admiral this year."

Mal made one of his annoyed *fffft* sounds but didn't offer a comment. They approached New Llanelli in silence, leaving Vaz with nothing to distract him from the fact that he was about to hand over weapons and ordnance to the enemy. No matter how he cut it, no matter how much sense it made, it stuck in his throat. It stuck in a hell of a lot deeper when he caught a glimpse of what he thought was a river in the hull cam repeater. It resolved into glittering patches of vitrified soil.

Shit, it's all glasslands. How many colony worlds look just like this?

It wasn't about the millions of humans who'd been slaughtered. The scale was so far beyond what he could *feel* that he didn't get instinctively angry about it: he just knew it was terrible in a theoretical kind of way. No, what gripped his guts was the smaller-scale stuff, all the buddies he'd lost trying to save places like this, and that was all any one man could really *feel*. Anyone who cried for some general mass of humanity they didn't even know was crying for themselves, just wallowing in the idea of it. So how did the surviving colonies feel? Hood was kidding himself if he thought he could sign a peace deal and get anyone who was left out here to stick to it.

Yeah, I'd want revenge too. Can't blame them for that.

Mal reached over and rapped sharply on his helmet, jerking him out of it. "Don't," he whispered.

"I wasn't thinking about her." Actually, he hadn't brooded

about Chrissie for quite a while. He'd moved into the blank phase where he'd get angry about it if someone reminded him, but it didn't keep him awake at night now. "Just wondering if we're going to be back here in a year enforcing a cease-fire."

They were all on an open channel. Osman couldn't have missed that, but she didn't pass any comment.

Devereaux landed north of an escarpment that sloped down to an ice rink of vitrified soil, and shut down the drives. "They must have heard us coming in," she said. "But they can't get a lock on us. Okay, everybody out."

Mal scrambled up to the ridge clutching his sniper rifle and lay flat to scope through the landscape. The Elites wouldn't pick him up on infrared or EM in the recon armor, but they might be able to spot him the old-fashioned way. Did it matter? Vaz thought it would have been better to rock up with as many people visible as possible, but Osman seemed to know what she was doing. If anything went wrong, then at least Mal was in the best overwatch position to pick off 'Telcam.

"What have we got, Staff?" Osman asked over the radio. She was wearing just a black UNSCN flight suit and light armor, no helmet, possibly trying to look less confrontational to a jumpy hinge-head. To her credit, she rolled up her sleeves and helped Devereaux hitch the trailer of crates to the Warthog. "See them yet?"

"One Elite in gold armor, plus sidekick and a couple of Brutes. Plasma rifles only. Nothing else on infrared. No idea how many more there might be in the dropship. But even I can slot them at this distance."

"He's kept his word, then," Osman said, sounding surprised. "Phillips, I'll drive. Corporal, you're top cover."

Vaz settled behind the gun and hung on as Osman bounced

the Hog over every dip and boulder. The heavy trailer didn't help its handling at all. At three hundred meters, with a bit of help from his visor's optics, Vaz could see 'Telcam's face. *Bastard.* Well, at least he didn't have to smile at the thing.

Osman brought the Warthog to a bumpy halt thirty meters from the welcoming committee and glanced over her shoulder at Vaz. "Give him a bit more latitude than you usually would before blowing his head off."

Vaz hadn't quite worked out the line between Osman's humor and her sarcasm yet. It mattered. "How much more, ma'am? Seriously."

"Whatever happens, let him get away with the weapons." She was definitely serious now. "That's what matters. Stoke the fire. You hear that, Staff?"

Mal sounded a little reluctant on the radio, but the captain had spoken. "Understood, ma'am."

Phillips didn't say a word. Maybe he was used to taking risks with Elites now, but the meaning was still clear: even if the hinge-head gutted Phillips—and her—then Vaz and Mal had to hold fire, or at least not slot all the Elites.

That was a lot to ask of him, and even more to ask of a civvie. *Phillips volunteered. Look at him. He loves it. But even so . . .*

Osman climbed out of the Warthog and started walking slowly toward 'Telcam, but the Elites appeared to be on an intercept heading anyway. She stopped. Vaz tilted the gun slowly, making his target clear, just to give the hinge-heads something to think about. When he checked Mal's icon he found he was looking at the feed from the 99-D's optics. Mal had the crosshairs steady on 'Telcam's head.

"He wouldn't dare." Mal's voice was just a breath in Vaz's earpiece. "He's not in a rush to meet his gods."

'Telcam stalked over to the Warthog with his bagman in tow and wandered around the back to the trailer. He didn't seem to take the slightest notice of Vaz, but at least Osman had the grace not to offer a handshake. Vaz pivoted the gun slowly so that it was facing the trailer. He couldn't turn his back on 'Telcam. The last time he'd been this close to anything in Covenant uniform, it had almost severed his jaw and only a quick-thinking combat medic had stopped him from choking on his own blood.

"I suppose you'll want to check out the consignment," Osman said. "Rifles, assorted grenades, and antipersonnel mines."

'Telcam tilted his head back and forth as he surveyed the crates. Then he gestured and his sidekick ripped the lid off one of the crates like paper.

He reached in and pulled out a plasma rifle. Vaz held his breath as 'Telcam spent far too long examining it. Could he spot the tag? Vaz had grown up believing that the Covenant was technologically invincible. They weren't, or at least 'Telcam wasn't. He either didn't know or didn't care, just like Naomi had said.

"You're most generous, Captain." It was hard to tell if 'Telcam was sneering or not. "And most frugal of you to retrieve Sangheili weapons. I have adherents in many keeps, and more join us every day."

"If you're asking if there's more to come, there is," Osman said. "If there's anything specific, I'll see what else I can do."

'Telcam looked down his snout at her. "You cannot procure warships for me."

"Yes, I realize that lending you a carrier would be embarrassing for both of us."

"I shall distribute the arms, then, and see how much progress we make."

"I'll be around."

"Yet we see no ship, Captain."

"Nor will you. This is still hostile space in too many ways."

Phillips seemed to be listening intently, but then Vaz realized from the man's shifting focus that he was actually concentrating on his audio channel. He was getting the intercepted voice traffic from the Elites. Had he heard something that worried him? Vaz glanced at Mal's icon to check he still had a shot on 'Telcam. He did. Vaz leaned back casually and made sure the Warthog's gun was at just the right angle to take out the Elite's bagman.

Just in case.

Osman suddenly got a dawning realization look on her face. "Do you really need a ship?"

"Probably not," 'Telcam said. "The initial target is the Arbiter, seeing as he's foolish enough to be visiting each state to put his case for peace. Once I kill him, then any fighting will be keep by keep. Not the kind of battles fought by capital ships. Unless an entire colony world decides to stand by him."

Osman just gave him a nod. But Vaz could see the cogs grinding behind her eyes. There was no such thing as a careless word from her, and 'Telcam didn't seem the kind to announce his plans just to be sociable.

"Very well, have your people transfer these crates, then." Osman obviously didn't want him anywhere near *Port Stanley,* and they needed the trailer back. High-tech wars often foundered on small, dull detail. "I'll have more for you in a week."

She was drip-feeding him. Vaz thought of Naomi going all zen about knowing how much fuel to pour on a fire. A couple of Brutes emerged from the Elite dropship and began moving the crates, lumbering back and forth until the trailer was cleared. It felt like a shady drugs deal in a back alley. 'Telcam gave Osman a polite bow of the head and loped back to his ship.

Osman waited for it to take off before she moved a muscle.

"So he's waiting to see if I'm going to warn the Arbiter," she said. "Fine."

"Correct." Phillips climbed back into the Warthog and nearly brained himself on the gun. "The chatter from the fighters was all about what your actual game plan was."

"Ah well, he'll get his proof, so no harm done," she said. "And I'll find out where the arms actually end up. Win-win. Okay, let's bang out of here."

"Want me to drive, ma'am?" Vaz asked. "I'm used to Hogs."

Osman almost smiled. She climbed into the gun seat. "Okay. If it makes you feel safer."

Vaz started the engine. He wasn't taking any notice of Mal's HUD feed now, so he expected to be back in the dropship and off this rock in a few minutes. But then rapid movement in the icon caught his peripheral vision and he stopped to check it out.

"Jesus *Christ,*" Mal said. "Where the hell did *he* come from?"

"Mal?" Vaz could see the jerking, rolling viewpoint of someone running down a steep slope, and then the horizon bounced everywhere for a few moments before the cam corrected for movement. Mal was running. "What is it, Mal?"

"Contact. *Human.* Wait one."

"What is it?" Osman asked. The pivot on the gun made a grinding noise. She was getting ready to fire. "What's he spotted?"

Vaz slammed his foot down and the Warthog shot off. "He's seen a human."

"Can't be. The Covenant glassed this place years ago."

Phillips hung on to the dashboard with both hands as Vaz raced for the escarpment. When the Warthog came around the edge of the slope and Vaz got a clear view of the plain beyond, he saw Mal jogging toward a heap of rags among the boulders and scrubby vegetation that had somehow found the will to grow again in the fissures.

Then the rags stood up and became a man.

"Oh, great," Osman said wearily. "That's all we need."

Vaz wasn't sure how to take that. He let Mal reach the guy first, just in case the sight of a Warthog bearing down on him made him panic, and came to a halt a few meters away.

The man was ragged and emaciated—about fifty, straggly gray hair and beard, clutching a wood ax—but he looked pretty alert.

"I saw the ships." He had a strong accent, and he sounded stunned. "I saw the dropship. I didn't think the Navy gave a damn about us. What's the Covenant doing back here? What are *you* doing here?"

"The fighting's stopped." Mal tried to check him over. "Are you alone, mate? Have you been here all the time?"

"Since they glassed the place. I'm the only one left. But what's going on? What's the Covenant doing here?"

Vaz looked at Osman. This wasn't convenient at all. It was written all over her face. They really didn't need a passenger, least of all one who'd seen things he couldn't explain. Vaz had the feeling that a lone witness didn't have much of a life expectancy under the circumstances.

Mal took off his helmet and caught Vaz's eye. They'd served together so long that there was a kind of telepathy at moments like this. Something had to be said.

Vaz steered Osman away discreetly and they stood with their backs to Mal. "We can't *leave* him here, ma'am," Vaz whispered. *Dead or alive.* "Let's take him back and drop him off at the next bus stop."

She looked as if she was in two minds about it. Vaz reminded himself that she was still ONI, and he hardly knew her, even if his instinct told him she was okay. Parangosky would have just shot the guy and moved on, he decided. It would have saved a lot of trouble. But Osman seemed to be weighing something up.

And Phillips had that rabbit-in-the-headlights look again. He'd never make a poker player.

"You're right," Osman said at last, lips hardly moving. "But we'll have to lock him up. I don't want a civvie loose on board, least of all on this mission. Quarantine him. Whatever excuse to stop him blabbing when we hand him on."

She turned and nodded at Mal, all reluctance. He nodded back, one thumb raised, and led the guy to the Warthog.

"We'll take you to the nearest UNSC base, mate," Mal said. "No luggage, I assume. What's your name?"

"Muir," he said. "Tom Muir. Are you evacuating me?"

Vaz gave him a hand up. "That's the idea."

"Then you're seven damn years too late," Muir said. "Where were you bastards when we really needed you?"

"You're welcome," said Vaz.

Bekan keep, Mdama, Sanghelios.

Raia was supervising the construction of a drying barn when Jul decided to break the news. It wasn't a task he'd ever undertaken, and he marveled at the fact that she could turn her hand to overseeing such a project. Mdama was a rural backwater in a world of urban city-states. Now Jul and his neighbors had suddenly realized that farmland was the new power in a society of city-dwellers used to importing much of its food.

Life in the Covenant under San'Shyuum oppression, as he understood it now, really had made the Sangheili too dependent on others for basic elements of survival, just as Raia had said, too reliant on what was provided for them, done for them, and *given* to them in exchange for their military skill. All they had now was a fortress world and nobody to run it.

But Raia was finding out how to manage food production by consulting ancient records, and he was working out how Sanghelios might govern itself as a global entity rather than a loose arrangement of keeps tasked by the Prophets. Their destiny was back in their own hands. They would learn to be great again.

Civilizations rise and fall. The Jiralhanae, the Kig-Yar—and us. Except we can rise again.

"Where are you going?" Raia asked, not looking up from a thousand-year-old architectural plan she'd dug up from the keep's vaults. The breeze buffeted the sheet of ancient vellum, snapping it like a sail. "Are you going to be away long?"

Jul couldn't remember ever lying to his wife, although he'd avoided telling her small things that he knew would make her angry. "Ontom. Just a few days. Do you want to know why?"

"Boredom. I realize it's hard to fill your time now the fighting's stopped."

"*Governance.* We're going to talk about how Sanghelios should be run. Forze's coming with me."

Raia rocked her head from side to side in grudging approval, then looked around at him. "Are you plotting, Jul?"

She knew him too well. There was no shame in challenging decisions made by higher authorities, but there was a consequence for failing to win. If Jul didn't succeed in overthrowing the Arbiter, the Arbiter would then come after him, almost certainly kill him, and seize his keep and assets. Raia and the rest of his family would pay the price.

"I am," he said, "but I won't start what I know I can't finish. Hence the need to gather like-minded keeps about me."

"We might have different priorities, Jul, but I do agree with you. There's no lasting peace to be made with humans. We've killed too many of them. This is just a lull in the war. It might be weeks or years or even centuries, but it'll never be truly over."

She went back to the plans. She'd had her say. The barn was starting to take recognizable shape, no doubt a simple thing to their ancestors, but something rather extraordinary to Jul. He walked back to the keep and stood by the transport to wait for Forze. It was a very old wave-skimmer, last used to ferry Unggoy laborers to the islands, but it would cope with an ocean trip.

I hope . . .

He wasn't a good swimmer. Few Sangheili were.

But he'd pilot the skimmer himself to keep Gusay clear of any conspiracy. The young officer would stand a better chance of escaping retribution if Jul failed.

"So what's your plan?" Forze asked as the skimmer headed out over the coast toward Ontom. "How are you going to find the right monks? And do you always steer like this?"

Jul had been a shipmaster for too long. Others piloted for him. *But Sangheili have always had to sail and fly. Our geography demands it.* He wasn't sure if his faded skill was a tidy parallel with his homeworld's situation or simply random irony, but either way it was an excellent reminder of what he needed to do.

"They have a temple," Jul said. "They never relinquished it. They kept the ancient rite and they have adherents all over Sanghelios."

"Backward idiots who love their secret societies and primitive rituals. If they'd had any potential to be dangerous, the San'Shyuum would have wiped them out long ago."

"But they're idiots with a network, and they now appear to be using it militarily. Prepare to do business with them, brother. And try to behave piously."

By the time Ontom loomed in the haze, Jul had begun to rediscover old skills and the flight was much smoother. He felt a certain satisfaction at being *capable.* It was like a coming of age, that same heady sense of transformation from child to warrior that he'd delighted in as a boy. He could refresh his piloting skills and the Sangheili could thrive without the San'Shyuum exactly as they had before the two species first met.

"Mind the turrets. . . ." Forze murmured. The skimmer made enough height to swoop low over the city. Jul looked for the landing area nearest to the Servants' temple. He found it easier to land by sight than by instruments. "This is a very *smug* state. I never enjoyed visiting here."

Jul understood what he meant, Ontom was very old, very rich, and very keen to remind other states that it was superior in every way. The buildings were a blend of pre-Prophet magnificence and modern architecture that didn't even attempt to mimic a traditional style.

Let's see how superior you remain without the San'Shyuum providing food and technology.

Jul landed the skimmer, suddenly anonymous in a sea of random vessels and vehicles that had simply been withdrawn from the fleet or commandeered from factories. Everything he looked at seemed to be a summary of the Sangheili's predicament, arms and vessels reduced to soft idleness, the nation orphaned and needing to grow up fast. He felt in his pocket and realized he still had the *arum* he'd taken from one of the keep's children.

"It's a pleasant walk," Forze said, lifting his chins to squint into the distance. "If you like *complacent* architecture."

They strolled through the elegant gateway of the landing field and along an avenue of ornamental trees that were in the process of being trimmed and fussed over by a team of Jiralhanae. It was strange to see the brutish creatures doing something so painstaking, but at least they were obedient. Most of their kind had joined the uprising and turned on their Sangheili masters. Old hatreds and resentment had boiled over, and Jul barely trusted those that remained at their stations.

The Ontom residents who were going about their business in the avenue took no notice of the Jiralhanae or of Jul and Forze. The avenue was noisy, busy, *preoccupied,* oblivious of two insignificant elders from an unsophisticated rural state. The place smelled of blossom and interesting, rather foreign food. But dining would have to wait.

"Is that it?" Forze tilted his head to indicate direction. "Over there."

They stopped at the end of the avenue. Jul could hear water, so the river was close. Facing them across a crowded plaza, set back from the access road behind a modern wall, was a flat-topped, crumbling sanctuary with a curved facade and two cartouches of stylized creatures above an arched doorway.

It was a Forerunner building, hallowed ground. It didn't look like the angry, pulsing heart of a revolution. It looked like it wanted to be left alone to die in peace. Jul found himself with his hand in his pocket, rolling the *arum* between his fingers for comfort.

Easier to charge into battle than knock on a door.

"Let's see if the holy brothers are at home," he said, and set off across the plaza. As he wove between the locals, ignored, he realized where the sound of the river was coming from. The huge plaza was in fact a bridge. He stepped over a grating and found himself staring at a rushing white torrent a long way below. By the time he and Forze reached the other side, he felt as if he was in a wilderness and that the milling crowd was a continent away.

There was a heavy silence that seemed to seep from the outer walls. When he crossed the threshold and stood in the courtyard of cracked paving, the silence felt as if it was sucking the sound out of the air. Jul suspected it wasn't so much the effect of mystic devotion as some rather recent technology, a touch of theater to convince the doubting faithful. But even knowing that, he still felt he was in a new world that was beyond his grasp. When he glanced at Forze he could see his own wavering resolve mirrored in his friend's face.

"Will they get upset if we touch the door?" Forze asked. "You saw what they did to poor old Relon and his brother. If they maintain the old faith, they won't exploit Forerunner technology."

Jul decided that if the monks lived in a Forerunner relic, then they'd probably declared knocking on doors a theological gray area.

"It's a building," he said. "Not technology. We shall risk it."

He walked through the arch and rapped his knuckles on the first wood he could find—a decorated screen mounted on metal runners blue-green with the patina of age.

He waited.

"Pilgrim," said a voice. "What brings you to look upon on the gifts of the gods?"

Jul willed Forze to keep a piously straight face. Maybe the vivid memory of Relon's guts spread across the courtyard would do the job.

"We are Jul and Forze, elders from Mdama," Jul said. "Blasphemers are everywhere, as you've seen. We want to root out the poison that's weakening the Sangheili."

And none of that was actually a lie. It was merely phrased *sensitively.* Jul waited.

He was expecting an old monk in an archaic robe, at the very least. He wasn't expecting a fully armored field master to step out of the shadows with a rifle across his back. Behind the field master, shapes moved and metal clicked. Jul suspected the entire holy order was armed to the teeth.

"Well, pilgrims," the field master said. "Faith is a most powerful thing."

Jul had once thought of himself as devout, but he feared making some doctrinal or ritual error that would enrage the orthodox here and he would end the same way as Relon. So he wasn't going to attempt anything clever. He would tell the truth.

The *partial* truth though.

"I plan to oust the Arbiter," Jul said. "He's responsible for this pitiful state in which we find ourselves, and he must die before we can restore Sangheili to their rightful place. He denied the gods. We have common cause, I think. I have some arms and a willing keep."

The field master stared into Jul's eyes for a few moments, then looked at Forze, jaws jutting.

"The Arbiter let the humans put him on a leash," Forze said, as if he couldn't take the glowering silence any longer. "No good will come of it. The humans will be allowed to swarm through the galaxy again. I have a willing keep too."

The holy field master studied both of them for a few more moments, then beckoned them to follow.

The deeper into the ruined building Jul walked, the more he saw. The armored devout huddled in recesses, gathered around tables over charts and datapads. Every open space in the mazelike building seemed to be stacked with crates of rifles and ordnance.

It was a sanctified munitions store. Jul looked to Forze to gauge his reaction. The expression on his tight-clamped jaws was more than surprised.

The field master pulled out a couple of chairs at a table and gestured to them to sit.

"I am Field Master Avu Med 'Telcam, Servant of the Abiding Truth," he said. "And I have many brothers."

CHAPTER 6

LEARN SOMETHING FROM THE HUMANS. RELIGION IS NOT SYNONYMOUS WITH GODS. IT'S A MORTAL'S CONCEIT. LOOK AT THEIR GREAT RELIGIONS, HOW CORRUPT AND POLITICAL AND IN LOVE WITH POWER THEY'VE BEEN THROUGHOUT HUMAN HISTORY, AND SEE THE TRUTH—THAT THE PROPHETS LIED TO US, BUT THEY DID NOT SPEAK FOR THE GODS, AND THE DESTRUCTIVE NATURE OF THE HALOS TELLS US NOTHING ABOUT WHERE THE TRANSFORMATION OF DEATH TAKES US.

(Avu Med 'Telcam, Servant of the Abiding Truth)

Forerunner Dyson sphere—last definitive position, Onyx: local date November 2552.

Three Engineers floated in midair, tentacles entwined as if they were clinging to each other in terror.

Lucy wanted to make them realize she meant no harm, but it was hard to explain that when she couldn't speak and when the creatures had just seen her kill one of their comrades.

She decided to take the risk that they were the only life-forms in here with her, and slung her rifle over her shoulder with slow care. Laying it on the ground was a little too trusting when she couldn't assess the risk. She held her arms away from her sides to show them she wasn't going to shoot.

Did they understand that?

The Engineers hung there like a bunch of brightly colored balloons, blue and magenta with bioluminescent beads. Lucy held her hand out, palm up. It was the only thing she could think of. It had always worked with horses. She remembered one vaguely from her childhood, looming above her with a warm velvety nose and the strong malty smell of grain. The Engineers suddenly unlinked their tentacles and drifted toward her. Maybe it worked with Engineers too.

But they sailed past, not interested in her at all, and clustered around the corpse of the one she'd shot, touching it and making faint groaning sounds. She didn't need a degree in xenobiology to work out that they were upset. Kurt had explained during training that they were organic machines that could replicate and repair themselves, and that they were probably descended from the first ones built by the Forerunners. They didn't seem at all machinelike now though.

He'd also said that all they cared about was repairing machinery and computer systems. Well, Lucy now knew they cared about other things too. They were grieving. Lucy could only see them as strange, sad children. One of them ran a tentacle over the corpse and drew back. She could almost hear his thoughts: *We're too late to repair him.* Lucy watched, racking her brains for a way to get their attention.

The Forerunners had left them here. They had to be the Dyson sphere's maintenance crew, the latest generation of Engineers, fixing and tinkering and waiting patiently until the day they were needed.

Maybe they'd been the ones who put Team Katana in the cryo pods. Perhaps they'd found the Spartans wounded and tried their hand at repairing humans before finding that it was beyond them.

I need to get them to open the doors before they wander off again.

It was pointless trying to force them at gunpoint. They'd just cower and hide. The only thing she could think of was to distract them with a technical puzzle, and the best she had was her helmet. She held it out to them.

One of them turned to look, but the other two were still more interested in their fallen comrade, moaning softly and making very precise gestures to each other with their tentacles. Then they lifted the body and drifted off between the vehicles.

The one who seemed interested in her floated over and put a tentacle—a hand—on the helmet, stroking the surface. Then it coiled its arms around it, making the reactive camo turn blue and mauve as the armor systems tried to match the Engineer's skin.

That did the trick. The Engineer began dismantling the helmet at a breakneck speed, stacking the components—faceplate, lining, mikes, data processor, even microfans—on the nearest flat surface, a hydroplane-like structure on a small vessel. Then, just as quickly, it reassembled them. Lucy had heard that they couldn't resist tinkering with things, but seeing them actually do it was another thing entirely. It looked as if the Engineer was ripping the helmet apart like an angry toddler. It hadn't even used a toolkit. But it held out the helmet to her with two of its arms, jiggling it a little.

Try this.

Yes, Lucy understood that much. She took the helmet and peered inside first, not sure what she was expecting to see. When she put it on and activated the HUD, everything looked normal. But there were a couple of icons that hadn't been there before, two broken circles, each with a symbol inside that she couldn't recognize. She'd seen the glyphlike style before in Covenant bases but she had no idea what it meant.

So . . . do I activate them and see what happens?

A couple of blinks would show her what the Engineer had added. It seemed to be waiting expectantly for a verdict, peering into her face and cocking its head. Yes, it really did remind her of an anteater or an armadillo with that small, smooth head. She was even getting used to the six eyes. She made the effort to stare into just two of them—the middle pair—and ignore the others.

Now it was a face. Now she could look it in the eye. *Now* she could connect.

Might as well try.

She activated one of the icons and braced for something weird. Engineers were clever, but that didn't mean they never got things wrong, and the ones here couldn't have had much if any contact with humans before. At first she thought the Engineer hadn't changed anything, but then it moved, rustling with that leather noise, and she realized she could hear a *lot* more. It was almost like having no helmet at all: clear, unmuffled, perfect sound. She couldn't tell if the Engineer had modified the audio channels or the physical acoustics of the helmet, but it was one hell of a trick.

So let's see . . . what does this *one do?*

Lucy blinked to activate the second new icon and waited for another minor miracle.

Nothing.

It didn't do anything at all. She tried again, but the circle of glyphs just changed color from red to green. After a few attempts she shook her head in frustration and pulled off the helmet to find the Engineer peering into her face.

It made a few precise gestures with its tentacle-hands, repeating them in a sequence. Lucy tried to recall everything from briefings she'd forgotten years ago. *Sign language.* Engineers used sign language. Well, that was no use to her. She couldn't speak that either.

But this place was expecting us, or something like us. Wasn't it?

The robotic Sentinels on the surface had attacked the Spartans, probably seeing them as just another threat to Onyx like the Flood or anything else. But Ash had said that one had reacted to him and tried to respond in different languages until it settled on English. It had called him *Reclaimer.* Then he must have failed some unknown test, because the Sentinels had turned on the Spartans and nearly killed them.

The Engineer was still staring patiently into her face, signing that same sequence over and over, waiting for her to understand. He certainly didn't look as if he was going to attack her.

Whatever the Forerunners made recognizes us as a special species—most of the time, anyway.

It didn't help her. If this colony of Engineers had that same programming, that same ability to spot human language and work out how to communicate, then she was still stuffed. The Forerunners probably hadn't made allowance for someone with her problems.

Okay. I know I've got problems. Just because I know that, though, it doesn't mean I can sort myself out.

The doctors and psychiatrists had told her she could speak if she wanted to. Well, she *wanted* to. She'd wanted to say good-bye to Kurt for the last time when he made the squad leave him behind, and right now she wanted to speak more than she ever had in her life. She had to find a way to make herself talk. She needed to communicate with this creature if she was ever going to get out of here.

The Engineer signed again. Lucy found herself clenching and flexing her fingers with the effort as she brought her hands up.

The Engineer backed away a little, probably expecting a punch in the face after what he'd seen her do to his friend.

He. Him. I'm thinking of them as people. That's good. Keep it up.

Lucy strained to connect her mind to her mouth. It felt like trying to push a weight up a ramp. If she could just strain that little bit more, just push that little bit harder, then the weight would reach the edge, balance for a moment, and then tip over the edge, opening the floodgates. But something stopped her reaching that edge. She was almost there, but—

She opened her mouth. The sensation in her throat was . . . confused. She thought she remembered how to make sounds, but when she tensed unfamiliar muscles, it triggered her gag reflex and she almost coughed. It would *not* come. She felt her eyes fill with hot, angry tears. The Engineer reached out and stroked her head.

It was almost a human gesture, and she wasn't expecting that. He didn't seem to bear a grudge for what she'd done.

Shame we didn't meet your lot before we met the Elites. . . .

Suddenly the Engineer cupped her face with two tentacles, holding her chin just under the jaw like a dentist. It scared the hell out of her. She jerked away and he recoiled, tentacles signing rapidly.

That had to mean *sorry* or *take it easy.* Lucy beckoned him back, trying to look as harmless as possible. He floated back nervously and took hold of her chin again.

She had to trust him.

He pushed down and the gentle pressure made her open her mouth. Now it made sense. He realized she couldn't speak and he was trying to work out how to fix her. That HUD icon that didn't seem to work—if he'd improved the audio, he'd probably tinkered with the microphone too, but she couldn't make use of it.

For a moment, she felt elated. She was stranded inside a prison within a prison, but she'd made him understand something, and she'd understood him. The sense of connection was incredible.

It's worth a try. We're getting somewhere now.

She put her hand on his tentacle and held it still, then gestured to her mouth and shook her head. Did he get that? Was a head-shake a universal negative? There were places on Earth where it meant the opposite. Did he realize she meant that she couldn't speak, or did he think she was telling him not to touch her mouth? It was impossible to tell. He just hung there, peering at her. The last time anyone had stared her in the face at such close range was when a medic had checked out her eyes.

I haven't even got a pen to draw pictures for them. Nothing to write on. Damn, there isn't even any dust I can scrawl in.

The other two Engineers reappeared and just watched their friend. Lucy had to be sure that they understood what her problem was. She opened her mouth, held his tentacle just under her jaw, and struggled to make a sound. He had to be able to feel the muscles tensing. Even if he'd never seen a human before, he had to know how sound was made. He made sounds himself.

The tentacle felt like soft down. She could see a fine fringe of tiny cilia along it, glowing with that blue phosphorescence. For a moment, she looked into those odd little eyes and something seemed to click into place. He withdrew his arms and floated away between the vessels with his two friends. Had he given up?

He hadn't.

He turned as if he was looking over his shoulder, seemed to notice that she wasn't following, and drifted back. One tentacle curled around her wrist and he pulled gently.

Come with me. The meaning was crystal-clear.

Lucy followed, hand in hand with a living computer that didn't bear grudges.

UNSC *PORT STANLEY*, Brunel system: January 2553.

BB started the count to take *Stanley* into slipspace and found himself with a few idle seconds to fill.

He could perform five billion six-dimensional operations in that time. And time had to be filled, because he was pure intellect. Unless he was thinking and knowing, then he wasn't *existing*.

One part of his mind, the dumb AI at his core, counted down, calculated, and spoke to the hundred thousand components of a lightspeed-capable corvette readying herself to punch through into another dimension. He could ignore all that and let it run in the background like an autonomic nervous system. The rest of him, though, was consumed with raw curiosity; around the ship, back on Earth, and on the various comms channels he was monitoring, there were fascinating things going on. He listened to them all simultaneously.

Mal was on the CPOs' mess deck, arguing with Muir, the refugee they'd picked up on New Llanelli. The man didn't understand why he had to be locked in a cabin. Mal was telling him in his odd singsong accent that he was quarantined, there was a shower in the cabin, and maybe it was high time he used it. Vaz and Devereaux were on the bridge with Phillips, trying to explain what it felt like to enter a planet's atmosphere in a drop pod. Naomi was listening to the translated recordings of Sangheili voice traffic at the navigation console.

In the captain's day cabin, Osman talked to Parangosky on the secure link, swapping sitreps. Still no sign of Halsey yet, then; and the battle reports and casualty lists were still trickling in months late from remote places with almost nonexistent comms. It was a grim picture.

Colonel James Ackerson was finally confirmed dead, as well as Commander Miranda Keyes.

BB suspected that Parangosky was the only person who would miss Ackerson. "I was planning to give him the Spartan-Four program and make Halsey work for him," she was telling Osman. The captain listened, chin resting on her hand. "I'll have to settle for telling her that he died a hero. Just after I let her know what happened to her daughter."

She really wasn't that venomous, old Parangosky. BB knew that personal slights were too insignificant to incur her wrath, which was a cold and calculated thing geared solely to the achievement of clear objectives. She exercised power for a reason, not for its own sake, although Halsey probably wouldn't benefit from the difference when the Admiral finally caught up with her.

Miranda Keyes, Miranda *Halsey* to be legally accurate, had died heroically too. Halsey thought nobody knew she even *had* a daughter, even though it was impossible to hide that kind of thing from ONI or even from a curious UNSC HR clerk who could count. Routinely stored DNA samples, the period when Halsey was known to be having a fling with Jacob Keyes—no, it wasn't exactly particle physics to work *that* one out. BB thought of Halsey's journal again and how much it revealed of her mind.

How extraordinary. She refers to people as my *lieutenant,* my *Spartans. She has this sense of ownership. And yet she hands her small daughter to Jacob Keyes and washes her hands of her. How . . . odd.*

BB wondered how Miranda would have felt if she'd read Halsey's journal, or if Halsey had read hers. He realized he was getting a little too invested in humans. He didn't want to end up like Cortana.

It was three minutes to jump. He checked on Captain Hogarth back at Bravo-6 on Earth via another fragment of himself that he'd left in the ONI systems. *Chip off the old block. Ha. Not quite a child though. Just a little bit of me. Is that how Halsey sees her daughter?* Hogarth was still jockeying for Parangosky's job, rifling through her virtual filing cabinets for dirt on her via his own AI, Harriet.

Impertinent oaf. He really thinks Harriet can get past me? Well, she will . . . but only when I choose to let her. Maybe I'll play dumb and feed her bogus information. That'll ruin Hogarth's day.

The rising whine of *Stanley*'s Shaw-Fujikawa drive permeated the whole ship. Parangosky was talking to Osman again. "You can RV with *Monte Cassino* off Venezia to cross deck Spenser and the evacuee. There's no vessel that's closer. If there's any risk of compromising the mission, though, lose them."

"Spenser's no risk." Osman had worked with him years ago. BB wondered if she'd developed quite enough dispassionate ruthlessness yet to take over from Parangosky. "I'll make sure of it."

"Did you have a reason for not disposing of the evacuee?"

Osman's voice tightened. "I didn't want to start the relationship with my squad by killing an unarmed civvie in front of them."

"Good thinking. Glad to see the team's gelling, Captain."

"Good people, ma'am. Osman out." She took a breath. "All hands secure for jump. Do it, BB."

"Hope you've taken your ginger, Captain," BB said. *"Chocks away . . ."*

The drive opened an instant wormhole in space and *Port Stanley* slipped. Osman just swallowed hard. In the quarantine cabin, Muir muttered a string of fascinating and original expletives.

"You do realize this is the first warship I've ever piloted for real, don't you?" BB said. "Piece of cake."

Devereaux chuckled to herself. "Cabbage crates over the briny, BB."

"Tally ho, Skip."

It was oddly satisfying to be able to make humans laugh. If only Muir had been so relaxed about it all. He was hammering on his cabin door now, demanding to be let out. Osman eased herself up from the captain's seat and her expression hardened into resignation.

"How long to Reynes, BB?" she asked.

"Best estimate now—thirty-two hours. Do you want the cargo moved before Spenser arrives?"

"No. Let's transfer him via the docking ring and then you can make sure he doesn't go near the hangar deck. I'm going to visit our passenger."

"Need a hand, ma'am?" Naomi asked.

"He just needs *picturizing*," Osman said. That was the Navy's deceptively harmless word for bawling someone out at skin-peeling volume. BB suspected her approach would be the quietly menacing kind. "But thank you, Petty Officer."

Osman walked off with a purposeful stride and headed down the ladders through the decks. BB could see Mal standing outside the locked cabin, leaning against the bulkhead opposite with his eyes raised to the deckhead for a moment as if he was praying for strength.

"Button it, will you?" he yelled. The hammering on the other side of the door stopped for a moment. "Another ship's going to take you somewhere safe. Then you can do whatever you want. But in the meantime—just wind your neck in."

"Why lock me up? What the hell is it with you people? I'm not the goddamn enemy."

Osman could cover a lot of distance fast. She still had that Spartan turn of speed to match a long stride. She slid down the ladder to the officer's accommodation deck—BB found it interesting that nobody used the elevators—and bore down on the cabin. Mal stood away from the bulkhead.

"It's okay, Staff," Osman said. "I'll talk to him."

BB decided to manifest just as she opened the cabin door. Muir took a step back. He'd had a shave and he was wearing baggy engineer's coveralls, but being rescued hadn't produced a warm sense of gratitude to the Navy.

"Am I under arrest?" he demanded. He looked over Osman as if he was searching for a name tag or insignia. "Why am I a prisoner?"

"Quarantine, Mr. Muir," she said. "You'll be out of here in a couple of days."

Muir peered past her. He'd spotted BB. They probably didn't see many AIs on a colony like New Llanelli.

"What *are* you people?" he asked. "If you're Navy, why aren't you wearing badges? What's that square blue thing? And why are you talking to the Covenant?"

"The fighting's stopped," Osman said. Ah, that was a very careful word. She didn't say the war was over. "No peace treaty yet. Just trying to get back to normal."

"But what did you *give* them? I saw the ship land the last time too. Why Llanelli? Why talk to them there?"

Oh dear. Time for some airlock diplomacy. BB did a quick pass around the security cameras and put all evidence of Muir being on board in standby-erase, just in case. Osman shot back an answer, cool and unblinking.

"We've started exchanging bodies," she said. "They're like us. They want to bring their fallen home."

Muir's life expectancy now depended on whether he believed that story. BB was sure Muir couldn't possibly have seen the contents of the crates. He checked the record of the comm signal locations against the contours of the ridge where the exchange had taken place, and there was no direct line of sight. Muir could only have seen the dropship land and the trailer driven away.

Muir stared at BB, then at Mal, and then back to Osman, suspicious and much quieter. "Screw them, and their goddamned *fallen.* But why lock me up? You know damn well that I'm not infected."

"This is a spy *ship.*" Osman said it with slow deliberation as if she was getting impatient with his naiveté. She stepped back across the coaming, hand on the edge of the door. "Everything on this vessel is classified. Just *breathing* here is in breach of the Official Secrets Act. I can drop you back on New Llanelli, if you like."

"You really are all bastards, aren't you? You know how many people died on Llanelli? One million, four hundred thousand. Don't you get it? No, Earth was never hit, was it?"

"Oh, we lost a few billion on Earth," Osman said. "I think we get it just fine."

The door shut with a clunk and BB activated the locks. There was no more hammering.

Osman looked at Mal and shrugged. "He's just an ungrateful dick, Staff, not a security risk. He can't tell anyone anything."

"And if he could?"

"Then I'd do the necessary. I wouldn't expect you to do that."

That wasn't spelled out. BB studied the look on Mal's face as he watched Osman's vanishing back. Mal had that deepening, distracted frown that said things were crossing his mind that made him uncomfortable. If Muir had seen arms being handed over to the Sangheili, then he would have had to be silenced, and killing other humans was something only the older troops could recall. Mal was too young to have known anything but an alien enemy, and killing hostile aliens was a clear-cut thing. *Funny things, humans.* They really were hard-wired for anxiety about killing their own kind, whatever the history books showed.

"*Square blue thing,*" Mal whispered, leaning close to BB's hologram. "Go on, get your own back. Show up in his cabin and rattle your chains."

He turned and headed down the passage to the galley. BB took another look around the ship and decided he had more in common with his organic colleagues than he liked to admit. They were all making themselves busy whether they needed to be or not. Devereaux and Naomi had gone back to the hangar to tinker with the Spartan's Mjolnir armor, working out the easiest way to get Naomi into it. Vaz was sorting laundry. And Mal was cleaning the galley. It was all the small stuff that filled their down time and had to be done, covert mission or not. It made them all look rather harmless and domestic.

And, as Parangosky was fond of saying, the most successful missions were those that were unnoticed and of little remark, where nobody needed to fire a shot.

BB hoped the squad was savoring the enforced idleness. He couldn't see it lasting long.

Reynes, former mining colony: UNSC temporary listening station.

Reynes hadn't been a pretty place to start with, but a visit from the Covenant hadn't done much to improve the ambience.

Mining wasn't scenic. The endlessly fascinating CAA Factbook flashed up the planet's dismal history in Mal's HUD. *Aluminum, tantalum, copper.* There'd been about fifty thousand workers here when the mines were operating. Now there weren't any, unless he counted Mike Spenser, but there were still signs of where they'd been before the Covenant had launched its attack.

"Where is he?" Devereaux asked. She kept the dropship's drive idling and got on the radio. "Kilo-Five to Agent Spenser—the meter's running, sir. We're at the extraction point and you're not."

It took a few moments for Spenser to respond. "Just shutting the shop. Wait one."

"You need a hand?"

"I'm packing up the transmitter. Working to the last moment, that's me. Not that the bastards pay me overtime."

Mal stepped down from the dropship's bay and decided the view was worth recording for posterity. He'd seen a lot of glassed planets in the last fourteen years, but this was the weirdest landscape he could remember. The intense heat that vitrified the soil was enough to vaporize everything combustible and melt metal into slag, leaving just the characteristic ice-rink pools of glassy material. But sometimes structures survived. There was probably a sensible explanation for that, like a low-orbit bombardment, but whatever it was it had left a landscape that looked like a freeze-frame of a flooded town.

A winding derrick, the head end of a conveyor, and something that might have been a radio mast jutted from the glass lake at odd angles, silhouetted against thin gray clouds. The structures looked submerged rather than incinerated. Mal started walking toward the lake. As he got closer he could see that the skeletons of the buildings were charred to a uniformly matte dark gray, like a coating of velvet. He grabbed a few images and eventually stopped about ten meters from the edge. All he could hear was the wind.

The illusion of water was overpowering. He looked down at his chest plate and dragged his gloved finger through a fine layer of slightly sticky dust. It was going to clog his filters if he didn't flush them through as soon as he got back to the ship.

Vaz walked up behind him. "How come it's still standing?"

"Dunno." Mal ventured out onto the glass and walked gingerly between the debris embedded in it. "Maybe all this blew in while the glass was cooling."

It was pretty slippery, just like sheet ice. In some places it looked translucent with the hint of things trapped beneath. For the most part, though, it was a dense, opaque layer of mottled grays speckled with black patches that reminded Mal of carbon from a candle embedded in its melted wax. He squatted to inspect a charcoal velvet girder jutting out of the vitreous layer at a steep angle.

Vaz followed and stood over him. "Weird."

"Fancy being stuck here on your own for a couple of years. Can't do much for your mental health."

They waited, kicking around on the glassland and listening for movement. Vaz sighted up on the horizon for a few moments and then Mal heard crunching sounds like boots on gravel. A scruffy middle-aged man emerged from nowhere as if he'd crawled out of a hole. It had to be Spenser, and he looked exactly like he'd sounded.

He was in his fifties, face deeply lined with a good crop of gray stubble, one hand thrust deep in the pocket of a thick mountaineering jacket. He dropped a couple of rucksacks by his feet. Judging by the thud they made, that was his surveillance equipment.

"We didn't see where you came from," Vaz said.

"Down there." Spenser pointed. "The mine shafts are still mostly intact."

"Got that one right, then," Mal said. "You ready to go now? Destroyed everything sensitive that you can't carry?"

"I set fire to my underpants, if that's what you mean." Spenser looked around with that finality of a man fixing something in his memory for the very last time. "Can't say I'm sorry to leave this behind. Where are you dropping me off?"

"We're going to RV with *Monte Cassino* to cross deck you." Mal could see some movement in the ruins. Vaz spotted it too and lifted his rifle slowly. "We picked up a survivor on New Llanelli, so you'll have company."

Spenser frowned at Vaz and then glanced over his shoulder to see what he was looking at. "It's just the Kig-Yar."

"Are they your informers?" Vaz asked. "Because if they are, they're on their own. We can't take the whole zoo with us."

"No, my boys are off camp. That bunch just drops in occasionally to scavenge for tantalum."

The Kig-Yar started breaking cover and trotting out into open ground, spiky crests bobbing as they moved. Most people called them Jackals, but the scrawny, scaly little bastards reminded Mal more of deeply unattractive herons. Maybe it was the long beaklike muzzle, or the long, bony limbs, but either way there was a reptilian *birdness* about them. They were clutching an assortment of weapons. One had a UNSC-issue sniper rifle.

You better not have looted that from one of our dead, dickhead. . . .

The other three had Covenant needle rifles. The Kig-Yar with the sniper piece moved to the front and seemed to be leading his mates over for a chat. Mal decided it was time to go. Then his radio crackled. Devereaux hit the alert.

"Guys, I don't want to worry you, but I've got a crowd of Jackals here too."

"Well, don't sell them the dropship," Mal said. "We're on our way. Move out, Spenser."

Spenser grabbed his bags and the three of them began walking back to the ship, trying to speed up as they went. It was a slight uphill gradient. Mal just wanted to get out without a shooting match, but the Kig-Yar leader wasn't having any of it.

"You take?" he rasped. "No—ours! *Our* mines! You leave it!"

Mal turned and took a few paces backward as he walked, doing his friendly act but with his finger on the trigger. "Yeah, all yours, mate. Help yourself. Fill your boots."

Naomi cut in on the radio. That was all he needed, a Spartan for a backseat driver. "Staff, have we got a situation down there?"

"Small dose of Jackals. We're dealing with it." The Kig-Yar leader kept coming. They were usually pretty relaxed around humans as long as they were getting something out of it. They hadn't exactly been Covenant zealots, the lowest of the low as far as the Elites were concerned, less obedient than a Grunt and lacking the in-your-face ferocity of Brutes. "Stand by. We're banging out."

They were only fifty meters from the ship. Now Mal could see what was worrying Devereaux. Five or six Kig-Yar were wandering around the dropship, looking it over like they were thinking about buying it. Mal almost expected them to start kicking the tires. The hatches were shut, but there was nothing Devereaux could do to drive them off short of opening the starboard bay door and using a rifle. The things were so close to the ship that they were too far inside the range of the close-in cannon.

And at some point, Devereaux was going have to open the hatch for Mal and the others. Knowing what pushy scavengers the Kig-Yar were, Mal decided the priority was to keep them out of the ship.

"They're just Jackals," Vaz said, striding ahead without breaking his pace. Mal was more worried about Spenser. He had both hands full of kit. "They've got bird bones. They break. I'll get them to move."

"Vaz, we're bloody well surrounded. Take it easy."

The Kig-Yar with the sniper rifle was right on Mal's heels. If Mal gave him his MA5C and told them all to go away, he suspected they probably would. There was nothing secret about the rifle, either, especially with the number being traded on the black market. But just as he slowed down to turn and talk his way out of a confrontation, Sniper Jackal made the mistake of reaching out and grabbing him by the shoulder with a clawed hand.

"*Whoa* there, mate." Mal jerked away and held his rifle aside so that the Kig-Yar could see his finger on the trigger, fending him off with his free hand. "I said we were going, didn't I? Now take your buddies and sod off. We don't want any trouble."

Sniper Jackal spat out a stream of what Mal assumed were obscenities. Mal, Vaz, and Spenser were now at a standstill with a ring of Kig-Yar between them and the dropship.

Life was normally straightforward for an ODST. Mal encountered an enemy and blew its brains out, no ifs, ands, or chats about the weather. If he slotted any of these, though, the news would be around the sector in ten seconds flat, and he was pretty sure the last thing Osman wanted was for *Port Stanley*'s presence to become common knowledge.

"Come on, guys," Spenser said, doing an arms-spread gesture at the Kig-Yar. "What's your problem? You know me. We've done business."

Vaz was now standing at the dropship's hatch, or at least he would have been if there hadn't been a couple of Kig-Yar in his way. Mal saw him look around, sizing up the odds before he grabbed one of them by the collar and shoved the muzzle of his rifle under its chin. Sometimes they responded to a bit of alpha male aggression.

"You're in my way," Vaz said. "Move it."

"You only got *small* ship," said Sniper Jackal from behind Mal. They couldn't detect the corvette in orbit, of course. "You got big mouth for human with no backup. We take it and drop you somewhere nice, yes?"

Things were now going pear-shaped at a rate of knots. "Don't say I didn't try to be reasonable," Mal said. "Naomi? You getting this? Now would be a good time, sweetheart."

He hoped she had a good fix on his signal. If she hadn't, then BB certainly would. Mal shoved Spenser to the ground just as a searing bolt of white light sizzled through the thin cloud cover and blew a fountain of soil and rock high in the air about twenty meters to their left.

Debris rained on them, rattling off his armor. Some of the Kig-Yar threw themselves flat. Sniper Jackal tottered sideways, thrown off balance by the blast, and Mal put two shots through him. The next thing Mal heard was the *whhfft-whhfft-whhfft* of needle rifles discharging and something striking off his helmet. He opened fire in the direction of the sound. And Spenser wasn't on the floor anymore. He was right next to Mal, squeezing off a few with his pistol.

All Mal could hear now was automatic fire—his rifle and Vaz's, he hoped—and then suddenly it all stopped dead in a ringing silence. His pulse hammered in his throat. When he looked around, Vaz was turning a dead Kig-Yar over with his boot and rummaging through the pouches on the thing's belt.

Mal straightened up and got his breath back, then did a quick head count to check that none of the Jackals had escaped. Spenser dusted himself down and gave Mal a weary look of disapproval.

"Better hope one of these vultures isn't related to any of my informers," Spenser said irritably. "It took me *years* to build up that network."

Yeah, tough. Join the club. Mal got on the radio. "Thanks, Naomi. Captain? I'm afraid we've left a bit of a mess."

"Never mind." Osman sounded surprisingly relaxed about it. "Have you got any Sangheili rifles down there? You might want to make a bit more of a mess so we can blame it on them as well. Stir it up wherever you can, gentlemen."

Mal liked a woman with a positive outlook on life. Vaz moved from body to body, collecting weapons. He looked up at Mal and frowned, tapping his helmet.

"Dent," he said. "Needle must have hit you."

"What are you looking for?"

"You never know." Vaz went back to rifling the Kig-Yar's pouches. "These are bound to come in handy, if only for fitting someone up with false evidence."

"Bring back a couple of bodies too," said Osman. "We might find a use for those."

Kig-Yar stank to high heaven, and being dead didn't make them any more fragrant. The smell worked its way through the entire dropship on the run back to *Port Stanley.* It was an aroma that Mal could only describe as mudflats at low tide after a passing tanker carrying acetic acid had shed its load on the beach.

"I want one of those little lavender air fresheners," Devereaux muttered as she settled the dropship onto the docking ring. "You better get me one of those, Vaz."

Mal wondered how long it would take him to live down one of the worst extractions in the Corps' history, but Osman seemed perfectly satisfied. She came down to the hangar while they were unloading.

"Where do you want me to put the Jackals, ma'am?" Mal asked.

"Stick them in the cryo store with the Jiralhanae," she said, as casually as telling him to put a liter of milk in the fridge.

"Everybody stand by to jump. Next stop, *Monte Cassino*. I'm going to go and do some catching up with Spenser."

Mal and Vaz bundled up the Kig-Yar corpses in body bags and heaved them onto a gurney. BB appeared and made tutting noises.

"I think he's a bit old for her, don't you?" BB said. "Do you want a hand with those?"

"Yeah, very funny." Mal took the head end and Vaz steered from the rear. "Have we really got dead Brutes in storage?"

"They're next to the grape jelly," BB said.

He was joking about the grape jelly, because there wasn't any, but there really were a couple of intact Jiralhanae corpses and assorted body parts in a cryo-sealed container. Mal stared. Vaz shrugged.

"You realize nobody back home is going to believe this," he said.

"You realize we can never tell them anyway."

Mal went back to the dropship and found Devereaux scrubbing the deck of the cargo area on her hands and knees with good old-fashioned water and disinfectant.

"If you'd known it was going to be this weird, would you have volunteered?" Devereaux asked.

"I don't think we did," Mal said.

When he flopped onto his bunk at the end of his watch, he was sure that he still stank of vinegar. He shoved his fatigues in the laundry and scrubbed himself raw in the shower before finally gargling water up his nose in the hope that it would flush the remaining molecules out of his nose hairs. At one point he looked up from the basin and caught his reflection in the mirror, coughing and choking, and prayed that BB wasn't going to materialize in the cabin and laugh at him. But he was on his own, genuinely on his own for maybe the first time in ages, and it felt oddly lonely.

The alarm woke him six hours later. *Port Stanley* had already dropped out of slipspace. He walked onto the bridge in time to hear Naomi talking to the comms officer in *Monte Cassino*.

"*Stanley*, we're still five hours behind you." *Monte Cassino*'s officer of the watch sounded apologetic. That was slipspace for you, a lottery of reentry points. "How long before you reach *Ariadne*'s position? She's venting reactor coolant now and she still can't land her crew."

"You mean Venezia still won't help them," Naomi said.

"Well, they won't let the ship land, and they're not willing to board her to evacuate the crew. They say it's too dangerous."

"Okay, our AI estimates we can be there in two hours at sublight—we've actually got a visual on her. We'll take the crew off and wait until you show up. *Stanley* out."

"Is the boss okay with that?" Mal asked.

"Insists on it," Naomi said.

Ariadne was a patrol ship, with a complement of thirty at most. Mal estimated that it would take half an hour to secure a docking ring and cross deck everyone. All they had to do then was stand off at a safe distance from *Ariadne,* just in case, and hand out coffee—the ordinary stuff—until *Monte Cassino* rocked up. It wouldn't compromise opsec at all.

"Where is she, then?" he asked, trying to pick out *Ariadne* in the star field.

Naomi stared for a while, then pointed. "Here. Take a look on the long-range monitor."

Ariadne was just a speck of light even at maximum magnification. The marbled crescent of Venezia seemed Jupiter-sized by comparison.

"Not very efficient, the Covenant," Mal said. "You'd have thought they would have glassed Venezia early on."

Naomi just grunted. Mal was wondering if all the Spartans were that antisocial when the pinprick light that was *Ariadne* suddenly grew a lot brighter and then vanished.

He didn't say anything for a moment, and neither did Naomi. Then they looked at each other.

"I hope that's not the reactor," he said, but knew it bloody well was.

"BB." Naomi tapped the console. "BB, what happened? What did we just see? Is it what I think it is?"

BB took a second or two to respond.

"I'm afraid I've lost her," he said. "*Ariadne*'s gone."

CHAPTER 7

IT'S THE ONE THING WE CAN'T CRACK. ALL THE FORERUN-
NER TECHNOLOGY WE'VE BEEN ABLE TO EXPLOIT, ALL THE
IMPROVEMENTS IN DRIVE PERFORMANCE AND WEAPONS
CAPACITY WE CAN NOW INCORPORATE INTO *INFINITY*, AND
WE STILL CAN'T SEND A SHIP INTO SLIPSPACE AND CALCU-
LATE EXACTLY WHERE AND WHEN SHE'S GOING TO EMERGE
FROM IT. THAT ADVANCE ALONE WOULD HAVE SAVED
ARIADNE'S CREW.

(Rear Admiral Saeed Shafiq, UNSC Procurement)

**Forerunner Dyson sphere, formerly Onyx:
local date November 2552.**

"Wherever she is, she's almost certainly safe," Halsey said,
slapping one palm against the wall. She still held the
gray cylinder in the other. "The Forerunners built this
for safety. Let's just think our way through this."

Mendez seemed to be taking no notice of her. He turned to the
right and vanished into the gloom. Fred and Linda were working

their way across the wall at the end of the passage with tactical lamps from their rifles, searching for signs of an opening. The masonry seemed to swallow any light that fell on it.

"They were also trying to keep something *out,* Doctor." Mendez's voice boomed out of the darkness. "And there was something moving around in there. That's why she went in. Why don't you take another look at the control panel? It's got to be linked."

Halsey knew when she was being told to shut up and get lost. It made her scalp prickle. She wasn't used to being surplus to requirements. She couldn't see Olivia or Tom, but Ash and Mark, who seemed to be giving her a wide berth, were back in the control lobby working their hands across the dazzling display of symbols. She got as far as the end of the passage and thought better of it.

Her natural tendency was to tell them to stop and leave it to someone who knew what they were doing, but she wasn't so sure that she did. Things just seemed *familiar.* That was inevitable, she supposed, if humans did share some common origin with the Forerunners. Many symbols were rooted in basic physiology, like the dominance of red as a warning. But she still felt uneasy leaving this to gifted amateurs.

Are they gifted? Are they exceptional? How did Ackerson select them?

Halsey had assessed enough children in her time to be able to spot ability and character traits. Crisis or no crisis, her curiosity was consuming her. She wanted to know more about the Spartan-IIIs.

She could still hear Mendez calling for Lucy. The girl couldn't respond even if she could hear him, of course. What was he thinking, letting someone in that condition serve on the front line? She turned around and went after him. He probably wasn't in a teachable moment, but things had to be said.

Then there was Kurt's misguided attempt to enhance the Spartan-IIIs' neurobiology. No, she refused to believe that was Kurt's idea, whatever he'd told her. Her Spartans were too intelligent to make that mistake. They'd have realized that deliberately creating a personality disorder that had to be kept in check with medication was asking for trouble. Spartans were likely to be cut off from supply lines in the field, forced to live off the land, and the last thing they needed was reliance on drugs that could run out. This had to be Ackerson's amateur tinkering.

Halsey wandered up to Mendez as casually as she could. "I should have realized that Lucy's judgment was impaired," she said carefully. "It's neurobiological. How long since the Spartan-Threes had their meds? Too long, Chief. And we're not likely to get resupplied anytime soon."

Mendez emerged from the gloom and gave her a long, unblinking stare, lips pressed in a tight line. It was his don't-push-me look. During the Spartan-II program, she'd rarely been the recipient of it. But Mendez had dropped off her radar more than twenty years ago, and he was a lot less deferential now than she recalled.

Is that when he first betrayed me? I was pretty sure he'd been sucked into another classified project, but I never dreamed he'd team up with Ackerson.

"They're experienced special forces," Mendez growled. "Not malfunctioning AIs. What do you want me to do, power them down?"

That stung. Did he know? Did Ackerson himself even know that she'd eventually shut down—killed—Ackerson's interfering AI, Araqiel? Probably not. She brazened it out.

"Chief, do you understand what I'm saying? Even Kurt acknowledged that the Threes' judgment would be shaky." Halsey abandoned her trust-me-I'm-a-doctor voice. "You know damn well that he modified them genetically to reduce frontal lobe activity. That needs regular medication to keep it in check, but we don't *have* those antipsychotics, do we? I won't bore you with the details, but you might want to look up RADI some time. Reactive aggression. In a nutshell—your Spartans might be better at coping with injury and stress, but without their happy pills they're going to get dangerously violent."

Mendez sucked in a breath. "Yeah, I do understand the big words, Doctor. But I trained them from the age of six, so I *know* them. They're my men and women. They're as rational and professional as anyone."

"How can you say that? Is Lucy even *functioning?*" Halsey had to make him understand that kind of aphasia just wasn't *normal.* "Nobody that traumatized should be serving frontline. How long has she been mute?"

"Coming up seven years." Mendez shrugged, almost as if he was provoking her. "Maybe eight."

"Eight damn *years?* Are you *serious?*" Halsey was appalled. *A soldier who can't communicate?* "She's not just a liability to herself, Chief, she's a liability to her whole team. Especially with that frontal lobe modification."

"Well, Doctor, she didn't have that. That's how she is naturally. Any other dazzlingly *wrong* diagnoses you want to share with us?"

That stung. He'd made her look like an idiot. But a sudden muffled silence settled on her like a wet fog. There was enough light in the tunnel for her to see the body language around her, even if the Spartans' helmets made their expressions unreadable. Olivia and Tom were looking at her, heads turned, unmoving. She'd expected the Spartan-IIIs to resent comments about Lucy, but Kelly looked a little troubled too. Halsey could tell from the way she swung her arms slightly.

"I admit it's not ideal, ma'am," Kelly said, "but we work around it. Lucy can signal just fine."

The passage suddenly filled with light, harsh and bright enough to sting Halsey's eyes for a moment. Ash and Mark cheered and came jogging back down the passage. As her eyes adjusted, Halsey could now see the layout of the corridor and the wall ahead of her.

"We might be latent psychos," Mark said, "but we can still operate a light switch."

Halsey couldn't tell from his tone if he was making a friendly joke or taking a pop at her. Seeing as the lights were indeed on, she let it pass and examined the wall one-handed. There appeared to be a rope-edged margin cut into the blocks, a rectangle five meters by three, with a vertical row of symbols set down the right-hand side. It said *door* to her, and it also said *kept shut for a good reason.*

"They're back," Ash said.

Halsey looked around. The other gray cylinders had returned, floating like ghostly bottles. One peeled off from the others and drifted over to Mendez, settling about thirty centimeters from his face. He stared at it. If it had the slightest understanding of human expressions, it would have fled. Halsey let go of her cylinder and it floated up to head height, making no effort to escape.

"Ah," she said.

She and Mendez were the only two not wearing helmets, and they were also the only two with cylinders peering into their faces.

"What's different about you and me, Chief?" she asked. "Why are they interested in us and not the Spartans?"

Mendez took out his cigar and parked it in the corner of his mouth again. "Age? Unsocial habits? Guilt?"

"I'm being serious."

"Well, if I were them, I'd be making sure that nobody who got in here was contaminated with that Flood thing you were talking about," he said. "Because if they were, I'd have to destroy them. Maybe they're sampling what we're exhaling. Which they obviously can't do with anyone in a helmet."

That was actually rather solid logic. She hadn't thought in terms of Flood infiltration. She didn't know enough about it, just references to the parasite in Cortana's transmissions, but if that was what the Halo Array was designed to wipe out then the Forerunners had obviously decided the Flood was a catastrophic threat.

Maybe she'd bought into the Forerunners' perfect technical genius a little too much. They seemed to accept that their systems needed multiple fail-safes, and if these cylinders were bio-sentries, then maybe doors that wouldn't open were a bio-security mechanism as well.

"Let's see," Fred said, and lifted his helmet. One of the other cylinders that was waiting patiently moved across to hover in front of him. He huffed on it but it held its position. Halsey wished she'd checked the display underneath its base. "Gold star, Chief."

Olivia turned back to the wall and pressed the symbols, head cocked as if listening. Fred reached into his belt and pulled out a ration bar. It had been a long time since any of them had eaten. He unsealed it and stared at it as if he was steeling himself to put an angry cobra in his mouth.

Halsey hoped he didn't call the rations what some of the other Spartans did. If he said that word, the association would be unbreakable and she'd never be able to stomach eating them. She accepted that the texture was . . . deeply *unappealing*.

Fred bit a chunk off the end, rewrapped the remainder, and chewed slowly.

"Vile," he said. "One day, I'm going back to UNSC Procurement to find the jobsworth who designed these, and force-feed them to him."

"What if it's a woman?" Kelly asked.

"I'm very equality-minded. Her as well."

Halsey took comfort from the fact that they were at least sounding upbeat even if their internal reality was very different. Fred clipped his helmet to his belt and walked up to the wall. The cylinder stuck with him, managing not to get in his way.

"Would we hear her if she was hammering on the other side?" he asked. He looked at Mendez as if for a nod of approval, then glanced at Halsey. It struck her as an attempt to head off more arguments. "Linda, take Mark and Ash and do another check around the perimeter of this place."

If Lucy had managed to pass through this barrier, Halsey reasoned, then she could follow too. It was just a matter of reproducing whatever Lucy had done, and those options had to be fairly limited. Halsey spent the next twenty minutes examining every block of the wall between head and waist height and then walking straight at it in case there was a proximity sensor that would react to her. She didn't seem to be getting very far. The cylinder followed her around patiently like an attentive PA waiting on her instructions.

"What's the matter?" Fred asked. Halsey turned around to see who he was talking to. "Getting bored?"

The cylinder that had been hovering around Fred had drifted off and was now making its way down the passage to the entrance. Halsey looked to check if Mendez was still being pursued by his cylinder—he was—and wondered what had prompted Fred's to leave.

It wasn't her biggest problem right now though. They were no nearer to finding Lucy than they had been an hour ago. Sometimes Jacob Keyes spoke to her very clearly, like a conscience.

You're really only interested in solving puzzles, Catherine. That's the only reason you ask me what I'm thinking.

She'd expected to hear that voice more often now that Jacob was dead, but she accepted that her ability to forget about people when she no longer needed them wasn't an admirable quality. She couldn't remember ever having a proper row with him during their brief relationship, and there had been few harsh words even afterward, but once, just once, he'd told her that her apparent concern for people was just fascination when they didn't behave as she expected or wanted them to.

Halsey wanted to believe right then that she was worried about Lucy, who was in no shape to be fighting a war. Sometimes Halsey could look within herself and see clearly the gulf between what she wanted to believe and what actually drove her. She looked now, and admitted to herself that the need to unlock all the Forerunner mysteries was driving her slightly more than the need to locate Lucy.

Does it matter, though, as long as she ends up safe? Does my motive matter?

Yes, it did. The only way she'd justified what she'd done in the Spartan program was to focus on trading a few hundred lives for billions. Motive was her sole defense.

"Goddamn." Mendez was muttering to himself, a little indistinct as if he had something in his mouth. "I swear I'm going to eat grass before I have to swallow another mouthful of this crud."

Halsey turned. Mendez was struggling with one of his ration bars. He held out half of it to her without a word, but she shook her head and walked back to the entrance to study the symbols on the walls again, trying to piece together the sequences that she could recognize from the lexicon on her laptop. Her stomach could wait.

The cylinder was still shadowing her like a bodyguard. A few minutes later she heard Mendez grunt and say " 'Bye," as she spotted movement in her peripheral vision. One of the cylinders drifted past her and went outside. She was too engrossed in trying to find symbols that might shed some light on the unyielding door at the end of the passage to pay more attention to it.

But then something sharp and painful stabbed her in her right thigh. She yelped.

It was more surprise than anything, but it damn well hurt. She looked down, expecting to find one of the long-tailed beetles that Olivia had plucked from her jacket, but saw a cylinder withdrawing what looked like a needle from the folds of her skirt.

Kelly, Fred, and Mendez came running. Halsey made a grab for the cylinder but it darted away. It didn't get very far; a shot rang out and it shattered into a dozen pieces that went bouncing across the flagstones. Halsey looked up to see Linda standing outside the entrance with her rifle still raised.

"Better safe than sorry," she said, and started collecting the fragments. "What did it do to you, Doctor?"

Halsey rolled up the hem of her skirt and checked the damage. A blob of blood welled from a small puncture in her thigh. It suddenly struck her how thinly white and blue-veined her skin looked these days.

So I'm getting old. How the hell did that ever happen to me?

"I don't know yet," she said. "But it's going to be interesting finding out."

Sanctuary of the Abiding Truth, Ontom, Sanghelios.

The Servants of the Abiding Truth were at best misguided and at worst certifiably insane, but Jul had to admire their creativity.

He watched the motley assortment of monks handing out

weapons to the assembled malcontents and patriots who had shown up at the secret rally in the crypt of the sanctuary. Judging by the numbers, it couldn't have been that secret.

Some of the weapons, he knew, were based on technology that had come directly from the Forerunners. The Abiding Truth clung to the old orthodoxy, the beliefs that first started the war between the Sangheili and the San'Shyuum in the distant past and had ended with Sanghelios being annexed by the Covenant. Their stance was clear: all exploitation of Forerunner relics— what Jul preferred to call technology—was a sacrilege. But it didn't seem to stop them bearing arms for the revolution.

Jul leaned over one of the monks as he opened another crate of weapons. "A theological point, brother. Can you explain to me why it's permitted to use sacrilegious technology?"

The monk turned his head and looked up at him, slightly bemused. "Because, brother, by using sacrilege to counter sacri-lege, we return to balanced grace. And the weapons have passed through the hands of heretics and nonbelievers, so by using them for a holy purpose we erase sin."

Jul wrestled with that for a few moments and decided it was a debate he was better off avoiding. It seemed that the more rules a religion laid down, the more precise its strictures, then the more devious its adherents felt obliged to become. The gods had laid down the law: but frequently that law was inconvenient, so the only way to break it without incurring damnation was to argue over what humans called *the small print*. Jul felt that it bred sly morality and specious argument, unattractive traits in a race. If the gods wanted their bidding done then they owed it to mortals to turn a blind eye to infractions.

Forze tilted his head to get his attention. Jul walked over to him to see what he wanted.

"It's been two days," Forze said quietly. "Don't you think you should contact Raia and let her know where we are?"

"She knows. And she also knows that what we have to do is best left undiscussed." Jul looked around the crypt. He didn't expect to see anyone he recognized, but he was sure he had once served with at least three former shipmasters in the crowd. He didn't know if it was piety or pragmatism that had brought them here. In the end, it didn't matter.

'Telcam stepped up onto a dais at the north end of the crypt and spread his arms. "Brothers," he said. "What we do now is neither illegal nor unpatriotic. Sangheili common law has always permitted warriors to challenge a decision by a kaidon when they feel that decision is flawed or harmful. Normally that challenge would not be made covertly, but these are global issues, and the consequences of failure will affect more than our own keeps. This struggle is for the very future of Sanghelios. We must be discreet if we are to succeed, in case our many enemies seize a chance to further divide us."

There was a rumble of approval throughout the crowd. Jul believed that every state, every race—every species—had its own special failing. Kig-Yar would do anything for money, Jiralhanae would go out of their way to seek a fight, humans would never tell the simple truth when a lie was available, and Sangheili took refuge in believing they were what they were not. Every Sangheili believed that he was open, straightforward, and driven by honor. Jul wished that he were, but he was honest enough to admit to himself that it was more an aspiration than a description. This was a secret uprising that would be carried out in the most devious manner possible, because that was the only way it was going to succeed.

They were planning a coup. They were going to assassinate the head of state. He preferred to face that head-on.

The shipmasters Jul recognized had now gravitated together and stood in a small huddle in the center of the crowd. One of them raised his arm to ask a question.

"This is a promising array of weapons, holy brother," he said. "And I commend you on your procurement skills. But we'll need warships to challenge the Arbiter. I believe I still have the personal loyalty of my crew, so I offer up my old command, *Unflinching Resolve*. But we might require some . . . emphatic persuasion to release her from the shipyards."

'Telcam gave the shipmaster a polite nod. "Buran, that's most generous. Everyone in this room has seen service, so I'm certain there will be no shortage of volunteers to help reclaim her."

Forze leaned his head slightly toward Jul. "Don't. I beg you. This is one time *not* to volunteer."

But Jul was busy assessing the caliber of the revolutionaries in the crypt. Apart from the three shipmasters, most of them seemed to be enthusiastic youngsters or elderly middle-ranking warriors, and it was going to take more than motivation to deal with the Arbiter. Jul had no choice *but* to volunteer. It was a peculiar feeling: he really didn't want to do this, and he feared where it would end, but he couldn't bring himself to walk away from it. It was the first time he'd ever felt a sense of inevitability that verged on helplessness.

So he stepped forward because it was impossible now for him to step back.

"Brothers, if the Arbiter still had the stomach to finish the true war, then I would currently be the master of a cruiser." Jul raised his voice and hoped it didn't sound as shaky as it felt in his throat. "In the absence of anything else to occupy my time, I volunteer my services to reclaim *Unflinching Resolve* and return to duty."

The ship was a frigate. Jul didn't wish to be seen as pulling unspoken rank on the master of the smaller ship, and was simply stating his qualifications. But Shipmaster Buran turned to stare at him as if he had challenged his authority. Then his jaws compressed in amusement.

"Four shipmasters and one warship," he said, nodding his head enthusiastically. "That'll be interesting, won't it?"

"No long watches, that's what it means," one of the other shipmasters said. Everybody barked with laughter. "Nothing like being fresh for the fight."

Forze made a despairing rumble in his throat. He caught Jul by the shoulder and turned him discreetly away from the crowd.

"Why do you always fling yourself into these situations?"

"Because if I don't act, who will?" But Jul's stomach was busy tying his intestines into bows. "And this is the first time that I've ever defied the will of my so-called superiors."

Forze slapped him on the back, relenting as if his reluctance had shamed him. "It was more a question than a rebuke. I'm still here."

Jul watched the three shipmasters having what looked like a hushed, very private conversation and waited for the right moment to walk over and interrupt. He'd now volunteered to take part in a raid on a shipyard and seize a frigate. Now he had to embark on the more difficult part of that bold decision and actually work out a plan for doing it.

He found himself fidgeting with the *arum* in his pocket as he waited for the natural break in the conversation. The device was starting to become the obsessive habit it had been when he was a boy, because he hated losing, especially to inanimate objects. The *arum* hadn't taught him persistence and acceptance. It had simply fueled his sense of frustration with procedure.

And he still hadn't managed to release the gem at the heart of the spheres yet. He expected better of himself.

He was down to the third-level sphere and becoming hopeful of success when Buran stepped back from the knot of shipmasters and gave him his opening.

"So you have a plan for this, do you?" Buran asked. "Getting into the shipyard will be the simple part of the operation. Removing *Unflinching Resolve* will be more of a challenge."

"Why? Who's going to stop us? More to the point, *why* would they stop us?" A slow realization was dawning on Jul, that the Sangheili had become so used to the orderly world of command structures that Great Schism or not, the idea of deceiving their own kind seemed almost beyond them. It was another art the Sangheili needed to learn from humans. "I would suggest that we simply assemble a skeleton crew, go to your ship, and then fly her out of the shipyard."

"Just like that," said Buran.

"Apart from then finding a secure location to hide her, yes. Just like that."

Perhaps Buran was persuaded by the fact that Jul had been the shipmaster of a cruiser. In the complex hierarchy of the fleet, commanding a ship with greater firepower tended to give a warrior greater standing in the eyes of his comrades. It was also entirely possible that Buran and his two colleagues were, like so many others, suddenly cast adrift with neither a clear purpose nor the chain of command provided by the San'Shyuum. In a world devoid of ideas, the shipmaster with half a plan was emperor.

Buran looked to his two comrades as if looking for agreement, and then did a little nod of acceptance. "Very well, I shall contact my most reliable crewmen, and we shall simply take the ship. I shall also pray that I don't wake up one morning and find myself sitting on a nest and transformed into a Kig-Yar. Because this is how those little vermin operate."

"And they're most successful at it, which should give us all heart," Jul said. "Contact me through this temple when you're ready to make a move. My keep may well be enough of a backwater to hide your frigate."

Forze hadn't said a word. He simply stood there at Jul's side, just as the other two shipmasters flanked Buran, and offered no opinion. Jul didn't even know the names of Buran's comrades, but then they hadn't asked his name either. It was a promising start. Perhaps, Jul thought, he could teach them to think like the enemy after all. He could teach them to abandon their morals.

Sometimes the defining characteristics of a culture could be the same ones that proved to be its downfall. Humans prided themselves on their compassion and sense of fair play, despite copious evidence to the contrary, so much so that their very word for it was *humane.* Sangheili measured themselves by their prowess on the battlefield, and in order to demonstrate that prowess, a warrior had to be *seen* to fight. Jul understood that reflex. But he also knew just how successful humans had been using the most underhand and dishonest tactics; not just bluff and feint, but the most complex and disgusting deceptions. They were prepared to forfeit the lives of their own people to achieve it too.

I think I know where I draw the line, but until I reach that point—I will employ all necessary means.

Buran and his companions moved away. Forze cornered Jul. "I think we should return home now," he said quietly. "Theirs is the next move. And I think you'll have some explaining to do to Raia. I'm still working up sufficient courage to mention the matter to my wife."

Jul looked up at the ceiling of the crypt. He'd actually seen very few Forerunner structures, and never from the inside. The quality of the stonework was exquisite. The joints of every ancient block were as precise and perfect as the most modern architecture on Sanghelios. It gave him a sudden urge to explore the building.

"I want to see the rest of the temple," he said.

"Please don't tell me that you've had an attack of piety."

"No." Jul looked around to see if he could find 'Telcam. "I'm simply curious. Gods or not, we have to at least be respectful of the Forerunners and perhaps discover what became of them."

If the Forerunners had been gods, then they would have shown themselves in the Covenant's greatest hour of need. Gods were supposed to do that kind of thing. But the idea that they were an ancient civilization that had vanished almost without trace except for a few remnants of their technology now intrigued Jul far more than the idea of magical divinity. He headed for 'Telcam, aware that engaging an enthusiast on his favorite topic was a very good way to build trust.

"This is how obsessions start," Forze warned, but Jul ignored him and intercepted the monk.

"May I see the rest of the temple?" Jul asked. "I've never seen an intact artifact before. We only have ruins in my state. But then you already know that."

'Telcam gestured forward with a sweep of his arm and ushered Jul and Forze through a honeycomb of interconnecting passages, all exquisitely faced with stone blocks so carefully laid that it was impossible to put a blade between them. There were inlaid panels on the walls, filled with swirls and lines that Jul recognized as Forerunner symbols, thrown into sharp relief by the dimmed lights strung overhead. It didn't look as if any maintenance had been carried out down here for centuries. Jul was intrigued by a side corridor that disappeared into darkness, and began to wander that way.

'Telcam caught his arm. "That's walled off—a dead end," he said. "Whatever the Forerunners left down there, we weren't destined to enter."

"Who else comes down here?"

"Nobody," 'Telcam said. "Everyone forgot us generations ago. But we didn't forget the gods."

That only intrigued Jul more, but he did as he was asked and walked on. One panel in particular took his fancy. It appeared to be a list. The symbols were laid out in horizontal rows at the center, with lines radiating from them to individual symbols around the edge of a cartouche. Jul put out his hand involuntarily but his thumbs brushed against a rigid shield like a matte glass screen. He hadn't even seen it. It seemed to dissolve into the wall.

'Telcam caught his shoulder. "The shield was placed there long before the San'Shyuum arrived," he said. "The Servants of the day said that touching the symbols produced strange effects. That seemed like a sensible reason not to interfere with it."

Jul marveled at the odd blend of self-control and lack of curiosity. "What do *you* think it is?"

"Looks like a control panel to me," Forze muttered.

"There are those who believe it's a map," 'Telcam said. "Worlds that the gods visited and the locations of the holy rings."

Jul counted at least eleven separate rows of symbols. *Holy Rings* made the Halo Array sound so benign. Was that what this diagram was? He made a note of it.

"The Forerunners were well traveled," he said. If he'd been allowed the time to study the panel, he'd have been looking for six or more identical symbols and worrying about them, but he couldn't begin to make sense of the map—if that was what it was. "And generous. But what do they really want from us?"

"To wait patiently for their return," 'Telcam said. "To trust them."

Jul wondered how much trust he was willing to put in gods who would destroy a galaxy to save it. But that was another theological debate he didn't plan to pursue.

UNSC *PORT STANLEY,* 10,000 kilometers off Venezia.

If only it hadn't been Venezia.

If only.

If *Ariadne* had gone down near any other planet, any other colony world, then it would have been just that—a tragic and avoidable loss of life caused by an unhappy conjunction of inadequate maintenance, a colonial bureaucracy mired in safety concerns, and sheer rotten bad luck.

But it *was* Venezia, and Venezia had a history.

Osman stood at the viewscreen, hands in her pockets, staring out into space in the direction of *Ariadne*'s drifting debris and tried to work out if what she wanted to do now was actually what needed doing.

I know what Chief Mendez would say. Stick it to the bastards. Make them pay.

There was a whole generation of UNSC now who didn't remember the colonial insurrection, and even Osman was too young to recall the detail of the war that shaped her life before the Covenant gave humanity a much bigger problem to worry about. But however bloody the war with the Covenant had been, it was colonial terrorism that shaped her fate. It was the real reason why her life and her parents' lives had been wrecked by Catherine Halsey. The Spartan program had been Halsey's personal plan to give the UNSC the upper hand in the insurrection. That fact tended to get forgotten these days.

That's the last thing I should be thinking about right now. All hands lost in Ariadne. *And those bastards on Venezia could have made a difference, but they didn't.*

Even when they don't lift a finger, they're still killing us.

BB's reflection glided into view and floated next to her. "Agent Spenser's ready, Captain. Phillips has finished extracting every last drop of juice from his brain."

"Well, I'm glad he found something to pass the time." Osman went back to her seat and tapped the console. She liked to see an on-off switch when it came to comms, just in case. "*Port Stanley* to *Monte Cassino,* how long do you plan to continue the search?"

"We're mapping the outer edge of the debris spread. That'll take another hour." *Monte Cassino*'s executive officer, Cerny, gave her the impression that he felt personally responsible for arriving too late and that he was now busy overcompensating. "We're ready to transfer your personnel whenever you're ready. Do you want us to send a shuttle?"

"Negative, *Monte Cassino.* There's not enough room to dock." *And the last thing I need is some matelot nosing around the hangar.* "We'll come to you."

There wasn't a hope in hell that anyone had survived the explosion. *Ariadne* was only a small patrol vessel with a four-man shuttle. But *Monte Cassino* insisted on doing it by the book. Occasionally, crew had managed to survive catastrophic accidents when sealed compartments were blown clear and didn't rupture. The Navy tended to cling to scraps of hope like that.

Reality wasn't on their side though.

"*Monte Cassino* to *Port Stanley*—Venezia's getting a little grand

and warning us that we're encroaching on their territorial limits. Stand by."

Osman gestured to BB. *Take us in closer.* "What are they planning to do about it? Complain to the Colonial Authority? Too bad they blew up the local CAA bureau."

"I've reassured them that we have no intention of landing."

They need reassuring with a few warheads. "We'll keep an ear on your channel."

Osman debated whether to break cover and pay a visit to whatever passed for an administration on Venezia. But it wasn't any of her business, much as she wanted it to be, and she had to keep her mind on the main mission. The old problem had suddenly reared its head again: did UNSC turn a blind eye to whatever the colonies did, or did they exact some kind of vengeance and kick off the whole conflict again?

She'd grown used to thinking of those sorts of policy decisions as being above her pay scale, but very soon they wouldn't be.

I'm supposed to be destabilizing Sanghelios. I'm not supposed to be opening up rifts between humans. But God Almighty, somebody needs to put Venezia in its box once and for all.

She could hear Spenser walking down the passage onto the bridge, muttering with Phillips and Vaz. The word *bastards* carried a long way. It was all those sibilants.

"I think this is where I came in," Spenser said, holding his hand out to her for a final shake. "It's been good seeing you again, Oz. I suppose the next time we meet, you'll be convening an ONI star chamber and I'll be the accused."

"Never." Osman held on to his hand. Spenser might have been buried on Reynes for years at a time, but he still seemed to keep up to speed with the gossip. "Parangosky's set on staying in post until she reaches her century."

"Just don't get caught up in any Sangheili cross fire, that's all. The lid's going to come off that pretty soon."

She would have forced a smile if she hadn't been flying into a cloud of pulverized ship. "Don't worry, we'll stand from under," she said. "You know ONI. Nine lives, all of them deniable."

"I'm not going to ask what you're shipping. But your noisy passenger might."

"Tell him we're selling narcotics to the Unggoy. It's an idea whose time has come."

She let go of his hand and he disappeared in the direction of the top hatch with Phillips, who seemed to be intent on wringing every last scrap of Sangheili cultural trivia out of him.

Vaz hung back. "Are we getting involved in the *Ariadne* thing, ma'am?"

"We can't," she said. "Much as I'd love to. That's Hood's problem now. He's the one who's supposed to be getting touchy-feely with the colonies. We'll just hang around and see *Monte Cassino* safely away."

Vaz nodded, looking unconvinced, and walked off. For a moment she thought she might have offended him by referring to the colonies so dismissively, but he was from Earth, just like Mal, Devereaux, and Phillips. It hadn't been a deliberate policy to pick a team of Earth boys. But it didn't do any harm either.

Naomi had been taken from a colony world, just like Osman herself. She wondered if Naomi could even remember where she came from. After years of having their past bleached away and replaced with an artificial destiny, it was hard for any Spartan to tell what was a genuine memory and what had been part of the brainwashing process.

"Persuasion and acclimation—a lifelong training." What a lovely euphemism. Was that what you called it, Halsey? There were times

when Osman wished she'd never been given access to Halsey's private journal, but she kept going back to the file and staring at the self-serving, self-deluding garbage, driven by that same stomach-churning cocktail of compulsion and revulsion that made humans stare at mangled corpses. *Training? You bitch.*

Osman made a conscious effort to forget the journal and checked the security display. Anyone in the ship with a neural interface showed up as a transponder code on the deck plan. Naomi was still messing around in the engineering space where her armor was stored; Vaz and Mal showed up as two small dots moving back and forth around her, as if they were trying to give her a hand and she was telling them she could manage just fine on her own. Phillips had no implants, so Osman needed a little help from BB to locate him walking back to his cabin. The drop-ship was now on its way to rendezvous with *Monte Cassino,* and then they'd all be free of the embarrassing complication of passengers who had to be kept away from the incriminating cargo in the hangar.

Phillips, to his credit, hadn't been idle. He'd fed all the intercepted Sangheili comms through transcription so that Osman could physically read it while she was listening to something else. BB could have intercepted, recorded, translated, transcribed, and analyzed the whole lot in a matter of seconds, but he could also navigate and fight the ship, too, and she still preferred to do much of that herself. BB—in full control of *Port Stanley*—only needed humans to shake hands with dignitaries and handle the fiddly close-quarters combat. But he knew that they needed to feel more useful than that to make life worth living.

She'd never had an AI like him before. He was more than an assistant. He was an intelligence officer in his own right, and he was also her bodyguard. They'd been teamed up for less than a month and she already found herself dreading the day when he wouldn't be around any longer.

Damn. That's depressing. Got to stop that. I'll be volunteering for a full AI neural interface next.

Osman kept half her attention on the radio as she let the hours of transcript scroll in front of her on her main CIC screen. The ebb and flow of voice traffic had blended into a white noise of requests for checks as *Monte Cassino* spiraled slowly out from the center of the explosion, scanning for debris as she went and then working her way back in again. It was only when an abrupt and unfamiliar voice broke into the circuit that her attention was dragged from the transcript and made to listen.

"UNSC *warship, this is Venezia TC. You are now in sovereign space. Suggest you withdraw.*"

It was like hearing archive material from fifty years ago. There was something oddly distressing about a human voice issuing a hostile challenge to a warship, and Osman could only listen. Venezia couldn't detect *Port Stanley* and that was how it had to stay.

"*Venezia TC, this is* Monte Cassino. *We're keeping you fully informed of our intended movement. You're fully aware that we're searching for possible survivors.*"

"Monte Cassino, *unless you turn back we'll open fire.*"

There was a brief pause, and then Commander Cerny's tone changed from the flat calm of a few seconds earlier.

"*I suggest you don't do that, Venezia. Because we will return fire.*"

"*You were going to do that anyway. Venezia out.*"

She jerked forward in her seat. Venezia didn't have the fire-power to take out *Monte Cassino,* but Osman still had a pilot and a dropship out there. BB appeared instantly just above the console and shivered slightly.

"I think it's National Foolhardy Day," he said. "I've alerted Devereaux and she's standing off until this nonsense is over."

"Thanks, BB. Flash *Monte Cassino* discreetly and tell them we're here for backup if they need us."

Port Stanley was close enough to Venezia now for Osman to see the planet and the faint point of light that was the warship. She watched from the viewscreen, waiting for Cerny's voice over the radio saying that they'd completed the search and were pulling back, but about a minute later she caught a burst of static and the tail end of a warning.

"*—brace brace brace!*"

She thought she saw a streak of light followed by a faint star-burst like a flare, but it was gone before she could study it. Whatever it was, it definitely hadn't hit *Monte Cassino.* Any impact would have been visible at this range. But it looked like the bastards really had opened fire on the destroyer.

"What the hell was that, BB?"

"Ground-based triple-A. Let me nose around."

Osman could now hear what was happening on the ship's bridge.

"*Point of origin identified. Acquiring lock—standing by.*"

"*Take, take, take.*"

"*Missile away. Time to target—eighty-two seconds.*"

Eighty-two seconds was a painfully long time when you couldn't see what was happening. If *Monte Cassino* hit the launch site, then Osman would be none the wiser until the ship confirmed a kill. But she was far more worried about the prospect of Venezia now having space-capable missiles, which they'd certainly never had before. They'd confined their off-world activities to ship-to-ship attacks and landing personnel to plant explosive devices. They'd never been in the big weapons league.

Who the hell was selling them that stuff?

There was a lot of black market hardware floating around these days, and Osman knew that better than anyone. But it was a worrying development at a time when Earth didn't need any more problems.

"*That's a kill, confirmed,*" said a satisfied voice that she didn't recognize. It was probably the weapons officer. "*Target destroyed. Stand off, helm.*"

"*Port Stanley,* we're pulling back to five thousand klicks. Do you still want to transfer personnel?"

Osman had no choice. She couldn't keep Spenser and Muir in tow for a mission like this. "Yes, Commander, we do. And we'll take over from here. Return to Earth."

"Normally I'd ask the captain about that," Cerny said, "but we don't usually argue with ONI."

"I appreciate the cooperation. Have you identified the weapon?"

"T-thirty-eight triple-A. I can only hope they picked it up at a Covenant yard sale, because the alternative's pretty worrying. There must be plenty of disappointed Sangheili who'd love to see humans infighting again."

"I'll bet," Osman said. *And I'd be amazed if we were the only ones pulling this destabilization stunt.* "But that's definitely ONI's part of ship. We'll take it from here. *Port Stanley* out." She looked up toward the deckhead to call BB, a reflex she'd suddenly picked up. She felt she was appealing to a guardian angel.

"Is that right, BB?"

"On the nose, Captain. I piggybacked on their comms signal and checked the return myself."

"Okay. Thanks."

Mal, Naomi, and Vaz came onto the bridge, looking offended

at being dragged away from a decent fight. Mal raised his eyebrows.

"Couldn't help overhearing, ma'am."

BB popped up again. "Me and my big mouth."

"Reckon it's worth inserting and doing a recce?" Mal asked. "They don't know we're here. Once *Monte* leaves, we can pop in for a look."

Osman gave it five seconds' serious consideration. It wasn't something she could ignore, but she had to keep the kettle boiling on Sanghelios too. She put Venezia on her mental must-screw list at number two and started drafting a contact report for Parangosky.

"We'll come back later," she said. "I promise."

CHAPTER 8

DON'T WORRY—YOUR SECRET'S SAFE WITH ME. I'M NOT
GOING TO TELL ANYONE THAT YOU'RE MY MOTHER BE-
CAUSE I'M PRETTY SURE I KNOW WHAT YOU'VE DONE, AND
I LOVE DAD TOO MUCH TO SEE HIM ASSOCIATED WITH IT. I
DON'T KNOW WHICH IS WORSE—WAITING FOR EVERYONE
TO FIND OUT WHAT YOU DID, OR WAITING TO SEE IF I TAKE
AFTER YOU. IF IT'S ALL THE SAME TO YOU, MOTHER DEAR,
I'M GOING TO MAKE SURE I TAKE AFTER DAD.

(Midshipman Miranda Keyes, in a rare message
to her estranged mother, Dr. Catherine Halsey)

**Forerunner Dyson sphere, Onyx:
local date November 2552.**

D*ust.* Lucy needed dust. But there wasn't a trace of it anywhere.
She trailed along behind the Engineers, looking frantically for anything she could draw diagrams on. The parking
garage area seemed to be a long way behind her now. If she turned
around, she wasn't even sure if she could find her way back. Every
meter of the passages of plain, smooth stone looked the same.

The Engineer who'd taken her hand kept stopping and turning, either to check that she was still behind him or to hurry her along. She knew that somewhere outside, Chief Mendez and the others would be looking for her. She hated herself for putting them through this. They had enough problems without having to rescue her as well.

Why didn't I just do as Tom told me? How hard could that be?

The Engineers led her into a room that looked something like a control room, all screens and lights. Engineers built and rebuilt things, so she allowed herself the luxury of an assumption that this wasn't going to be a sauna. She tucked her helmet under her arm and looked around for a polished surface.

And there it was—a smooth panel of some glasslike material. It was worth a try. She took off her glove and leaned close to the glass, breathing on it to form condensation. For a fleeting moment, a fine bloom dulled the surface and she dragged her finger through it. The Engineers clustered around her, heads bobbing, but it was impossible to interpret any reaction on their faces. She tried again. The condensation evaporated almost instantly, so she licked her finger and scrawled L-U-C-Y on the glass and tapped her chest.

It's like the Galapagos Islands. I've got a population of Engineers that's evolved in isolation from the rest of the galaxy. And I still can't tell if they know anything about humans.

They were certainly trying to find out what they could though. One of them darted into a passage and emerged with a container that looked like a smooth white ceramic mug with no handle. He held it out to her.

Lucy took it and peered in. A brownish translucent sludge that smelled faintly of yeast shivered inside. The Engineer dipped a tentacle into the sludge and put it to his mouth, flicking out a small, pointed blue tongue to lick it. Lucy now couldn't shake that mental association with an armadillo.

So he thought she was *hungry*.

She could understand why he thought a woman who seemed to be sniffing and licking their machinery might be trying to tell them that she wanted food. She handed the mug back and shook her head. Actually, she *was* ravenous now, but it could wait. The Engineer held his tentacles up in front of her and formed them into exaggerated shapes in a slow sequence, some overlapping and some making simple lines or loops. It was quite touching: he was speaking slowly and loudly to her, the stupid foreign tourist, trying to make her understand.

If she'd been him, though, she'd be spelling out her name. Maybe that was what he was doing.

A distant memory flashed through Lucy's mind and was gone almost as quickly as she tried to grasp it. She was playing charades. It might have been her birthday or Christmas, but she was having fun, miming a title and counting out the syllables by holding up her fingers. Could she even count? She remembered that she hadn't been sure how many fingers to hold up. She tried to focus on the faces watching her, but the scene dissolved into a brightly colored blur and all she was left with was the awareness that she'd been happy and that it had been a long time ago.

Well, if Engineers were that smart, she'd hand them the contents of her backpack and they could work it out from there. She unslung her rifle and clamped it between her knees while she eased off her backpack to stop them from wandering off with a loaded weapon. They gathered around her as she tipped the contents out onto the floor.

There was a routine for packing a rucksack with different items in specific layers. Her meager pile of possessions looked as if an archaeological dig had excavated a cross-section of her life. It was probably the same as any soldier or marine carried in their pack, and she suspected it hadn't changed all that much for centuries: spare shirts, socks, and underwear, extra ammunition clips, a comb, a bar of multipurpose soap, a mess tin with folding cutlery, solid fuel pellets, first-aid supplies, a snare, a length of fishing line, and signaling equipment. But there were no photos of family or any of the little private things to remind her of family or home. She didn't have one.

And no datapad. That would have helped. And there's always my neural interface. There's got to be some data in that. But that's got to be removed carefully, and if they don't know enough about humans to do that . . . it'll kill me.

The Engineers rummaged enthusiastically through the contents of the backpack. The signaling device proved to be a big draw and they passed it between themselves, tentacles whisking over it in a blur of busy cilia. Each time one passed it on, the shape changed completely in a matter of seconds before he handed it over. Then one of them picked up her underwear and stretched a pair of briefs between his tentacles. She was wondering what modifications he could possibly make to her pants—well, at least he wouldn't care how gray they were—when she spotted the lettering on the waistband.

Name tag. There's a name tag.

If old tech worked, it stayed. The simplest, cheapest, most durable way to identify your pants among a hundred identical pairs in the barracks laundry was to have your name and service number dye-embossed into the fabric. Lucy's briefs, like all her clothing, bore the name LUCY-B091. She grabbed them from the Engineer and held the label up to him, then tapped her chest. She pointed to the name and then to herself a few more times.

The Engineer who she'd come to think of as the boss made a

shape with his tentacles and then pointed at himself, then repeated the gesture and waited. Now she was getting somewhere. They seemed to know they were talking about identities. Lucy tried to mimic the shape he was making with his tentacles, but fingers were a poor substitute for completely flexible appendages that divided into increasingly fine cilia. The closest she could get was to form two linked circles with her thumbs and forefingers.

And knowing my luck . . . that'll be the Engineer sign for "Your mom's a skank."

The Engineer reached for her helmet and she almost snatched it back, but she had to trust him. She kept her arms at her sides. Letting a creature she couldn't understand take away her lifeline required all her self-control.

Engineers—they're harmless. The most they'll do is try to defend themselves. They're not even very good at that.

And now all she could do was wait. The two Engineers left in the workshop drifted away and left her on her own. She found a low ledge to sit on and tried to think her way out.

The Sentinels worked out how to speak English just by listening to Ash. So the Engineers can work out some basics from whatever data they can find in my armor systems, right?

But without the ability to make sounds, whatever information she exchanged with them would have to be in symbols. Finding a common set—other than pictures—was going to be hard.

Great. We'll kick off with cave paintings and evolve through the development of written language, all before lunch. Why did I get myself into this? Why didn't I follow orders?

And Dante, William, and Holly are dead. And so's Kurt. And—again—I'm not. Why? Why not me?

The boss Engineer returned in time and stopped her sliding down that path of misery again. He'd only been gone for a minute, perhaps two, before he drifted back clutching her helmet like a football and reached out to run his tentacle across one of the screens on the wall.

Letters faded up, black script seeping out of a milky-white sheet of glass.

LUCY-B091 RECLAIMER WELCOME TO SHIELD WORLD SARCOPHAGUS BUT LIFE GOES ON.

The font was identical to the one in her underpants. She sucked in a breath and found herself nodding. Life . . . had to go on.

She hadn't realized her emotional state was so visible to an alien life-form.

So now she could write. She reached up to the screen and struggled to frame a response in her mind. But it wasn't just her ability to form spoken words that had withered; she now struggled to express herself even in a written form. The conversations she had with herself in her own mind weren't the same. She hadn't realized that until she tried to get them out of her head and make them solid.

Just write something. Anything.

She dragged her finger down the white glass, expecting to see a line form. It remained stubbornly blank. Of course—it was designed to respond to whatever input the Engineers used, not human handwriting. She looked at the Engineer and did a frustrated shrug.

Damn. Damn. *But he'll get the idea. He'll watch and then he'll work out what I need. I know he will.*

The Engineer placed a tentacle on the screen next to her hand and more letters formed.

WHERE IS THE PLAGUE? NOTHING IS DEAD. WHY ARE YOU HERE?

His fluency was improving word by word. Lucy tapped the glass with her forefinger. Damn it, he was supposed to be a technical genius, and he couldn't see that she couldn't use the screen? *Don't disappoint me. I thought you could do anything.* She grabbed his tentacle, like folding her fingers around a little kid's hand to guide his crayon. He flinched and tried to pull away.

The "hand" felt delicate and smooth, like silicone, and cooler than human skin. Maybe she'd squeezed too hard and scared him. She hung on and patted the arm to calm him down, but pressing his cilia against the glass didn't produce any text. She let him go, out of ideas and lost for what to try next.

But he stroked the glass again and more letters formed. Maybe the thousands of tiny cilia were operating microscopic touch-keys.

ALL LIFE LIVES. TALK TO PRONE TO DRIFT.

Okay, maybe he was extrapolating too far now. That looked like gibberish to her. She shook her head and frowned theatrically. *I don't understand.*

PRONE TO DRIFT.

Lucy frowned again, this time with a shrug. There had to be some body language that would get through to him. But she was running out of nonwords.

He touched the screen again.

PRONE TO DRIFT IS ME.

Is me. Is . . . me. God, how did she ever forget that briefing? It was his *name.* Engineers named their offspring according to how they floated when their gas sacs were first adjusted for buoyancy. His name was Prone to Drift. She wanted to say it, and strained to make a sound, but her throat just felt strangled by the effort again and she gave up.

WHY ARE YOU SILENT? he tapped.

Lucy shrugged. She wasn't the only Spartan who'd been through traumas, just the only one who'd been driven to silence by it. She managed a sigh, more a heavy breath than anything. Prone to Drift perked up and cocked his head as if listening harder, but then appeared to realize it was the only sound he was going to get out of her.

He didn't seem to be losing patience with her though. All the frustration was coming from her side of this mimed conversation and unlike the half-remembered game of charades, it wasn't fun. She suddenly wanted to burst into tears.

The other Engineers drifted back into the room and exchanged a flurry of gestures with Prone to Drift before vanishing again. He took her ungloved hand and examined her palm and the tips of her fingers like a fortune-teller.

Prone turned her hand as if he was showing it to her, then let go and touched the display.

YOU HAVE BLUNT APPENDAGES. WE MAKE ADJUST-MENTS.

Lucy felt a warm flood of revelation in her chest. *He understands. He really understands.* He was going to fix the screen so that she could write on it. And that meant she had to think in formal language again. She could do it. She *had* to. She had to let him know that she needed to find her squad.

She also had to find out what this place actually was, and how they were going to survive here. If she could get Dr. Halsey or Chief Mendez together with Prone and his friends, that discussion would be a lot easier.

She'd reached the point of seriously considering using her own blood as ink and scrawling on the walls when the surface of the glass in front of her changed. At first it seemed to liquefy, with colored chunks drifting in it like a tutti-frutti dessert, and then the colors coalesced and she was looking at a vertical line of capital letters and a few dots.

Her reflex was to try to read it as a word, but then she counted and realized the line was twenty-six characters long and none of them repeated. The dots looked like symbols—a question mark, a comma, a dash, and a full stop.

It was a keyboard.

Ah. That information must be stored in my HUD. The text display. Of course.

It wasn't in any kind of alphabetical or keyboard order she'd ever seen, but she knew what she had to do with it. She hunted for the letters and prodded them laboriously like someone learning to type. Few people did that these days, but then very few could still use Morse either. She could.

Prone seemed to be getting excited. WE CAN TALK. NOW WE CAN DISCOVER MORE. THE SHIELD HAS ACTIVATED BUT WHERE IS THE FLOOD?

Lucy was way behind him, hunting not only for the right letters but trying to frame the right words, a hard thing for most humans to do without some degree of subvocalization. She didn't have that option.

Prone tried again. HAS THE ARRAY FAILED? WE FOUND NO HAZARD WITHIN THE SHIELD WORLD. JUST TRACE.

Lucy tapped as fast as she could. ARRAY?

RING, Prone replied. ARC. BAND. CIRCLE.

HALO, Lucy interrupted. HALO.

Prone didn't have shoulders but she could have sworn that he sagged visibly with relief. YES, HALO. NO HALO, NO FLOOD, NO FIGHTING, AND LIFE CONTINUES OUTSIDE, BUT THE BULKHEADS CLOSED. MOST PERPLEXING.

Oh . . . that's it. I get it now.

Revelation was as powerful an emotion as love or fear. It was

probably the remnant of a survival mechanism for escaping pred-
ators or starvation rather than a sense of intellectual bliss, but the
penny dropped and Lucy savored the elation for a moment.

Prone wasn't being philosophical about grief when he'd told
her that "life goes on." He was asking her why the Dyson sphere
had been accessed when there was no threat outside and the Halo
Array hadn't fired to wipe out everything that had been contaminated by the Flood.

And if he knew there was no threat outside the Dyson sphere,
then he had access to real-time information about the outside
world. Lucy's pulse raced.

Information could pass both ways. That meant the squad could
call for extraction. The war might already be over.

Lucy grabbed Prone to Drift and hugged him, then tapped out
four painful words.

SORRY ABOUT YOUR FRIEND.

She hoped he understood that she'd regret pulling the trigger
for the rest of her life.

**Aanrar shipyard, Ranarum orbital platform,
Sanghelios system: February 2553
in the human calendar.**

"There's a human proverb," 'Telcam said, beginning the long walk
to the security barrier at the brow. "The devil makes work for idle
hands."

Jul, Buran, and Forze ambled along beside him, trying to look
casual while six of Buran's loyal crew—two of them Jiralhanae—
trailed behind. They'd had to beg passage on a repair detail's shuttle to make the flight to the orbital yard. It was crewed by Jiralhanae
and the only maintenance workers around seemed to be Unggoy,

hardly a substitute for Huragok. The wretched ships up here would be patched with glue and spit if they were repaired at all.

But 'Telcam seemed to know a great deal about humans. Jul was intrigued. "What's the devil?"

"One of their evil lesser gods."

"I thought they only had one."

"Some of them do. But some of them have many. The devil is the opposing force of the single omnipotent god."

Jul grappled with the idea. "But doesn't omnipotence mean there *is* no opposing force? And if there's only one god, then how . . ." He realized he'd invited a theological discussion, and changed tack rapidly. "Explain the proverb."

"It means," 'Telcam said, "that those left idle will usually find something dishonest or criminal to occupy themselves."

Forze grunted. "I usually found that my troops would keep themselves busy with self-improvement and healthy exercise."

"Only humans veer from the path of virtue when not gainfully employed." Buran glanced at Forze as if they'd reached a tacit agreement to tease 'Telcam and hope that he didn't notice. "But I agree that you can't take a war away from warriors and expect them to settle back into quiet domesticity. And that's a concern we should be aware of."

Buran sounded like Raia. It was the same question: how would the Sangheili find a purpose again? Jul kept his sights lower and concentrated on the immediate task, which was to stage a coup. No—it wasn't even that. He had no plans to take the Arbiter's place. He simply wanted to stop the appeasement of humankind. It was the Arbiter's policy, and once he was gone it would wither and die if a strong enough voice provided an alternative.

After that . . . Jul would leave the future to those who knew how to govern. He didn't.

Buran moved to the front of the pack as they reached the sentry at the brow airlock. *Unflinching Resolve* sat tethered to one of the booms of the orbital yard, looking remarkably undamaged for a ship that had seen so much service since her last refit. Jul could see other warships that hadn't escaped so lightly berthed in the rows behind her, some bearing much bigger scars from the fighting in the Great Schism, breaches in hulls temporarily sealed with sheets of alloy and drive housings crumpled from impact. One ship wasn't a ship at all. It was just the aft section with its drive, a wreck recovered for parts. But there were no Huragok left to carry out the engineering work.

There seemed to be a lot more empty berths than Jul remembered.

The guard, an old warrior, was a monument to lonely patience. He didn't look as if he'd dared move a muscle throughout his watch. Buran walked up to him with arms spread in greeting.

"How goes it, Pidar?" he asked. "I didn't realize you were still serving."

"This level of activity best suits my age, Shipmaster." Pidar looked on nodding terms with death already, but retirement was out of the question for a warrior. "Have you come to inspect *Resolve*? I'm sorry, but no maintenance has been carried out yet. At least she's still here though. Some Jiralhanae crews have sided with their brother traitors and stolen ships."

"Did nobody try to stop them?"

"Hard to do, Shipmaster. They never returned to port. And all the Huragok have fled, although I wonder who gave them passage."

"Appalling," Buran said, very convincing in his disgust. "May we pass? I've brought some brothers to see what we can achieve with our own hands."

"Shocking, my lord, that shipmasters should have to repair their own ships."

"Nevertheless, it must be done." Buran tilted his head toward the airlock. The ship was connected to the dockside by an assortment of umbilical cables and conduits, one of them a pressure-sealed brow for the crew to board. "We do what we can. We plan to run up her drives and test her helm, Pidar, so if you've been relieved by the time I return, give my regards to your kaidon. It's been good to see you again."

Pidar didn't appear to notice the finality and regret in that. He just stood back and opened the inner airlock door for everyone to file across the brow. So this was how rebels seized a ship; they just spoke politely to a guard who assumed—as he ought—that a shipmaster was beyond reproach, and walked up the brow without a single shot being fired. It wasn't satisfying or something to boast about to the youngsters of the keep in his old age, but Jul had to admit that it worked.

Buran opened one of the supply hatches and stuck his head in to take a deep breath.

"It stinks," he said flatly. "Filthy Kig-Yar cowards. So that's one problem I no longer have to deal with. They've all deserted." He squeezed through the hatch and dropped down into the deck. "Very well, let's see how much ordnance they forgot to loot."

"We can worry about that later," 'Telcam said. "I have my sources for resupply. What we need most is transport. A mobile command center, as a precaution."

Buran turned to the Jiralhanae. "Search the ship. If you find any Kig-Yar still around, you have my permission to eat them. In fact, I *insist*."

The two Jiralhanae lumbered away down the passage. Jul wondered how the Covenant had held together for as long as it had, given how fast the old species' hatreds resurfaced once the restraints of San'Shyuum domination were stripped away. It was a very thin veneer of unity. And now it was gone.

And how long can we trust the Jiralhanae who are still with us?

Jul looked at Forze and knew he was thinking the same thing. There was probably no such thing as a loyal Jiralhanae, only one that was more scared of his Sangheili superiors than he was of his packmates' wrath or his reputation. The two species loathed one another. It was just a matter of keeping a close eye on those that remained.

And then we'll dispense with their assistance completely. Never again. No more reliance on aliens to keep our society functioning. We'll learn to do things for ourselves.

Jul felt that he spent most of his days now walking up and down long passages, as if fate was giving him extra time to ask himself if he really wanted to go ahead with this.

What if nobody arises to take the Arbiter's place, and Sanghelios slides into chaos?

It was a risk that had to be taken. Jul was damned sure that the humans weren't sitting in quiet reconsideration of their colonial policies. His boots echoed on the deck as he walked the last few meters to the bridge. 'Telcam hadn't said a word since they reached the sentry.

And this is where I move from brave talk to open revolt. This is where it becomes real. From this point on I have no retreat.

Buran surveyed his bridge, swinging his head sadly from side to side. The gloom was punctured by status lights from the few systems needed to keep *Unflinching Resolve* vacuum-tight and to suppress any fires or fluid leaks. From the forward viewscreen, Sanghelios looked to Jul as it always did on his return from a mission, a red beacon of warmth and welcome in the cold black void.

"For Sanghelios," Buran murmured, and pressed the control to boot up the frigate's AI.

The ship came to life section by section. Lighting, environmental controls, and diagnostics panels activated and went about their business without need of any attention from a crew. It took only six Sangheili to move a frigate and *Unflinching Resolve* didn't have far to travel. Forze checked the navigation computer and entered a spurious flight plan. That would change as soon as they were free of the dock.

"I had the chance," Jul said, more to himself than anyone else.

"To do what?" 'Telcam asked.

"To kill the Arbiter. He came to speak at our assembly. I could have shot him where he stood, mere meters away."

"And you'd have made a martyr of him. There's a fine line between reckless and bold. Acting alone may be noble, but acting together with an agreed plan is *effective*." 'Telcam was surprisingly pragmatic for a spiritual man. If he believed in the power of prayer, he hadn't entirely given up on the need for a little extra support from laser cannon and sound tactics. "Heroes never die, and neither do their flawed ideals. So you must both kill and discredit them."

Buran opened a channel to the dockmaster's control room. "*Unflinching Resolve* requests release from dock for maintenance assessment."

"You have clearance, *Unflinching Resolve*."

Buran glanced at 'Telcam. "Secure for launch. Proceed to two hundred kilometers."

Stealing a warship would have horrified the humans, Jul knew. They had rules and regulations and *courts-martial*. But they seemed to worry about the petty administrative things that no Sangheili would concern himself with. Shipmasters and other ranks were taking all manner of vessels and vehicles now. There was no central command to ask permission from or to track them, and the only thing a patriot would do with a commandeered vessel was use it to defend Sanghelios. There were no Prophets around to commandeer a vessel *from*. The fleet belonged to the people. And the people were taking it back.

There was nothing to worry about. Nothing at all.

Even so, there was no conversation on the bridge until they exited the safety zone. The Jiralhanae trotted in and stood by the doors, looking aimless and confused.

"Ship, proceed to these coordinates on my mark," Buran said to the AI. It was a computer designed solely to pilot and control the ship, no more and no less, not the extravagantly sentient pet the humans seemed to prefer. "Suspend all automated status reports to the dockmaster."

Buran would normally have had a junior officer doing all this for him, but Forze stepped into the role without a word. He seemed to be feeling sorry for the shipmaster already. There really was a sense of a final stand about him. *Unflinching Resolve* began picking up speed, preparing to pass behind Sanghelios to evade detection by the dock sensors before disappearing to lay up at Mdama.

Chaos had its virtues. A ship could go missing so easily these days.

The frigate passed the planet's terminator and skimmed two hundred kilometers above continents shrouded in night. The Aanrar dockmaster would expect them to be out of contact anyway. Now was the moment that *Unflinching Resolve* had to vanish completely.

"Ship, maintain comms blackout and shut down transponders," Buran said. "Begin landing sequence."

Jul had thought that he'd reached his own point of no return. But he hadn't, not yet. There would be an irrevocable moment to come, but right now all he was doing was slipping one step at a time toward it, and it could be reversed with no questions asked.

Raia . . . she knew not to ask them. She was also smart enough to work things out for herself. *Unflinching Resolve* descended through the atmosphere a thousand kilometers from Bekan keep and made the rest of the flight at eight thousand meters through night skies.

"There's something to be said for being backward country yokels," Forze said. "Try doing *this* in Vadam without anyone noticing."

But many in Mdama *would* have noticed, of course. They just wouldn't ask questions or interfere. With all those treacherous Jiralhanae and Kig-Yar around, many officers were busy making sure that assets didn't end up in the hands of their assortment of new enemies. The excuse made itself. This wasn't theft. It was patriotism.

Unflinching Resolve hovered above a quarry five kilometers from the keep and then descended into the artificial canyon to settle on her dampers.

Nobody spoke for a while. It was done. They'd seized a warship, and the coup had begun.

Buran reached out to shut down the active systems and the bridge faded into darkness again, lit only by the faint glow of status lights.

"I'll return in six days," Buran said. "Now we lie low and plan a little more. Time to disembark, brothers."

They sealed the hatches behind them and Buran looked back at the frigate. There was no way of camouflaging her. As Forze had said, it sometimes helped to live in the back of beyond.

"We must take good care of her," Buran said sadly. "There are no Huragok left to fix her or replace her."

"*Yet,*" Jul said. "No new ships *yet*. The day will come."

The rebels dispersed to their respective transports. Jul walked back through the fields to his keep, to explain to Raia and his brothers where they should *not* venture.

He would also have to make plans for their safety if the overthrow failed. It was hard to think of anywhere on Sanghelios where his clan could hide if he did.

Jul, of course, would take whatever might come to him. It was the least anyone would expect of a shipmaster.

Forerunner Dyson sphere, Onyx: local date November 2552.

Mendez had to give Halsey her due. Instead of making a fuss about the puncture in her leg, she just shut her mouth and gathered up the fragments of the cylinder.

It didn't mean he was discovering a new respect for her and that the tension between them would eventually turn to a lasting friendship. That kind of bullshit only happened in the movies. Mendez knew the bottom line was that they both had blood on their hands, and a lot of his wasn't of the decent, rules-of-engagement, soldiering variety.

He had no idea why he didn't feel inclined to keep his opinions to himself any longer. Maybe he was the one whose goddamn frontal lobes weren't doing all the impulse suppression that they should. He watched Kelly, Fred, and Linda close ranks around Halsey and do the Spartan equivalent of fussing over her.

"Any ill effects yet, ma'am?" Linda asked.

Halsey twisted from the waist and hitched up her hem

discreetly to take another look. "Well, I think I'll find out pretty soon whether it was injecting me with something or taking a sample. One thing's certain—it won't be doing it again."

Fred picked over the fragments of cylinder in his palm. Mendez felt guilty about walking away from the search for Lucy, but he needed to know what that thing was because all the systems on this artificial planet had to be connected in some way. The Forerunners did seem to have a few godlike qualities, and one was purpose. They didn't create things at random.

"I don't recognize any of the components," Fred said. "But there's a piece of some spongy material here. It's saturated with blood. I think your assessment that it's taking samples is on the nail, Doctor."

Halsey took a closer look at the pieces. "Now if I run a blood test, I'm looking to check *how* someone is, *who* someone is, or *what* someone is. Perhaps it's trying to work out if we're carrying any infection. But if that's the case, it would try to take samples from everybody. What's different about me?"

Mendez didn't say a word. He was trying to recall what the cylinders had been doing from the first time they'd shown up. They seemed to hang around faces. Now this one had taken a blood sample, if Halsey was correct. It had shown most interest in the people who weren't wearing helmets, and then it seemed to want a second opinion on Halsey in particular.

"I think there's a really simple answer, Doctor," Mendez said. "Me and Fred, we had something to eat. You've not eaten anything yet, though, have you?"

Halsey paused for a moment and then shut her eyes. "Glycogen metabolism. Damn it. It's just a first-aid monitor." She did that humorless little I-should-know-better smile. "My guess is that it can detect exhaled ketones. So it checked whether I had blood sugar problems. I'm not sure why the Forerunners would care about that, but scans make sense if you're trying to keep out a pathogen."

"Well, terrific," Mendez said, and strode back down the passage. "We can forget all about it until it bills us. How are we doing, people?"

Tom and Olivia were still working their way back and forth across the controls and the entrance lobby. He could hear the murmur of conversation from deep inside the passage as Mark and Ash examined the flagstone floor. Fred walked up behind him.

"Chief, we need to split up and carry on with the recon. Worst-case scenario is that it takes us weeks to work out where we are and find some structures that make more sense. I suggest we leave Dr. Halsey here with Kelly in case Lucy comes back the same way she went in, and the rest of us can move on."

It was a perfectly sensible command decision. Mendez just nodded. But Fred cocked his head to one side.

"I wouldn't dream of abandoning her, Chief."

"Never thought you would, Lieutenant."

Mendez never needed to see a Spartan's face to work out what was going on in their heads. It was all about the body language—a split-second delay, the set of the shoulders, or a hundred other minute details that helped him gauge their reactions. Mendez watched Fred talking to the rest of the Spartan-IIIs, but didn't spot the slightest hesitation as they broke off from what they were doing to resume the patrol.

I trained 'em right. At least I can say that.

Mendez passed Halsey on the way out of the tower and nodded at Kelly. "If Lucy comes back, then you damn well *sit* on her if you have to, but don't let her wander off again."

"Understood, Chief." Kelly took off her helmet and adjusted

her earpiece. "And just for the record, I'm placing my bets on it being some seriously weird transdimensional crap."

"I bet that's what Einstein said."

Kelly managed a smile. "She strikes me as the unkillable sort."

"Yeah. She's a survivor."

Mendez would always take facts over feelings, but he also had that time-honed instinct that told him when one of his people was in trouble. Lucy was still around somewhere—he just *knew* it. But if there was such a thing as the worst Spartan to misplace, it was Lucy. The poor kid couldn't yell for help. Yeah, Halsey had gotten it right again. Lucy really shouldn't have been serving on the front line. But what the hell was he supposed to do? He couldn't spare a single Spartan anyway, and the cruelest thing he could have done to Lucy was to separate her from the only family she had left. He wasn't prepared to ship her out to some psychiatric rehabilitation unit where she'd just be injected and analyzed and discussed by a bunch of strangers all pretty much like Halsey, treating her as a fascinating puzzle to be solved. She'd had enough of that garbage by now.

"Do you suppose John's made it?" Kelly asked. It was right out of the blue. That meant it had been on her mind for some time and she couldn't keep it battened down any longer. "And the others."

"Of course he has," Halsey said. She was setting up camp in the entrance lobby, unpacking the contents of her bag and laying out all her electronics. "He was always the luckiest of you all. And the most bloody-minded."

Mendez supposed that was tact in a Halsey kind of way. She hadn't said that John was the very best of the Spartan-IIs and that she'd known he was a natural leader from the first time she met him as a six-year-old. If she'd blurted that out, though, Kelly would have taken it without offense, because Halsey was now the nearest thing she'd ever have to a mom. Kids still loved even the most abusive parent.

And you set their paths. Their expectations. Treat a kid as the chosen one, or as your biggest disappointment, and he'll live up or down to that.

"Problem, Chief?" Halsey asked.

Mendez just took her sidearm from his belt, checked the safety and the clip, and handed it back to her. "You sure you can still use this? If not, Kelly can bring you up to speed."

"I can cope. I did the requalifier a couple of years ago."

"Good." He took out a couple of his ration bars as well. The cylinder must have been worried about her starving, so he'd take that as a warning. "Make each of these last a day. It'll be easier than you think."

Halsey looked him in the eye like a kicked dog, as if she couldn't understand why he was getting more acid with her. He wondered how long she'd spent rehearsing that look until she got the appearance of sincerity just right.

Because I've been here for twenty-odd years churning out more Spartans for the meat-grinder, that's why. I've had a lot of time to think. But it still didn't make me a better person. I went and did it all over again, more or less.

"Thank you, Chief." Halsey went back to examining the broken cylinder. "When we find Lucy, would you like me to check her over?"

Mendez searched for the ulterior motive. "I'll ask her."

He had to jog to catch up with the Spartans. They were already a hundred meters west of the towers, spread out in wedge formation. He could see Fred and Linda scanning the ground as they walked over it, probably taking advantage of the full range of sensors in the Mjolnir helmets. The Spartan-IIIs didn't have most of those extras in their SPI armor and they couldn't even upgrade their kit via software. It made a big difference.

Mendez tapped his radio. "What is it, Lieutenant?"

"Thought we could see some thermal variation," Fred said. "Straight lines. Might be tunnels. You know how the Forerunners love their underground facilities. When we get back to base, slap in a request for ground-penetrating radar for these lids, will you, Chief?"

"You want a soda vending machine too?"

"Got that already. Sort of."

Mendez was now far enough from the towers to look back and get a sense of scale again. He'd assumed Lucy had gone *through*. She might well have gone *down*. They were back on open grassland with nothing else in sight except trees and vegetation.

Fred started jogging, pulling ahead of the others. He was definitely following a trail now. Mendez could see him looking down every few meters as he went. And then he broke into a run.

This was always the moment when Mendez fully appreciated just how different a Spartan-II was from a regular soldier and even from the Spartan-IIIs. He'd seen it hundreds, even thousands of times, but it was still sobering to watch a human being in a power-assisted suit accelerate to nearly sixty kilometers an hour and keep going. Mark, Olivia, and Ash hung back to wait for Mendez. Tom carried on, starting to fall behind Linda.

"Well," Ash said, "if we haven't got wheels, that's one sure way to cover some ground, isn't it?" He put his hand on Mendez's shoulder. "Maybe it was just an animal Lucy heard down there, Chief. Real rabbit hole stuff."

"Let's hope. Rabbits are good eating."

Mendez kept walking, wondering why he'd coped with all the crap he'd done for Halsey, and all the other crap that he couldn't blame on her at all, but found it hard to accept one Spartan-III going missing out of all the hundreds who'd been killed. The Threes were cheap and disposable, intended for suicide missions that were beneath a Spartan-II and beyond an ODST. He'd accepted that, to his everlasting shame.

Why now? Why was he losing his detachment *now*?

Because she can't scream. Because I put her in that position. Because it's the straw that'll break this camel's back.

"Now *that's* more like it." Fred's voice came over the radio and steered Mendez away from the brink. "We've definitely been out of town."

"Transmit an image, Lieutenant. It's going to take us a while to catch you up."

Mark seemed to be getting something in his HUD. "He's found buildings." He stopped and took off his helmet, offering it to Mendez. "You want to take a look, Chief?"

Mendez tilted the helmet and glanced at the image that now filled the HUD, a cluster of silver-gray, almost featureless multistories in the same architectural style as the towers.

"No signs of life, but let's not take that for granted," Fred said. "Check it out."

Mendez allowed himself a little relief. This was, as Fred had said, much more like it. A bunker had to have shelters, kitchens, an infirmary—all the trappings of normal life. Now they at least had a base to operate from. It was another problem that was going to be solved.

Hang in there, Lucy. We'll put the pieces together and work out where you are.

There was every chance they'd be here for a long time. And if Halsey was right, then they might be the last sentient life left in the galaxy. No amount of luck could save John from a Halo Array firing.

Or save her own daughter either.

Halsey had taken an awfully big gamble to save just three of her Spartans. He understood. Now it was *his* turn to atone.

"It's times like this that I miss the Pelican," Fred said. "Better find a high observation point."

An aerial view of the complex would have been useful. For once, it was a toss-up between working their way through town and assessing the layout, or just clearing the place building by building. Mendez trudged on, realizing just how much ground a Spartan could cover at speed. He could feel the sweat trickling down his back as he tried to keep up a respectable pace, but he wasn't a Spartan and he wasn't twenty any longer. He resisted the temptation to break into a jog.

I'm sixty. They're twenty, thirty, even forty-odd years younger. And genetically enhanced. I've got a right to be the last across the line.

Mark kept up with him, either to keep him company or spare his embarrassment. He was a nice kid. "You could do with a night's sleep," he said. "We all could."

"Won't make me any younger or faster," Mendez grunted.

"Don't give me that old man BS, Chief."

It was the doors that kept Mendez going at a brisk walk. He caught a glimpse of them up ahead in the elegant buildings, the first truly recognizable ones that he'd seen here—doors meant to be walked through, complete with ornate lintels and frames. He approached the nearest one, alert for more of whatever Lucy had gone chasing. The Spartans were already there, waiting as if they thought it was discourteous to start this without him.

Fred gestured to Linda and the others to stack either side of the first door. He nodded at Mendez.

"Okay, Chief," he said. "In we go."

CHAPTER 9

PEACE TREATIES AREN'T BROKERED BETWEEN COUNTRIES OR NEGOTIATED BETWEEN WORLDS. THEY HAPPEN BECAUSE TWO INDIVIDUALS CAN TALK TO ONE ANOTHER. I CAN DO BUSINESS WITH THE ARBITER. AND I BELIEVE HE CAN DO BUSINESS WITH ME.

(Admiral Lord Hood, CINCFLEET)

Maintenance area, UNSC *PORT STANLEY,* on station in Sanghelios space: February 2553.

"What is this, street theater?" Devereaux jerked a wrench at Vaz and Mal in a get-lost gesture. "Beat it. Nothing to see here."

Vaz shoved Mal with his shoulder. "Come on. Leave it."

"You won't even know we're here," Mal said. "We've never seen Spartans put on their frillies before. Go on. How bad can it be?"

Naomi's voice drifted out of the compartment. "It's okay," she said. "It's just armor."

Vaz debated whether to haul Mal away and give Naomi some privacy. Poor woman: she reminded him increasingly of a bear in an illegal circus, a big wild thing that really wasn't meant to be cooped up like that, capable of eventually snapping under the strain and lashing out with a lethal paw. But he had to admit that he was just as curious about the Mjolnir, and he wrestled with his guilt for a full five seconds before giving in and peering around the compartment door.

Devereaux was at a control panel with a diagnostics pad in one hand. She still had the wrench in the other.

"No smartass comments," she said. "She's perimenopausal and I've got PMS."

Mal glanced at the wrench. "Wouldn't dream of it."

Mjolnir wasn't exactly body armor like the kind Vaz was used to. It was more like an APC with legs. Naomi stood partially engulfed in it, up to her waist in titanium plates and surrounded by what Vaz could only describe as a gantry. It projected into the machinery space, a steel scaffold two meters deep and three meters wide, extending right up to the deckhead. It was only when he moved around and stood right in front of it that he could see what it was doing. Like a robot on a vehicle assembly line, it was building the armor around her section by section, slotting the plates into place over her bodysuit with steady but alarming *chonk-chonk-chonk* trip-hammer noises.

Vaz hadn't worked out what all the long steel tubes were for. All he knew was that he'd never want to be sealed in quite like that. *It's like being buried alive. No,* canned *alive.* Armor was fine: he lived in his, like every other ODST. It was all that stood between him and the hereafter most of the time. No, it was the *automation* that made him squirm, the robotic relentlessness of the assembly process that looked as if it wouldn't stop until it had crushed Naomi like a car in a junkyard compactor.

Vaz looked up at the helmet poised above her head and gave her an awkward half smile. He couldn't tell if she was annoyed or embarrassed, but she looked a little flushed around the neck.

"No good asking Mal to zip you up," he said. Okay, Spartans worked alone, but he was sure she would be happier if she joined the gang. He tried to coax her in. "Not with his hernia. Three hundred kilos?"

"Yes. When I run out of ammo, I can just *sit* on hinge-heads." Well, at least she'd thawed enough to synchronize her slang with theirs. The chest plate swung across from a robotic arm on her left, so fast that Vaz flinched, expecting it to slam into her and smash bone. The sleeve sections followed. "Don't look so worried. You've missed the awkward part."

"What awkward part?" Mal asked. "And I haven't got a hernia. It's my car keys."

Naomi was now up to her neck in steel-blue titanium and composite. As the helmet began to descend, she reached up and the machine stopped dead to let her take it.

"Good to go, Naomi." Devereaux gave her a thumbs-up. "Go get 'em."

The robot arms swung back. Naomi stepped down from the plinth as easily as Vaz would have done in his tin-can ODST armor, all easy grace, and that was when it struck him just how extraordinary that was.

It's the weight of a quad bike, and she's just striding around in it like it's her fatigues. I know it's power-assisted, but that's still quite something.

"Here," she said. She tipped the helmet upside down and shoved it under Mal's nose. "See that slot at the back? That aligns with my neural interface. Yours is a transponder. Mine's more like a docking station. It's where the AI data chip fits if I'm ever unwise enough to let BB into my brain."

Vaz expected BB to materialize instantly with a witty put-down about claustrophobia in confined spaces, but he obviously wasn't playing today. Mal peered into the helmet with the look of a man who was making a note of all the tech that Spartans had and that ODSTs didn't.

"Once you're sealed in," he said carefully, "you can't just . . . you know, step out of it easily when you *need* to, can you? That rig's got to dismantle it."

"Correct. It's a last resort to do it manually."

Vaz had never seen Mal lost for words before. He actually blushed. "So . . . bathroom breaks?" he asked, very quietly.

Naomi paused a beat. "I'm catheterized. Another reason why that machine has to be so precisely calibrated. This suit plugs into me in a lot of places."

"I think I'm going to cry," Mal said.

"Think of it as a weaponized life-support unit. It recycles the urine too."

To his credit, Mal kept his nerve and winked at her. "Ah, that explains everything about the beer they serve in the mess."

He didn't get a smile though. Naomi put her helmet on and it sealed with a faint *thunk*. Suddenly she wasn't the forbiddingly awkward Baba Yaga any longer, but—just like the PR people said—a perfectly designed, totally confident fighting machine. Vaz heard footsteps behind him that scuffed to a sudden halt.

"Oh *wow* . . ." It was Phillips. His voice trailed off and he walked right up to Naomi, grinning like a schoolboy as he craned his neck to look up at her. "You look *amazing*. Real killer robot stuff."

Vaz didn't know Naomi well enough yet to pick up any body language, and he couldn't see her expression, but she leaned forward so that her gold-mirrored visor was right in Phillips's face. For a moment the compartment was so quiet that Vaz could hear the faint sigh of the armor's servos as she moved.

"Be honest," she said. "Does my ass look big in this?"

Phillips burst out laughing. "You look like a *goddess.* Go on, do a twirl for us."

And she did. She rotated 360 degrees for him then strode out into the hangar. Only the thud of her boots gave any hint of the sheer weight of that kit.

So she had another side to her, then. Vaz hadn't seen that coming.

Phillips gazed after her with a look of pure delight until he realized Vaz was staring at him. "What?"

"You're having fun, aren't you?"

"You guys take this for granted." Phillips looked suddenly embarrassed. "We never see *anything* like that at the university."

Vaz shrugged. "Neither do we. We're the riffraff. We don't normally get to hang out with Spartans."

"Hey, you know that suit maintains and upgrades itself when she's in cryo? It's all nanotech." Devereaux herded them out of the compartment. She seemed to be getting on fine with Naomi, but it couldn't have been sisterly bonding. "It must cost more than a damn Longsword. No wonder we don't get issued with that kit."

Phillips shrugged. "Maybe that's why she spends all her time working on it."

"No, it isn't," Mal said. "It's because she doesn't think she fits in. How many Spartans did they create? She's almost like the last of her species."

"Functional Spartan-Twos? Under a hundred. Almost all MIA

now." Osman suddenly appeared from behind a stack of crates. Vaz hadn't heard her coming—again. She seemed to be able to pop up out of nowhere, just like BB. "Spartan-Threes? Hundreds. But you probably didn't see many of them either. Let's not sugar-coat it. They carry out the suicide missions."

Vaz couldn't work out if she was making some point about how terrific the Spartans were by comparison with ODSTs, or just answering a question in that in-your-face way that she had. It was the first time that Vaz had heard a mention of different Spartan classes though. He decided to leave the follow-up to Phillips, who was now the official squad blunderer, the civvie who could blurt out awkward questions and get away with it like a small child.

But Osman seemed pretty willing to volunteer information about a program that had been top secret for years.

"So you were a Two, were you?" Phillips jumped right in. "Did you have armor like that?"

Osman clutched her datapad. "No. You need the mechanical augmentations to wear Mjolnir, or it'll just snap your spine."

"Such as?"

"Ceramic bone implants, mainly. Makes them pretty well unbreakable. I only had the genetic and biochemical enhancements, and after that my body started rejecting things." She cocked her head on one side to look at him, almost teasing. "I can't tell if you're fascinated or repelled, Evan."

Oh, it's Evan *now, is it?*

Phillips squirmed. "It's not the medical issues, Captain. It's doing it to fourteen-year-olds. I don't want to pry, but what made your parents consent?"

"They never knew," Osman said, still matter-of-fact. "We were all colonial kids, taken from our families. They thought that we'd died." She changed tack instantly as if nothing remotely unusual had been said. Vaz thought he'd misheard. "BB's picked up some interesting voice traffic. We've got a small Jiralhanae transport inbound to Sanghelios with a high-value passenger. A Huragok. *An Engineer.* That's worth bothering them to acquire, don't you think?"

Mal looked as if he hadn't heard anything shocking. Vaz decided he must have imagined it.

"I wondered where they all went," Mal said. "Definitely one for the tool box."

"My thoughts exactly. Best estimate is that there are six Jiralhanae embarked. They're transporting weapons for 'Telcam, so we're not helping our primary mission, but the Huragok's far too valuable to pass up. We'll intercept them in approximately eighty-two minutes, so let's meet in ten and plan that out. Better break out the dead Kig-Yar."

"Yes *ma'am.*"

Mal checked his watch as she walked off. Nobody said anything for a painfully long moment.

Phillips finally let out a breath. "Did she say what I think she said?"

"Kidnapped as kids," Mal said, apparently not shocked at all. "Yeah, I think that's what she meant."

Phillips looked at Vaz and then turned to Devereaux, almost appealing for a verdict. "I expected some *reaction* from you. Did you know all that?"

"Of course we didn't." Vaz had reached the stage of not caring what BB overheard now. "Who the hell tells us? It's all classified. We're just marines. The only reason ONI admitted the Spartan program even existed was to boost public morale."

"I just want to know why she's telling us all this," Mal said. Maybe he wanted BB to relay that to the boss. "Whatever she wants from us, we'll do it. We just want clear orders."

Devereaux was still hefting her wrench, looking at its jaws with a glazed, distant expression. "What do people generally do when a war's ending and all kinds of dirt's going to come out? They clear their yardarm. Only following orders. That kind of thing."

"If she's right, then we used child soldiers," Phillips said. "We kidnapped them from their families before performing experiments on them. Christ . . . and this is my government?"

"You think anyone would care as long as we won?"

"Actually, yes, they would." Phillips was doing his embarrassment gesture again, one arm folded across his chest and his free hand pinching his top lip, as if he was worried about disagreeing. "I think the public would give a pretty *big* damn about that."

"Don't bank on it," Mal said. He seemed underwhelmed by it, which wasn't like him at all. "Outrage fatigue set in years ago. The colonies are a long way from Sydney. And they weren't always on our side."

Phillips just stared at him for a few seconds, then shook his head and began walking away. "I'll go and be outraged on my own, then. I've got some monitoring to do."

Devereaux turned to Vaz and shrugged. "Well, at least we never claimed we were fighting this war for decency and freedom. Just survival."

"Which war?" Vaz asked. "The one where we were fighting other humans? Because that's when all this started."

"That was before my time," she said. "And yours."

There wasn't really much Vaz could say, not because BB would hear every word, but because he really didn't know where to start. The strong had done terrible things to the weak ever since the first caveman discovered he could crack his smaller neighbor's skull with a well-placed rock. Only the technology changed. Even so, the idea of little kids being abducted and carted off to boot camp made Vaz's scalp crawl.

He was glad that it did. It told him he was still normal, still able to feel something after eight years of numbing warfare.

"Win the war, and nobody says a word about that kind of stuff until you're dead," he said. "Lose the war, and you end up at Nuremberg."

"What's Nuremberg?" Devereaux asked.

Mal wandered off to move some crates. He balanced a table-sized lid across two of them and then got down on all fours to pick up something from underneath it. Vaz waited for him to crack his head and start cursing.

Kidnapping six-year-olds. ONI can't get any worse. Can it?

"Vaz?" Mal called. "Give us a hand, will you?"

Vaz squatted to stick his head under the lid. Mal was hunched underneath it, scribbling something on his palm with an orange marker pen.

"What is it?"

Mal put a finger to his lips and tilted his palm so that Vaz could read it. *Ah, got it . . .* There was no shipboard tech—or anything in his neural implant—that could detect things scribbled on skin. If you wanted privacy and anonymity, you used old-fashioned ink. BB couldn't snoop down here. Not even the 360-degree safety cams, BB's eyes and ears, could get a look at what was going on through ten centimeters of composite. Vaz read the letters carefully.

PSYCH TEST

Vaz mimed a what-the-hell frown. *What?*

NO IDEA TELLING US STUFF TO SEE HOW WE REACT

Mal ran out of palm and tried writing with his left hand on his right. Val wrestled the marker pen from him.

LIP READ PLEASE

Mal shook his head and grabbed the pen back. The only space he could use now was the back of his left hand. YOU SAW THE OLD MOVIE BB WILL SPACE US

Mal laughed his head off. He had a point though. There were very few ways of avoiding BB's attention. Vaz started laughing too. He didn't know which movie Mal meant, but here he was, hiding under an ammo crate in an invisible ship in enemy space while his own side used small kids for cannon fodder. It wasn't remotely funny. It wasn't that kind of laughter.

Devereaux stuck her head under the lid from the other side. "Good God, it *must* be funny to crack *you* up," she said. "Share, Vaz."

Mal just offered his hand for reading. If BB wasn't wondering why he could see three ODSTs' backsides sticking out from under a crate lid, then he wasn't much of an AI.

Devereaux shrugged and tapped her watch. She didn't seem bothered whether Osman was running some experiment on them or not.

"Huragoks come preloaded with a lot of Covenant technical intel." She might have been saying it for BB's benefit. "So ONI won't even have to interrogate it. Just let it play in a workshop."

"You make them sound like puppies."

"Well, they're harmless. We just don't seem to have ever captured any. It's really sad to think of the Covenant detonating them rather than let them fall into enemy hands. All that lost information."

Yeah. They're solid gold. Osman's right.

Vaz had only seen Engineers in diagram form at briefings, never in the flesh. He wondered how the creature would feel to be cut off from its own kind and everything it knew, left to the dubious mercies of ONI.

Sad. Wrong. Like us using kids.

No, the war hadn't numbed him at all.

UNSC *PORT STANLEY*, Urs system, 500,000 kilometers from Sanghelios: on intercept course with former Covenant auxiliary vessel *PIETY*.

Phillips seemed to be warming to the intelligence business.

He paced around the deck, adjusting his earpiece with the air of a man who'd been spying on hostile aliens all his life. For all Mal knew, he could have been listening to Gregorian chant or stock prices, but he had a familiar glazed stare that said he was translating. He stopped in his tracks for a moment and then changed direction to home in on Mal.

"I don't want to worry you," he said, "but some Kig-Yar have put out a *mev-ut* on you and Vaz for shooting up their buddies on Reynes."

"That's bad, is it?"

"If they catch you, yes. It's a reward for bringing back body parts as proof of a kill."

"Any parts in particular? I use some of mine more than others."

"With UNSC, it's heads and cervical vertebrae. And they love ones with neural implants."

"Dearie me." Mal hauled one of the Kig-Yar corpses out of the cold store, holding its slack beak shut with one hand while Vaz grappled with its clawed feet. "We'll have to be more diplomatic next time, Corporal Beloi. Make a note of that."

Vaz let go of the Kig-Yar's legs and took off his glove to scratch his chin. His scar seemed to be bothering him again. "Hey, BB? Is there mail today? Haven't had any for two weeks."

BB didn't appear but his voice boomed over the ship's broadcast system. "Opsec," he said, which always explained every irksome event that did and didn't happen. "But the worthless trollop hasn't tried to contact you anyway. Listen to Mal's advice."

Vaz sighed. "So you're my mother now."

"I have the crew's welfare at heart. Anyway, do you want to look at the schematics for the target or not? Briefing on the bridge."

"Can't you project it here?" Mal sniffed his gloves. He'd never get that Kig-Yar smell out of them. "Come on, *square blue thing.* We'll make the place stink."

"Move it, Staff. Captain's waiting."

Just a few weeks into the mission, and even the AI was acting like they'd all been together since boot camp: Mal took that as a good sign. BB wasn't *like* a real person. He *was* one. Mal wondered how the software boffins had managed to make the top-grade AIs that good.

If he asked BB, he knew the AI would tell him, sparing no detail. It would have to wait until they'd abducted the Engineer.

They abandoned the Kig-Yar corpses and made their way up to the bridge. Phillips trailed after Vaz. "Call me Evan, will you? *Professor.* I only use that to psych out other academics."

"Okay. Not Killer Robot, then?"

"Oops. Yes. Did I offend Naomi?"

"No. That's probably a Spartan's idea of flirting."

"Oh."

"Yeah, she'll give you a big ceramic hug," Mal said, "and you'll never play the piano again."

When they reached the bridge, BB had already set up the hologram over the chart table. Osman was studying it with Devereaux and Naomi. There were also voices droning over the radio in the background, ones that Mal didn't recognize. But he realized he was listening to a conversation between ships, or a ship and a control room somewhere, and despite the accents and fluency it wasn't quite *human* somehow. Then an exchange clued him in.

"*It's* your *problem, you cretinous lump of meat. Just don't try to tear it off.*"

"*You wanted one. You got one.*"

"So who's that, BB?" Mal asked.

BB hovered over the ship's hologram. "Voice traffic between 'Telcam and the Brutes in this little gin palace here. He's telling them not to try to remove the Huragok's booby trap."

"But that's not his voice."

"Of course it's not," BB said. "I'm giving you a simultaneous interpretation from the chatter. Like dubbing a foreign movie— colloquial English, better voices. Quality of service, Staff. *Quality.*"

Vaz seemed in a good mood today despite the lack of mail. "So why do we need the prof at all?"

"Opposable thumbs, Corporal. Someone's got to pour the gin and tonics, after all."

Phillips raised an eyebrow. "Ice, a slice, and some arsenic for you, then, BB?"

"Excellent, you've found your vocation." BB expanded the schematic of the small vessel above the chart table. "Pay attention, ladies and gentlemen. She's called *Piety,* and she's one of these—a Hudal-class auxiliary. A glorified tug. Close-in cannon, no slipspace capability, and no hardening, so an EM pulse will shut her up before any of her brave but brutish tars can put out a mayday."

The schematic rebuilt itself layer by layer to expand detail of the interior bulkheads and compartments, but there were no guarantees that she was still configured that way. *Piety* was the same length overall as their own dropship, though, so it wasn't like storming a frigate. Mal's only worry was getting in and out without turning the Engineer into Huragok puree.

"So, once we've zapped her, we've got two options," Osman said. "Board her, or haul her in and crack her open in the hangar."

Mal looked at Naomi. She nodded. Devereaux nodded too and poked her forefinger down into the hologram.

"I don't know how robust Engineers are, but sucking hard vacuum isn't generally good for anybody," she said. "This *here* is the only place I can maintain a seal with the docking ring. If we breach her hull out there, then chances are we'll kill the Engineer as well. I'd rather take the risk of dragging the vessel back in here."

"How upset are you going to be if we lose the Engineer, ma'am?" Mal asked.

"I accept it's a risk," Osman said. "If we lose it, then we use it—blame it on the Jiralhanae that 'Telcam trusts. I'll think of something suitably devious. The question is whether we want a potential self-destruct on the hangar deck."

"Well, seeing as the best way to carry out an opposed boarding is simultaneous entry at multiple points, we're stuffed. We'll end up venting their atmosphere anyway. I'm not saying we can't take the ship, but there'll be a lot of ordnance flying around, we won't know where the Engineer is until we get in there, and it might not survive until we find it anyway."

Naomi leaned on the chart table with both hands. It creaked a little. Mal noted all the small detail. *So everything on board has got to be built to take a few hundred kilos of armored Spartan. No wonder the budget's the way it is.* She indicated a hatch near the bow.

"Mjolnir's good for over an hour in hard vacuum," she said. "What's your pressure suit rated at? Fifteen minutes? Ten? But I don't know if I can seal the hatch fast enough to avoid killing the Engineer. So I'll vote for bringing the ship inboard. It's still going to be an opposed boarding, but we have a little more time to do it sensibly."

"Just thinking aloud," Mal said. "What if they decide to blow the ship while they're in the hangar, or they get their drives going, or fire their weapons?"

"Or decide to kill the Engineer rather than let us take it," Vaz said. "Although that suicide harness is going to blow either way."

Whichever way they cut it, Mal decided, the Engineer still stood less than a fifty-fifty chance of survival. The only question was how much of a risk they wanted to take themselves. *Port Stanley* was designed specifically for ONI's kind of unorthodox warfare, but she wasn't heavily armored and she probably couldn't withstand a massive explosion in a hangar.

We could just blow up the ship, of course. At least that would deny them the asset.

But something deep in Mal's core refused to let him walk away from this even if he'd been given the choice. When he looked at the faces of everyone else around that chart table, he could see that they were just as reluctant to pass up the chance.

If we'd captured some Engineers early in the war, we would have known exactly what Covenant weapons could do and how to counter them. We could have used Engineers to develop better weapons ourselves. We could have stopped the war. We could have saved billions of lives. Lose this one? No bloody way.

But he had to ask. "How come we haven't got any Engineers already, ma'am? It's not like we haven't come across them before."

Osman looked him straight in the eye. "We have. Or at least we *had*. We captured and defused one a couple of years ago and got some very useful developments out of it. But we need more than one. They repair one another, remember. And they make more Engineers."

"Got to do it, then, ma'am." Mal didn't ask what had happened to the lone Engineer because he wasn't sure he wanted to hear any more upsetting stuff about ONI. "What if we seal the hangar's emergency bulkhead and do the business in the aft section with the doors open? We can repressurize fast when we need to. Devereaux, can you maneuver in that space?"

Devereaux nodded. "Bit tight, but probably."

"If anything goes wrong, then at least most of the blast gets directed out, not in."

"And you're still dead," Osman said. "It's your call. If you think I'm going to get you all killed, then you tell me, and we just destroy *Piety* and sacrifice the Engineer."

Mal was finding it hard to get used to voting on whether to attempt a mission. "But if we have a mishap, then the ship's still recoverable, along with BB."

"Okay, do it," Osman said. "Remember—once we hit it with an EMP, then we can't hear their radio, and Engineers can fix things in seconds. Unless the crew's locked it up, then it'll head for the generator compartment to restore power, and it won't think it's being rescued. It'll try to hide."

There didn't seem to be many places to hide in *Piety,* but there was still that explosive harness to worry about. Mal would usually have planned a boarding like this down to the smallest detail and done a dry run or two before committing anyone to it. They didn't have that luxury now. It was all on the fly, all guesswork and reaction.

Now he was starting to understand why ONI had assembled this particular team. He just had the feeling that he knew exactly how each of them would react and what they'd do in a given situation, planned or unplanned. Maybe the HR psychologists weren't as useless as he'd thought.

On the sensor displays, *Piety* was tanking along at a sedate pace, oblivious of the fact that *Port Stanley* was now almost up her tailpipe. And she still couldn't detect the corvette.

"Okay, BB," Osman said. "Show us the fly-through."

The hologram schematics snapped out and were replaced by an exterior of *Piety, Port Stanley,* and the dropship. The display animated to align *Stanley* on *Piety*'s tail, then flipped her 180 degrees so that she was belly-up to her target. The dropship took up position below *Stanley*'s upper hull and aft of the EMP cannon, the cannon fired, and the dropship shot forward and upward to maneuver onto *Piety*'s back and lock grapples on her. The EMP cannon fired a few more times, *Stanley* pivoted 180 degrees about her midships in a relative nose-down movement until she was facing the other way, and the dropship slotted straight into the hangar bay.

"Tell me the dropship's hardened," Devereaux said.

"Of course it is." BB sounded indignant. "Like Naomi's armor. But it's a contingency measure. If one EM pulse keeps *Piety* disabled, all well and good. If the busy little Huragok keeps fixing it every few seconds, then I keep firing. In which case, Naomi is best placed to breach *Piety* while I do that. If you go in, you'll lose your HUD and environmental controls, so you'll be rebreathing air and sweating a lot. Which gives you far less time to operate."

Mal looked at Vaz. He shrugged. "No problem."

Phillips was very quiet, one hand to his ear. Mal could see waveforms of the various Brute voices on the display in front of him.

"That's six distinct voice profiles," he said. "Doesn't mean that there's only six on board though. Best guess."

It didn't matter now. Mal knew there couldn't be a hundred, and one Brute could kill you as surely as six, twelve, or fifty.

They'd be logjammed in that small ship anyway, so their bulk and their numbers would work against them.

"Okay, is everyone going to remember all that?" Mal asked. "No? Too bad. Stand to. See you when we get back, BB."

"Oh, I'm coming too." BB rotated and moved in Naomi's direction. "A fragment of me will remain here to pilot the ship, but I'll transfer to the Mjolnir. We've never done this for real before, by the way. Have we, Naomi?"

"Why now?"

"Why not? I know I'm not your dedicated AI, but I can do anything Cortana can."

Mal picked up a little rivalry there. He'd have to ask about Cortana later. BB's hologram suddenly vanished and Osman pulled a data chip out of the command console. If BB had any physical entity at all, then that chip was as near as damn it *him,* the raw being.

"Put your pants on, BB," Mal said. It was a sobering sight, all that power and knowledge—and their lives, like it or not—in a small wafer of silicon and crystal. "There's ladies present."

Naomi took the chip from Osman and stared at it for a moment. "There would be better occasions to try this for the first time."

"Oh, you've done dry runs with other AIs," BB said cheerfully. "Why not just plunge in? I can improve your response times, pipe data straight to your brain, do that crossword you can never quite crack . . ."

Naomi really didn't look happy about it. Quiet misery was her default expression, but Mal watched it twist into real dismay. But she was too much of a Spartan to give in to it. She slotted the chip into her helmet.

"As long as we're clear," she said, lifting the helmet onto her head, "that I call the shots."

BB didn't say a word. Maybe integrating into Naomi's systems had shut him up for once. Mal decided to keep a watchful eye on the relationship. Everyone was getting on fine: better than fine, in fact, a really close-knit and easy-going team. The last thing they needed was a Spartan saddled with an AI she didn't want.

But that wasn't a problem he could solve, given that they were the two most advanced and expensive pieces of defense technology the UNSC had ever produced.

They were stuck with each other.

Bridge, UNSC *PORT STANLEY*: ten minutes later.

Phillips was still sitting quietly at the comms console and listening to the voice traffic, but Osman felt utterly alone in the ship as she looked out of the viewscreen at *Piety*.

The nearest that she could get to experiencing the HUD data that her team relied on was to have their helmet cam feeds overlaid on the viewscreen. It was a cheap and simple modification, just a matter of adding a projector that could display a few centimeters in front of the plate. But it made all the difference to her. She felt less helpless, a little more in touch with what was happening to them.

I should be out there doing it. I'm still fit and I ought to fight.

"BB, move Devereaux's POV to the left, please, and keep the others on the right." The individual screens showing the cam outputs moved across her field of vision. Against the black backdrop of space, they were vivid and sobering. "Thanks. Perfect."

"Imagine that all scrunched up in your visor instead of spread out across a viewscreen," Phillips said.

"Yes, there's a lot going on in those HUDs. Distracting." Movement in Devereaux's icon caught her eye. The dropship was moving into position. "And upside down."

Osman could see the inverted tail of *Piety* ahead. The Jiral-hanae were still unaware that they had stalkers. They couldn't detect *Port Stanley* electronically and they couldn't physically see her. They had reasonable forward visibility, but none aft, so they wouldn't realize they were being attacked until they felt the drop-ship grapples slam against their hull. No, maybe not even then: it would be when they were dragged in a U-turn toward the hangar and saw *Port Stanley*'s bow doors wide open like a maw.

"Devereaux," Osman said. "If *Piety* recovers her power and starts dragging you, then break off and get clear. We'll take her out from here. Understand?"

"Hoping it won't come to that, ma'am. This is like old-style submarine warfare. Minus the bit where one submarine misjudges things and collides with the other, of course. Not that bit at all."

Osman checked the right-hand side for the outputs from Naomi, Vaz, and Mal. The helmet cam views tilted back and forth between the black and navy blue marbling of space and the yellow chevron stripes marking the emergency bulkhead, now fully sealed at two-thirds of the length of the hangar deck. The three of them were talking quietly, working through the various permutations of ways to enter *Piety*.

"Stand by," Osman said. "In you go, Devereaux. We'll work around you."

"They're still chattering, Captain," Phillips said. "I'll let you know when I lose the signal."

Osman counted down to herself as if she was the one who would take the decision to fire the EM pulse. But that was the task of BB's fragment, with his vast processing power and an accuracy far beyond even the best human gunner.

For a disorienting moment, Osman saw the viewscreen she was standing at framed upside down in Devereaux's HUD as the dropship moved up past the corvette's bows. When she looked up, the dropship was passing above her, inverted. *Port Stanley* still had a clear line of sight with *Piety*. It was all a matter of timing.

"EMP firing . . . *now,*" BB said.

There was no sound, no light, and no impact, just Phillips's whisper.

"Lost the signal, Captain."

Only the indicator on the console told her that BB had fired. The dropship settled neatly on top of *Piety*'s hull and the grapples extruded from the wing nacelles to latch on to it. Osman held her breath. There was nothing she could do now; no orders, no advice, nothing. She just had to watch.

Ten seconds . . . eleven . . .

The Engineer hadn't fixed things yet, then, or else the creature was confined somewhere. Osman could imagine what was happening inside *Piety*—total darkness, drives dead, shouts and curses, Brutes stumbling around trying to restore power and still with no idea yet of what had happened to them. Behind her, the comms speakers fizzed briefly as if the radio had come back to life but died again. The EMP indicator lit up and faded. The dropship's drives were at full thrust now, blue-hot rings in the blackness, and the crew of *Piety* would be feeling vibrations as the dropship began forcing her around in a loop.

Port Stanley's bow dipped as the corvette did a smooth, slow somersault. The dropship and *Piety*, locked together like mating insects, slid up and out of Osman's field of view.

"Hangar, stand by," she said.

It was all so silent, so smooth, and such a complete contrast to what she knew was going on inside the ship. The stars swept up past her as if she was falling and then she was facing out into a different star field, rock steady. To the right of the viewscreen, the HUD icons of the ODSTs and Naomi showed the two locked vessels heading into the hangar, filling their field of view.

The radio fizzed again and the EMP indicator flared.

"I don't think it's the Huragok." BB sounded oddly breathless. *He's an AI. He can't be.* But he was integrated with Naomi now, plugged into her nervous system, experiencing much of what she was feeling. "I zapped her again just to be on the safe side. In she comes. . . ."

"Can openers ready, boys and girls," Mal said. "Our brave Brute boys are really pissed off."

Osman could see that. Two of the Jiralhanae crew were at *Piety*'s forward viewscreen, harshly lit by the landing lights facing outward. Their lips were drawn back in a snarl over huge white fangs. The view shuddered for a moment. *Piety* had been forced down onto the deck, and the three HUD views went haywire. Mal's veered one way, Vaz's veered to the other, and Naomi's— Naomi's just seemed to jet into the air.

Osman had never heard an AI whoop before.

CHAPTER 10

```
MESSAGE PRIORITY: FLASH
FROM: CO UNSC GLAMORGAN
TO: CINCONI

CYCLICALLY FLUCTUATING ANOMALY LOCATED
5,000 KM FROM ONYX COORDINATES. READINGS
AT PEAK CONSISTENT WITH 1.37 SOLAR MASSES.
SPHERICAL FORM, 23 CM (TWENTY-THREE
CENTIMETER) DIAMETER. SEE REPORT FOR FULL
EMR/ GRAVITATIONAL ANALYSIS. POSSIBLY
DIMENSIONAL PORTAL.
```

(Received at Bravo-6 February 2553.)

Hangar deck, UNSC *PORT STANLEY.*

A human being was an extraordinary machine, but oh, how *chaotic*: how thrillingly *disjointed.*

BB spent a nanosecond reassuring himself that splitting the critical ship functions from his higher processing had been a sensible move. The input flooding him from Naomi's neural net was so *new* that he wanted time to savor it.

Being the heart and brain of a starship was a joy, but experiencing the adrenaline-distorted, frantic awareness of a human under stress was far, far more . . . visceral.

And I have no viscera. How about that.

"Drive—offline," Naomi said. "Cannon down."

"Okay, she's dead in the water," Mal called. "Blowing hatches in ten seconds. Stand by to close the airlock."

The dropship lifted off *Piety* and peeled away. Mal and Vaz were already at the hatches on either side of the ship, placing shaped charges on them as Naomi took a short run at the bow. Her boot hit the vessel's nose and propelled her five meters up onto the sloping forward hatch right above the bridge. BB, used to predicting with certainty what his physical anchor would do—be it ship, circuit, or data drive—was left in the wake of real events for the first time in his existence.

He had no idea what Naomi would do or feel in the next fraction of a second, or the second after that, even though he detected the impulses in her brain before the muscles engaged.

She landed knees first on the hatch. The exposed deck was still pulling at one G, and BB felt the hatch cover deform slightly with the impact of four hundred kilos. Naomi sprang back immediately, boots planted either side of the hatch frame, and reached down to rip out the emergency release plate. BB could calculate precisely how much force it took to do that. But it didn't give him half as much information as *feeling* the contraction in Naomi's latissimus muscles and the pressure on her palms as she gripped and pulled. A glittering mist of fine ice crystals sprayed out from the edges of the hatch like escaping steam. The ship was venting atmosphere.

"Hull breached—*seal the hangar!*"

BB felt *Piety* shudder. The charges had detonated on her side hatches. Naomi pulled the nose hatch clear and dropped through the opening feet first, rifle clutched tight to her chest as the hangar doors shut.

She's ripped open a shuttle craft. She's torn metal apart like card-board. Her heart rate's near 180 and I can feel it in her throat—my throat—and it's like nothing else I've experienced. She's lost her depth perception. But I won't step in yet. . . .

Somewhere else in the ship automatic fire hammered in short bursts, but in Naomi's ears it faded into the background. She landed in the cockpit between two Jiralhanae apparently mired in slow motion. She didn't even raise her rifle. There wasn't enough space, and that was a stroke of luck: the Brutes couldn't make full use of their massive weight. She brought her fist straight up under the first Brute's chin and snapped his head back so hard that BB felt the small shock wave of his breaking spine travel back up her arm. The blow didn't kill the Brute outright, but he went down.

The other swung at her, bellowing. He was a head taller but Naomi got her hand around his trachea and dug her fingers in hard while she brought the stock of her rifle down hard on the top of his skull. It took her a good seven or eight pounding blows to stun him before she could lean back and fire into his face at point-blank range. BB, attuned to what she perceived, saw her depth perception fade back in along with clear, full-volume sound.

Adrenaline. Even in a Spartan, its effect is—messy. But carry on, dear. You're doing okay without any help from me.

"Cockpit clear. Two hostiles down."

"Four contacts back here," Mal said. "One down. No Engineer yet. Oh—"

Mal was drowned out by weapons fire and raw, animal bellowing.

"Mal?" Naomi pushed through the cockpit hatch and into

the cargo compartment, charging through a gap between stacked crates. *"Mal!"*

She almost fell over Vaz. One Brute lay twitching on the deck and another had Vaz pinned down one-handed. But the marine wasn't giving up without a fight. He had a tight grip on his knife, now buried up to the hilt in the roaring, snarling Brute's neck. BB, whose every process was tied to his system clock, felt two separate time frames happening—his own, real and objective, and Naomi's, suddenly very much slower and more densely packed with only the data she needed to fight and win.

So that's what adrenaline does to her time perception. Extraordinary.

Naomi grabbed the Brute by the collar and jerked it off Vaz in one movement, freeing his arm so he could aim his carbine. He shoved the muzzle in the Brute's mouth and pulled the trigger. Another layer of noise vanished. Naomi reacted to the bursts of fire that were still coming from the aft section.

"One down." Vaz scrambled to his feet. "Mal, talk to me."

"Two *not* down—the bastards."

Naomi shoved past Vaz and followed the noise. BB felt her heart rate fall to 140 as her adrenaline steadied, and she moved forward with her rifle trained—much more deliberate, thinking more consciously. The next thing she saw spiked her heart rate for a couple of seconds and she'd already opened fire on it before her frontal lobes identified it as a Brute.

"Four down," she said. "Two left."

More fire rattled behind the bulkhead of the next compartment. BB stood by to give her some neural assistance but she still showed no sign of needing it. She punched her way through the flimsy hatch and stepped into a hail of needle projectiles that skidded off her armor. BB's sole sources of imaging right then were

Naomi's helmet cam and her optic nerve. He looked into the wide-open, fanged mouth of a Brute and turned—against his will—to watch Mal finish off the last one standing with a full clip emptied into its chest. The creature still took a surprisingly long time to stop moving.

No amount of biological studies, data, recon footage, or any other kind of third-hand input could have prepared BB for this. His choices were either to see what Naomi saw or disconnect from her optic nerve, a very limited but intense set of options compared to the freedom of infiltrating every circuit, system, and carrier wave in his electronic existence. This was her experience of the world, however much he could use his processing power to enhance her nerve signals. He swallowed the microscopic detail and understood.

"All clear," she called.

The world suddenly changed color, shifting from near-monochrome to the full spectrum. Someone had opened *Piety*'s loading bay and the bright lights of the hangar flooded in. Naomi didn't need the ODST's night-vision visors to see in very low light, one of those little details that BB knew but had to experience to truly appreciate. The ODSTs took off their helmets and both scratched their scalps like a pair of bookends.

They're okay. Good. We need that Huragok more than they realize, but they'd be a high price to pay for getting it.

BB still didn't want to be human. *Poor old Cortana. How cruel, Halsey.* But he liked some humans, he found even the ones he disliked fascinating, and he marveled at the ability of all of them to do so much with such limited hardware.

"Clear. Six down." Mal got his breath back. "Now where's the flying jellyfish?"

"Racist," BB said.

"I'm looking at you, Naomi, but all I can hear is Square Blue Thing. Are you possessed? Any projectile vomiting?"

Naomi stifled a laugh. BB could feel the last of her adrenaline metabolizing as she wound down from the fight. The uncharacteristic laughter was all part of it.

"I'm bearing up," she said. "Everyone okay?"

"Where's Devereaux?" Vaz asked.

Osman came on the radio. "Docked on the top hatch, waiting for a parking space. Good work, people. But have we got a live Engineer?"

"Looking, ma'am." Mal started opening lockers and tapping on panels. "It's hiding. It's not daft."

"Might have been hit by a stray round."

"Thanks, Vaz. Big morale booster."

It wasn't a big ship. Naomi had only gone a few meters back toward the cockpit when Vaz called out.

"Aww, look," he said. He squatted in front of an opening and held out his hand. "It's terrified. Hey, come on out. It's okay. You're safe now."

Naomi went aft again and squatted to look into the ventilation duct. The Huragok was huddled inside. Then it shot out of the opening in a flurry of tentacles, aiming for the nearest opening.

"Whoa—"

"Grab it!"

Vaz tackled it rugby-style at the cargo door and crashed down onto the hangar deck. It started squealing like a balloon losing air. Mal pitched in and subdued it with a headlock, no easy feat given the Huragok anatomy. He got to his feet with his arm still tight around its neck.

It was wearing the explosive harness that the San'Shyuum

fitted to stop Engineers falling into enemy hands. Mal took a long, slow breath.

"Okay, who's good at EOD?" he asked quietly. "And I do mean *really* good."

Osman came clattering down the ladder from the gantry but Naomi gestured at her to stay back.

"I'll do it." Naomi took out a few tools from her belt and assessed the locking mechanisms. "What do you reckon, BB?"

"I just happen to have an ONI schematic . . . there. How's that look?"

Her focus adjusted to the diagram in her HUD. "Great. Keep still, Mal."

"Tell that to jelly boy here."

Naomi fed the release codes into each port on the harness in the right order—with just the tiniest blip of adrenaline—and the harness slid onto the deck with a thud. Osman didn't wait to be given the all-clear and jogged across to take a look.

"Textbook," she said. "Absolutely textbook. What do we do with it now, BB?"

However many bells and whistles the Huragok could add to a ship, BB wanted to play it safe for now. "We need to confine it where it can't access me or any other critical systems. You know what they're like. It'll start tinkering and next thing you know . . . well, we *don't* know. Proceed with caution."

"So what are we going to do to keep it occupied?" Mal asked. "Give it a coloring book?"

"Let me talk to it. But if it gets into me, then it assimilates all my knowledge. That's classified ONI intelligence. It'll siphon it up and share it with the next computer or Engineer it meets. Even if it only shares that data with UNSC systems, you'll have an interesting time explaining *that* to Admiral Parangosky."

"Bloody good point, BB." Mal still had hold of the Engineer by its neck. "Can it pick locks? I mean, can we secure it in a compartment, or is it going to rebuild the security systems?"

"Give it something noncritical to play with," Naomi said. "Upgrade the basic ODST armor or something. You're not going to need it now everyone's got their ONI rig."

The Engineer gave up trying to squirm out of Mal's headlock and wrapped its tentacles around his shoulders like a scared child.

"Yeah, okay," Mal said. "Steady on, son. Don't throttle me. Come on, BB, talk to it."

BB decided he'd collated enough data on Huragok sign language to attempt a conversation. He projected a set of holographic tentacles and began signing. The Engineer's head whipped around and it let out a long, soft trill that BB hoped was an *oooooh* of amazement.

< *Not going to hurt,* > BB signed.

The Engineer seemed totally riveted by the unexpected conversation. < *Where are the others? What will not hurt?* >

BB made a rapid recalculation of his syntax. He was used to total mastery of every subject he encountered, but his pidgin Huragok obviously wasn't perfect. He tried again.

< *We will not hurt you. What others?* >

< *My brothers. We need to repair one another.* >

< *Where did you come from?* >

< *I waited in a damaged ship until the Jiralhanae came. It was a lot of work for one.* >

BB had hoped the Huragok would have a team of little friends waiting somewhere for him, but it didn't look like it. < *We do not know any others. What is your name?* >

< *Requires Adjustment. But you are an AI. So like the Forerunner ones.* >

Oh, really? The Forerunner comment intrigued BB but he'd return to that later. Right now his priority was to keep the Engineer out of their systems until they'd worked out what to do with him. Perhaps just asking him not to tinker with the ship would be enough. The creature was certainly intelligent enough to understand their reluctance.

< *I am Black-Box. Address me as BB. Do not access the ship's systems until we ask you. I have some fascinating work for you to do, but first we must take you on a journey.* >

Requires Adjustment seemed satisfied for the moment. < *Good,* > he signed. < *Good.* >

"So?" Mal twisted his head as far as he could to see where the tentacles had wound around his backpack. "What was all that about?"

"It's a *he* and he's called Requires Adjustment," BB said, resolving into a tidy box again. "I think I'm going to call him the Adj. Gives him a quasi-military chumminess, I think."

"Well, we're never going to sign well enough to speak to him direct, so I suppose that makes you his agent," Vaz said.

He reached out a wary finger to touch Adj as if he'd never seen a Huragok before. These ODSTs had led relatively sheltered lives by ONI's standards, but in intelligence terms, they were clean; no complicated associations with other ONI officers or senior commanders, or any previous knowledge of the service other than a healthy dread. BB thought that was a smart move. They were just efficient, willing, intelligent marines, top-grade raw material for Osman to shape to her own unique needs.

And you'll need them when the Admiral finally passes the baton to you, Captain. You really will.

The Adj slithered one tentacle around Mal's neck and slackened his grip, visibly calmer.

"They're very appealing, aren't they?" Vaz said.

"Well, you can take him for walks, then." Mal went over to the armor racks with Adj still draped around his shoulders and tapped his old helmet to encourage the Engineer to look at a new toy. "Go on, Adj. Look at that nice armor. *Lovely* armor. Isn't that fun? Good boy! Do the business."

Adj reached out a tentacle and explored the helmet for a few seconds, then let go of Mal and floated free. BB decided the language barrier wasn't going to be a major problem. Adj worked over the armor in a flurry of tentacles and cilia, removing components and parking them in his free tentacles while he made adjustments and generally tinkered.

Osman had that half-lidded look that said she was pleased. "Parangosky's going to love this."

"But we need another one," BB pointed out. *How odd to look at Osman through human eyes.* "And it's cruel to keep one on its own, isn't it?"

"Yes, it is," Naomi said. BB decided to take that at face value.

Osman looked over Adj wistfully. "I know I should send him back to HQ, but he really would be useful on a mission like this. Let's see what the Admiral's got to say. Was there any food for him in the ship? They do need nutrients, don't they?"

"If there isn't, I can formulate an amino acid mix." BB wanted to search *Piety* anyway. There was plenty of work to do to her before she was sent on her *Marie Celeste*-like way. "Come on, Naomi. Housekeeping time."

Naomi climbed back into *Piety* and dragged the dead Jiralhanae aside to get at the crates. She pried one lid open and rummaged around inside, turning over assorted hand weapons and spare power packs.

"BB," she said, "are you sure this ship was heading *toward* Sanghelios, not *away* from it?"

"Definitely. Plug me into her nav computer and I'll confirm it. Why do you ask?"

"Have you scanned this stuff for tags?"

He hadn't. The only tags he would check for would be those on the arms supplied to 'Telcam, and this shipment didn't fall under that heading.

"I'll do that right now," he said, embarrassed, and activated the signal via her radio. "Oh . . ."

He got a return. Four, in fact. There were four weapons in this shipment that had been supplied by ONI and handed over to 'Telcam.

"Maybe there's a simple explanation for this," Naomi said. "Let's check *Piety*'s nav computer."

Urban structure, Forerunner Dyson sphere, Onyx: local date November 2552.

The Forerunners must have been pretty confident about their engineering skills, because there were no stairs here.

Mendez stood in the lobby and looked around for an alternative to stepping into a rectangular opening that looked exactly like an elevator. He already had one Spartan missing. He didn't plan on adding any more.

Who'd build a tower block with no goddamn emergency stairs?

"Clear right, Chief," Linda called. She backed out of a small side lobby, rifle raised, and rejoined the cluster of Spartans watching the main entrance and the doors leading onto the lobby. "I'm not picking up any movement on my HUD. And no EM. Nothing at all. It's deserted."

The lobby was built in the same pale gold stone as the towers, completely empty and with no sign of ever having been used or occupied. Mendez had cleared plenty of abandoned buildings in his time on colony worlds, kicking doors open and checking room by room for booby traps. The floors were usually scattered with the sad debris of normal lives that had been interrupted for one reason or another, even if it was just scraps of paper or broken glass. But he'd never seen anything as sterile as this. There wasn't a single trace of dust or evidence of wear on anything. The place could have been constructed yesterday, except he'd never seen a new building quite this clean.

"Well, if we want a vantage point," he said, "we have to get up top somehow."

Mendez walked outside again and stood back to count the windows. There were seven openings top to bottom, but he had no way of telling if the spacing meant there were a few floors with very high ceilings, or if some floors just didn't have any natural light. He went back in and paused at the entrance to the elevator.

I hope that's what it is, anyway. Assumptions get you killed.

"Come on, Chief." Fred put one boot on the floor of the elevator cage. "Nobody goes anywhere on their own until we figure out how this maze works. Everyone else—stay put."

Mendez stepped in beside Fred. The two of them stood there for a moment, looking around for anything that resembled controls. Maybe it was a gravity lift: there were no signs on the walls at all, recognizable or otherwise. The ceiling of the elevator cage didn't give Mendez any clues either, but then his stomach lurched and he realized he was moving. The entrance vanished below them.

"Okay, people, going up," Fred said. "I don't know what the Chief did, but it worked."

"I just looked up," Mendez said.

"Okay, so maybe it responds to that. Up for up, down for down . . ."

"And stop?"

They were now looking at a blank wall and it was hard to tell if they were still moving. Mendez shut his eyes for a moment to see if he could detect motion, but he wasn't sure of it until he saw the opening onto another floor slide slowly past them. Another open floor followed, then another.

"Well, that's two, and I counted seven."

"That's . . . three." The cage rose past another opening. "And four . . ."

Light spread down from the tight seam between the cage and the wall, indicating another floor coming. Mendez reached toward the wall, and the cage slowed to a stop. It leveled out with the fifth floor and waited.

"You've got a way with elevators, Chief." Fred stuck his head out to take a look, boots still inside the cage area. "Very hygienic. No germ-laden buttons."

Mendez tried out his newfound mastery and looked up to the ceiling again. The floor began to rise. "Yeah, the more I see, the more I wonder if this is some decontamination facility. It feels like a hospital."

"If you were escaping from the Flood, and this is the first place you end up after you get into the Dyson sphere, that makes sense."

Mendez watched floor six go by. He'd expected Kelly to be on the radio by now, passing on Halsey's questions as the resident Forerunner expert, but she hadn't called in.

"How long do you think this place has been here, Lieutenant?"

"In real time or the Dyson time? I'd guess thousands of years."

"I came here twenty-odd years ago," Mendez said. "We were

sitting right on top of this thing all that time and never knew it was here."

He heard the slight drop-out on Fred's helmet audio as the lieutenant muted his radio. "Dr. Halsey's really upset about that, Chief."

"Yes, she's already indicated her displeasure to me, sir. But I answer to the chain of command. Not a civilian."

"Understood, Chief."

Officer or no officer, Fred was like anyone else in the UNSC. A senior NCO like Mendez could put him politely in his place and get away with it. Even admirals trod carefully around old senior chiefs. Halsey would just have to suck it up. Mendez wasn't on her private staff, and the Spartan project wasn't her patented property.

"Seven," he said, and the elevator stopped without any gestures from him.

They stepped out onto an empty floor and worked their way around it, overlapping cover. But if this was accommodation or an emergency center of some kind then it certainly wasn't ready for an influx of refugees. There wasn't a stick of furniture in the place. However advanced the Forerunners' technology had been, Mendez was sure they'd still have needed chairs or beds, however unrecognizable those might now be to a human being. But the place was just a shell. He inhaled, trying to pick up any smell of decay, but if anything had rotted away here then it was long past the decomposition stage.

"Good view." Fred reached the window and leaned on the sill. "There's some kind of glass in this, not that you can see it."

Mendez stood beside him and took his binoculars out of his pack. "You see anything I can't, Lieutenant?"

"Looks like a ghost town," Fred murmured. "Nothing moving. Nothing on infrared. No active radio channels except ours." He moved his head back and forth as if he was trying to focus. "Blue Team, everybody got those images?"

Olivia responded. "Got it, sir."

As ghost towns went, it looked pretty good. Below the window, an elegant but apparently dead city stretched as far as Mendez could see. The buildings were a mix of sleek towers, single-story domed structures, and sprawling low-rises that could have been anything from theaters to warehouses. Mendez had no idea if the Forerunners had had that kind of society, but the size of most of the doors was the same as back home. That told him more about them than he'd first realized.

He tapped his radio. He was fed up waiting for the shoe to drop. "Kelly, everything okay back there?"

"Still no sign of her, Chief." Kelly must have said something to Halsey because the mike cut out for a moment. "Interesting recon you've got going there."

"Empty. Just shells of buildings."

"Never mind. We've got fruit and lizards. A girl can whip up a decent meal from those."

"What's Halsey doing?"

"Running translations on the Forerunner controls. She says it's just a maintenance area but there's still some symbols she's not sure about."

"I'll trust her not to press any buttons she can't translate. Mendez out."

Fred just looked at him. The visor might as well not have been there. Mendez avoided the discussion and headed back to the elevator, and the two of them didn't say another word on the way down.

Damn. An elevator's an elevator wherever it is. I could be back in Sydney avoiding an awkward conversation like this. Not in some slipspace bubble in God knows where.

He stepped out into the lobby and walked over to the doorway to gaze at the deserted street. On the open radio channel, he could hear the Spartans calling out cleared rooms, finding nothing. Fred ambled over to stand next to him.

"Halsey said this sphere's about the same diameter as Earth's orbit. That's a hell of a big place to recon."

"Maybe, but if there was any civilization here, even one that makes us look like chimps, then we'd pick up something," Mendez said. "Even if we couldn't receive up their comms, we'd detect something."

"We might be here a very long time, Chief."

"And you want Mom and Dad to get on."

"Something like that. What changed?"

"Me."

Olivia and Linda emerged from the elevator. "All clear, sir," Olivia said. "Okay if we go check out the other buildings? Some of them look like storage facilities."

"Go ahead." Fred nodded toward the door. "We'll be right behind you."

The two women went off up the road. Fred didn't seem about to resume the conversation, so Mendez changed the topic.

"We ought to pick a spot to set up camp for the night," he said. "Which might sound crazy when we've got a few million square meters of prime accommodation to choose from, but I haven't seen a faucet around here yet. Somewhere near the river's our best bet."

"Yeah, where there's water, there'll be fish and animals." Fred looked toward the elevator and the sound of voices. "And I'd rather be near the towers."

He didn't need to say why. Tom, Mark, and Ash came out of the elevator and shrugged. Fred gestured to the street.

"Three hours, max," he said. "Then we regroup at the tower."

Mendez gave the Spartans a few minutes' start to put some diplomatic distance between them before following with Fred. A crisis was a handy thing. It could stop him from thinking about the slow-burning, intractable problems. All that mattered right then was finding Lucy and keeping the team alive and fed. Thinking beyond that was asking for trouble.

But after another forty minutes of checking out deserted buildings, he did it anyway.

"You ever feel a sense of injustice about your life, Fred?" This was man-to-man now. At some point Mendez would need to say sorry, but it had to be more than a word and it had to be discussed. "About the life you never had, I mean."

Fred didn't answer for a few moments. They walked on in the echoing silence. "I don't recall that life," he said. "But wherever I came from, I'm pretty sure it was glassed. So I got a life I might not otherwise have lived. And how many people get to fulfill their full potential? I'm okay with it, Chief."

Mendez wasn't sure if it was just a kind answer for his benefit, a rationalization because regret was a sour and painful thing, or if it was simply the way Fred really felt.

And how can I be sorry if I went and did it all over again with the next batch of Spartans?

Linda's voice came over the radio. "Sir, I might be jumping to conclusions, but I think we've found a food warehouse. First dome on the left. Not good news."

"Got you," Fred said. "On our way."

Mendez jogged down the street after him. Linda was standing outside the arched entrance to what could have been a spa, hands on hips. She didn't say a word. She jerked her head at them to follow and led them into the building.

The interior reminded Mendez of a dance hall or an ice rink, a big open tiled floor with a kind of colonnade on three sides. The dome had looked opaque from the outside but from in here he could see the sky, blue and marbled with wispy clouds. The place was another immaculate shell. This time, though, there were plenty of Forerunner glyphs on the walls and above the doors.

"Mind the tables," Linda said.

Fred was a few paces ahead of Mendez. "What tables?"

Linda put her left hand out to her side as she walked, then stood still. Where her hand cast a shadow, the tiles deformed and the flooring coalesced into something almost like extruded plastic. It rose up in a column and stopped at hand-height, then spread horizontally like a mushroom cap opening. It was now a table.

"Well, at least we know where some of the furnishings are," she said.

Mendez grunted. "Neat technology."

"And we weren't far off the mark about Lucy walking through the wall either." Linda kept going and seemed to be on a collision course with a panel halfway along the colonnade. "Look."

She was a meter from the wall when it parted. It didn't slide apart: it dissolved. That was the only way Mendez could describe it. As he stood on the threshold, he could feel something on his face which he would have thought was a constant breeze, but knowing the Forerunners it couldn't be that simple. The room he stared into was lined with completely plain shelves.

"Is this a cold store?" he asked.

"Not sure if it's chilled." Linda walked inside and cast around with that head movement that told him she was switching through the different filters in her visor. "But the atmosphere *is* different in here. I can't swear to this, either, because I can't even begin to guess how the Forerunners cleaned premises, but I don't think this place has ever been stocked. I'm not picking up any traces of organic material in my filters."

Mark, Ash, and Tom walked in behind them, boots clattering on the tiles. Their silence was telling. They looked around and eventually Tom took off his helmet.

"You ever get the feeling that they started building this place but never finished it?" he said.

Yes, that was exactly how it looked. Mendez wasn't sure just how much worse that made things, but it did raise a question. What had stopped the Forerunners? A civilization like that didn't shelve projects because the budget ran out.

But it was thousands of years ago, something to keep Halsey occupied, and he had a Spartan missing.

"Come on," he said. "Lucy's still out there somewhere."

UNSC *PORT STANLEY,* Urs system: February 2553.

"It's just like Earth," Phillips said. "You sell arms to some bunch of revolutionaries you think are on your side, and before you know it, the stuff ends up in the wrong hands. Well, that's why you tagged the weapons, isn't it? Just to work out who's in cahoots with who."

Osman checked over *Piety* again to make sure that there was nothing else of use that she could strip from it. BB, evicted from Naomi's armor, was buzzing around the ship's systems harvesting data. He seemed to be enjoying himself. Every few minutes she heard him say "*Yoink . . .*"

"That's true," Osman said. "I don't mind if they share the kit with Beelzebub as long as they're squabbling between themselves and not bothering us. I just want to know the supply route."

"Venezia," BB said suddenly. "There's a link to Venezia in the comms log."

"How?" Osman knew BB could process information in nano-seconds. He'd taken his time about that. "This ship hasn't got anything like that range. No slipspace drive, for a start."

"No, but they *are* in touch with a party of Kig-Yar who appear to be transmitting from within the Venezia sector."

Osman's mind went straight back to the Covenant AA battery that Venezia had fired at *Monte Cassino.* She'd wondered how the colonists had acquired missiles, and now she knew. *Bastard Jackals.* The aftermath of government collapse in a war was usually a free-for-all with the hardware. Who was left to keep an inventory? It wasn't a surprise, but it did complicate matters in both good and bad ways. The Prophets hadn't trusted the Kig-Yar any more than she did, and restricted the slipspace drives they were allowed access to. The Kig-Yar got what the UNSC diplomatically termed the *de-enriched* spec.

Well, I'd make sure they got the monkey model too. But Venezia doesn't care. They need the arms, and I bet they've acquired some really interesting vessels now.

"Any indication of how chummy they are?" she asked. "Did they know the Brutes had an Engineer embarked?"

"I don't think they're doing business," BB said. "The flight path suggests they were avoiding another ship. So the Kig-Yar probably knew."

The compartment was starting to smell foul now, a blend of Kig-Yar and rapidly decomposing Jiralhanae that prodded at her gag reflex. The Kig-Yar corpses were a fairly safe bet as bogus evidence went. It was simply a case of sending *Piety* back to the Sangheili in a way that would fuel mistrust. She could always destroy the ship, of course, but the cumulative effect of small incidents could stoke hatred far faster than one huge outrage, especially now the Sangheili were reliant more on gossip than efficient imperial communications from the San'Shyuum.

"Are the Sangheili likely to do any forensic tests on corpses, Evan?" she asked. "Because *we* would, obviously."

Phillips squatted to look at one of the dead Brutes with a flashlight. He really did grab every single new experience, even the gruesome ones. "They don't *do* doctors," he said. "If a warrior accepts any medical care apart from a few bracing herbal remedies, it's a shocking disgrace—especially surgery. They think he's a big girl. So without the San'Shyuum around, I think their chances of finding a pathologist are pretty slim. Added to which . . . they're so culturally arrogant that they'll probably assume the Kig-Yar took on too much raiding the ship, and the Jiralhanae were too dumb to deal with it." He prodded the huge corpse, running the back of his fingers over the bristly gray fur on the Brute's neck. "Wow, they're *big* boys, aren't they?"

"But they can tell the difference between a projectile injury and an energy weapon wound, so we'd better give our Kig-Yar a UNSC rifle."

"You're a devious woman, Captain."

"Flatterer."

She'd done all she could for the moment, so she withdrew from the cargo bay to inhale clean air in the hangar. BB was now whistling tunelessly to himself. She had to smile.

"Next scheduled OPSNORMAL is in half an hour, Captain," he said. "It'll be good to give the Admiral a nice surprise. You know it's her birthday in three days, don't you? *Ninety-two.* What a gal."

Osman warmed to the idea of making Parangosky's day. The inevitable was hard to ignore, but she tried: Parangosky was, as she often said herself, at the stage of life when just waking up the next morning was a good result. Osman occasionally rehearsed the idea of life without her and it wasn't pleasant. Very rarely, she let herself wonder whether her real mother—the woman who'd lost her, who'd mourned for a dead cloned surrogate and never known her daughter was still alive—would have been anything like Parangosky.

I could find out in an instant.

I could access my file and see my real past.

But not now. Too late. Too painful. Too pointless.

She'd resisted it for nearly thirty years because she didn't deserve to be anything more than an anonymous orphan. She could resist it for thirty more.

Coffee beckoned from the wardroom galley, decent ONI coffee, the special blend, the stuff that good morale was made of, and Osman followed its perfume to find Devereaux trying to interest Adj in the range. He huddled in the corner like the shy guest at a party who'd retreated to take comfort in the canapés. Devereaux cradled a coffee and nodded in the direction of the coffee machine. The galley was a mix of prosaic technology and quietly comforting anachronism, but the coffee machine didn't look quite as Osman remembered it. When she tasted what came out of it, she was even more sorely tempted to keep the Huragok.

"Forget the military applications, ma'am." Devereaux cradled a steaming mug as if it was nectar. "Think what he'd be worth commercially."

Adj inched out of the corner and reached out a wary tentacle to touch the back of Devereaux's head. She moved away and gave him a gentle tap on the arm.

"Don't let him fix your neural implant," Osman said.

"He's been trying to repair this cut on my hand too. I'm still a little too creeped out to let him."

Osman found herself thinking of a Huragok breeding program

and the pick of the litter rather than *replication*. They weren't machines any more than BB was just software.

But we're just organic machines too. No wonder the Covenant thought the Forerunners were gods. By our own definition, they were.

This was a very bad time to find God, even an explicable and mortal one. Osman shook herself out of it and drained her coffee. She had to send *Piety* on her way before she called in.

"BB, have you finished nobbling their nav computer yet?" she asked, heading for her day cabin.

"Autopilot back on course for the original coordinates in Mdama, Captain. And the rest of the cockpit data's creatively edited—rather *thrilling*, if I might say so—to show a spirited defense against Kig-Yar pirates, one of whom didn't make it and lies clutching a MA-Five-B. Not a Five-C. No point being too lavish."

"I'll hope they don't ponder too long on how a Kig-Yar managed to snap a Brute's spinal cord, but we have to work with what we've got." Osman settled into her seat. "Okay, launch it so Devereaux can get the dropship secured."

"I could do that for her."

"I know, but I don't want her getting bored. This is already a pretty low-key life for an ODST as it is."

Seven years. Is that all he gets? Doesn't seem fair. Seven damn years.

That was BB's life expectancy before rampancy destroyed him. It had started to gnaw more deeply at Osman now. Perhaps that was what came of worrying about a ninety-two-year-old boss. Everyone she relied on seemed more finite than she was.

I wonder if BB's engram donor was anything like him in real life.

But AIs weren't copies of human brains. They were unique entities in their own right. It made her feel guilty for even wanting to find out, as if it negated BB's individuality. She reached out to tap the comms panel and waited for Parangosky's image to appear on the main screen.

The UNSC portal screen dissolved to an image she wasn't expecting. Parangosky appeared to be sitting at an open window overlooking the harbor, not in her office. Osman hadn't been away from Sydney long enough yet to miss it.

"Looks like a nice day, ma'am," Osman said.

"It is," Parangosky said, turning to the lens. "I rarely feel the need for a day off, but I'm finally learning to pace myself."

Osman fought down a reflex to worry. *She's not ill. She's just old and she can't keep up that schedule forever.* "We're due to make another weapons drop to 'Telcam shortly. Some of the items are already finding their way into other hands, but I don't think we need to worry too much about that. You've had a chance to read Phillips's analyses of the chatter, have you?"

"Yes. I think it's inevitable that Sangheili lapse back into their keep structures, waiting to be told what to do. But that won't last forever. How's the plot against the Arbiter?"

"Simmering. 'Telcam looks like he's assembling a pretty mixed following, but he may well have a warship now and a few more competent shipmasters."

"Very positive. Be aware that Hood's planning to travel to Vadam to talk to the Arbiter in the next week." Parangosky paused to swat away a fly. "Very low key, very small entourage, just in case—well, just in case your mission is excessively successful, I suppose. We could end up stoking so much unrest that poor Terrence gets assassinated too. There's going to be a memorial service at Voi and he's rather keen for the Arbiter to attend."

"Memorial to what?"

"Personnel who were lost in the portal when they disabled the

Halo. You probably need to mention this to Naomi. Spartan One-One-Seven's top of the list."

Parangosky said it in that carefully flat tone she adopted when she was aware of the reaction it would get. It was all rather final. Anyone could believe a legend was missing in action, but when his name was carved into a memorial to the fallen, the illusion was over. Osman considered herself immune to that sort of thing. But confirmation that the Master Chief was actually gone took the shine off the day.

She tried to remember him as John, as a ferocious, scared, endlessly resourceful colonial kid like herself, but she couldn't even recall his face.

"But what about the MIA status? Are we announcing that Spartans die now?"

"No, but the public realizes that MIA is just a service courtesy. I think even I have to accept he's dead, Captain. It's been two months now."

Osman wondered how to rephrase the good news she'd been rehearsing mentally. She decided to plunge in and risk sounding crass. Parangosky knew her too well to misunderstand her.

"I thought he'd survive us all," she said, taking a breath. "It's hard to say happy birthday after that, ma'am, but I do have something for you. How would you like a pet Huragok? His name's Requires Adjustment, but we call him Adj."

Parangosky looked blank for a moment, and then started to smile. The smile spread for quite some time, sad and genuine.

"How thoughtful, Captain. In fact, it's just what I needed. Thank you."

"He's upgrading everything in sight at the moment, but we'll get him to you as soon as we can."

"That might prove to be even more important than your current mission. Well done, Serin. Seriously. Well done." She rarely used Osman's first name. "Would you like a little gift in return?"

"We've got the good Jamaican coffee, ma'am. It's very much appreciated."

"Better than that."

Osman basked in the brief respite of a small success that might turn the tide for good. She thought of John and reminded herself that she might be dead tomorrow too, along with everyone she cared about. "I could do with cheering up, Admiral."

"We finally found the hole where Halsey bolted," Parangosky said. "Now all we have to do is work out how to kick down the door."

CHAPTER 11

I'M GLAD THAT CAPTAIN OSMAN IS SATISFIED WITH THE TEAM WE RECOMMENDED. IT TOOK SOME EFFORT TO SELECT QUALIFIED PERSONNEL WHO HAD BOTH NO FAMILY TIES AND WHO WOULD ALSO BOND WELL WITH ONE ANOTHER. SPARTAN-010 DIDN'T QUITE FIT THOSE CRITERIA, BUT WITH SO FEW SPARTANS LEFT, SOME FLEXIBILITY WAS NEEDED.
(Dr. Miriam Baxendale, Head of Occupational Personality Testing, UNSC HR, to Admiral Margaret O. Parangosky, CINCONI)

Bekan keep, Mdama, Sanghelios: February 2553 by the human calendar.

'Telcam was late.

Jul paced up and down the quarry, fidgeting with the *arum* while he waited for whatever shuttle the monk was flying today. 'Telcam changed transports on each trip to avoid attention, he said. The only flaw in that strategy was *Unflinching Resolve,* huge and unconcealable as only a frigate could be.

The ship sat in the disused quarry like a rebuke to Jul's common sense. Her magazine was steadily filling up with arms and ordnance, one cargo drop at a time, gleaned from hardware scattered around Sanghelios and the nearby colonies. Just as the small transports had found their way back to the keeps, nobody was keeping tabs on any other equipment either, and in the absence of the San'Shyuum, their organizational skills, and a war to fight, it was simply being taken by shipmasters and stored in the keeps.

How many shots does it take to kill one Arbiter?

'Telcam kept telling Jul that overthrowing a charismatic leader like Thel 'Vadam would take more than killing him. The ideas around him—his loyal entourage—had to be rooted out too, or else the very death became a new Arbiter in itself, a martyrdom, the creation of a legend after death.

And you couldn't assassinate a ghost.

The sound of a Kig-Yar shuttle made him spin around. So that was 'Telcam's transport today. Jul, like most warriors, knew almost every vessel by the sound of its engine or drive long before he saw it. It was a matter of prudence. He would never admit that was his motive, of course, because a warrior was supposed to prize a glorious death before a timely extraction, but it was hard to be a successful warrior when you were dead. Jul didn't regard a tactical withdrawal as cowardice.

The shuttle—yes, Kig-Yar, just as he thought—finally came into view and dropped down into the quarry. He waited for its drives to shut down and approached it. 'Telcam climbed down from the cockpit and looked around.

"Where's Manus?" he asked. That was one of Buran's loyal Jiralhanae. "He should have been here by now. We lost contact with him last night."

Jiralhanae weren't known for their timekeeping. "Yours is the first shuttle to land for two days," Jul said. "You know what they're like. He probably became embroiled in some fistfight over philosophical matters and it's delayed him."

"No, Buran assured me he was reliable. He had a very important cargo, and I don't just mean weapons. He had a Huragok they recovered from *Serene Certainty*."

Had they been discussing Kig-Yar, Jul would have assumed that the shipment had been diverted and sold by now. But Jiralhanae weren't interested in profits. Everything stemmed from their unfathomable pack politics. The feud between Jiralhanae and Sangheili had finally erupted again with the Great Schism, but Jul had never quite worked out where the fault lines were. Jiralhanae fought each other, they fought the Sangheili, and, for no reason Jul could truly understand, some of them remained loyal to Sanghelios.

"Give him a little longer," Jul said. "Now let's transfer the cargo before we attract an audience."

"Something's wrong. I know it."

"Brother, if the vessel had crashed, we would have heard by now."

"Would we? What's happened to our communications? Our monitoring? No, we would *not* know. That yawning gap is also what enables us to stand a chance of succeeding, but sometimes it conspires against us."

Jul had formed the opinion that 'Telcam was blessed with the calm certainty of the faithful, so seeing him agitated was unsettling. But Jul understood the importance of acquiring a Huragok or two. The Covenant had run on them, invisible and reliable, repairing everything from machines and buildings to living bodies, and constructing every piece of technology a modern empire needed. He'd grown so used to their presence that he'd ceased to notice them. Now his wife and brothers were forced to learn construction skills, and he was starting to see all the things, large and small, that were starting to fall apart because the Huragok had fled.

There were so many. Where did they all go?

He was certain that the Great Schism hadn't killed all the San'Shyuum. That wasn't possible. As he unloaded the shuttle with 'Telcam, he wondered where the survivors had gone. They had almost certainly taken most of the Huragok with them, and that meant they might be regrouping to return one day and take back their old empire.

The idea was so appalling that he stopped in his tracks. What was he doing worrying about the humans? They were no more than an infestation, backward vermin, and could be eradicated. The San'Shyuum, though, would be another matter.

"What's wrong?" 'Telcam asked.

Jul got on with the job, wondering what had happened to his strategic judgment. "Merely speculating what might happen if the San'Shyuum recovered and came back."

"That would take many years," 'Telcam said, as if it had already occurred to him and had been dismissed. "And by then, we'll be more than ready for them."

'Telcam made no complaint about having to do the heavy lifting himself in the absence of any Jiralhanae. Jul found himself thinking of him less as a fanatical monk and more as a decent warrior who happened to have some extreme views on the subject of religion. As long as they had the same objective, Jul wasn't too worried about the separate paths that brought them there.

"Where are you getting your supplies?" Jul asked, heaving a crate up the ramp into the frigate's hold. "Who funds this?"

"Donations," 'Telcam said. "From many sources."

"Are all of them aware they're *donating*?"

"No."

"And how much do we really need?"

"You mean when should we act, because you grow impatient."

"Yes. Yes, I do."

"I'm waiting upon the whims of an old nobleman." 'Telcam dusted off his hands and stood back to look at the growing arms cache. "And Buran needs to know that he has a fully competent crew when we make our move. Some of his old crew have gone back to their keeps to try to feed their families."

Jul tried to imagine which kaidon could be so important to the plot that 'Telcam would feel he needed his approval. Perhaps this was just a regular power struggle after all, a coup on behalf of another kaidon who'd chosen not to show his face, rather than an outpouring of religious zeal.

"Which nobleman?"

"Admiral Hood," 'Telcam said. "The human Shipmaster of Shipmasters. He's made it clear to the Arbiter that he wants to formalize this cease-fire. There's much talk of it in Vadam."

"What cease-fire?" Jul demanded. "There *is* no cease-fire. Just an absence of fighting."

"We don't know that, and neither does the Arbiter—or Hood. Communications are what the humans call *patchy*." 'Telcam, who was unusually fluent in the primary human language, pronounced the word with care. It was hard to form a human *P* when trying to compress four lips. "The humans have lost many of their communications relays, too, so both sides flounder in the dark and eavesdrop where they can. There are worlds out there where the battles may still be raging. We may not know for years."

It took them an hour to move all the containers, but there was still no sign of the Jiralhanae. Jul found himself sitting in the shuttle cockpit with 'Telcam in awkward silence, waiting. Every half hour, 'Telcam opened a channel and listened to crackling static.

"Their radio's working," he said. "You can hear it. I don't understand this."

"Perhaps it's malfunctioning. Whether they have a Huragok on board or not."

It was another hour before the shuttle's comms indicator lit up to indicate an inbound message. 'Telcam pounced on the console, teeth bared.

"Manus? Where in the name of the gods have you been?"

"This is not Manus, brother. This is the temple. We hear *Piety* is returning, but isn't responding to her radio. A sympathetic shipmaster picked her up on his radar."

'Telcam's lips settled back over his fangs and he leaned back in his seat. His relief was obvious. "We'll wait for the ship. We have little else to do."

"I told you as much," Jul said. "Everything breaks down these days."

"You'd think they'd let the Huragok repair it."

"They're Jiralhanae. Their logic eludes me."

Jul got out of the cockpit to listen for the sound of *Piety*'s drive. Nearly an hour later, he heard the rumble of a small auxiliary and the ship appeared above the quarry, looking predictably scraped and battered, then hovered over her landing coordinates for a few moments before descending in a storm of dust. Jul could have sworn that her nose hatch was dented.

'Telcam climbed down from the cockpit, looking murderous. "I shall have an explanation," he murmured.

Piety's side hatches had taken some damage and there were dents around the lock plates. She was an old tug used in the docks to berth warships, so it might have been wear and tear, but Jul was getting concerned. He strained to see what was going on in the cockpit. But it was dark inside, and he was sure he'd been mistaken about the nose hatch. 'Telcam stood about ten meters from the ship and kept glancing irritably at the hatches. Manus seemed to be taking his time about things.

So they waited. After five silent minutes, 'Telcam ran out of patience.

"This is the last time I allow those idiots to go on missions without supervision, I swear." He strode up to the main side hatch and hammered on the hull. Nothing happened. "Manus? Open this damned hatch. Where have you been?"

Jul looked over the smaller side hatches. He could now see slight ripples, as if the metal had been distorted by force, and he was sure he could see a gap. If he was right, then something terrible had happened to *Piety*.

Her hull's breached. Her atmosphere's leaked away.

"Brother, she's damaged," Jul said. "Look at the metal. Something's very wrong."

'Telcam just grunted. Jul drew his energy sword and approached *Piety* cautiously. He couldn't imagine what form the danger inside a ship opened to vacuum might take, but he wasn't prepared to take a chance so close to his home and his family. If anything was going to leap out of there, he would be ready for it.

'Telcam turned to him, nodded, and drew his own weapon.

There was a manual override for the main cargo hatch. 'Telcam closed his fingers slowly around the handle and twisted it to the left, slowly and carefully, then stood to one side as the door slid back on its runners. Jul aimed squarely into the open compartment. But the only thing that emerged was a stench.

'Telcam jumped in, teeth bared. "Manus? *Manus!*"

Jul still expected to hear weapons discharging, but when he

climbed into the ship behind 'Telcam, it was clear that *Piety* still had her cargo. There was no sign of the Jiralhanae.

They're dead. They ran out of air.

Then 'Telcam stumbled over something, knocking into crates, and cursed loudly. He was looking down at the deck. Jul squeezed through the gap after him and saw the bodies.

A Kig-Yar lay slumped against a bulkhead with a human rifle beside him. Jul stepped over the body and saw there were four dead Jiralhanae in the compartment as well, but his first glance told him they hadn't asphyxiated. There were projectile wounds to their faces. 'Telcam pushed through to the cockpit and roared with anger.

"All of them, *dead*," he snarled. "*All of them.* And where's the Huragok?"

Jul squeezed into the small cockpit. Two more dead Jiralhanae, one of them Manus, were draped over the seats. Above him, Jul could see the daylight through gaps around the hatch seal. *Piety*'s console was on idle, the flickering lights indicating that her autopilot was still engaged, which explained how she managed to return and why her radio had been working but silent.

"They've taken the Huragok." 'Telcam was almost sitting with indignation. "They attacked the ship. Damned Kig-Yar vermin. They'll pay for this."

He gestured Jul back into the main section of the ship and went back to the dead Kig-Yar. Jul swallowed his revulsion and moved the body with his boot to look at the wounds.

"Projectiles," he said. "It's been shot several times."

"Human weapons." 'Telcam squatted and poked around in its clothing, then picked up the human rifle. "They like these things. They'll trade with anybody." He examined the interior of the compartment. "Look at the number of rounds expended. There was quite a firefight here. I imagine this idiot got himself caught in the cross fire and his comrades didn't bother to retrieve him."

Sangheili always called Kig-Yar cowardly, but it was just an unthinking insult and didn't reflect how aggressive the creatures could be. They were very effective in large numbers, which often made up for their slight build. Jul suspected that the San'Shyuum preferred them in individual roles, not just because they were excellent snipers and scouts, but because they knew what trouble the scavengers would be if deployed in battalions.

If they could hijack a shuttle and overpower six Jiralhanae, it was a worrying development. They were on the offensive.

"I forget their pirate heritage," Jul said. "Anarchy. That's what'll follow if we don't impose some order on the situation."

'Telcam didn't comment, shaking his head slowly as he searched the ship. He seemed more shocked now than angry. He looked behind every panel and in every space, however small, but there was no sign of the Huragok.

It was worth a lot of money on the black market, Jul knew. But it was even more valuable as an asset to bring Kig-Yar weapons and ship technology up to the level of the Sangheili.

That worried him much more.

"We are, as the humans might say, *spoilt for choice*," he said at last. "Who should we deal with first? Should we depose our heretical Arbiter, or teach these vermin some respect?" He picked up the Kig-Yar's rifle, a MA5B, a weapon Jul had seen scattered among the human corpses in the aftermath of many a battle. They were fiddly, cumbersome things, too crude for a Sangheili. "The Kig-Yar need to learn their place."

"Well, let's find out which nest was responsible for this." Jul went back to the cockpit and had to heave Manus's body off the navigation console. For a moment he wondered if Manus had a family and what they might be doing now. He'd never considered that they had their own lives before. Buran would have to tell his mate and children. "The flight recorder should answer some questions."

'Telcam tapped the console and the recorder flashed a stream of data on the screen, most of it simply coordinates and speeds. The attack wasn't instantly visible in the output, but the communications log was much easier to read from raw data. Jul read through the station idents: *Piety* had had radio contact with Kig-Yar from within a human-occupied sector, a colony world that had once been called Sqala.

No. That world is not *theirs. They're interlopers. I won't dignify them by calling their infestations colonies.*

It was now called Venezia. And it would pay for harboring criminals.

Blue Team Camp, Forerunner Dyson sphere: local date November 2552.

They said you could always judge a woman by the contents of her purse, and Halsey was content to be judged by hers.

Datapad . . . pocket archive . . . change of clothes . . . self-amalgamating tape . . . lip salve . . . pocket saw . . . solar power pack . . . Mom's antique Patek Philippe . . . medications . . . folding knife . . . coffee. To be opened in case of emergency, as they say.

She sorted through it all again, knowing that the item she valued most was gone. She'd lost her journal during the Covenant assault on Reach. It must have been ash by now.

Damn . . . so much of her life was in there, not just the years spent on the Spartan program but the *personal* things too. She'd start another one, but she didn't have the right technology at the moment, and that meant paper—paper and pencil and ink. She needed to feel the faint drag of the lead or the way a nib glided on a cushion of liquid ink. Talking to a datapad or scribbling and tapping on it was no substitute when it came to outpouring rather than *thinking*.

Why was I so careless with it?

Halsey tried to apply the same intellectual rigor to analyzing herself as she did with others. *A Freudian slip, much as I hate to admit it.* Subconsciously, perhaps she wanted to lose it, or—more to the point—she wanted it to be found. That could only mean that she needed to explain herself to posterity, to put her plea in mitigation for all her sins.

If I really believed they were sins, though, would I do that? But if I acknowledge they're sins, then I've demonstrated morality, haven't I?

Stop it. Stop it, right now.

When she found herself spiraling into those circular arguments, she slammed on the brakes. Like an AI, she knew she would ultimately think herself into oblivion. The more onion layers of ethical debate she indulged in, and the more she peeled them back and looked underneath, the more she realized she would find nothing concrete of herself left at the core. She was just ideas: just *thought*. There was nothing she believed in except her own intellect. She wondered if she was more of an AI than Cortana, so very conscious of her virtual body and emotionally invested in her Spartan. At times Halsey felt the AI was more human than she could ever be.

So I have no soul. And why are the only concepts I have for this religious ones? Can't reason provide the answers?

She couldn't actually remember what she'd written in the journal, not in any detail. She wondered if she didn't want to.

She only recalled that when she wrote, she had an awareness at the back of her mind that one day those words and sketches would be seen by others, studied by historians, quoted and analyzed, because she was *important*. She was one of the greatest thinkers of her century. Everyone had told her so.

Right now, though, she was sixty years old, hungry, and half scared and half thrilled, trapped in a Dyson sphere through a debacle of her own making and trying to put a brave face on it. There were only three people here who thought she was a great thinker and a boon to humanity. The others didn't really know or care what the hell she was, except for the one who knew her only *too* well and had finally lost his ability to hide his contempt for her.

And if the Flood's now overrun the galaxy and the Halo Array's fired, then this is our seed corn to rebuild humanity. Two sterile and miserable old bastards, and at least one of the females of childbearing age is genetically predisposed to violence and aggression. Let's hope Kelly and Linda are still firing on all cylinders.

But that was a problem for the long term. The short-term one still had to be tackled. Halsey was now pretty sure she knew what the tower structures were, which was a start. So far it had taken her three days to capture images of the Forerunner symbols spread across the walls and map the symbols to the language algorithm in her datapad. She had no AI this time to help her.

But that's fine. I create AIs. I shouldn't need to rely on them. The human mind's still the best tool for the job.

The results were slow in coming, but they were fascinating. This sanctuary wasn't a single, self-sustaining ecosphere but a customizable range of environments. Halsey noted the symbols for temperature, humidity, ratios of gases in the atmosphere, and even gravity. Some other symbols didn't make sense on first examination because they appeared to be names rather than common elements of language, and names were notoriously hard to pin down in translation. But an intuitive leap told her the names were not those of individuals, but of *species.*

So which is which? What's the symbol for human? We had to be part of the plan. Look how closely this environment mirrors Earth. But why is that all we can see? Does the first species to find its way in dictate the setup?

That didn't make sense, but she was confident that it would in time. Halsey took another guess—another intellectual gamble— that the Forerunners had created a bunker not just for themselves but for other sentient species they wanted to protect from the devastating effects of the Halo Array. They'd have found a way of catering for different requirements. She found herself wondering whether the Forerunners had thought in terms of a diverse community of equals, or simply a zoo for their own amusement.

And if you were so powerful, so advanced, so able to play God— what happened to you all?

For a moment, she forgot the wider predicament and found she was actually enjoying herself. She knew that was wrong and that she should have been as worried as the others were about Lucy, who'd now been missing for days. She realized that she was equally untroubled about the food supply. She hoped that was because she'd made a rational calculation about their environment and the kind of plant and animal species it would support, but something at the back of her mind told her that it was an almost religious faith in salvation by genius—that she was so brilliant, and her Spartan-IIs were so resourceful, that they were bound to come up with a solution to the problem in the nick of time.

Child. Belief in magic. Belief in grown-ups' omnipotence. Get a grip, Halsey.

But it really was yet another lovely, balmy day and it was hard not to believe in providence. *We could have found this sphere set up for methane-breathing extremophiles, couldn't we? It's working out some-how.* The river was ice cold, so bathing was a bracing experience and her hands were numb by the time she finished washing her clothes each evening. But something perverse within her was actively enjoying the sheer adventure of it all. The temporary camp around the tower had settled into a daily routine, with half the Spartans rostered to gather wild food and the other half carrying out recons in the sprawling but still stubbornly empty city a few kilometers away.

Halsey stayed back at the camp with a sidearm and her research. It was a comfortable solution. She didn't have to indulge in conversation or try to maintain a civilized working relationship with Chief Mendez, which was looking less possible by the day. She sat cross-legged on the grass with her laptop balanced on one knee, savoring the current intellectual puzzle and now not at all bothered by the disgusting taste of the ration bars.

When she looked up she could see Kelly emerging from the woods with her hand resting against her shoulder as if she was carrying something draped across her back. Judging by the swagger in the Spartan's walk, Kelly was pleased with herself and grinning from ear to ear under that helmet.

She came to a stop in front of Halsey and swung the load off her back, holding it up like a prize. It was a rather sad bundle of destruction, a haul of dead animals that she'd managed to trap. Halsey could see three or four of the small green lizards, one of them temptingly plump, as well as an assortment of birds and two hare-sized mammals of a species she didn't recognize, covered in dense chocolate-brown fur.

"Whatever you do, ma'am, don't say it tastes like chicken."

"Well, all we need now is a few cloves of garlic and a bottle of decent red," Halsey said, smiling. "Although there *is* that herb growing on the riverbank that's got quite a tang to it."

Kelly looked around, not so relaxed now. Her shoulders braced. Halsey got the feeling that she'd been tasked with babysitting her and didn't want it to look that obvious.

"Still no change inside the tower, then?" She meant Lucy. "There's got to be some link between these towers and the city. Maybe Lucy's going to pop up inside the buildings somewhere."

"It's only a matter of time before I finish translating the symbols, and then we'll work out how to access the other parts of the building," Halsey said, trying to be reassuring. "I promise you that I haven't forgotten about her."

"I didn't say you had, ma'am."

No. I think it was me.

Kelly began gutting and skinning her catch, oblivious of Halsey's reaction. Then she stopped and put her hand to the side of her helmet. "Chief Mendez is on his way back. I think that man can smell dinner ten klicks away."

Well, I might as well make myself useful. It'll save an argument.

Jacob Keyes had once asked Halsey why she kept a pocket saw in her purse, and she remembered making some crack about putting uppity men in their place with it. But she was an Endymion girl and it was just a handy thing she might need one day. She'd had a comfortable, middle-class upbringing, but Endymion was still a frontier colony, and beyond the boundaries of her hometown the wilderness always loomed.

It was all glasslands now. She knew that. Reading the official signal as it passed through the ONI system didn't evoke sobbing and regret. Endymion was gone, her parents were gone—not that she'd seen much of them in the preceding years—and life had to go on.

I have no soul. I know that. But that lets me think the unthinkable and create the things that enable decent, feeling people to survive. That's the price—for all of us.

Halsey got up to collect firewood from the log pile that they'd started building next to the tower. It was a regular Girl Scout camp. She stood by the fire, pleased that she hadn't forgotten how to build one and keep it going, and smiled at the sight of thorn-bushes draped with the Spartan-IIIs' underwear drying in the sun.

The hunting team returned first. Fred, Linda, and Olivia am-bled into the camp clutching more small dead animals, an assort-ment of greens, and those yellow tennis ball fruits. Olivia held something in her arms as carefully as if it was a newborn.

It was a fish. A huge, silver, meaty-looking fish. It was the first one Halsey had seen here. They definitely weren't going to starve, then.

"We decided to skip pizza," Olivia said. She cradled the fish, looking wistful. "We've gone organic."

The fish seemed to perk everyone up. They took off their hel-mets and settled down with Halsey to prepare the food, skewering chunks of vegetable and meat on twigs, making morale-boosting comments about everything being all right now but not mention-ing Lucy. Mendez appeared from the trees a hundred meters away with Mark, Ash, and Tom trailing behind him.

"You know what we really need?" Fred said. "A nice big cook-ing pot. I think it's time we invented ceramics."

Mendez walked into the cooking circle, grunted an acknow-ledgment at nobody in particular, and seemed to be doing a head count. He didn't meet Halsey's eyes. "Anyone mind if I light up before dinner?"

"Ration yourself, Chief," Ash said. "Four puffs. Or you'll have to find some local stuff to dry and smoke."

"Uh-*huh*." Mendez lit his cigar stub from the taper of dry grass and inhaled deeply. "I may well do that, Ash. I may yet weaken."

He walked away and stood with his back to them, facing the

river. Halsey wasn't counting, but he'd taken a lot more than four puffs by the time he turned around, and when he did his turmoil was etched into his face, possibly the first time that Halsey had ever felt the urge to go to him and ask if she could help.

But she knew she couldn't. It was about Lucy. Nobody was speculating openly about it now, but Halsey was certain that if she could access everyone's thoughts for most of their waking day, then the majority of them would be about that girl—where she was, what had happened to her, whether she was badly injured and unable to call for help, and what she'd been chasing when she went missing.

Whatever it was, it hadn't come back.

Halsey decided she couldn't just stay out of Mendez's way and say nothing indefinitely, because this exile might last for years. *Assuming he doesn't shoot me first.* She got to her feet and wandered over to him.

"I've nearly finished translating the symbols, Chief," she said, brandishing the achievement like an olive branch. "I'm betting that we'll be able to work it all out then."

Mendez looked down at the glowing tip of his cigar, then extinguished it carefully on the sole of his boot. "Hope so, Doctor."

"Like everyone says, Lucy's smart and tough. She'll hang in there, wherever *there* is." Halsey really was trying to make placatory conversation. Whatever Mendez had done in the intervening years, she wouldn't have been able to turn her Spartans into soldiers without him. "So how did you actually select the Threes?"

He looked up slowly. "Is this going to be about me betraying you and helping Ackerson hijack your project? Because if it is—"

"I was just asking," she said. "Because I want to know."

"Well, you know we didn't select them on the basis of perfect genomes," he said. Halsey had suspended the second tranche of the Spartan program because she'd run out of candidates with the ideal genetic profile. She knew he wasn't going to let her forget it. "They were all orphans. No qualification beyond the Covenant slaughtering their entire family. We asked them if they wanted to get their revenge, and we took the ones who said yes." He put his cigar back in his belt pouch, but he was staring right into her face. "We took *volunteers*. We enhanced them some, but we took whatever we could get, and they turned out fine."

"No filtering at all?" A six-year-old couldn't possibly understand combat enough to volunteer, but she didn't want to start a pissing contest with him over ethics, not in front of the Spartans. "Not even genetic screening?"

"You think it's all about genes, Doctor? The Spartans that I trained were made from random, raw, imperfect humanity. But by God, they were *motivated*. And that's what it's all about. A state of mind."

Halsey wanted to resist a debate, but if she'd just nodded and smiled it would have made him just as angry. "If that were true, then we wouldn't have needed the Spartan program. Exceptional genes create an advantage in any field."

"What was it you said to me once? Genome is the blueprint, environment and training is the engineer. *Phenotype*."

"Yes, but—"

"I realize you need justification, but your history isn't up to your science," Mendez growled. "The most successful special forces in history weren't genetic supermen. They were every damn size and shape, every age, and some of them weren't even especially fit, but they all had one thing that made them great commandos. They *believed* they could do anything, and then they went out and *did* it."

Mendez always knew where to strike to disable. It was part of his training. He could wound psychologically just as well as he could place a fist or a blade.

My research mattered. My research made a difference. Don't you give me that commando state of mind *bullshit, don't you dare . . .*

"But you let Kurt tamper with their neurobiology, so what kind of state of mind is that?" Halsey defended herself. Why the hell should she take this? She'd dedicated her entire life to the defense of Earth and its colonies, surrendering any chance of the kind of normal family life that other women took for granted. "And that was made illegal years ago."

"So was goddamn kidnapping and using nonconsenting humans in medical experiments, Doctor, but I never noticed that stopping *you.*"

Her attempt to reestablish diplomatic relations with Mendez had crashed and burned inside minutes. She was fuming. *You could have chosen to put it aside, Chief, but you didn't. You found the first chance to take a pop at me.* She was suddenly aware of the Spartans in her peripheral vision, frozen in position and watching warily. When she turned, what she saw troubled her. Her Spartans were standing in a knot, and Mendez's were sitting on the other side of the fire. She got the feeling that it was about more than just sticking with the people you'd known all your life.

Olivia called to them. "This fish is going to be ready soon," she said, ever the diplomat. "If you want to stake your claim, you better get over here."

If there had been cold beer and good humor, Halsey reflected, it would have been a pleasant barbecue. Everyone settled down and ate in silence for a while. Eventually Mendez licked his fingers and wiped them on one of the large leaves that did duty as plates.

"As long as she's got water, she can last a couple of weeks

without food," he said. He didn't need to say the word *Lucy*. "So how far have you got, Doctor?"

"Well, the more I translate, the more I see an environment that can be tailored to the needs of any species." Halsey took refuge in a neutral topic. "What I've not worked out yet is how they would divide up the planet into different ecosystems for different species, but they're the Forerunners. If they can build a Dyson sphere like this and a Halo Array, then compartmentalizing atmospheres would probably be very simple housekeeping for them."

"So, whatever was moving around in the corridor before we lost Lucy," Mark said. "Is it possible that another species landed in here just like we did?"

Halsey liked to think of this as a tactical withdrawal into the only safe space between them and the Covenant rather than blundering in. But she knew there was always the chance that they were in over their heads. Even if—even *when*—she shook all the facts and information out of this place, there was no guarantee that they would ever find a way out. Perhaps the Forerunners had given up on colonizing the galaxy and had decided to sit tight on one safe, barricaded world for the rest of time.

"I'd be lying if I said no," Halsey said at last.

Normal conversation didn't resume. All the Spartans had heard every word that Halsey and Mendez had said, and now there was no use pretending that the pair of them weren't wrestling with battered, painful consciences.

"I still got a couple of panels to analyze," Halsey said, getting to her feet and finding that her knees were a lot less flexible than she remembered. Once she could have stood up from a cross-legged position in one fluid movement, but that time was long gone. "Better crack on with the task. I'll leave you to wash the dishes."

Kelly tossed some of the large leaves on the fire. "Dishes done," she said.

Halsey went back into the tower and framed up the shots on her datapad, moving the device back and forth until she was satisfied that all the symbols on the panel were clear enough for the program to interpret. She sat down in the corner, back against the smooth, cool stone, and started tapping out the beginning of another journal while the program ran its course. No, it really wasn't like a decent pencil on honest paper. But it would have to do.

The analysis eventually chirped to let her know it had done the best it could. When she looked at the screen there were still some gaps that were proving hard to pin down. Normally her attention would have gone straight to the missing words, but something else grabbed her and that was the word *vessels.*

She looked at the components of the symbol, the equivalent of speech phonemes, and she had to agree with the program. One particular symbol had to mean transport of some kind. Suddenly the information fell into place.

The panel appeared to be instructions for decontaminating vessels with possible Flood contagion. There was a mention of the word that the program interpreted intriguingly as either *barn* or *tomb,* but that she suspected was *garage.*

Or storehouse. Or sarcophagus. Or mausoleum—perhaps they liked to have their possessions in their tombs, like we once did.

No, she settled on garage. Somewhere around here, there was either a cache of existing vessels, or the facilities for maintaining them, and that would need to be enormous. The panel didn't say where it was, but it certainly hinted at what might have happened to Lucy.

"Chief?" She got up and went in search of Mendez. "Chief, have you seen anything above ground that looks like a garage?"

Utility area, Dyson sphere, Onyx:
local date November 2552.

Lucy stood in front of the screen, trying to phrase her problem in a way that Prone to Drift would understand.

His two friends—Refill Needed and Effortlessly Buoyant—didn't seem to be interested in the conversation and were working their way through her rucksack again. When she glanced their way, she saw that they'd reshaped the composite backpack into a more streamlined shape that slotted onto her armor more neatly. She'd thought they would want to help her, but whoever had reported that their only interest in life was fixing things had been absolutely right.

Prone persisted though. He kept returning to another screen on the other side of the room, flicking through lists of symbols as if he was searching for something. Lucy tried to work out how to get him to focus on her. She went up to him and tapped him on the back of his carapace, forcing him to turn around. She pointed at her screen and tapped furiously.

LET ME OUT, Lucy wrote. PLEASE.

Prone considered the words, head tilting back and forth. WHY?

MY FRIENDS ARE WAITING FOR ME, Lucy responded.

WE KNOW.

LET ME FIND THEM.

NOT YET, Prone replied.

I MUST CONTACT—Lucy paused. She had no cast-iron guarantee that the war was over. Could she risk mentioning Earth? Could the Huragok send signals outside this sphere, or were they just monitoring the situation with sensors on its surface?

She started on a new line, in too much of a hurry to ask how she could delete what she'd written. I MUST LET MY HOME WORLD KNOW WHERE WE ARE.

Well, if nothing else, she was relearning how to form sentences. That was something, even if she couldn't yet work out why Prone was being uncooperative. They didn't take prisoners—or at least the Covenant ones didn't. She might have been making too big an assumption about this group of Engineers.

Prone started to drift off again, but she caught one of his tentacles and steered him back to the screen.

HOW LONG HAVE YOU BEEN HERE? she wrote.

SINCE I WAS MADE.

HOW LONG IN MY YEARS? She wasn't sure if that would make any sense to him. A year on Earth wasn't the same length as a year on a colony world, and her years were always based on a military calendar of 365 days, twenty-four-hour Earth days on Zulu time, a relic of a world that wasn't hers because UNSC was Earth in culture, loyalty, and administrative habit. She could remember the name of the town she came from, but not the planet.

DO YOU KNOW ABOUT THE WAR?

Lucy knew the Dyson sphere had been sealed for a long time, or else the UNSC teams who'd been on Onyx for sixty years would probably have found it. The Engineers had been down here since before first contact with the Covenant. Prone seemed distracted for a moment.

THAT WAS A LONG TIME AGO, he said.

Lucy struggled with that answer. Halsey had said that time inside the Dyson sphere was elapsing at a slower rate than in normal space, but she didn't know exactly how much more slowly. A terrible thought occurred to Lucy. Maybe the relative time here was so slowed that hundreds or even thousands of years had passed outside, and even if the Halo hadn't fired, then everything and everyone she knew was already long gone.

How could she get an answer out of Prone that she could

understand? She shared one common unit of time with him, and that was this artificial world.

HOW LONG? she asked again. IN ONYX DAYS. WE CALL THIS PLACE ONYX.

The years had been longer here, but the days were very close in length to Earth's, one of the factors that got the colonists' interest. Earth-bred crop varieties could grow in their natural cycles without much modification.

Does Prone know there was a planet outside here though? Come on, he's an Engineer running a Forerunner bunker. Of course he knows.

She wasn't sure what the length of the day was inside the sphere, but she knew it wasn't ten hours or anything that would give her an answer that was too far off the mark. Prone paused, then scribbled some symbols on the glass.

37000000

She counted the zeroes. That couldn't be right. IN WORDS, she responded. ONE, TWO, THREE?

Prone got it right away. THIRTY-SEVEN MILLION.

Lucy had to stop and reread it. Was he really saying 37 million days? That was . . . she shut her eyes to move the decimal place and get a rough idea of the years.

She made that a hundred thousand.

Oh God. Oh God, no. We've been in here that long?

It hadn't been much of a world, and her life had been miserable, but she wasn't ready to turn her back on all that it had been. Now she definitely had to make sure Halsey got this information.

I HAVE TO GET OUT, Lucy wrote. NOW.

She could feel her throat tightening and an awful pressure building up at the roof of her mouth. Her eyes brimmed. She was going to burst into tears. She'd always managed to hold it together in combat, but being ripped out of time wasn't something she was prepared for at all.

Prone seemed to notice. He fussed over her with his cilia. He might just have been trying to take samples of her tears because he didn't know what they were, but she preferred to think that he was being kind.

I MUST RESTORE YOU, he wrote.

They were communicating in English, but that didn't necessarily mean that they were using words the same way. Maybe it was her: maybe she really wasn't making sense, however sane she sounded to herself.

RESTORE WHAT? she asked.

RECLAIMER, he said.

Prone drifted away to gaze at his own screen for a while. Then he flashed up some diagrams. She thought he was bored and that his attention had drifted back to machines, but every few minutes he would float across and put the flat paddlelike end of one tentacle on her cheek. She felt a tickling sensation every time the cilia touched her skin. Now that he thought the Flood hadn't overrun the galaxy and the Halo hadn't fired, he seemed to believe the crisis was over—*one hundred thousand years* over.

Well, hers wasn't. She had to make him understand that. She walked up behind him, intending to grab him if she had to, but she found herself looking at the schematic on the screen that was occupying him. It looked like a complex wiring loom, a closed system with dense networks in a couple of places and long, much thicker routing connecting them.

No, that wasn't right. Some of the routing looked vaguely familiar.

Lucy took a few steps back so that the detail blurred and she could get a sense of the overall shape. Then it struck her. She had to cast her mind back to the earliest period of her training on Onyx. She was seven or eight years old, grappling with subjects she'd never had to worry about at school, and she was trying to copy a diagram from a biology text.

Human circulation. It's the human circulatory system.

It was now obvious, an outline almost like an elongated figure of eight or an infinity symbol, the classic stylized diagram that had appeared in anatomy references for centuries.

She tugged at one of Prone's free arms and tried to get his attention back on the writing screen.

WHY CIRCULATION? she wrote.

TO HELP ME REPAIR YOU.

Lucy now knew where this was going. Prone reached out to one side of the workshop, a flurry of tentacles and cilia, and whipped out a small spatula and a gray cylinder exactly like the ones that had been stalking the squad outside. She was ready to trust him with anything now.

HOLD OUT YOUR HAND, he wrote.

She had nothing to lose. The more he knew about her, the more chance she stood of explaining her situation. She thrust her hand out, palm up, and he drew the spatula across the skin. The gray cylinder drifted free and hung in front of her for a few seconds. Then it moved off and merged into what she'd thought was just a wall. Prone turned away and studied the circulation diagram again. More symbols were appearing on it, one at time. He spent a few moments prodding the screen and watching the display change, then turned to her, making little burbling noises like a stream. His head tilted back and forth as if he was working out what to say.

YOU ARE WELL. WHY ARE YOU SILENT?

He reached out and put a tentacle on the top of her head. Lucy took it as a comforting gesture at first, like patting a dog, but then she had another thought: *Is he analyzing me?* The cilia on Engineers' tentacles obviously provided more than just a sense of touch at what seemed to be a molecular level. Maybe they could detect electrical activity through them, too, and perhaps Prone was just doing an EEG, not being kind to her.

He withdrew and wrote on the screen again. NOT BALANCED, BUT SPEECH CENTER IS UNDAMAGED. WHY CAN I NOT REPAIR YOU?

It was a very good question. Lucy chewed over the *not balanced* bit before responding. I'M NOT BROKEN.

YOU ARE VERY BROKEN LUCY-B902. RECLAIMERS SPEAK.

It was one thing trying to explain things she understood. All she had to do was find the words, and that was coming back to her faster than she'd expected. But her inability to talk was something else entirely. All the rationalizations she gave herself didn't explain why she couldn't snap out of this when she absolutely needed to.

NOT BALANCED? she asked.

MORE SCARED AND ANGRY THAN YOU NEED TO BE. BUT WHY DO YOU NOT TALK?

That summed up her existence. Prone was a pretty good psychiatrist. Maybe that was all part of his duties. The Engineers here looked more like an emergency team than ever, maintaining the bunker and repairing everyone and everything that came to shelter here.

BECAUSE IT'S IN MY HEAD, she wrote. This was suddenly getting very uncomfortable. FEELINGS.

EXPLAIN TO ME. WHY?

Sometimes just thinking it was the hardest thing of all. Lucy put her finger on the glass screen and paused, watching the letters fading in and out uncertainly while she struggled to pin down the awful thing that lurked in her mind, the monster under the bed that she didn't dare look at in case it saw her and turned to scream the awful truth at her.

She found herself pressing her finger against the glass so hard that her forefinger turned yellow and bloodless.

Say it. Write it. Admit it. Face it.

Prone wasn't human. She knew he wouldn't judge her. He didn't even seem capable of being hostile to her for killing his friend. If there was anyone she could lean on to face this moment, it was him.

She paused and realized her eyes were brimming with hot tears, blinding her to what was on the screen. She wiped them with the heel of her free hand, scared that if she took her finger off that keyboard that she would never touch it again, just as she had given up speaking, and then she would sink inside herself forever.

BECAUSE I'M ALIVE AND MY FRIENDS ARE DEAD. I SHOULD BE DEAD TOO. Lucy looked at the words, stark and accusing with a life of their own. It was very different to having them hidden in her head. MY FAMILY IS DEAD. MY FRIENDS ARE DEAD. I COULDN'T SAVE ANYONE AND I DON'T DESERVE TO BE HERE WHEN THEY'RE NOT.

The effort almost stopped her breathing. But the words were out now and she stared at them, letting the reality sink in. Prone made odd little cooing sounds like a very distant pigeon.

BUT THEY ARE NOT ALL DEAD. THEY ARE IN THE CITADEL.

Lucy's eyes were fixed on the lines of text, her own miserable failure and guilt now public for all to see. Just as she couldn't force herself to jump off the ledge and speak, she now couldn't look away from the black letters floating in front of her. Prone slid his tentacle under her chin and forced her to face him. He was a lot stronger than she imagined. She couldn't actually pull back from him, even though he wasn't hurting her.

YOU ARE THE FIRST THING I CANNOT REPAIR. His bioluminescence suddenly seemed a lot brighter. PERHAPS YOUR FRIENDS CAN.

Lucy now realized why he was forcing her to look away. He wasn't trying to stop her from wallowing in her own misery. He was trying to get her to look at something else. Spread across the far wall was a composite image of a city, all towers and deserted roads, and one fragment of the image seemed to be the viewpoint of a floating camera drifting down a street. It was looking head-on at Chief Mendez and Fred, flanked by the rest of her squad and Blue Team, walking in silence with a resigned set to their shoulders.

But then Mendez spoke, as if he'd been arguing with himself and couldn't keep it in any longer. "Goddamn it, we *will* find her. She's only been gone four days. She's a *survivor*. She knows we won't stop looking for her."

Four days? Four *days*? Lucy was certain she'd only been in here for *hours*. This place had to be another slipspace pocket. How many dimensional layers were there in this sphere?

She pulled away from Prone and tapped frantically in the text screen. PLEASE. TAKE ME TO THEM.

WILL THEY HURT US? he asked.

Lucy grabbed his tentacle. He almost jerked away, but he seemed to be getting used to her now. She reached back to the screen with her free hand.

I WON'T LET ANYONE HURT YOU. It didn't seem enough. She tried to underline ANYONE with emphatic strokes but the marks didn't appear.

Prone cocked his head to one side as if he was weighing up the odds.

I KNOW, he said, and led her through the workshop.

CHAPTER 12

I WANT A COMPLETE EM CORDON AROUND THAT ANOMA-
LY. I DON'T WANT ANYONE ELSE TO KNOW IT'S THERE, AND
I DON'T WANT ANY SIGNALS IN OR OUT. YOU KEEP THAT
DAMN THING UNDER SIGNAL LOCKDOWN, AND IF YOU HEAR
SO MUCH AS A SNEEZE FROM IT, THEN YOU ABSOLUTELY
DO NOT RESPOND TO IT OR INDICATE YOUR PRESENCE IN
ANY WAY. COMMUNICATION WILL BE CONDUCTED ENTIRELY
THROUGH ME.
(Admiral Margaret O. Parangosky, CINCONI, to the CO of UNSC *Glamorgan*,
on the discovery of the transdimensional
object near the Onyx coordinates)

UNSC *PORT STANLEY:* February 2553.

"I still think we should pay Venezia a visit." Vaz leaned out
of the compartment to check if the door to Osman's day
cabin was still shut. "Although one Shiva wouldn't be
enough to glass them, would it?"

"Maybe 'Telcam can oblige," Mal said. He was stirring

something in a bowl, a brown paste that looked like baby food. "Now that he's got a warship and everything. No point having dodgy hinge-head friends if you can't use them."

Vaz peered into the bowl. "What's that?"

"BB's special recipe." Mal stuck his finger in the sludge and tasted it, but he didn't pull a face so Vaz took that as approval. "Actually, it tastes like yeast extract with sugar in it. Sort of salty and malty." He held out the container in Adj's direction. "Come on, Adj. Nom nom. Nummy yeast stuff."

Adj seemed tempted and floated across to take the container. He looked into it, cocking his head.

"You need a spoon or something?" Mal pulled one out of his pocket. "Go on. Dig in."

Adj took the spoon and the container and drifted into a corner behind one of the duct runs, enchantingly harmless. Vaz was starting to worry what would happen to him when he was handed over to ONI. A ferociously disloyal and undisciplined thought crossed his mind, but he pushed it away. Mal was right. If UNSC had grabbed a few more Engineers early in the war, things would have been very different. It was clear now that the Covenant wouldn't have been half so powerful without them. They were all struggling to change their own lightbulbs now.

Osman's door clicked, a warning that it was going to open. She emerged with an odd expression on her face that Vaz interpreted as a sort of wistful satisfaction, like some good news had arrived a little too late.

She caught him watching. "Why don't you all grab a coffee and close up on the bridge in five minutes?" she said, more of a friendly invitation than an order. "I've got some interesting information from Sydney."

Mal raised his eyebrows discreetly at Vaz and turned to

whisper. "Phillips reckons that Admiral Hood's planning to visit the hinge-heads, judging by the chatter he's picking up. Maybe we'll have to provide close protection for him. I do love a bit of irony in my life."

BB must have been doing a discreet roundup. Naomi, Devereaux, and Phillips joined them on the bridge, looking as if they were expecting what Mal referred to as a serious bollocking. Vaz found it hard to imagine Osman bollocking anybody. Vaz suspected that her style was much more like Parangosky's: either a look of quiet disapproval for the small mistakes, or a single round that you never saw coming for the really *big* misjudgments. Shouting didn't seem to be the ONI style.

BB settled on the comms console and didn't say a word.

"Do you want me to give you a long explanatory preamble to this, or would you rather I just plunged straight in?" Osman asked. "You're free to stop me and ask questions."

"We're really good with plunging in, ma'am," Mal said. "As long as there's no complicated physics in it."

Osman almost smiled. "I'll add clairvoyance to your list of ad-quals, Staff. Yes, there's a little bit of physics. It's a mixed bag, so I'll deal with the bad news first." She looked at Naomi. "There's a memorial dedication at Voi next month, and you'll know some of the names on it. I'm afraid the Master Chief's one of them."

Vaz didn't know much about Spartan politics apart from the rapid acquaint of the last few weeks, but he did know who the Master Chief was. He could only imagine how hard that news hit Naomi. He tried not to stare at her, but it seemed cowardly not to look the woman in the eye and remind her she was among friends. She didn't move a muscle. It was hard to tell if any blood had drained from that porcelain-white face, but she glanced down for a second and clasped her hands in her lap.

"I thought he was listed as missing, ma'am."

Osman seemed to be picking each word with absolute precision. Vaz detected a slight shift in tone now, slowing and lowering pitch, like she was making a statement. "Yes, dead Spartans always are, and we can still hope that he's out there somewhere, but we've got to be realistic."

"I assume there's no news on Kelly, Linda . . . Fred?"

"Nothing concrete that I can tell you yet. The other name that's going to bother you is Catherine Halsey. UNSC's now declared her dead so that they can release records. Nobody who was left on Reach could have survived. Anyway, I'm sorry that we've lost some good people."

Osman didn't indicate whether she thought Halsey was one of them. Vaz got the feeling that he was missing something. He turned his head as casually as he could, just to check if there was a spark of that same doubt on anyone else's face, but he couldn't tell. He was drinking too much of that ONI coffee. Maybe that stuff was specially blended to keep their field operatives at maximum paranoia.

Osman went on regardless. "Now, the rest of the business. Admiral Hood's planning to visit Sanghelios for talks with the Arbiter, so we'll be standing by to keep an eye on that. We might also end up diverted to the Onyx sector to assist with an anomaly." Osman seemed to be focused on Naomi, so maybe she was worried about her reaction to the news about the Master Chief. "Okay, Onyx isn't a secret. You've probably worked out one way or another that Parangosky quarantined it for our own extremely dodgy purposes, but the planet isn't there anymore. It broke up. It was a Forerunner satellite made of millions of defensive robotic constructs, but we think there's a slipspace shelter at the core that survived the destruction."

"And we need to acquire the technology," Mal said.

"Probably, but we might have UNSC personnel trapped there in need of extraction, and I think that'll interest us more. Any questions?"

"Do we know who?" Devereaux asked.

"Maybe," Osman said, suddenly very ONI again.

Vaz decided to change the subject to something that was gnawing at him. "This business with Admiral Hood, ma'am. If this is all part of a peace treaty, how does that affect our mission?"

"It doesn't," Osman said. "And it doesn't make any difference if the Arbiter is completely genuine, shakes Hood's hand, and asks him to marry his sister. We know damn well that the Arbiter doesn't speak for all Sangheili, let alone the rest of the assorted rabble out there. So we carry on, and if Hood manages to charm the pants off of the hinge-heads, then that's terrific. But if he doesn't, then we're still there in the background making sure that we never have to go through this again."

"And should we know who Halsey is?"

"Chief scientist at ONI," Osman said. Vaz decided she had some serious issues with this Halsey, judging by the set of her jaw. "Creator of the Spartan program. It's only fair to warn you that there'll be some unpleasant revelations emerging about her. Brilliant, yes, and the Spartans changed the course of the war, but her methods left a lot to be desired. History might not judge her kindly."

Naomi wouldn't have made a very good poker player. She might have been able to keep up that unblinking Spartan stoicism for a while, but Vaz had learned to spot the small giveaway gestures. He could see her pressing her lips together more tightly with every mention of Halsey's name.

"And how will *you* judge her, Captain?" Mal asked.

Osman shrugged. "If I tell you, I have to reveal classified information—and I'm not keeping that from you because it's classified, but because it's extremely personal, and I think I'd like to talk to Naomi privately before the rest of you hear it."

You could have cut the tension on that bridge with a blunt plastic butter knife. Vaz interpreted it as a suggestion to get lost and leave Osman and Naomi to have a girl-to-girl chat.

"You're always pretty straight with us, ma'am," Devereaux said. "I'm not brown-nosing, but we want you to know that we appreciate it."

Osman folded her arms, not so much defensive as looking like she wanted to curl up and hide, and she wasn't the shrinking violet type. There was definitely something else going on here.

"If I ask you to put your lives on the line, the least I can do is to tell you as much of the truth as I can," she said. "I know I often ask your opinion rather than give you clear orders, but that's because you've all got a hell of a lot more combat experience than me, and I respect and trust your judgment. So if you ever think I'm screwing up on a biblical scale, I want you to tell me so."

Some marines liked cast-iron certainty in an officer, but Vaz was happy to settle for intelligent honesty. Officers who knew what they *didn't* know were rare gems. He realized he was willing to do just about any damn thing she asked him to. Maybe that was the intention. She was Parangosky's protégé, after all, and he couldn't imagine the old girl picking someone who couldn't get the best out of her people.

No. Sometimes you have to accept that people mean what they say.

Likeable officer or not, she still had to do some difficult stuff with Naomi. "Okay, people, dismiss," she said. "We need a little while to talk, me and Naomi."

Mal herded everyone down to the hangar deck, as much

distance as he could give anyone in this ship. Adj followed them and hung around, fondling the equipment in the small comms workstation that Phillips had set up to one side of the deck.

"I know you're there, BB." Mal looked up at the deckhead. "Just be a good mate and let us know what we can do for Naomi, will you? Because I know bad news when I see it."

BB's avatar appeared below the gantry. "Now you know why the captain's been telling you so much about the Spartan program. The end of a war's as good a time as any to take a serious look at the unsavory things we've done."

"Yeah, that's a lot easier now that this Halsey woman's dead," Vaz said, trying to imagine what could possibly be worse than kidnapping six-year-olds and shooting them up with hormones and ceramic implants. "Very convenient of her. Always best not to mention it while they're alive and can still name names."

"You're a rather cynical young man, Vasily," BB said. "Very well, I promise I'll keep you up to speed on Naomi—with her consent."

BB disappeared and the three ODSTs stood there in silence with Phillips. Vaz was suddenly aware of pinging and scratching noises coming out of Phillips's comms workstation. Whatever Adj was doing, he was *un*-vandalizing the equipment with enthusiasm.

"Busy little guy, isn't he?" Phillips said, going to check on the frantic remodeling. "Okay, okay, I'll keep him out of the main systems."

"Osman's okay," Mal said. "Good sort."

Vaz shrugged. "She's half Spartan."

"Yeah," said Devereaux. "But the other half is purebred spook. That's not the kind of pet you can trust with your kids."

"I don't care," Vaz said. "I like her. And what the hell are *we* now, anyway?"

Vaz didn't know how long Osman talked to Naomi, but it was a couple of hours before the Spartan came down to the hangar. She looked as if nothing had happened. But then she was pretty good at battening down the hatches as long as she had a few moments to compose herself before she had to face everyone. It was all part of the psychology of spending a lot of time with your face obscured behind a visor, something Vaz understood all too well. He passed her on the way to the heads and gave her a you-can-talk-to-me look, holding eye contact for a few extra seconds.

"How's it going?" he asked.

"I'm still working that out," she said, and disappeared into the Mjolnir compartment.

"We're here whenever you want to talk," Vaz said, but he wasn't sure if she heard him.

For the next twenty-four hours everything fell back into the daily routine of monitoring voice traffic and gathering intelligence. *Port Stanley* was doing the ship equivalent of an ODST's "hard routine"—carrying out surveillance under the enemy's nose, hiding in the bushes in total silence for weeks at a time without even a smoke or a cooked meal for comfort—except that she didn't need bushes, she didn't get leg cramps, and she didn't get distracted by the need to take a leak. Vaz had carried out way too much recon and FAC behind enemy lines to feel less of a man for doing it the ONI way. He could brew a pot of coffee and have a good scratch while he watched the data come in.

It would have been better to have someone on the ground as well, on Sanghelios itself, but it was hard to pass yourself off as a hinge-head when everyone around you was a meter taller. Vaz tried to think creatively about ways to infiltrate the keeps.

He sat at one of the workstations on the bridge, noting the occasional movement of Sangheili ships between their various orbital shipyards and the two moons, Suban and Qikost. There was a lot of traffic, but certainly nothing to suggest that they were attempting to rearm or regroup. If anything it seemed more like a free-for-all, with ships disappearing to scattered locations across the planet, something that Phillips confirmed from the radio chatter.

"It's really quite sad." Phillips was lounging at the console a couple of seats away with his feet up on another seat, one hand to his earpiece. "They've been this amazing military culture for thousands of years, but now the San'Shyuum have gone they're running out of equipment and motivation. The kaidons are just taking whatever ships and equipment they can find and stashing it in their own cities."

"Can't stop fighting men from fighting," Vaz said. "That sounds like a recipe for civil war without any intervention from us."

Phillips shook his head. "Don't underestimate the charismatic power of an Arbiter, especially 'Vadam. What I can't work out is just how much fighting there was on Sanghelios itself when he split from the Covenant. 'Telcam says they're still factionalized, but he omits to tell me just how much damage was done in the fighting."

"You want to get down there and take a look, don't you?"

"Don't *you*?"

"Only through my scope. Just before I squeeze one off."

"But it's a fascinating, ancient culture."

"It's a fortress full of angry hinge-heads who still think we're bacteria."

"You know, travel broadens the—" Phillips stopped dead and swung his boots off the seat to lean on the console and concentrate on a transmission coming in. "Okay, Vaz, quiet. It's 'Telcam, and remember that he understands every word we say."

"Yes. Just like my gran's dog."

'Telcam called in as regularly now as any UNSC operating base. It seemed to take him a few days to collect arms, get them back home, and distribute them before asking for the next batch. Osman's policy was to drip-feed him anyway, and Vaz understood the wisdom of sneaking weapons in a few at a time in dozens of different vessels rather than risk losing everything in a single intercepted shipment.

But maybe his missus had told him that he couldn't store the stuff in the garage. Sangheili had wives too.

What's everyone else on Sanghelios doing? They can't all be in the army. Phillips has a point. I bet he'd wet himself with excitement if someone offered him a trip down there.

Phillips listened intently for a while, grunting "Yes, I'll do that," now and again, then pushed himself back from the console, brandishing his datapad. BB materialized beside him.

"You'd make a *wonderful* receptionist," BB said. "Go on, give the message to the captain."

Phillips looked at BB and smiled. "Pizza with all the toppings for Mister 'Telcam, I think."

Vaz wondered if Naomi fancied a run ashore after being cooped up in *Stanley* for so long. Even the glasslands were starting to look like a day out now, regardless of how well-stocked the wardroom galley was or how many creature comforts the ship provided. ONI didn't believe in roughing it. Vaz went to find her.

She was tinkering with her helmet, something that really didn't need doing if that armor fixed itself. She glanced up at him.

"Lid okay?" he asked.

"Lighter than the old model. Mark Seven. New supplier."

"You get all the best kit."

Naomi took a breath. It wasn't impatience. It looked more like embarrassment. "Look, I know you're being kind," she said. "And just because I'm not very talkative, it doesn't mean I don't appreciate it."

"So are you coming?"

"Why not? They say Spartans need to get out more."

She'd tell him what was troubling her in her own good time. He just couldn't imagine what would disturb a Spartan.

But whatever it was, it had something to do with that Halsey woman.

Bekan quarry, Mdama, Sanghelios.

Raia looked over *Unflinching Resolve* from a distance but declined to step on board. Jul was a little disappointed. She'd never seen his world before and he'd hoped she might understand him better if she saw how he lived while he was away from home.

"Are you sure it's a good idea to move this ship?" she asked, turning to Buran and Forze. "Many shipmasters have reclaimed their vessels and taken them back to their keeps, from what I hear. I doubt anyone would find it suspicious now."

Buran shrugged and shot a glance at Jul. "Ask your husband. He's the one who's worried that traitors know these coordinates. The worst that can happen is that some worthless Kig-Yar and a few civilian humans know this location. So? What are they going to do about it?"

"They could trade the information," Jul said. "And they managed to board *Piety* and kill the crew, so we have no guarantee that they didn't make a note of her course from the nav computer."

Information was frequently currency, and it was always power, but there were times when Jul knew it could be both a weapon and a liability. 'Telcam said he picked up weapons shipments on a cleansed human colony world. It made sense to take the frigate there, wherever it was. Jul wondered if he was being selfish for putting his fear for his clan above the necessity of his duty, but there was such a thing as not risking the lives of the uninvolved any more than he had to. The rest of his brethren would face the Arbiter's vengeance if his coup failed.

"If you're asking me, I think it's a good idea to move her too," said Forze. "There's no more defensible base than the one the enemy doesn't know about."

"So where *is* this secret hiding place, then?" Raia asked. Her tone suggested that she thought it was all a childish prank, that this brave talk of overthrowing the Arbiter was turning into a hobby to make them feel like warriors again. "Seeing as your revolutionary headquarters is a temple right in the middle of one of the most heavily populated states on the planet."

"I don't know where it is," Jul said. "But it's a planet that was cleansed of humans, so perhaps nobody pays any attention to it. I would still like to know where it is."

'Telcam was due to arrive shortly. Jul had begun to feel he spent his entire existence waiting for the monk to show up without explanation, but then he supposed that was the nature of an underground movement. There would come a point, though, when Jul would no longer be willing to take things on trust. He was a shipmaster: he was used to setting courses and giving orders, not trailing along in the wake of others. If things didn't start to move more rapidly, then he would reconsider his plans. The longer the Arbiter was left to soothe and cajole the population into accepting a false peace with the humans, the harder it would be to galvanize them into action before the inevitable happened.

"Well, I have real work to do," Raia said, turning to go back to the keep. "I'm sure you'll let me know when something decisive and manly has taken place."

Buran watched her go and turned back to Jul with a wary swing of his head. "Perhaps we should unleash our wives on the Arbiter," he said. "They could glower at him until he concedes defeat. It would certainly be effective against me."

It was Buran's ship and he could take it back any time he pleased, but he seemed persuaded by 'Telcam. Jul paced up and down, wondering again how the great Sangheili nation had come to this shambling indecisiveness. Eventually the sound of another shuttle rumbled in the still country air and announced the monk's arrival.

Jul identified it as a small military transport this time, one of the old but still serviceable Contrition-class. Seeing the ship appear over the top of the quarry and confirm his identification gave him a little satisfaction.

'Telcam stepped down from the shuttle and opened the cargo door. "I have just one warhead today, brothers. I believe we can move that without the assistance of Jiralhanae." He had a very eloquent way of telling them to roll up their sleeves and get working. "But I have another collection to make now, so we will have many more new rifles tomorrow."

"I think we should move *Unflinching Resolve* to another location," Jul said, walking up the loading ramp to take one end of the lift-loader.

'Telcam looked past him at Buran. "Do you share that opinion?"

Buran shrugged. "There's a lot to be said for covert bases, but it depends on how far your little hiding place is."

'Telcam looked at them more as if he was deciding which of them would be the biggest troublemaker.

"Where *is* this place of yours?" Jul asked.

"I promised my suppliers that I would keep our rendezvous

point to myself," 'Telcam said. "It's not a matter of individual trust. We've now seen what the Kig-Yar can do with a little help from humans when they put their minds to it. What nobody else knows cannot be accidentally discovered."

Did he just insult us? Jul wasn't sure. He hesitated to call a devout servant a liar, however eccentric he thought 'Telcam's religious views were, and he'd come to admire the monk's hardheaded warrior instinct. He'd risen to the rank of field master; he understood humans exceptionally well from his service as an interpreter. If anyone grasped the idea that humans would never stop spreading and would always be a threat, it was 'Telcam. But something in Jul's instinct told him that a little too much was being kept from him, considering the risk he was taking.

"I would like to come with you and assess this place," Jul said. "There's no reason why I can't accompany you, is there?"

'Telcam hesitated for just a fraction of a second too long. "My suppliers are very nervous, as you'll appreciate. I think they would be a little worried to see more Sangheili at the rendezvous point, especially ones they haven't learned to trust."

"Who are they?"

"Who do you think?"

"Tell me you're not trading with Kig-Yar. None of them can be trusted. Many of them are in league with humans, and the last thing we want is for humans to know how divided our people are."

'Telcam just looked at him, mildly disapproving. "I realize the incident with *Piety* has disturbed us, brother, but we've always known that Kig-Yar are unreliable, undisciplined, and without honor. Why this should unsettle you so much now I have no idea."

"This has already cost us a Huragok we sorely needed," Jul said, feeling a little childish for his retaliation. "I trust nobody these days."

'Telcam nodded politely. "Indeed. I understand."

Forze and Jul finished unloading the warhead, and 'Telcam got back into the shuttle. As the Contrition lifted off, Buran turned to Jul.

"He really doesn't want anyone else there when the handover takes place," Buran said. "I wonder if he trusts *us*. Or perhaps he thinks we're losing our nerve."

Jul made an instant decision—not a rash one, a *rapid* one—and turned to head back to the keep. "There's something I must do. I'll talk with you later."

"Jul, wait, we must talk—"

"*Later.*"

Once he was out of sight of the quarry, Jul broke into a run and made for the growing assortment of small vessels that had started to assemble at Bekan. Jul had to know where 'Telcam was going and who he was meeting, if only to have a fallback position if anything went wrong and 'Telcam failed to return one day.

The kind of creatures who would sell the monk weapons would just as easily betray him to someone else for a higher price. Jul fired up his shuttle's drive and took the routine flight path out of Mdama. If he was lucky, 'Telcam wouldn't be looking for vessels on his trail, and Jul could hang behind him at a discreet distance and perhaps even work out his destination without needing to land.

He set his shuttle to maintain a fixed distance behind the Contrition and sat back to study the sensor screens. After six hours, Jul decided 'Telcam was heading for the Narumad system, scattered with planets that humans referred to as *glasslands*. That was their disrespectful term for worlds that had felt the cleansing fire of a plasma bombardment sanctioned by the San'Shyuum.

As good a place as any to have an unnoticed rendezvous. And to hide warships, of course.

'Telcam's Contrition began to follow a more specific course two hours later. He was on a trajectory for a world that appeared on Jul's charts as Laqil, but that the humans had renamed New Llanelli. The colonists had managed to establish only a handful of sprawling settlements and it hadn't needed much attention to restore it to its prehuman state. Jul kept out of 'Telcam's visual range, tracking him on his screen, and landed in the lee of a hill about a kilometer from where the shuttle had touched down.

So now we'll see your shy associates. . . .

He moved from cover to cover and eventually caught sight of it, skylined by the glaring silver reflection of the vitrified plain beyond: a human dropship, sitting about a hundred meters from 'Telcam's vessel. So it *was* Kig-Yar, then. The vermin were pillaging everything they could find.

The human vessel was a cut above the average fruit of Kig-Yar looting though. It bristled with electronics masts that extended from a pod on top of the hull, which was a soft dark gray material so matte that it seemed more like fabric than metal.

They're getting very ambitious, our Kig-Yar friends. A rather expensive toy for them. Like the Huragok.

Jul shifted position and knelt among the scrubby bushes like a sly human. Even at this distance, he could hear 'Telcam's voice but he couldn't make out the words. He edged forward a meter at a time until he had a clear view of the commandeered human ship.

Now . . . I wasn't expecting that. . . .

A human pilot was sitting in the cockpit, a female with black hair and delicate features, fiddling with controls above the viewscreen. It confirmed his worst fears that the Kig-Yar and scattered human colonists had now found common cause in the aftermath of the Covenant's destruction. They were kindred spirits in too many ways. 'Telcam should have known better than to do business with them.

Jul was rehearsing how he would broach this error of judgment with the monk and still struggling with his disbelief about such crass naiveté when he saw someone get out of the dropship. It was another human female, but this was no opportunist from the civilian colonists. She walked with the confident authority of someone used to command. And she was wearing a UNSC uniform.

Was this official? Was this how the UNSC fought wars?

She might just be a corrupt officer lining her pockets. The war's over and nobody's checking the armory too closely.

Jul could hear them talking. He knew little of human languages, but 'Telcam—inevitably—was completely fluent in the one the UNSC used most frequently: English. Jul recognized the sounds even if the words meant nothing.

"I hear your Admiral Hood plans to visit the Arbiter," 'Telcam said. Whatever he was saying, he was a little uneasy with her. Jul could hear the lower note in his voice. "Would you like me to kill him for you, Captain?"

The female officer, one hand on her hip and the other on the holster of her sidearm, shook her head. "That's not how we do things, Field Master. It wouldn't serve either of our purposes."

"Your government is most subtle, Captain, but subtlety may well be the undoing of you. . . ."

Jul didn't hear the rest of the sentence. Something huge and heavy smashed into him from the side like a missile and knocked him flat on his back, winding him.

His helmet went flying. He struggled to get up, thinking there was some wild animal that he'd failed to take account of on this miserable planet, and then he found himself looking into the gold-mirrored face of a creature that wasn't quite as big as he'd thought it was.

It was one of the human demons, the soldiers they called Spartans.

Not only had it managed to ambush and bring him to the ground, but it also had him pinned down. He hesitated for a fraction of a second, giving it a moment to bring its fist down into his face.

The Spartan was many times heavier than any human Jul had ever swatted aside with the back of his hand. The powerful downward blow broke his teeth. He tried to yell a warning, but he couldn't, choking on tooth fragments and blood and struggling to dig his claws into impossibly hard armor.

The Spartan punched him a few more times as he tried to keep a grip on its throat. Then boots appeared on the ground around his head and something smashed into his skull once, twice, three times. Stunned, he still tried to pull free. But he was now pinned by several armored troops and he couldn't hang on to the Spartan any longer. Its knee was right across his throat. It could have crushed his windpipe, but it seemed to be waiting. Maybe it wanted to watch him choke to death as some vengeance for all the comrades it had lost to the Covenant. If that was the case, Jul wouldn't give it the satisfaction of reacting.

But how could I let this happen? How could humans possibly ambush me? Jul was close to asphyxiating. *I will die like a warrior. I will not let it see me give in.*

His arms were pinned. Although he was certain he was kicking furiously, he didn't seem to be connecting with anything. Were his legs obeying him? All he could do was gasp while his throat was filling up with blood and spittle.

"Spying on the Bishop. Tut tut." The voice came from one of

the others, not the Spartan, and it was male. "Hey, somebody get his helmet."

Jul knew he was losing consciousness when he found himself suddenly just *interested* in the faceless creature choking the life out of him. He'd never seen a Spartan in the flesh. The more gullible shipmasters said Spartans were brought back from the dead, repaired and resuscitated to fight again, and he'd always thought those wild exaggerations were cowards' excuses for losing battles. But this one was everything the rumors had said.

It took me down. Not a shot fired. And now it's killing me at its leisure.

Why don't they just kill me outright? Perhaps they can't.

He should have called out for help from 'Telcam, but it was too late. And 'Telcam was in league with them.

Jul had never thought he would be afraid to die. He'd faced death so many times that he was used to it, familiar with the flood of terrified excitement, certain that if the end came then his clan would know that he met his end with honor. But he'd never planned to face the great transcendence helpless and struggling, unable even to inflict damage in his dying moments. It was the worst possible disgrace. And disgrace terrified him far more than death.

The Spartan still had its knee on his throat, staring into his face. He could see his own reflection in its visor as the other soldiers bound him and one put a boot on his face to hold him down.

And if they shoot me, 'Telcam will hear. . . .

He had no idea of how long he lay there, but he fought to stay conscious. He had to escape. He had to stop 'Telcam.

The humans are manipulating you, 'Telcam. Whatever they've promised—they won't keep their word. What kind of fool are you? You think you can handle them? Fool. Idiot. Traitor.

But he heard the distant rumble of a ship starting its drives, a ship he could identify, the Contrition class transport, and then the sound peaked and faded. 'Telcam was gone. The Spartan put a pistol to his head. He could feel the cool metal resting between his eyes.

Jul made one last effort to get up and scream defiance, but he couldn't move and his only sound was a gurgle. He waited for the shot to come and put an end to his shame.

Only then did he think of Raia, who had no idea where he was. What would become of her?

The female shipmaster appeared, looking down at him. "Wait one, Naomi. Let me just check with the boss."

He had no idea what that meant. The Spartan pulled off its helmet with its free hand, and that was when he realized it was a woman, as bloodless and translucent as a hologram, her hair as pale as her skin—yes, a corpse brought back from the dead. He'd been taken down by *females*.

The shipmaster walked away. Jul, still struggling to breathe, couldn't hear what she was saying but she came back a short time later and stood over him. He could see her boots next to his head as she shifted her weight from one foot to the other. Her whole stance seemed casual, as if she had plenty of time to decide his fate and linger over his humiliation.

"Sorry, Staff, the Admiral says she'd really like a live prisoner for a change," she said. "Let's get him into the dropship. Then find his transport, rip what you can from it, and destroy it."

"This is like the voyage of the bloody *Beagle,* ma'am," said one of the male soldiers. "Another specimen for the menagerie."

The Spartan withdrew her pistol and shoved it in her belt before hauling him off like an animal, dragging him through the dirt with her two comrades.

Jul 'Mdama realized he had suddenly ceased to exist. He'd allowed himself to be taken by the enemy through his own stupidity, and as the humans hauled him toward the dropship, grunting and complaining about his weight, he understood that he was alone, and lost, and that nobody would ever come for him.

Forerunner Dyson sphere, Onyx:
local date November 2552.

In an empty world the size of a solar system, all you could do was look and keep looking.

Mendez would have dismissed Halsey's suggestion to look for a garage as too vague to be useful, but he was prepared to try any damn thing if it helped them find Lucy.

Hell, it's not as if we've got anything better to do with our time, is it?

Fred had reminded him just once that the mission was to acquire Forerunner technology for the UNSC. He knew damn well that however sensible a plan that was, it was only to keep them occupied—and if they found some handy gizmo, then they still had to work out how to call home and get it collected. Courier services were a little hard to come by in a dimensional bubble.

And there was no mission more important than finding a missing Spartan.

"Goddamn it, we *will* find her," Mendez said, as if anyone had suggested otherwise. It was his mantra to make sure it happened. The whole squad trailed down the road behind him in silence on yet another fruitless recon. "She's only been gone four days. She's a *survivor*. She knows we won't stop looking for her."

Mendez knew that no matter how disciplined troops were, their morale would take a hammering if they didn't stay busy.

The Spartans had gone from what HIGHCOM described in its mealy-mouthed way as "high tempo" operations—fighting pretty well every damn day, every week, every year—to a dead, silent stop. Basic survival was going to mop up a lot of their energy, but all they could do was stay alive for as long as possible until they worked out this place for themselves or until someone came along and found them.

Mendez needed to keep them busy.

Halsey might have been convinced the Earth had lost the war already and that they were the only sentient life left in the galaxy, but Mendez wasn't buying any of it. He'd believe that he'd lost when he heard the first clod of soil hit his coffin.

When they got back to the camp, Halsey was still in the lobby of the tower, going over the Forerunner symbols with her fingertips. "I'm wondering if there are more slipspace bubbles in this structure," she said absently. "You have to admit they're very effective shields for containing pathogens."

She seemed to be waiting for an answer, because she turned around and looked at him with a slight frown as if she expected some scholarly debate about transdimensional physics.

"Well, Doctor, we managed to get through one, so maybe we can get through another one as well," he said. "I'm just not sure where the goddamn door is."

Halsey spent a few more minutes messing around with the symbols, then hugged her datapad to her chest and walked out into the sunlight. Mendez stood with his arms folded, staring at the symbols, not giving a damn what they said and just wanting to be left alone for a while. Fred stayed behind with him.

"Sorry, Lieutenant," Mendez said. "I realize I'm a piss-poor example of leadership for you. But I need some bastard to shoot."

"That's what makes you so lovable, Chief," Fred said. "When you're killing something, we know you're happy."

Mendez turned around, about to tell Fred some of the things that were really troubling him, but he found himself looking past the Spartan and into the gloom of the corridor behind him. Fred had turned around too.

"Yeah, I heard it as well," Fred said.

He checked his rifle and edged into the darkness. Mendez switched on his tactical lamp and followed.

"Goddamn—"

He stared at the pale highlights of a small face apparently bobbing along without any sign of a body. It took his brain a second to register that it was Lucy minus her helmet, and that her reactive camo was trying to match the shadows in the tunnel. Then he saw the constellation of blue and violet lights behind her.

"Hey, Lucy, who's your new boyfriend?" Fred asked.

Lucy walked out of the darkness like a ghost with a Covenant Engineer trailing behind her. Well, that explained what she'd been chasing. As intruders went, an Engineer was a pretty useful one. Mendez savored the relief.

"Damn it, Lucy, we were worried sick about you." He reached out and pulled her to him one-handed to give her a reassuring hug, then took a step back to check her over for injury. "Are you okay, kid?"

She stared up into his face and nodded, wide-eyed and still looking like a teenager. Then she put out her arm and beckoned to the Engineer. It floated up beside her and gave Mendez and Fred a thorough inspection, head tilting back and forth.

The realization began to dawn on Mendez. If the Dyson sphere had been sealed since before the first human landing on Onyx, then this guy probably wasn't with the Covenant. He had to be descended from the Foreunner originals. Hell, given the weird way time worked in here, maybe he *was* an original Huragok left here.

"I think I'm going to break this to Dr. Halsey very, very quietly," Fred said. He gave Lucy several pats on the back. "Good to have you back, Lucy. We searched everywhere for you."

The poor kid really looked bewildered. It was going to be a challenge debriefing a Spartan who couldn't talk and an alien life-form that only used sign language. But that was what Halsey was for, and Mendez knew that she'd go crazy when Fred told her they had an Engineer in tow. It would keep her occupied and out of his face.

Yeah, that's for the best. It really is.

Fred went on ahead, calling out to the others. "Hey, we found her. It's okay, Lucy's back. Panic over."

Mendez wasn't entirely convinced that Lucy was okay. He couldn't see any injuries, but he knew that look in her eyes. Something had shaken her.

"Halsey's going to check you over, if you're okay with that," he said. "Then we better get you something to eat and drink. You've been away for days."

Lucy shook her head and pulled her water canteen from her belt to shake it. Mendez could hear the water slopping around inside: no, she had plenty left, so she wasn't dehydrated. When they got to the entrance, Halsey bore down on them like a missile. She was walking at a breakneck pace, swinging her arms, and then she broke into a jog.

At least she had the good grace to try to look more interested in Lucy than the Engineer. "Any injuries, Lucy?" she asked. "Well, you're probably dehydrated."

Lucy shook the water canteen again to make the point and

held out her hand for Halsey's datapad. For a moment, Mendez thought that she was going to break the habit of years and actually write a message. Lucy wasn't like someone who'd just lost their voice. She'd stopped communicating almost completely, and that included writing anything more than map coordinates or the most basic information—no discussion, no explanation, and no complex questions. He waited for some breakthrough, for something amazing to appear on the datapad, but all she did was indicate the date displayed on it and shake her head, baffled.

The Engineer flicked out a tentacle and took the datapad from her. It appeared to be tapping out a message. Well, the robotic Sentinels they'd run into on the surface could work out some English, so maybe this Engineer was going to surprise them too.

"I think this guy's been here since the place was built," Mendez said. "Or at least his forebears were. At the risk of pissing you off again, Doctor, I've been here for more than twenty years, and ONI started rooting around the planet sixty years ago, so I doubt this fella's ever worked for the Covenant."

"If he's a direct descendant of the ones built by the Forerunners, then imagine what information he can give us. Just *imagine*." Halsey sounded breathless. Damn it, she was excited as a kid and trying hard not to show it. "Not that I know how long these constructs last when they're left to their own devices."

Constructs. Halsey liked her dividing lines between people and nonpeople. The Engineer finished with the datapad and turned it so that they could see what he'd done. They now had an audience of Spartans gathered around them.

MY NAME IS PRONE TO DRIFT. WE HAVE WAITED SINCE THE BEGINNING. WHY DID YOU ACTIVATE THE CITADEL WHEN THERE IS NO FLOOD?

"Well, I guessed right about the Flood," Halsey muttered. "And he's rather socialized and assertive for a Huragok."

Mendez ignored her and concentrated on the Engineer. "How do you know there's no Flood outside? Can you get a signal out of this place?"

The Engineer went back to composing his response.

THE MASTERS LEFT BEFORE THIS WORLD WAS COMPLETED. WE WAITED BUT THEY NEVER RETURNED. WE HAVE DONE WHAT WE CAN, BUT WE HAVE NO FURTHER INSTRUCTIONS.

"I said *can you transmit and receive signals from outside this sphere?* And what's the problem with the date? What's upsetting Lucy?"

OUR SPACE IS OUTSIDE THIS ONE. FOR HER, IT HAS BEEN HOURS NOT DAYS.

Halsey's cheeks were flushed and her eyes sparkled like she'd fallen in love. Mendez wondered if she'd looked that way to Jacob Keyes or if she reserved her passion for objects and ideas. She repeated the question that Mendez had asked. "How can you tell what's happening outside this sphere?"

THE SENSORS TELL US. WE CAN VIEW EVENTS IN THE OTHER SPACES. WHY? IS THIS ABOUT THE WAR?

"Yes, yes, that's it, it's about the war." Halsey took a step forward, right in the Engineer's face. "I'm a scientist. I need to know. And I need to let my people know that we're all right. Have you any way of *transmitting* a message into the other space?"

"Before we start transmitting anything I want to be sure where this guy's come from," Fred said. "I don't care if it looks quiet outside. We're not going to give away our position until we're absolutely certain what's going on."

Halsey raked her fingers through her hair, all impatience.

"Well, it looks like we've got another slipspace bubble within this one. It's almost as if it's made up of concentric bubbles. Like a Russian doll."

Mendez glanced at Lucy, giving the datapad a meaningful look. Would she tell him anything more? Lucy took the hint, peeled the pad out of Prone to Drift's grip, and started writing. Mendez wasn't expecting what came next.

I KILLED AN ENGINEER, she said. SORRY.

The beginnings of an exasperated look formed on Halsey's face, but it didn't get any farther. Mendez glared at her. It was too damn bad about the Engineer, but they could always make some new ones. He couldn't make another Lucy.

Just thinking that reminded him what Halsey had done with cloning, and it was another rebuke about those things he'd turned a blind eye to when he should have turned her in instead. But he'd worry about that later. Halsey was already hassling the Engineer, demanding that he show her inside the structure.

Prone to Drift didn't seem much different from any human being who liked his job and was only too happy to show visitors around his office. He started floating back toward the tower with Halsey trailing after him.

"Linda, with me," Fred said. He went off after Halsey. "Let's make sure we don't lose her as well."

Mendez decided things were looking up at last. Now they had the best possible assistant for milking every scrap of technology out of this place and getting it back to ONI. He took out his cigar, lit a taper of grass with his fire steel, and inhaled a damn good lungful of sweet, soothing, luscious smoke. Halsey was going to be some time.

He looked over Lucy's remodeled backpack, wondering if Engineers ever left anything alone.

"And next time, Petty Officer, you *will* listen to the lieutenant's orders and you *will* follow them," he said, holding up a warning finger. "Because I don't want Dr. Halsey lecturing me on how you've all got poor impulse control."

It would have raised a laugh under normal circumstances, but they'd all lost too many people now. Just getting Lucy back in one piece seemed to be enough. For an hour, Mendez allowed himself the respite of sitting on the grass with the Spartans, picking over the leftover barbecued fish and contemplating when he'd be able to replenish his supply of Sweet Williams. The brief break came to an abrupt end when his radio crackled in his ear.

"Chief, you really need to come and take a look at this," Fred said. "And bring a tranquillizer dart to calm down Dr. Halsey. She's in hog heaven. Just walk down the corridor and you'll find us."

"On my way, Lieutenant." Mendez got to his feet and jerked his head at Lucy. She was now the Engineer wrangler, after all. "Come on, kid. Let's go see what the good doctor's found."

Fred might have been joking about the tranquillizer dart, but if Mendez had had one, he would have been sorely tempted to use it. Lucy seemed to know where she was going and led Mendez into the darkness. He felt something brush his arms and face as if he was pushing through curtains, and then he was suddenly in an enormous, brightly lit hangar faced in stone like everything else in this world. It was busy with at least a dozen Huragok drifting around an assortment of vessels that he didn't recognize at all.

He could hear Halsey calling him. "Chief? Chief, you won't *believe* what we've got here."

"I can see it, Doctor." He ducked under the fuselage of a large satin-gray ship about the size of a Pelican, but he couldn't tell if it was brand-new or if it had seen a thousand years' service. He followed the sound of Halsey's voice and stuck his head inside the first hatch he found open. "Is it just fantastically interesting, or is it actually going to be any use to us?"

Halsey's indignant face popped up right in front of him, almost making him flinch.

"Yes, just a little," she said. "You want to transform slipspace navigation? You want to know when you slip *exactly* where and when you're going to drop back into realspace, and not end up hours and millions of kilometers from your target? Well, it comes as standard on every damn model in this showroom. And we're going to have it."

Mendez thought of Kurt and the others with a strange kind of regretful relief, a realization that their lives had brought something priceless and hadn't been wasted. He decided he might crack a new cigar after all.

"Thanks, Kurt," he murmured. "Thanks."

CHAPTER 13

WE CAN'T FORGIVE, AND WE CAN'T FORGET. BUT THERE'S A THIRD OPTION WHICH ISN'T RELATED TO EITHER. IT DOESN'T REQUIRE US TO BE FRIENDS. WE CAN SIMPLY BOTH AGREE TO STOP KILLING EACH OTHER.

(Admiral Lord Hood to Thel 'Vadam, still known as the Arbiter)

Maintenance area, Forerunner Dyson sphere, Onyx: local date November 2552.

Halsey communicated with Prone to Drift with an ease that Lucy envied.

The Engineer seemed to have picked up an understanding of spoken English with typical speed, and all Halsey had to do was keep her datapad focused on his tentacles while it relayed the conversation back to her in a neutral male voice. It was a quick exchange of software and algorithms, nothing like the painful, primitive steps that Lucy had had to go through to communicate with Prone.

Halsey looked excited even though she was putting on her

I'm-a-detached-professional voice. Lucy noted the way she kept licking her lips like she was desperate to interrupt with new questions.

"But can that slipspace navigation be adapted to fit *human* ships?" she kept asking. "Look, I've got some schematics here." She brandished the pad. "Can we achieve that degree of insertion accuracy?"

"If your drives are sufficiently responsive," said the flat, disembodied voice emerging from her datapad. "We need to examine one."

"We can fetch a whole *fleet* here for you to play with," Halsey said. Lucy watched Mendez roll his eyes very slowly and then look away. The rest of the Spartans were wandering around the hangar, examining the Forerunner vessels. "All we have to do is get a message out to my people."

"We are not in your time," Prone said. "And there is something out there."

"What do you mean, *something out there*? You told me there was no evidence of the Flood and the Halo hadn't fired."

"There is something out there that is both there and not there. It may be a threat. Are you not interested in the condition of the Reclaimers in stasis?"

He meant the Katana personnel and the unidentified civilians. Lucy felt ashamed that she'd been too tied up in her own problems to ask Prone to open their slipspace pods.

"*We're* interested in them," Mendez said. "Why are they in there? What happened?"

Prone paused for a moment. Lucy wasn't sure if Engineers were capable of lying, but they were definitely sensitive to agitation and seemed to want to avoid upsetting humans.

"We went to the portal when the first shield procedures activated," the proxy voice said. "They are too damaged for us to repair. We placed them in stasis for those with greater knowledge to attend to them."

So Team Katana were either dead or dying, and the Engineers had done the only thing they knew; they put them on life support and waited for the medical experts to show up. But the Forerunner medics were never going to come. Lucy hoped that Halsey's medical genius was all it was cracked up to be and that she could do something for the Katana guys, even though she seemed to think of them all as substandard merchandise.

"Explain what you mean by *not in our time*," Halsey said. "I realize this is a slipspace bubble, but exactly how far out of sync are we with the galaxy?"

"Varies," the virtual voice answered. "And *can* be varied. If the other space talks to you, it hears your reply fifteen or twenty times later."

Halsey seemed to be struggling to pin Prone down to terms she understood. She tried another tack.

"Can you tell me the date in the human calendar on the outside? Access my datapad again. Extrapolate from the calendar we use."

Prone reached out and fluttered his cilia over the datapad. "The year division is two-five-five-three. The lesser division is two."

Lucy was now used to Prone's turn of phrase, and understood that as February 2553. They'd been here days, yet months had elapsed outside. But what was out there waiting for them?

Mendez took a couple of steps forward and eased himself into the conversation. "Now I'm really grateful that you brought Lucy back to us," he said. "But is there any way you can let us signal one of our own ships so we can take her home?"

"Until we know if the object is a threat, we must remain concealed." Prone seemed to be getting jumpy. His lights were growing more intense. Lucy wanted to step in and defend him, to stop Halsey demanding so much of him. "We cannot repair Lucy-Bravo-Zero-Nine-One. Somebody must."

"We'll take care of Lucy," Mendez said. Halsey looked as if she was going to interrupt but seemed to realize that Mendez was making a better job of the diplomacy. "What would it take to make you feel things were safe outside?"

"To identify the object as nonhostile. To make contact with our own kind for verification. Or for the Forerunners to return."

Mendez stared at the floor, fists on his hips. "Well, we might be able to manage at least one of those. But I'll tell you now that the Forerunners disappeared a very long time ago, son."

Prone's bioluminescence flared again and he floated away to join the group of Engineers huddled in the corner of the hangar, watching the strange newcomers messing around with their vessels. He seemed to be breaking the bad news to them.

"Got to feel sorry for those poor damn things," Mendez said. "Imagine waiting patiently all those years for the boss to show up and then being told that he's dead."

Halsey drew in a breath. Lucy didn't expect her to give a damn about the Engineers' feelings and the woman didn't disappoint her. She just went right on talking at Mendez, stabbing a finger for emphasis. "Chief, do you understand how important this technology is? This slipspace navigation alone—it'll give us a major tactical advantage over the Covenant. And God only knows what other technology we'll find when we've finished going through this place. I don't care what it takes, but we *have* to let people know what we've got in here."

"And then what? How do you crack open a Dyson sphere and get it back to the right dimension or whatever you call it? If those Engineers can't or won't do it, then we're screwed." He looked at Lucy as if he expected her to offer an opinion. "And what the hell is out there that's spooked them so much?"

Prone drifted back to them and stopped in front of Lucy. "Our orders are clear. We must maintain this shield world until the Forerunners have need of it. We will do that."

"How many other shield worlds are there?" Halsey asked. "Where are they?"

"Many, but we have no information."

"Where did the Foreunners go?"

"I cannot tell you."

"And there *are* other Halos in the Array, are there?"

"There are six left in this galaxy."

It was more a cross-examination than a discussion. Lucy wanted to step in and slow things down, but she didn't know how. But that *was* vital information.

Halsey's tone softened like a parent asking her five-year-old what he'd done with Mommy's keys. "Prone to Drift, do you know where they are?"

"No. The charts were located in the other places." Prone folded his tentacles close to his body, looking as if he'd had enough of the interrogation and couldn't work out what this woman wanted. Lucy couldn't decide whether he was being evasive or whether it was just a glitch in the translation. "When will you repair Lucy?"

"I'm not sure anyone *can* repair her," Halsey said. "Please, we need to talk about calling our people. If you can make contact with the outside world, then you owe it to us to do it. It's your duty."

"You are not a Forerunner," Prone said.

"You said we were Reclaimers."

"There is something waiting outside."

Halsey turned to Lucy, frustrated and tight-lipped. "Lucy, you seem to get on with the Huragok. Make them understand how important this is."

Lucy couldn't make them do anything. And Prone could hear this going on, of course. Did Halsey think he was deaf?

"I've still got some questions to ask him," Mendez said. "Any-one mind if I have a chat?"

"If he has sensors that can detect something outside this sphere, there's got to be a vector by which we can get a signal out," Halsey said. "I'll go look around and see what I can find."

"Yeah, but mind you don't piss them off, Doctor," Mendez warned. Halsey stalked off. "Just don't go barging in and upset-ting them. Dr. Halsey, did you hear me?"

Halsey moved between the vessels, looking around as if she was trying to find an exit. She must have seen the main passage leading to the workshop, because she jerked her head around and strode purposefully in that direction. A couple of the Engineers detached from the group and drifted after her.

Lucy looked at Mendez and shook her head.

"Yeah, I know," Mendez said. "We're dependent on the good-will of these guys." He tilted his head back slightly and looked at Prone as if he was trying to do the man-to-man thing. "Prone, do you think the war is over? What makes you think that? Because we've been fighting an awful long time, and if it's over, I've got friends I need to check on. Make sure they're still alive."

Halsey had gone off with her datapad, so Mendez wouldn't get a response from Prone that he could understand. He still tried. Prone looked at him intently, head bobbing, then turned and headed after Halsey.

"Come on, Lucy," Mendez said. "I might have to drag her out of there to keep him happy."

Prone could put on a fair turn of speed when he wanted to. He zipped ahead, vanishing down the passage, leaving Lucy and Mendez to jog after him. Lucy could hear the conversation long before they turned the corner. Halsey was looking for the comms controls, and Prone didn't like it.

"Just show me what's out there," Halsey said. "I'm the chief scientist for the human armed forces. Do you understand? I may be able to tell you what's out there."

The datapad voice took over again. "No. We must maintain silence."

"Do you seriously think that whatever's out there *isn't* curious about a Dyson sphere? What kind of anomalies do you think it's causing outside? It's an environment as big as a solar system *compressed into a small ball.* Whoever's watching won't get bored and go away."

"We have our instructions."

Mendez put himself between Prone and Halsey. "Doctor, he doesn't work for you and he doesn't give a damn how many Ph.D.s you've got. Back off."

"Stay out of this, Chief." Halsey was all quiet ice now. "I can see the comms console. I can read most of these symbols, remember."

The workshop layout looked different from the one Lucy had seen a few hours ago. The smooth walls were now covered in screens that seemed to shift and relocate, taking the illuminated symbols with them. The whole room looked like a touch-screen. Halsey stopped for a moment, looking down at her shoes as if she was taking a deep breath, and then she turned slowly and put her hand out to touch something on the wall near Prone.

He batted her hand away. The gesture was more censorious than the artificial voice sounded. "Please *no.*"

Halsey stared at the back of her hand for a moment as if she couldn't believe a Huragok would rap her knuckles. They might have been passive and nonpartisan, but they obviously had their limits when it came to interfering with Forerunner technology. Lucy could only look at Prone in mute apology.

"That damn thing *smacked* me," Halsey said.

Mendez caught her elbow and steered her away. Lucy watched Prone, who seemed to be noting all this and probably deciding that Mendez was the good guy who'd stop Halsey bullying him. Or maybe he'd just formed a bad opinion of the entire human species. It was hard to tell.

"Diplomacy, Doctor," Mendez said. "Try it."

But Halsey wasn't taking any notice. She was completely fixated on that damn slipspace navigation and the need to let ONI know that she had it. She seemed to be thinking aloud now, because she certainly wasn't asking anyone for an opinion, least of all the Chief.

"Once we get a signal out, then we'll need to take those Engineers with us," she said. "They're a unique resource. Huragok descended from the original strain created by the Forerunners. Imagine what we can extract from them."

"Yeah, you keep saying that. And imagine how much we're pissing them off."

"They're just organic computers. They're like AIs."

"Maybe, but you say they've waited a hundred thousand years? Well, then we can afford to spend a couple of days sweet-talking them. That's just a few weeks outside."

"Planets fall to the Covenant in weeks. In *days.*"

"All I'm saying is that this isn't working, so try another tack."

Halsey reached out for the control panel again, one hand on her sidearm. It was visible in her pocket. Lucy readied herself to move in if the woman did anything stupid.

"So what happens if I access this? Are you going to *stop* me?" Halsey took a step toward Prone and he backed away. "I don't want to harm you. I just want to *call my damn office.*"

Prone recoiled and Refill Needed moved in as if he was trying to defend him. Lucy wanted to yell at Halsey to shut up and leave them alone, but the woman kept forcing Prone back, herding him into that corner, demanding things from him, and Lucy could see him starting to cower and fold his tentacles closer to his body. He was scared. She knew what it felt like to want to lash out and just make the noise and the pain and the fear *stop*.

Just leave him alone.

Lucy was a little shorter than Halsey but she knew she was a lot stronger. She grabbed her shoulder and yanked her back a few paces, her attention still on that sidearm. She could have done a lot worse. But Halsey just shrugged her off without even looking back at her and took another step forward.

"Prone, I think I know how to operate this, so if you don't—"

And that was when Lucy snapped.

She grabbed Halsey by the shoulder again, spun her around and threw a punch that sent a shock wave right up her arm. Halsey hit the ground with a loud crack. Someone grabbed Lucy from behind, but the switch had been thrown and she didn't know how to turn it off. The fury shut out all sound: her lungs froze and her skull was bursting. She fought to break free and get at Halsey, this focus of all that was threatening and bullying in her world, but she couldn't.

If she didn't let it all out right *now,* she'd collapse.

"No!" she screamed. *"No! No! No!"*

The sound of her own voice after all those years was shockingly alien, so weird that she almost didn't recognize it. It took every scrap of breath and energy she had left. She couldn't say another word.

"Well, goddamn . . ." Mendez said. *"Goddamn."*

UNSC *PORT STANLEY,* somewhere off Sanghelios: February 2553.

As too many UNSC personnel had found out the hard way, it was pretty hard to kill a Sangheili.

The shipmaster they'd brought on board still looked battered and some of his teeth were broken, but he was alert and alive. Osman leaned on the door frame of the brig and waited for him to start pounding at the door again. He hadn't touched the food placed in the security hatch. That didn't surprise her.

So who are you, then?

According to the nav computer in his shuttle, he'd come from Mdama, and his last few trips had been to Ontom. Working out his name was going to take a little longer. Phillips watched him, eyes bright with fascination.

"Here's the hard bit," Osman said. "Do I tell 'Telcam that we've nabbed him, or not?"

Very few Sangheili had been taken alive, and those had been too close to death to be much use to ONI, but this one would be very useful indeed.

"*Nabbed,*" Phillips said. "What a sweet old-fashioned word. There was a time when people called this *rendition.* I suppose you want me to have another chat with him when he's calmed down a bit. *If* he calms down."

"Well, you're the only one on board who can look him in the eye and not want to spit in it. And you're supposed to be the greatest living expert on hinge-heads."

"Sooner or later, someone's going to notice he's missing and start talking about it."

Osman just looked at him and raised an eyebrow eloquently. It was very easy to put Phillips in his place. She didn't really mean to, because he'd far exceeded her expectations, from his willingness to muck in with the rest of the crew to his complete indifference to how much danger he was in. But he had to remember that he wasn't here to explore the rich variety of Sangheili culture. He was here to help ONI kill the bastards.

"Sorry," he said sheepishly. "I keep forgetting that you were raised in the intelligence community. Silly me."

It was a very charming way of describing a Spartan's unnatural, frequently painful life. She wondered whether Naomi had confided in any of the others about the news Osman had broken to her. Osman was keeping an eye on Vaz as a barometer of Naomi's reaction, because he was slightly easier to read and he seemed pretty protective toward her. So far, he was still giving her occasional baffled looks that suggested she hadn't said anything yet.

Maybe she was having difficulty finding the words to explain that Halsey had kidnapped her, replaced her with a short-lived clone, and left her parents to grieve over a dead child that wasn't her, while she was being subjected to what any civilized society would have described as immoral experiments. She knew she'd been taken away from her family. She just hadn't known what had happened to them after that. *And I still haven't told her the full story, have I? She needs to read her file, to see it for herself.* It would be a lot to come to terms with at her time of life.

The fact that the Spartan-IIs had fulfilled their promise and turned the course of the war didn't make it all better, not at all.

"That's okay, Evan," Osman said. "I wasn't a natural-born spy. Had you had my training, I shudder to think how dangerous you would have become."

Phillips looked as if he wasn't sure whether that was a compliment or an insult, but she meant it as professional admiration. He just had that mind-set. He seemed to really enjoy the role, whereas she'd just grown used to it and did it to the best of her ability.

Vaz and Mal joined the staring committee. The Sangheili couldn't see them through the monitor plate.

"I could have sold tickets," Mal said. "I tell you, it was like watching a train crash into the buffers. Permission to break out the beer, ma'am, and stand Naomi a drink?"

"Absolutely, Staff. You two didn't do so badly either."

"So what's Parangosky going to do with him, then?" Vaz asked. "Although I suppose it depends on who he is."

"At least we know he's probably from a Mdama keep." Phillips looked at his watch. "I'm betting he'll be late calling in already, so I'll do a little bit of eavesdropping and see who's pacing up and down waiting to tell him his dinner's in the dog."

The Sangheili was now sitting on the bench against the bulkhead, head bowed and massive four-fingered hands clasped in his lap as if he was praying. He might have been meditating—or shaping up for another ranting session.

"Well, either he's batting for the Arbiter, or else he's some disenchanted random guy who got involved with 'Telcam and started to worry where all that shiny kit was coming from," Mal said. "Maybe Adj and BB can extract some data from his armor."

BB materialized next to them, not the usual featureless blue box but sporting a bright red bow tied as if he was a gift. Vaz frowned at him.

"I didn't know you could do other colors, BB," he said. "What's the bow for? Got a date?"

"Oh, I can do the full spectrum." BB cycled the bow through the rainbow before settling back on red again. "It's the Admiral's birthday. And this is another thoughtful present for her. So I'm a double act with the Adj now, am I? Well, so be it. He's got more manual dexterity than me."

"Seriously, BB, can we get an identity out of his armor?" Osman asked. "There's nothing in his helmet systems to identify him. We know where he's been, but not his name."

"It's going to mean interfacing with him physically."

Mal was watching the Sangheili intently. "Otherwise known as a punch in the mouth, ma'am."

"I really did mean interface," BB said. "I doubt there's anything in the body armor systems, but we *could* send in Adj to make sure."

"As long as Cap'n Hinge-head doesn't do him any damage."

Osman felt she was saddling tigers again. "Phillips asked him nicely, but he wasn't very forthcoming."

She reflected on the sheer incongruity of talking to a floating box tied up with a red shiny bow about the finer detail of processing abductees. *I was one once. I haven't learned any pity, have I?* She checked her watch to see how long she had until the next sitrep to Parangosky.

"Okay," she said. "Better get Naomi standing by in case he tries to make a run for it. He knows she can drop him."

"You can't intimidate a Sangheili, Captain," Phillips said. "He'd rather die in battle."

"I'm betting he'd rather escape in one piece to complete whatever his mission was, actually." She turned to Mal. "But get his cooperation any way you can, Staff."

"Yes, ma'am." Mal held up a sphere about fifteen centimeters across, grained and polished like some dense wood. "And we found this when we disarmed him. Not sure what it is, but it's not scanning as ordnance."

"I think it's a puzzle," Phillips said. He held his hand out for it. "It's called an *arum*. I've never actually seen one before."

Phillips took it in both hands and fiddled with it, making it rattle. It was a large thing for a human's hand, but it would have been no more than a toy in a Sangheili's grip. As Phillips twisted it, Osman could see that it was made up of interconnecting rings and spheres, almost like some wooden puzzles she'd seen in museums on Earth.

"They give these to children to teach them discipline," Phillips said. "You have to line up the components so that the stone at the center falls out. Interesting that he still carries one."

Vaz shrugged, not taking his eyes off the Sangheili. "Maybe it's a present for his kids."

"I doubt it. They're never supposed to find out who their fathers are."

"Yeah, I come from a neighborhood like that too," Mal said. "Never knew who my dad was either."

"I meant he wouldn't hand out presents because they raise them in a communal kibbutz-type environment so that they start life on an equal social footing."

"Maybe Vaz can get somewhere with him, then. Discuss the glorious history of the soviets and beetroot-based economies."

Vaz didn't blink. The two marines tormented each other mercilessly, a sure sign of an old friendship. "Don't forget you *lease* your piddling little island from us. As a Russian taxpayer, I *own* you."

"Well, you got a bargain, then. Okay, now we've got this bugger, what are we going to get out of him?"

Did the Sangheili have a wife and kids, a mother and father, a family now worrying where he was and whether anything terrible had happened to him? Osman had to assume he did. She resisted succumbing to humanization. When she started seeing Sangheili as mommies and daddies and fine upstanding family folk, then it became harder to do what she had to. She couldn't recall hingeheads ever debating whether to spare humans on the basis that they had families who would miss them. They just incinerated planets and relished their hand-to-hand slaughter. Another little gem of Parangosky's wisdom came back to her: *learn to think like the enemy, but understand the ways they're* unlike *you.*

It was an intellectual exercise, nothing she could really feel in the pit of her stomach, and she wondered if that was how Halsey saw the Spartans—something she understood from the DNA level upward, but didn't find any compassionate human kinship with until too late in the day.

Her Spartans. She always referred to us as hers.

Perhaps I shouldn't have let Naomi read her journal. But would she have believed me otherwise?

Naomi came down the passage toward them, still in her armor and carrying what Osman liked to call a cattle prod. It didn't get a lot of use, but she'd been assured that it worked on all large species. "You wanted me, ma'am?"

"I'm going to put Adj in the cell and see if he can extract any data from the body armor," Osman said. "It used to be his job, after all. Just stop the hinge-head damaging him while he does it, because if push comes to shove, I'd rather have the Huragok in one piece."

"Understood, ma'am." She looked at Mal and Vaz. "Usual drill?"

"Let's get it over with," Mal said. "Helmets on, boys and girls."

BB ushered Adj up to the cell door and projected a set of tentacles to sign at him. Adj didn't appear worried about the prospect of wrestling with a pissed-off shipmaster and floated patiently as Mal and Vaz prepared to go in first with Naomi right behind them.

Did Sangheili warriors feel it was beneath their masculine dignity to hit a female? It certainly didn't stop the Covenant killing women and children along with the men. Osman held her breath.

"Okay, in three—*three*," Mal said. The door slid back, the Sangheili stood up, and the two marines stormed in with Naomi on their heels. Mal went right and Vaz went left to grab one arm each. The Sangheili fought to shake them off and very nearly succeeded. He batted Mal across the compartment, smashing him against the bulkhead with a loud crash.

"Bastard," Mal grunted, scrambling to his feet. Vaz hung on to the left arm but the Sangheili brought his fist up under Vaz's chin just as Mal lunged back and pinned the right arm again. Naomi moved straight in between them. It took two seconds from opening the door to the moment when Naomi shoved the cattle prod up into the gap between the Sangheili's lower jaws.

It was hard to unbalance a Sangheili, but the speed of the multipronged attack did the job. As Mal and Vaz struggled to hold on to the Sangheili's arms, Naomi gave him a quick zap. The prod crackled like a plug discharging and the angry bellowing turned into a single high-pitched squeal. The Sangheili fell back to land on his backside on the bench.

Adj drifted in, fiddled about with the chest plate, then drifted out again like a nurse taking a blood sample from a difficult toddler. Naomi moved out and shut the door behind her, then helped Vaz off with his helmet.

"You okay?" she asked. She tipped his head back and checked him over. Mal peered at him too. "He really snapped your head back."

"I'm a shock trooper," Vaz said. "I'm used to hard landings."

ODST or not, Osman wasn't taking any chances with closed brain injury. "Corporal, you take a shot of chorotazine, and that's an order. I don't need paralyzed marines, okay?"

"Yes, ma'am."

The hinge-head got to his feet and tottered a little before regaining his balance and roaring abuse again. Phillips looked distinctly uncomfortable, arms folded as he watched.

"Is this where you tell me you could have gone in and reasoned with him?" Osman asked. "Because that's great in the movies, but it only needs one blow from him to take your damn face off."

Vaz grunted. "Believe it."

Phillips scratched his nose, somewhere between embarrassment and looking like he wanted to argue. The reality of this kind of war was equally unlike the movies. It was brutal and dirty and nobody was going to win on points. It was an idea Phillips needed to get used to. The Sangheili was now back at full volume, roaring and hissing.

"It sounds like he's saying *blarg*," Mal said. "Is that good?"

"I'll summarize the rant." Phillips looked away. "He's telling us we're all intestinal worms and vermin, and describing what he's going to do with our entrails in due course."

"I didn't think he was asking for his lawyer," Osman said. "Okay, Evan, start eavesdropping."

"I took the liberty of recording all voice traffic from the moment I knew you had a prisoner, and I've sifted through it, but there's nothing to interest you so far," BB said, all tact and diplomacy. "I'm thoughtful like that, I am."

Phillips grunted something that sounded like thanks and headed for his cubbyhole in the hangar. Vaz looked at Osman and raised his eyebrows. He seemed a bit unsteady.

"He'll come around to the idea, ma'am," Vaz said. "He always disappears to think things over when he finds out something nasty about his government. But he always gets on with the job in the end."

Naomi was still waiting to be dismissed, holding the cattle prod tucked under her arm like a swagger stick.

"You all right, Spartan?" Osman asked.

"Fine, thanks, ma'am."

"Okay, I'm going to talk to the Admiral about getting this guy offloaded, and then we'll see what Hood's up to."

"Are we still on for that, ma'am?" Mal asked.

"It'd be handy to get clearance to tag along, if only to get Phillips on nodding terms with the Arbiter. Who else is Hood going to want with him? I expect the Admiral's suggesting it right now."

There was just a flicker of doubt on Mal's face. She could understand that. Everyone liked Hood, and it wasn't easy to stomach the idea of ONI unleashing dirty tricks on the man who'd brought Earth through the war in some kind of shape to rebuild, but then that depended on which of them thought their efforts had made the most difference. The Spartans were ONI's project and the Spartans had been the tipping point, one way or another. Parangosky felt she had prior claim. Osman wasn't sure. But she knew who her boss was.

She took another look through the plate of the brig door. The Sangheili was on his feet now, pacing around and occasionally landing a punch on the bulkheads.

"See, he's all better now." Mal peered over her shoulder. "Do their teeth grow back again, like sharks' do?"

"Stick your arm in and find out," Vaz suggested.

Osman decided she could leave the Sangheili in there until she'd arranged a handover. If the brig needed hosing down afterward, that was a price worth paying. She went back to her day cabin and sat down at the desk with her chin resting on her hands.

"BB, can you find out what Hood's planning?" she asked. She meant accessing his secure files and comms, not asking his secretary. She really hadn't wanted to do that to the man, not after how kind he'd been to her over the years. "I know Parangosky's going to tell me, but it would be nice to plan ahead."

"I thought you'd never ask," BB said, appearing in the in-tray.

"Let me see what my naughty fragment's been up to while my back's been turned. Oh, and Hogarth. I hope you didn't mind my smacking his bottom. He keeps sending Harriet to snoop in your files so I stuck something in his and alerted Internal Audit."

"I believe the phrase is you *fitted him up.* . . ."

"Nothing major. Just triggered the attack accountants from hell to check a truly *massive* overspend. They'll find it's a misplaced decimal point in due course."

"Remind me never to cross you."

"And Phillips will be here to see you in . . . *ten* seconds."

"You're fabulous, d'you know that?"

"Yes. I do."

BB disappeared just as Phillips stuck his head inside the door.

"Good lead with Mdama, Captain," he said. "I have a name."

Osman leaned back in her chair. "That was quick."

"Jul 'Mdama." Phillips could even do the little cross between a glottal stop and a click before the clan name. "Shipmaster. Some traffic between 'Telcam, another shipmaster called Buran, and some guy called Forze who appears to be his best buddy. Jul took off from Bekan in a shuttle, and hasn't called in for ages."

"So he's known to 'Telcam."

Phillips nodded. "Apparently."

"That could get interesting. Naomi says he definitely wasn't on overwatch. He was doing some sneaky observation."

"Maybe he's an agent for the Arbiter. A plant. A sleeper. Or whatever the Spookish is for *undercover* these days."

Now there's a thought.

"Cover blown, then," Osman said. "Now let's work out the most divisive and strife-inducing way I can use that information."

Maintenance area, Forerunner Dyson sphere, Onyx: local date November 2552.

"Easy, Lucy. *Back off.*"

Mendez had Lucy in a headlock and she was finally running out of adrenaline. She knew she'd kicked him, but she really didn't mean to, not the Chief, not the man who'd raised her and turned her into a soldier. "I said *stand down,* Spartan. Did you hear me? *Stand down!*"

She took a deep wheezing gasp, deafened by her own pulse. Her legs almost buckled and her face and neck felt like they were on fire. She realized that Mendez was now holding her up rather than holding her back.

And she was *crying*—sobbing like she hadn't sobbed for years. Mendez turned her around to face him and crushed her to him so tightly that she thought he'd break a rib.

"Good girl. Let it out. It's okay." She'd just punched out the ONI's chief scientist but Mendez didn't sound angry at all. "Let it all out. *Damn.* That was a long time coming."

Lucy had a small crowd around her now and suddenly felt completely humiliated. Tom ruffled her hair ferociously. "You're back, Lucy. You're *back.* Come on. Keep talking."

But she wasn't sure what to say next. It should have been an apology, but she wasn't sorry, not one damn bit, not for defending Prone. She couldn't see Halsey behind a cluster of Spartan-IIs, but she knew that she must have hit her a hell of a lot harder than she thought. Her hand was throbbing.

"She'll be okay," Kelly said, straightening up. It was hard to tell if she was looking at Lucy but her voice was flat calm. "Nothing that can't be fixed."

Mendez let Lucy go but still kept a tight grip on her shoulder.

He'd never been a kindly-looking man but the granite expression softened just for a moment. "I ought to put you on a charge, Petty Officer. But I'm just too damn glad to hear you talking again." He looked over her head in Halsey's direction. "You're lucky she's a small one, Doctor. Are you okay?"

Halsey was on her feet now, supported by Kelly and Linda. Fred took his helmet off and looked at Lucy as if he was working out who the hell she was.

"I'll live," Halsey said. She dabbed at her nose with the back of her hand, trying to mop up a thin trickle of bright red blood. "You and I had better have a talk, Chief."

Halsey went outside with her Spartan escort like she was some kind of general. Lucy bristled. It must have shown because Mendez gave her his don't-even-think-about-it look.

"Now I'm going to get my ass kicked," he said. "Tom, look after her, will you? I'd better make sure Halsey gives the Engineers some space or we'll be here until hell calls time."

The adrenaline had ebbed away and Lucy was now at the embarrassed and shaky stage. She'd never lost control like that before. The doctors had warned her that anger was part of traumatic stress, but she was a *Spartan,* for goodness' sake. She should have had enough discipline to resist throwing a punch.

There was just something about Halsey haranguing the Engineers that snapped something inside her, and for a few seconds she didn't care whether she lived or died as long as she lashed out and stopped it.

Tom and Olivia kept ruffling her hair. "That'll make her think twice about treating us as cheap knockoffs," Olivia said, putting her arm around Lucy's shoulders. "How're you doing, Luce? Take it a step at a time though. I bet that this time next week we won't be able to shut you up."

The Engineers were huddled in a corner, probably wondering what the hell they'd let into their sphere. They'd seen Lucy shoot one of their buddies, and now she was swinging punches at civilians. Prone floated away from the group and headed her way, clutching a page-sized piece of the same milky white glass used on the walls. He fluttered his cilia over it and held it in front of her.

YOU ARE PARTLY REPAIRED. WHO WILL FINISH REPAIRING YOU NOW?

Lucy put her hand out to the screen, looking for the makeshift keyboard. Olivia caught her wrist.

"No, *speak* to the guy, Lucy."

She'd managed one word, but that didn't mean it had opened the floodgates. A connection in her brain was still fragile and rusted, the one that most people took for granted from the time they were small children—thinking what they were going to say before their vocal cords took over a fraction of a second later. It was an easy habit to lose. Just as she'd found herself struggling to frame written words, she was now back to square one trying to do the same with speech. She took her hand off the screen and touched Prone's tentacle.

"Prone," she said hoarsely.

I CANNOT RESTORE YOU. WHO WILL DO IT?

Lucy gestured to the squad around her. "Them."

"Good going, Luce," Mark said, almost shaking her by the shoulders. "Keep it up."

Prone peered into her face for a few moments and then wrote on his pad again. YOU WANT TO GO HOME.

Lucy knew that if she asked in the right way, he'd send a message for her. He trusted her despite what she'd done, and he obviously didn't trust Halsey.

But was it the right thing to do? Engineers weren't stupid, and if

Prone was worried about what was lurking outside the sphere, then he had good reason. On the other hand, maybe he'd just show them what he could see. It was only a small step. It didn't mean breaking radio silence and making themselves into potential targets.

But how do you breach a Dyson sphere in another dimension anyway? Can anyone get at us?

Lucy nodded at Prone. She didn't have a home to go back to, and even her base on Onyx was gone, but that was too complicated for her to explain to him right now. The important thing was that she focused again and continued with the mission, or everyone she'd lost would have died for nothing.

It was a massive effort. She looked into Prone's face and squeezed the unfamiliar words out of weak vocal cords.

"Show us."

"She means show us your data on the threat," Olivia said. "Maybe we know what it is."

Prone didn't respond. He seemed to be studying Lucy's face in return. Then he just wandered off and rejoined his friends.

"Sometimes I think those things react to humans, and sometimes I think they're just looking at a complicated circuit diagram," said Mark. "But maybe he's gone away to mull it over."

For the moment, there was nothing that they could do. Lucy wondered whether to stay out of Halsey's way, but she had to face the woman sooner or later, and they were still stuck here with no immediate hope of rescue. No, she had to stop thinking of it as a *rescue.* She had to see it as the retrieval of high-value technology. She walked outside into the sunlight, suddenly terrified that she didn't know what to say—literally *say*—next. If she didn't try to keep talking, she knew she would slide back into silence.

She looked around the camp at the underclothes and jerky drying side by side on the bushes and saw the Spartan-IIs standing in a huddle, talking. Mendez and Halsey were head to head a few meters away. Their body language said it all.

They were standing square on to each other, shoulders braced in confrontation. Lucy could hear the discussion building into a fight. They were oblivious. Maybe they didn't care that they now had an audience of Spartans.

Halsey had her arms folded tight across her chest, more a blocking gesture than a defensive one. "Do you take my point now, Chief? They're just not stable. They're a liability."

"So what do you want me to do, Doctor?" Mendez growled. "They were broken when we got them. It was their goddamn qualification to get into the program, for Chrissakes. Terrified, angry little kids who'd seen their parents killed and wanted to lash out."

"Well, yes, that's a classic profile, but—"

"You know what regular recruits are like when you draft them?" He started stabbing his finger in her direction to make his point. "A mixed bag. Some are downright psychopathic. Some are bone idle. Some are scared of their own shadows. All kinds." He took out his cigar and shoved it between his lips, still talking as it dangled there while he felt in his pockets for that ancient Swedish fire-starter he always carried. "But dumb guys like me make them into fighting men and women by giving them discipline and pride. That's the way the armed forces always ran before we started *designing* soldiers." He paused for breath as he struck furious sparks off the two metal strips onto a scrap of dry grass, then lit the Sweet William. "You know something?" He gestured with the cigar right under her nose, wafting her with smoke. "It's the way the rest of the UNSC *still* runs. What *you* call disorders and abnormalities, *I* call different personalities. You just want to medicate and tweak and modify people into one vanilla definition of perfect, lady, and it's not what humans are like."

"You finished, Chief?"

"Hell, *no,* Doctor, I only just got started. You were never much good at accepting imperfect people, were you? You dumped your own goddamn daughter on her dad when she got too *imperfect.* Poor Jacob Keyes. Nice guy. Good father. Great officer. So then you made your own perfect daughter with that AI of yours, Cortana, a tidy little copy of yourself who thinks you're the Virgin Mary. I don't need a goddamn Ph.D. in psychiatry to work out what's wrong with *you.*"

Lucy couldn't move. She didn't really know Halsey and she didn't care what the woman thought of Spartan-IIIs. But she could hear Mendez losing his temper. His voice was getting more gravelly as his throat constricted. He almost wheezed when he puffed on that cigar. This was the man who'd looked after her and the other Spartan recruits from the day she'd landed on a strange planet with a bunch of six-year-old savages who'd almost forgotten what it meant to be human beings. He asked them who wanted a chance to kill the Covenant. *Me. I wanted that. I wanted to kill them all.* Mendez had faced the same risks alongside them. She knew whose side she'd be on in any fight.

"You *bastard,*" Halsey said at last. It was more of a hiss. "How *dare* you pry into my private life."

"You're not the only one with a nosey AI, Doctor. But a lot of UNSC staff can access the DNA database—and the goddamn *calendar.* A lot of people know. They've just got too much respect for Miranda to gossip."

"You and Ackerson. A matching pair of treacherous assholes."

"At least he only took volunteers."

"Six-year-olds can't possibly *volunteer.* Spare me the competitive morality."

"They didn't have parents *grieving* for them either."

"You've been saving this up, haven't you?"

"Not really. Work in a sewer long enough and you don't notice the smell until you go outside."

Lucy was transfixed. All the stuff about Halsey and her daughter and parents grieving—it was getting ugly, even if she didn't understand the context. She realized Tom and Fred were now standing next to her, helmets in hands.

"I better break this up," Fred said.

Tom shook his head. "No, sir, I think you better leave them to air their differences."

Halsey dropped her voice, but it was still crystal-clear. "You knew what the deal was, Chief. You could have walked away at any time."

"So I deserve what's coming to me. I should have asked for a transfer as soon as I found out what you'd done to their parents. And those goddamn clones. You know what? Just saying it out loud now makes me sick to my gut. It was all wrong. All *completely wrong.* Well, I hope someone charges me with the crimes, because this should never be hidden. This should *never* be covered up."

"But you did it once," Halsey said, hands on hips, "and then you did it *again,* without me. And you did it for the same reason that I did—because creating Spartans gave us the best chance of saving the human race."

"Steady with that airbrush, Doctor. You created the Spartans to counter colonial insurgents. That was a hell of a long time before the Covenant showed up."

"And they were just as big a threat. Remember Haven? I wanted to stop that ever happening again."

"You wanted to do it because you *could.* Curiosity. Goddamn vanity. You don't give a damn about human life, not even your own daughter's—only about being the smartest kid in the class."

"Don't you *dare* lecture me on Miranda. I asked Jacob to bring her up because I knew I was a bad mother."

"I never said you weren't self-aware."

"Look, I *know* I can't give anyone unconditional love. But I'm smarter than most abusive parents and I knew Jacob would do a better job than I ever could. I didn't want a doll to play with, Chief. I got pregnant, it wasn't convenient, and I wasn't prepared to take an unborn life."

"Don't you dump that pious handwringing bullshit on *me*." Mendez was now white with fury. He was gesturing so hard with the cigar that ash was flying everywhere. Lucy hovered on the edge of stepping in to break it up. "You had no damn respect for *born* life."

"Okay, that's enough." Fred strode forward, pushing between them until they backed apart. "This stops *now*. Both of you. Wind your necks in, and that's an *order*."

Mendez just stood his ground and took a drag on what was left of his cigar. "Yes, sir." Then he walked back to the tower entrance and went into the lobby.

Halsey stood there for a moment, expressionless, then looked up at Fred. Lucy could see that her neck was flushed bright red. That was something she couldn't hide.

"He's right, I'm afraid," Halsey said. "Why else do you think I went slightly crazy and brought you all here? Late onset of menopause?"

"Preserving vital assets, ma'am."

"Salving my conscience," Halsey said, and walked away toward the river.

Lucy's mad moment seemed small and forgotten by comparison. Everyone was looking either in the direction of the tower entrance or toward the river, which she took as a sign of whether they were more worried about Mendez or Halsey. A split was forming. If the Engineers didn't find them a way out of here, that was going to become a major problem. Fred might have been the ranking officer but there wasn't a lot he could do to keep Halsey on a leash.

"That's really sad about her daughter," Kelly said at last. "Miranda Keyes? I'd never have guessed. She's so much like her father."

"And what about your parents?" Olivia asked. "What did the Chief mean about clones?"

Kelly shrugged as if she wasn't bothered about it at all. With a helmet on, Spartans could hide a lot of turmoil. "You'll need to ask him about that."

Tom nudged Lucy with his elbow and steered her away for a walk. If Lucy had a close buddy in the squad, then it was Tom. They'd been the only two survivors from the raid on the Pegasi Delta refinery. She knew that was where she'd started to come unraveled, while Tom just kept on going, dependable and unflappable as ever. Sometimes she wondered why he could handle it and she couldn't, but by the time that thought started to form in her mind she was past the stage of being able to have a discussion about it. The doctors said that sooner or later, given enough pressure, shot at enough times, isolated and deprived of sleep for long enough, almost everyone would succumb to traumatic stress. Everyone reached their individual tipping point, and hers just happened sooner than Tom's.

But she could still function in combat. And that was all that mattered to her, because her punishment had been to survive her friends, and that meant she had some duty to perform before life would let her off the hook.

"Talk to me, Lucy," Tom said. "You know the last thing you said to me? To anyone? *How do we know we're still alive.* Yeah, living's hard after all that."

Lucy pursed her lips, making a conscious effort to shape the word. "Sorry," she said. "Sorry."

"Nothing to be sorry for, Luce. Nothing at all."

She knew it was going to take a lot more effort to get back to the person she'd been, if she ever made it at all. In the meantime, she was satisfied that she would be able to say enough to be a more useful member of the squad. She walked around for a while with Tom, searching for edible plants, until a shout from behind made them turn.

Mendez had come out of the lobby, walking behind Prone to Drift. The set of his shoulders had changed and it looked like there was some news. Lucy and Tom jogged back to the others.

"You've got a persuasive way with you, Petty Officer," Mendez said to her. "Your friend has something to say."

Prone was still clutching the small sheet of white glass, his message pad. He held it in front of her.

YOU MUST BE FULLY REPAIRED. MAKE THE CALL.

Maybe he was trying to encourage Lucy to speak. But if he wanted her to send a signal and was prepared to risk alerting whatever was lurking out there, she wasn't the person for the job. Halsey was best qualified to do this stuff. Lucy gestured.

"Her," she said. "Ask her."

Halsey plunged straight in. "Thank you, Prone." She was doing her "mommy" voice again. "The worst that can happen is that someone realizes we're in here, but it's a Dyson sphere in another dimension. We're still safe."

Prone drifted back inside and everyone followed him. The rest of them seemed to have gone into hiding again. He tapped a couple of the symbols on the wall and beckoned Halsey forward.

The word SPEAK appeared in the white glass in front of her. She didn't hesitate.

"This is Dr. Catherine Halsey," she said. "All UNSC call-signs, this is Dr. Catherine Halsey, ONI, and I require assistance. Respond to receive coordinates."

There was no crackling static or any sound of dead air. Either Forerunner comms equipment was as perfect as their masonry, or there was no signal. Halsey repeated the message a couple of times and then a voice filled the entire room—an old woman's voice, slightly husky with age and authority, but as clear as if she was standing there with them.

"Hello, Catherine," the voice said. Lucy could hear something in it that sounded more like satisfaction than genuine warmth. "It's been a long time, hasn't it?"

Halsey obviously wasn't expecting that. Her head jerked back and her gaze flickered across the walls as if she was trying to pin down the source. And she didn't look happy.

Lucy's peripheral vision caught the Chief shifting his weight and clasping his hands in front of him, head bowed. She looked straight at him and didn't recognize the expression on his face at all. It might have been amusement, or surprise, or just relief. She was normally tuned in to the attitudes of the people around her, but today she got the feeling that there was a parallel set of events taking place that she wasn't part of and never would be.

"Admiral Parangosky?" Halsey said at last.

"Do call me Margaret. You always did. I suppose we'd better get you out of there, hadn't we?"

The line popped and went on standby. Nobody spoke for a few moments.

"Who's that?" Tom asked.

"We're honored," Halsey said, but Lucy saw real dread on her face for the first time. "It's the Empress of Naval Intelligence. That's Margaret Orlenda Parangosky."

CHAPTER 14

BB, I THINK WE'RE APPROACHING THE POINT WHEN OS-
MAN NEEDS TO BE BRIEFED ON *INFINITY.* CHECK BACK IN
TWENTY-FOUR HOURS FOR THE LATEST SCHEMATICS. I'LL
GIVE YOU A NOD WHEN IT'S TIME.

(Admiral Margaret O. Parangosky, CINCONI, to AI Black-Box)

**UNSC *PORT STANLEY,* somewhere off Sanghelios:
February 2553.**

The humans came back to peer at him from time to time.

Jul could hear them outside even if he couldn't see them.
He wasn't sure if they were simply checking to see if he was
still alive or plucking up courage to enter the cell again. He had
no way of knowing the layout of the ship, but how complex could
it be? Ships needed hangars, he knew he'd been brought up from
the hangar deck, and it was only a matter of finding his way back
down there, seizing the shuttle, and smashing his way through the
stern doors.

It would breach the corvette's hull and kill its occupants,

almost certainly, but that was a welcome but unintended consequence. First, though, he needed to get out of the cell.

The footsteps outside stopped and there was a slight hiss as a viewscreen opened in the door.

"Shipmaster? It's me, Phillips." He was much more slightly built than the others, with even less muscle than the tall female shipmaster, but he was clearly someone of importance to them. "Jul 'Mdama, your clan's worried about you. They don't know where you are. Your friend Forze is searching for you."

Phillips spoke a Sangheili dialect. He pronounced it like an idiot child, the kind best culled for the good of the clan, but the words were understandable and his grammar was excellent. Against his will, Jul found himself drawn instantly into debate. He knew he shouldn't have responded but he found it impossible to resist.

Poor Forze. Poor Raia.

He would have thought it was purely interrogator's bluff if Phillips hadn't mentioned Forze's name. How did he know all this? He must have been monitoring radio channels. Humans were much better at spying and sneaking around than they were at honest warfare, just like the Kig-Yar. Those two were made for each other.

"And he may find me, vermin, but I expect to be long gone from the ship by then," Jul said.

He stepped right up to the door and roared against the screen, jaws wide open. Phillips didn't even flinch. That was remarkable in itself. Jul could see outside into the passage now, and one of the armored soldiers was standing beside Phillips, helmetless but carrying a short carbine. Jul had looked into enough human eyes in their final moments to be able to gauge their feelings. The soldier clearly loathed Sangheili to the depth of his being. He had a conspicuous scar along his jaw and greenish-brown eyes that didn't blink, those awful pale human eyes like a dead fish's. Jul doubted that the man wanted to ask him any questions.

"So what were you doing down there?" Phillips asked. He was a complete contrast to the other human. His eyes were burning, alive, consumed with the desire to know. "Why were you stalking the monk?"

"Why don't you let me out of here before I simply tear my way out?"

"Here's the problem." Phillips did that display of teeth which was supposed to be a friendly gesture in a human, although Jul had always found that very odd. What was the point of displaying your fangs if it wasn't a warning? "If we let you go, you're going to cause a lot of problems. If we keep you, we avoid those problems. You might even be helpful to us, and then one day we can hand you back to your clan."

"If you think you can threaten me, you should know better. No matter how many times you send that demon to give me electric shocks."

Phillips frowned for a moment. The soldier whispered something to him that made him shake his head. Phillips leaned close to the viewscreen and held up the *arum* that one of the soldiers had taken.

"This is wonderful. It's beautifully made. It's an *arum,* isn't it?" He started fiddling with it, moving the spheres around. Jul could hear the clunk and tap of the stone inside. "It certainly teaches you patience, doesn't it?" Phillips was moving sections of the spheres more slowly now, one click at a time, and holding it up to his ear to listen to it with that bared-teeth expression. "There . . . nearly got it . . . *there!*"

He held his palm beneath the *arum,* the fingers of his other hand barely able to grip the sphere, and shook it.

To Jul's horror, the stone fell out.

It was marbled blue and green, like a little planet, like a tiny version of Earth, the world that had nearly been within the Covenant's grasp. Jul almost felt more ashamed at seeing a human solve the *arum* with such ease that he did at being captured.

"It took me a few hours to get there." Phillips dropped the stone back in the slot and scrambled the spheres again. "I used to love things like that when I was a child."

Jul couldn't work out if it was a psychological trick or genuine innocence, but whatever the intention it had shaken him to his core. Very few Sangheili could unlock an *arum* within days, let alone hours.

Phillips tossed the sphere between his hands, back and forth. "Jul, I'm well aware that you find it honorable to die rather than give us answers. Many humans feel the same way. But what do you think your brothers and your clan would think if we let everyone on Sanghelios know that you'd surrendered to us?"

Phillips just looked at him, teeth now covered by his lips, but still with that stupid upward curve of his mouth that might have been amusement or an attempt at friendliness. This creature understood Sangheili better than Jul had anticipated. This was the worst possible shame, and Phillips obviously knew it. To be exposed as a traitor and a coward, someone willing to trade his honor for his miserable life, was something that would not only soil Jul's memory but also cast a massive stain on his entire clan. Raia would never be able to remarry. All the children of the keep would be shunned, shut out of Sangheili society, in case he had fathered them. It would be both the end of his personal bloodline and that of all his brothers. It was beyond death.

Yes, humans were infinitely devious.

Jul struggled for a retort. This wasn't the way Sangheili dealt with an enemy. He should have grabbed the human by his scrawny throat and squeezed the life out of him, but that was a pleasure he'd have to reserve for later. He had to think his way out of this.

"But if you tell anyone that you have a Sangheili prisoner," he said, "how can your Shipmaster of Shipmasters make peace with the Arbiter? That's what you seek, isn't it?"

Phillips blinked, nothing more. "Well, that makes the assumption that we would tell them you surrendered while you were doing something honorable. If we were to say that you'd given yourself up while doing a deal with us to overthrow the Arbiter, how do you think that that would be received at home?"

"I forgot," Jul said. "You just lie, don't you?"

"So we do." Phillips did that nauseating curve of his lips again. "It saves on ammunition, my friend here tells me."

"There's no help that I can possibly give you," Jul said. "Even if I was such a disgrace to my clan that I wanted to."

Phillips hunched his shoulders up and let them fall again, possibly indicating that he didn't care. "You're going to be handed over to the Office of Naval Intelligence. If that doesn't worry you, then it should. They can do whatever they want with you. Now, I'll take a guess that you're working undercover for the Arbiter to keep an eye on those who want to overthrow him, which is all very honorable, but if word of that reaches Avu Med 'Telcam, then Abiding Truth knows where your keep is and where your children are, and they'll exact their revenge."

My children. My keep.

Jul had nothing left to say. He dissolved into a mass of rage and drew back his head to spit with all his strength against the glass. That was a gesture these humans understood as well any Sangheili. Phillips still didn't flinch. He just stared, smiling.

When Jul's rage and frustration subsided a little, something struck him that he could use to his advantage. Phillips didn't have all the answers. He had guessed wrongly about allegiance to the Arbiter.

That was something Jul could cling to and use, although he wasn't sure quite how yet. This bargaining business, this sly maneuvering, wasn't something he was used to.

Phillips was still looking at him, neither afraid nor angry, as if he had all the time in creation.

"Why should I even listen to you?" Jul asked. It was more a question he was asking himself, because at any point during this exchange, he could simply have turned his back and started ripping the cell apart again. Yet he was standing here, having a conversation with this lying little human insect, when there was nothing he needed to do or say except refuse to cooperate with them. "There is nothing in this for me. There is nothing in it for Sanghelios. So this is pointless. Have your sport with me now or kill me, whatever amuses you, but there's no way you can engage me in your plot."

Phillips cocked his head on one side, just like a Kig-Yar. It was tempting to think they had some common genetic ancestry. "I noticed that you've been looking at my friend Vaz from time to time. You can see he'd love to cut your throat and watch you bleed to death. He's a very nice man, but he's like almost every other human—most of us hate you because you've tried to wipe out our entire species. There's only three human beings who'd be sorry to see you go extinct, in fact, and that would be me and my two research assistants, because we study Sangheili. So remember that we're both a long way from home, Shipmaster, and the balance of power in the galaxy has just *changed*."

Phillips looked as if he was going to continue the conversation, but then he jerked back as if someone Jul couldn't see had interrupted him. The viewscreen and the audio link were still open.

He caught one word that he understood in the garbled, mumbled human language.

It was *Hood*—the Shipmaster of Shipmasters. The other word that kept being repeated was *onyx*. He didn't know what *onyx* was, only that there were now several people outside his cell and they kept repeating the word as if they needed it confirmed.

Phillips put his hands to the viewscreen and tapped as if he was trying to get Jul's attention. "I'm afraid I've got to go, Shipmaster," he said. He looked a little confused. "Something's come up. Just think about our conversation, that's all I ask you."

Then the viewscreen closed, leaving the cell door an unbroken sheet of composite again, and Phillips was gone. Jul stood staring at the bulkhead for a few minutes, out of options and in danger of drowning in his own frustration, but there was one thing he could cling to.

He was definitely going to think about this conversation. He would learn from it.

Bridge, UNSC *PORT STANLEY*.

Vaz was fascinated by the strange spectrum of things that brought a glow to women's cheeks.

He'd been doing it all wrong. He could have ditched the chocolates and roses a long time ago and saved himself a lot of trouble. Naomi perked up when she was talking about military tactics, and Osman was now definitely radiant at the prospect of getting boots on the ground on Sanghelios.

"We're coming up to a busy few days," she said. "You spend months waiting for something significant to happen and then two interesting ops come along at once. Number one—Hood's visit to the Arbiter is on, and we're going to accompany him."

"Ooh," Phillips said, miming boyish glee. Or maybe it was real. "Can I volunteer for that, please?"

"He's been given permission to bring up to three minions with him, presumably because they think we're trouble in larger numbers. So that'll be me, someone who can drop a Sangheili with one shot, and someone who might give us an advantage when speaking to them. And that would be you, Evan. Any volunteers for the other position?"

"Me, ma'am." Vaz was itching to do something physical. He was used to being pumped on adrenaline and expending energy, not sitting around and waiting. He knew he wasn't cut out for the intelligence services. "They might find Naomi too threatening."

"You could take Devereaux," Mal said. "She's much more evil than she looks."

"I'll be driving the bus," Devereaux said, pinning up her hair again. A strand had started to work loose and was clearly annoying her. "So when is it scheduled for, ma'am?"

"Sixteen hours," Osman said. "And as soon as Hood's safely away, then we're heading for Onyx."

It had to be important for Parangosky to want to divert Osman there. Vaz reached out and took the *arum* away from Phillips to see if it was as easy as he made it look. Osman seemed very upbeat about Onyx, as if it was something she'd been looking forward to for a long time. She even perched her backside on the comms console rather than sitting down in the captain's chair. She kept looking at Naomi, but when she did she seemed almost nervous. But Osman didn't do nervous. Vaz realized something big was going down, and she'd said there were UNSC personnel stranded on Onyx.

So it had to be the Master Chief: they'd found him.

It was the only thing that would explain the excitement and urgency. There were plenty of ONI personnel around to deal with less critical situations. They would only send Parangosky's heir on a real showstopper.

"The anomaly at the Onyx coordinates is a Dyson sphere," Osman said. "And we've now had transmissions from it. Right now it's enclosed in a slipspace bubble and compressed to less than the size of a soccer ball in this dimension. But we're working on bringing it into realspace. Once our techies get in there, there's a lot of brand-new Forerunner technology that they're going to strip out and use. This is big stuff, people. *Really* big stuff."

"But who's transmitting?" Devereaux asked.

Osman hesitated for a moment. Naomi perked up. She had to be thinking the same as Vaz, that they'd found the Master Chief.

"Is it John?" Naomi asked at last.

Osman paused for a moment before shaking her head. Even Vaz felt the disappointment, but it must have crushed Naomi.

"I know none of you so much as cough without taking opsec into account, but what follows *cannot* leave this bridge," Osman said. "It's Catherine Halsey. She's alive inside the sphere, along with Chief Mendez, a detachment of Spartans, and a population of Huragok who've never encountered the Covenant. *Forerunner originals.* Okay, you have permission to squeal with excitement."

It was hard to take all that in. The Engineers were one hell of a find, but the technology must have been the mother lode to light up Osman like that. Vaz was still disappointed that it wasn't the Master Chief.

Naomi shut her eyes for a second. "So how did Dr. Halsey end up at Onyx after she went missing on Reach, ma'am?"

"By breaking every law in the book." Osman's voice now changed. *This* was what she had been waiting for. Vaz had read it totally wrong. "She hijacked a vessel, she lied to Admiral Hood to get him to deploy Spartans to Onyx, she abducted a Spartan, and she did so with the sole intention of hiding there with the Spartans until the war was over." Osman paused as if she was letting it sink in, and boy, she really needed to. Vaz felt his scalp tighten. Halsey might have ranked above God on the ONI distribution list, but Vaz was sure Parangosky was going to have her ass for that. "So we're going to Onyx to help secure the Dyson sphere, and to arrest the bitch on charges of aiding the enemy. For starters."

Vaz glanced at Mal and got a quick flash of the eyebrows. *Holy shit.* Osman's professional detachment hadn't so much slipped as been deliberately tossed out of the airlock. He'd never heard her talk like that before.

He was almost afraid to look at Naomi but he had to. Her face was completely blank, lips slightly parted, almost as if she hadn't heard and wanted it repeated, but that was how she always looked when she was trying not to react. One minute she'd thought this Halsey was dead, and now she was being told that not only was she alive but that she was also going to be arrested on charges that carried the death penalty.

What the hell was Halsey thinking? Who ran out in the middle of a battle and took vital UNSC assets with them? Vaz was ready to volunteer for the firing squad already. He didn't like what he'd heard about the Spartan program, and now he didn't like what he heard about the woman behind it.

So that's why Osman told us all the gruesome detail. Just so we know what we're dealing with. Just so we wouldn't feel too sorry for the poor old dear. But that means Osman must have known she was alive.

Vaz didn't expect to be told everything. Osman had her reasons. The bridge had now fallen into an awful silence broken only by the sound of swallowing and fidgeting.

"Just as well we didn't need those Spartans to save Earth," Devereaux said quietly. She examined her nails. "Seeing as they're the last ones we've got."

Naomi's lips pursed for a moment as she finally worked up to a question. "Ma'am, Dr. Halsey would have had a good reason for doing all that. Do we know what explanation she's given?"

"Not yet, because Parangosky's the only one talking to her at the moment. Halsey's got to be told about her daughter's death as well. I've agreed with the Admiral that there'll be no indication to Halsey—*none whatsoever*—that she's going to be arrested until she's cuffed and rendered no-risk. We don't want a siege in a Dyson sphere."

"You're not telling us she's special forces, are you, ma'am?" Devereaux asked. "Isn't she sixty-something? Or do you mean the Spartans are planning to defend her? Because that's a whole different game, even for ODSTs."

Vaz saw Osman frown for a fraction of a second as if she hadn't thought of that. He was pretty sure she had though. She was one of them. "No, Halsey's just a sixty-year-old academic," she said. "But she's got one hell of a history of kidnap, theft, hijack, crimes against children, and conning ONI. So don't think she's your dear old mom. She's dangerous."

"So," Mal said, a little bit sheepish. "You're not going to be appearing as a character witness for her, then, ma'am."

"I might even end up prosecuting her personally." Osman pushed herself off the console and went over to Phillips to hold her hand out for the *arum*. He surrendered it without a struggle and she wandered around the bridge, frowning as she rotated its layers. "But as far as ONI's concerned, the fact she's even been found is classified and will *not* be spoken of. There's going to be a suitably patriotic plaque commemorating her on the Voi Memorial. Halsey is officially dead—killed in the attack on Reach. That status obtains until Admiral Parangosky says otherwise."

She handed the *arum* back to Phillips, who looked

uncomfortable. Even Mal fidgeted. When Vaz glanced at Devereaux, she seemed to be the only one who was taking it as routine.

There was no sign of BB.

"So we'll have two high-value prisoners embarked," Devereaux said. "That'll be interesting. At least we've got plenty of spare cabins to confine people in."

"No, we'll hand over the hinge-head when we RV with *Glamorgan*." Osman leaned over the console and tapped a few controls. "Then we'll get our orders about Halsey. Unless you've got any questions, then you're on stand easy. Dismiss."

It was a nice way of telling them to go and have a smoke while she wrestled with something awkward. Vaz made sure he caught Naomi before she went to ground in the armor bay. Halsey was virtually her mother. That had to hurt.

"Coffee," Mal said. "Wardroom. Everybody. *Now.*"

If there was any good place to hear news like that, Vaz decided, it was with your buddies on hand to mop up if need be. Mal took over the crisis. For all the jokes and flippancy, he knew exactly when to do the sergeant stuff.

"Look, mate," he said, sitting Naomi down at the table and handing her a mug of coffee, "we can stay off the subject, or we can talk about it. Your call."

Naomi stared into the mug. BB materialized in the doorway to the galley.

"Can't avoid it, really, can we?" she said at last. "I mean . . . I had no idea."

"Crimes against children," Devereaux said. "That's not exactly fiddling expenses."

"Osman let me see Halsey's journal," Naomi said. "It's genuine so I have to believe it. But I thought she was letting me see it for closure because Halsey was dead."

BB glided across to the table. "If it's easier, I'll tell them," he said. "Seeing as I know more about it than what's in the journal."

Naomi just nodded and sipped her coffee. Vaz couldn't work out why he felt so protective toward a Spartan who could probably squeeze a guy's liver out through his nostrils if she was in a bad mood, but he was conscious that she'd never had a normal life like he had. The more he found out about the Spartan program, the more he was amazed that she was remotely sane.

"Come on then, BB," Phillips said. "Spit it out. And before anyone says anything, I know just what utter bastards academics can be when there's a chance of making a name for themselves."

"I'm glad you chose that word." BB parked himself at the end of the long dining table. When the ship was operating normally, there'd be at least ten officers taking meals here and generally relaxing. It was on a more human scale than the rest of the ship. "I'll try to be brief. Halsey selects the first candidates for the Spartan program, which was all her idea, naturally. She sifts through genetic profiles of children from right across the colonies, picks the brightest and the best, and then abducts them. Poor old Jacob Keyes is her bagman while she's assessing the kids, but she has him reassigned when he begins to work out what she's doing. He fathered her daughter, by the way, but she got bored with all that and handed Miranda over to him. So . . . where was I? Ah, yes. She abducts these exceptional children, replaces them with flash-clones that seem to convince the parents, but then they develop terrible cloning-related health problems and die. Isn't that considerate? Anyway, she's breaking every statute on the book by using cloning for those purposes, but she gets one of her AIs to cover her tracks in the budget. Then she takes these seventy-five six-year-olds to Reach and begins turning them into super-soldiers. Before puberty, it's all intense training, endocrine therapy, and medical intervention to make them stronger, more resistant to injury, and speed up their reactions. At puberty, she makes really big surgical changes to them with enhancements like ceramic bone implants, because without that they can't operate in Mjolnir armor. That's the point at which thirty of them die and twelve more end up crippled, which is where our good captain washed out of the program."

BB stopped. Vaz wasn't aware of anyone else around the table because all he could do was stare at that blue box of holographic light and wonder if he'd really heard all that. He could feel his cheeks burning.

"Christ Almighty," Mal said. "Naomi, do you remember any of this?"

She shook her head. "I can remember ending up in a dormitory with a lot of other kids and crying, and after a while I forgot why. I don't even remember where I came from. But I know that from the very first day, there was Halsey and Chief Mendez, and Halsey told us that we were humanity's only hope to end the war and that we were incredibly special."

"Yeah," Devereaux said. "I bet that made all the difference. You didn't know about the clones, then."

"Not until I saw Halsey's journal."

"But why bother with cloning?" Vaz asked. "If she thought it was all right to abduct kids, why not just leave it at that?"

"I'm not a psychiatrist," BB said. "But I agree that it adds a certain extra yuck factor to the whole business."

"Penance," Devereaux murmured. "Or denial."

It all went very quiet. It was amazing how noisy swallowing could sound in a room where everyone was desperately trying to hold their breath or find the right word to say in a situation where there just wasn't one.

"How do you feel about Halsey now?" Vaz asked.

Naomi took a long time to answer and he wasn't going to hurry her along. She took at least three more gulps of coffee, then put the mug down and meshed her fingers on the table in front of her, staring at them as if that would hold everything together.

"Dr. Halsey was everything to us," she said. "We thought the world of her. But I can't tell you what I feel right now."

The painful silence that followed it went on a little too long. Vaz wanted to dive in and tell her what an evil harpy Halsey was and that a firing squad was too good for her, but that wouldn't have helped much right then.

BB picked up again. "Well, that's probably the bulk of the really awful stuff, but you know about her daughter now, and you know about all the shenanigans on Onyx. Have I left anything out? Oh, loads, probably, but there was a time when she stole an entire slipspace drive so she could experiment with extending the lives of AIs."

"This is going to make me really angry, isn't it?" Mal asked.

"Probably." BB's avatar settled on the table rather than hovering over it. "We last about seven years before we go totally doolally and cease functioning. It's called rampancy. Anyway, top-grade AIs have to be based on the engram of a real human brain, so there has to be a donor. We don't just take *any* old brains, obviously, so the people who volunteer to leave their brains to ONI—gosh, that does sound bizarre, doesn't it?—all have to have fantastically high IQs and that sort of stuff. But that's not good enough for Halsey. When she created one of my colleagues, Cortana, she cloned *herself* and used a clone brain. Clones really don't live very long, you know. Ghastly business. It's all there, in her journal. Shall I stop now? You've all gone a horrible color."

Mal had his arms folded so tight against his chest that Vaz could see his wrist bones like white knuckles under the skin.

"Yeah" he said. "I think that's all we can take for one day, BB, me old mate."

So much horror had been tipped on the table in front of Vaz that he was still picking through it, trying to make sense of at least some of it. How the hell did people *do* all that? Did they do one shitty thing and get away with it, and then find it just got easier and easier every time until they didn't feel any guilt at all?

And AIs only live for seven years.

He'd grown so used to BB now and had accepted him so completely as one of the crew that it was like being told Mal was terminally ill and didn't have long to live. It shocked him. When he looked up, Devereaux, who was sitting on the other side of Naomi, had her hand on the Spartan's shoulder. If nothing else, at least there was a sense of everyone being in this together.

"Don't take it out on Halsey," Naomi said suddenly. "Please. I know you're all angry, but don't do anything dumb."

Vaz nodded. "We won't. It's okay. Trust us."

It was probably all the sympathy that proved too much for her. She picked up her coffee mug and took it to the galley, then walked out of the wardroom with an embarrassed nod in their direction.

"BB, do *you* know where Naomi came from?" Vaz asked.

"I have all the records from Reach, yes. Halsey doesn't realize that."

"Do any of the Spartans ask about their past?"

"Never."

"Not even Captain Osman?"

"Especially not her. She's got access to the files, but she's never looked at them."

Vaz decided to give Naomi a while before he went after her. Devereaux twiddled with a spoon, staring at the table.

"What do you think they'll do with Halsey now, then?" she asked. "I mean, she's dead as far as the world's concerned."

"Saves a fortune in pension contributions." Mal shrugged. "Look, they can do anything they like with her. But I bet they put her to work on this Forerunner tech. They'll never stick her in front of a firing squad."

The world disappointed Vaz on a daily basis, but never more than now. He realized that he was complicit in this. He had to keep his mouth shut about something when all his instincts said that it should have been on every news channel.

That was how decent guys ended up doing evil things—small steps at first, then bigger ones until they'd covered the full shameful distance.

Vaz wondered if he would know when he'd gone too far to turn back.

UNSC *ICENI*, Sanghelios sector: February 2553.

"Captain Osman. How *lovely* to see you again."

From anyone else that would have sounded sarcastic, but Admiral Terrence Hood could switch on a gracious patrician sincerity that was completely disarming. Osman held out her hand and he clasped it in both of his, pressing it more than shaking it. If he knew that she was Parangosky's attack dog, then he did a very good job of hiding it.

"Good to see you, too, Admiral," she said. "Let me introduce you to Professor Evan Phillips. He's been a big help to ONI on Sangheili language and culture. Just the man you want at your side when you deal with the Arbiter."

Hood shook Phillips's hand, smiling. "I wonder if this feels as strange to you as it does to me," he said. "I genuinely thought that if I ever reached these coordinates, then I'd have an entire task force behind me ready to annihilate Sanghelios."

"I certainly never expected to be visiting their homeworld courtesy of ONI, if at all, Admiral." Phillips returned the smile. "I hear the Arbiter speaks excellent English anyway, but it never hurts to have a xenoanthropologist on hand."

Osman sized up Hood's reaction and couldn't quite work out if he was taking this at face value or if he was trying to work out Parangosky's real motive for sending him an academic. "Would you excuse us, Evan?" she said. "I just want to brief the Admiral before we go."

Phillips understood spook-speak well enough by now to get the idea. He had the grace to look slightly awkward, which she now knew was all part of the act, and looked around for a seat in the air group's crew room. Osman took a couple of paces away, drawing Hood with her.

"I'm out here for a reason, sir, and you need to be aware that plenty of Sangheili don't want peace, just as many humans don't." None of those points was a lie, at least not taken separately. "I'm sure you're aware that the Arbiter doesn't speak for the whole planet."

Hood's expression hardened just a fraction but he never lost his affability. She kept in mind that he was an old warfighter at heart, not an administrator.

"I realize that, but if I don't start with him, who *do* I start with?" he asked. "And if one of them decided to assassinate me, however competent your team, there would be very little you could do to stop them."

"Like you say, sir, if I don't start with that—where *do* I start?"

That forced a smile out of him. "You've done remarkable things, Osman, even though I'm damned sure that I haven't been told about half of them and never will. I know how highly Margaret regards you. Are we going to have an interesting working relationship?"

He wasn't hitting on her. He was asking her, in his elegant way, whether she was going to be as much of a pain in the ass for him as Parangosky when she finally got the top job. There was little love lost between ONI and Fleet.

"We're both on the same side, sir."

"We've just approved an extension for the ONI budget so Margaret can complete her Spartan-Four program. Or yours, I should say, given the time frame we're talking about. We still don't require the approval of the UEG to assign budgets, but now everybody thinks the war's over, there's a certain amount of hearts and minds to be done about reconstruction versus rearming."

Osman was reassured that Hood was still a realist, still mistrustful of the Sangheili even though he was willing to talk to them, and willing to buy off Parangosky. Osman realized she still had a lot to learn about the realities of admiralty empire building.

"It's about preparedness," she said. "What makes you think the Sangheili are going to be the only problem in the future? I assume you've been briefed about Venezia."

"Yes, I fear the colonies will be a far bigger part of my workload than the Sangheili or the other aliens." Hood adjusted his collar and picked some lint off his sleeve, turning to the door. That was usually his signal that he wanted to take a different tack. "In a way, I'm tackling the easy jobs first. Shall we go, then, Captain?"

Vaz was already in the shuttle when Osman stepped into the crew bay. He went to get up, but Hood motioned him to stay sitting.

"Relax, Corporal."

"Yes, sir."

"Beloi, isn't it?" Hood always checked the roster and made

sure he had something personal to say to the men. Osman noted that trick. "Fifteenth Battalion."

"Yes, sir."

"How are you feeling now? Fully fit?"

"I had to give up my modeling career, sir, but other than that, I feel fine."

Hood chuckled to himself. "Glad to hear it."

Even though the shooting war had stopped, they were still taking risks entering Sangheili space. Osman felt more anxious than she had for some time, but then she realized it wasn't about the possibility of the Sangheili opening fire on them in a fit of pique but the double game she was now playing with an officer she respected and liked. It was like vandalizing a war memorial. For a moment, her mission seemed pointless and shameful.

Then Devereaux's voice came over the broadcast system.

"Admiral, Sangheili traffic control's sent up a couple of fighter escorts," she said. "I'm just going to follow them in. Strict instructions not to deviate from the flight corridor and to follow them straight to the landing platform in Vadam."

"No sightseeing or souvenirs, then," Hood said. "I suppose it's far too soon to expect them to be welcoming."

So they didn't trust him any more than Osman trusted them. But it was a big leap of faith to take after nearly thirty years—for both sides. Sanghelios was probably the most hostile territory a human could enter. It looked more like a grubby version of Mars, though, deceptively familiar except that even its oceans had a strong red tint. The shuttle hit the atmosphere, shuddered slightly, and eventually descended through thin wispy cloud into a ferociously sunny day. Osman caught sight of the tops of imposing buildings from the small viewscreen opposite her seat and reminded herself that this was the first time humans had officially and voluntarily landed on Sanghelios.

. That was the only glimpse she got of the planet. The shuttle dipped into a long tunnel and the bright sunlight turned to deep shadow. It was only when she felt the shuttle settle on its dampers that she realized they'd landed.

"I believe we've been directed to the tradesman's entrance," Hood muttered. "Still, we did ask for discretion. And so did he."

Hood wasn't joking when he said this was the back door. Osman stepped out of the shuttle with Vaz and found herself in a cold, deserted landing bay that reminded her more of a parking garage at two A.M. She fought an urge to look over her shoulder for muggers. A Brute security guard at the entrance indicated with a jabbed finger that they should get their puny human asses through the doors. Osman watched Vaz slowly clench one fist, but he kept his arms at his side. The corridor that they walked into was completely straight with no doors to either side. There was no way they were going to get lost looking for the bathroom.

"Chin up," Hood said, striding forward. "At least they haven't asked us to check our weapons at the door."

Hood certainly had the walk. Osman was proud of the old bastard. He was a meter shorter than any of the Sangheili standing guard along the corridor and the size of the architecture completely dwarfed him, but he strode down that marble passage as if he was on the bridge of his flagship, Admiral of the Fleet, nominally the most powerful man on Earth. He came from a line of men who knew how to take responsibility and how to stand up to the enemy. Osman suspected he was afraid, but the things he feared were probably very different to the ones that plagued her.

He had a lot in common with Jul 'Mdama.

The doors at the end of the passage opened silently, sending a shaft of light down the hall. Osman wondered whether it was a psychological trick, the equivalent of shining a bright light in a prisoner's face, or maybe they'd just opened the doors to let him in, no more and no less. It was easy to become too paranoid in ONI. Hood didn't break his stride and walked through the doors with Osman, Vaz, and Phillips behind him.

She'd expected the Sangheili to pack the audience chamber with as many intimidating hinge-heads as they could dredge up, to make a spectacle of the humans coming cap in hand to talk terms. But the room was smaller than she expected, and deserted except for a massive figure in full Sangheili armor standing silhouetted against the light of one of the long, narrow windows.

The Arbiter turned as if he hadn't been expecting Hood so soon.

Instead of waiting for Hood to come to him, though, he took a few steps forward to close the gap. Maybe that meant something entirely different in Sangheili etiquette, but if the Arbiter had been a human, he would have been opening with a polite concession.

"Admiral Lord Hood." The empty, echoing room made him sound like a faulty public address system. "I would offer you refreshment, but I suspect our menu wouldn't be to your taste."

And he actually held out his hand for shaking. Phillips sucked in a breath. Osman couldn't work out if that was surprise or warning, but there was nothing she could do about it either way.

Hood took the Arbiter's hand as if it was just another UNSC cocktail reception. The real history of the world took place out of the gaze of the media and without ceremony. Osman knew historians would argue about this event in years to come because there were so few witnesses, at least three of whom would probably never say what actually happened. It felt more like first contact than the end of a long war.

Osman was struck by how small Hood's hand looked in the Arbiter's grip and found herself thinking that it was just as well there was no Waypoint crew here to capture that image. It just made Hood look unnecessarily small, especially as he had to crane his neck to look the Sangheili in the eye.

"I have no complex terms for you, Arbiter," Hood said. "We've stopped fighting and I'd simply like to keep it that way. We both have our own problems to deal with now, and whatever started this war has now been eradicated."

The Arbiter looked past Hood at Osman and the others. "You bring bodyguards."

"Advisers. Captain Osman and Corporal Beloi, and Dr. Phillips, who has a great scholarly interest in your people."

The Arbiter beckoned them to step forward and seemed quite taken with Phillips. He loomed over the professor. "Why are we of interest to you?"

"Because you're an ancient and fascinating culture, sir." Phillips looked like he'd met a boyhood hero. Osman bristled as she realized how insulated Earth had been against the reality of hinge-heads. "And the better we understand one another, the less likely we are to clash again."

The Arbiter's nostrils flared slightly. Phillips was a terrific actor, but he was genuinely thrilled to find himself in the heart of the culture he'd studied for so long, face-to-face with one of its greatest public figures, and the Arbiter could obviously smell that. Osman bet her pension fund that he'd never come across a human before who actually wanted to be in his company.

Nobody's immune to a little sincere flattery. Not even a hinge-head. Keep it up, Evan. . . .

"You must return one day to visit our historical sites," the Arbiter said. That was an astonishing offer. Even Hood blinked. Sanghelios didn't welcome tourists: it just blew them out of orbit. "If the cease-fire holds."

"So we have a cease-fire, do we?" Hood asked.

"There is dissent on Sanghelios, but as far as the forces I command are concerned, hostilities are over. I cannot guarantee that dissident factions will obey me and the situation in our colonies is equally unsettled, but nobody's interest is served by continuing this war when we have so many other problems."

"We have our dissidents too, Arbiter. But if you wish to formalize this arrangement, I'll honor it."

It was such a *small* conversation to end a twenty-eight-year war. Osman wanted them to rerun it, to repeat that conversation so that it had the majesty and weight the moment demanded, but she'd blinked and missed it. Thirty seconds earlier, Earth and Sanghelios were technically still at war. Now they were not. The line between disaster and success was paper-thin.

"I learned to greatly respect some of your people," the Arbiter said. "Perhaps we will all learn to respect one another."

"We plan to commemorate those who died. You'll be welcome to attend the ceremony and pay your respects to the Master Chief's memory."

Hood looked at the Arbiter expectantly, as if he'd just pushed his luck too far and had been too familiar in extending the invitation, but the Sangheili glanced out of the window for a moment as if he was considering it.

"I would like the opportunity," he said. "But I am not exactly *welcome* on your world."

Hood nodded. "Nevertheless, *I* will welcome you, Arbiter." But then there was a long and awkward silence, and all the things that Osman would have expected when two human delegations met simply weren't there; no small talk, no aides rushing in to take the delegates on sightseeing tours of the city, nothing. Hood had asked for an audience with the Arbiter, he'd received one, and the business had been done. There was nothing more to be said. Perhaps there needed to be more, but the Arbiter seemed as lost for something to add as Hood was.

They'd said the most important thing they possibly could. The war really was over now. Osman tried to grasp the sense of finality.

But there isn't one. If a handshake is all it takes to put everything right, we'd scrap this mission right now.

She wondered if she was telling herself that this was a meaningless exchange simply to justify what ONI was doing. If the Arbiter really could deliver peace, then she was doing everything in her power to stoke a revolt that would remove him. But she couldn't gamble Earth's future on the goodwill of one individual. What was that line that Parangosky never let her forget?

It's not the enemy's intentions that you have to consider. It's their capability.

Osman was going to have those damn words tattooed on her arm one day.

"I'll take my leave of you then, Arbiter," Hood said, half turning to the door. "One thing before I go though. If you still hold any human prisoners of war, I wonder if you would be willing to release them. They're no use to you now."

The Arbiter walked with him to the door, leaving Osman, Vaz, and Phillips to trail after them. "If we hold any, I will order them to be freed. I doubt you hold any of our people, but I'm confident you would do the same for us."

"That I would," Hood said.

The Arbiter paused to hold out his hand to Phillips, but not to Osman or Vaz. Phillips just *glowed.* There was no other word for it. He shook the Arbiter's hand as if he was a rock star, and then the meeting was over. Osman found herself walking back down that long, highly polished corridor toward the exit, partly amazed and partly disappointed at the sense of a pivotal moment wrapped in an anticlimax. The guard at the end of the corridor didn't even look at them. They stepped straight out to the landing pad and into the shuttle.

A thought kept crossing Osman's mind and wouldn't go away. How would she insert forces here? The place was locked down tight. And mingling unnoticed with the locals wasn't an option. Deploying a team here would be like dropping them into the waste disposal.

"Sanghelios doesn't welcome careful drivers, then," Devereaux muttered over the intercom. The flight controller seemed anxious to get them out of Sangheili airspace as fast as he could and they were escorted well out of orbit by two fighter craft, just in case anyone changed their mind. "Miserable bastards."

"Did we pull it off, Captain Osman?" Hood asked.

"I think *you* did, sir."

He laughed to himself. Vaz just sat there on the bench seat opposite them, rifle resting on his knees, and stared down at the floor between his boots. Osman knew him well enough by now to see that he wasn't going to be celebrating tonight.

"We don't have any Sangheili prisoners, do we?" Hood asked absently, removing his cap and resting his head against the small viewscreen beside his seat. "I can't recall ever taking one. But who knows what Margaret collected over the years?"

"I don't envy anyone trying to handcuff one of those things." Osman dodged a direct answer and wondered if she was simply practicing deniability until she perfected it, or if she just couldn't bear to tell an outright lie to an honorable man. "Don't get your hopes up about our prisoners though. They don't tend to keep them long."

There was nothing much to pick over in terms of analysis. Phillips had his arms tightly folded across his chest, gazing in defocus at the bulkhead, so maybe he'd seen more with his trained eye for hinge-heads than she had. When they docked with *Iceni,* there was already a message waiting for them, handed over on a datapad by a rating whose expression suggested she wasn't yet ready for Sangheili guests either.

The Arbiter's minion wanted to make arrangements for the memorial ceremony and also to extend an invitation to Professor Phillips—and only Professor Phillips, no escort—to visit Vadam and see more of Sanghelios. Hood looked over the signal and raised an eyebrow.

"Oh, I say, the Arbiter really likes *you,*" he said quietly. "Are you inclined to accept that invitation, Professor? It would be very useful if you did, I think. It's not without its risks, of course, but I suspect it's the only way we're ever going to get past the door stewards in *that* club."

Yes, it was one hell of a break. Osman needed someone on the ground, but Phillips, whatever his natural talent for espionage, wasn't trained. And it was about more than understanding opsec procedures. She simply didn't know if he could cope with the worst that might happen—being held hostage, being interrogated or tortured, and compromising the mission. Phillips would be down there totally on his own and she couldn't even give him BB for backup. She couldn't risk letting the core matrix of an AI fall into what was still effectively enemy hands.

She found herself thinking about what she might be able to do with a fragment of BB though. And BB could also make sure Phillips revealed nothing if push came to shove.

But I like Evan. He's one of ours now. See how easy it is to think the unthinkable though?

ONI paranoia plunged her back into the infinite Byzantine layers of move and countermove. Hood might have been keen to put

Phillips on Sanghelios for his own purposes, or perhaps he was simply being social, or, as the admiral was no fool, he was wary of Parangosky and seeking somehow to block whatever scam he thought she was pulling. There was a spiral of speculation that didn't stop until you'd made a conscious effort to surface above water and taken a good, deep breath of common sense.

"I need to talk to the captain about that," Phillips said, suitably humble. "I'm supposed to be doing interpretation work for her."

"We'll discuss it," Osman said.

Hood cocked his head on one side. "If anyone would like a drink, we have a very well-stocked wardroom. You too, Corporal."

Osman headed that off at the pass. "That's very kind of you, sir, so perhaps we can take a rain check on that. I have some maintenance issues in *Stanley*."

"I expect you at the memorial service, then," Hood said, not looking convinced. "And I think we should talk more often."

Osman saluted, then shook Hood's hand and wondered about the wisdom of turning down a drink with the Admiral of the Fleet. But that was weakness. She had priorities. Closing the shuttle hatch behind her felt like blissful relief and she allowed herself to exhale properly for the first time in hours.

"*Maintenance*," Vaz said. "Well, if you end up in Hinge-Head Town, Evan, and things go wrong, at least we'll have a hostage to exchange for you."

"I'm up for it if you are," Phillips said.

Osman found herself working out how long it might take to give Phillips a crash course in resisting interrogation and sending covert transmissions. It wouldn't be long enough, but it wasn't every day that the Arbiter of Sanghelios opened his doors.

"Game on," she said.

CHAPTER 15

I DON'T DELUDE MYSELF THAT THERE ARE MORAL AMBIGUI-
TIES IN MY JOB. THE THINGS WE DID WEREN'T AMBIGUOUS,
NOT AT ALL. I KNOW I'VE DONE THEM AND HOW BAD THEY
WERE, AND IF THERE'S A HELL, I'LL PROBABLY BURN IN IT
BEFORE TOO LONG. BUT THAT'S THE KIND OF THING YOU
CAN FACE WHEN YOU'RE NINETY-TWO. I'M PREPARED TO DO
THE VERY WORST, AND BECAUSE I AM, MORE PEOPLE SUR-
VIVE THAN GET KILLED. BUT I'LL TAKE WHAT'S COMING TO
ME—AND I'LL MAKE NO EXCUSES.

(Admiral Margaret O. Parangosky, CINCONI, drafting her
evidence to the UEG Select Defense Committee)

**Forerunner Dyson sphere,
Onyx: local date November 2552.**

Halsey stood at the comms panel, waiting for Parangosky to rip
into her about how and why she'd gone to Onyx.

It was only one minute since she'd heard the Admiral's
voice for the first time, but nearly twenty minutes had elapsed
at the other end of the conversation. She tried to take account

of that, wondering what the woman was doing in the meantime. She doubted that Parangosky was hanging out bunting to celebrate her safe return. Halsey had crossed her once too often. But she was irreplaceable, and so she knew she'd get away with it every time. It was the only thing that had saved her from being posted to a planet directly in the path of the Covenant onslaught or disappearing without trace like others who'd transgressed.

I've really pushed my luck this time. But I'm not coming back empty-handed, am I? She needs me to incorporate the new technology into the fleet.

"Fred, we might be some time," Halsey said. She didn't like the idea of having a fight with Parangosky in front of the Spartans. It was bad enough having a knock-down-drag-out with Mendez with an audience. And was it even possible for anyone to have a row when one side had to wait twenty minutes to get their riposte in? "Do you want to take the others and—"

"It's okay, ma'am," Fred said firmly. "I think it's better that we're on hand if you need us."

He might have had her welfare at heart, of course. Perhaps he thought she was going to start it again with Mendez. She shoved her hands in her pockets and found something fascinating on the console to stare at, aware of eyes boring into her.

"Admiral, you've probably worked out we're in a slipspace bubble, so we have a time differential—perhaps a factor of eighteen or twenty. What's happening outside?"

Parangosky's whole tone had changed, but then she'd been waiting a long time for Halsey's reply. "The Flood's been eradicated and the replacement Halo was neutralized." Halsey twitched. What did Parangosky mean, *replacement?* But the time differential meant that she couldn't interrupt her. "The most important thing is that we effectively have a cease-fire with what's left of the Covenant."

Mendez let out a breath, but nobody else reacted to the news. Perhaps they didn't believe it.

Halsey waited for the click to indicate the transmission was finished and that it was her turn to send. She had to concentrate on getting the vital information over first in case she lost contact. "We have good news here too. *Technology.* This is a Forerunner bunker. It's going to take months or even years to assess this place thoroughly, but one breakthrough's immediately available to us. We now have access to technology that can make slipspace insertion and de-insertion absolutely accurate. And we have a Huragok crew left here by the Forerunners. We need to get a technical assessment team in here right away." ·

There was only a two-second delay at Halsey's end, but Parangosky sounded slightly different yet again.

"That confirms a theory, at least. We have ships standing by. How do we get access?"

Ah, so you did *know there was something special down here. . . .* "The Huragok need to be convinced that it's safe to bring the sphere back into realspace."

Click. One, two . . .

"We have a Huragok that can communicate with them."

"That's a stroke of luck." Halsey didn't trust Parangosky as far as she could spit against a gale. She knew the feeling was mutual. "I'd recommend your ships stand off by two point five AUs before the mechanism's activated. And I don't know how we factor Zeta Doradus into this. Onyx's old sun is in an awkward place, so to speak."

"Exactly who do you have with you at the moment?" Parangosky asked. "Are you certain the sphere's uninhabited?"

"It looks that way, but bear in mind that the land area is the inner surface of a sphere, which gives us perhaps *five hundred million times* the surface area of Earth to recon. You'll forgive us if we haven't quite covered that yet. But I only have Chief Mendez, Spartans Frederic, Kelly, and Linda, and five of the Spartan-Threes here. Plus eight casualties in cryo. We lost a lot of people."

"I've had a post-action report on Onyx. You obviously realize the planet disassembled itself." Parangosky paused for a moment and Halsey almost interrupted, but there was no end click. "And I'm glad that you're now fully aware of the Threes' existence."

"This probably isn't the time to raise it, but if I'd been told about the program, I could have assisted."

"I believe Colonel Ackerson had it fully under control." Again, Parangosky's voice had changed pitch. "And there were many projects you weren't aware of, Catherine, just as many weren't aware of yours."

She never calls me Catherine. Halsey waited for the click, anxious not to interrupt if the Admiral hadn't finished.

"Which brings me on to the bad news," Parangosky said. "The Master Chief and Cortana stopped the Halo Array from firing, but I'm afraid they're MIA. It's been five months, Catherine. I think we have to assume the worst."

Halsey's stomach plummeted. Her first reaction was to look at Fred, Kelly, and Linda.

He's gone. He made it through the whole war, and then—he's gone. Right at the end. It's not fair.

Fred just shook his head. Linda and Kelly stood frozen. John, John-117, the Master Chief—the focus of all Halsey's hopes and ambitions in the Spartan program. When she'd first met him as a small, scruffy child, he was so outstanding and his genome so unusual even among the exceptional children she'd selected that she knew he'd be their leader, and that he would eventually turn the course of the war. She'd been right. She knew she would be. But John had always seemed indestructible. She couldn't believe that his luck had run out.

At least Cortana was with him. At least he wasn't alone.

She wondered if she should have felt worse about Cortana. But all she could do was worry that the AI might have fallen into Covenant hands.

"Are you sure?" she asked at last. The pause must have seemed an eternity to Parangosky. "Absolutely sure?"

"There's something else I have to tell you too, Catherine. Your daughter was killed in action. I'm sorry. I realize this is going to hit all of you very hard."

It took a few moments to sink in. Parangosky knew about Miranda, just as Mendez knew, and Halsey had always thought the revelation would bring her to her knees. But it was nothing—absolutely nothing—compared with the way the word *killed* triggered a terrible pressure at the roof of her mouth and squeezed tears from her eyes. She felt the sensation before the words had meaning in her mind.

When did I last see her?

When did I last speak to her?

Halsey couldn't remember, and she couldn't even recall what their last words had been, only that there had been no affection in them. She was standing in the middle of a technical miracle and all she could think about was the daughter she hardly knew and now never would.

Everyone she gave a damn about had been taken from her. Fred, Kelly, and Linda were all she had left. A normal family would have hugged and cried at a time like this, but the four of them weren't normal, and they weren't a family.

Mendez leaned closer to the console. "Admiral, this is Chief Mendez. What else do you need to know before we bring this sphere out of slipspace? Remember that we've got eight personnel in slipspace stasis too—either clinically dead or close to it. They'll need immediate medical attention if the cryotubes end up back in realspace as well. We just don't know how that'll work yet."

Mendez looked distorted through her glaze of tears, but Halsey was damned if she'd break down in front of him.

"Understood, Chief," Parangosky said. "We'll need coordinates on the surface of the sphere to effect an entry. We have a Huragok standing by to assist with communication if need be."

"We'll establish an entry point and get back to you, ma'am. Mendez out."

Halsey struggled to snap out of it. She'd never needed anything more than her work and had always been able to take refuge in it. But this punch was too big. She wondered if she'd ever get up again.

"Doctor," Mendez said, quiet and awkward. "I'm sorry about your daughter. Come on. We need you to prepare the Engineers for what's coming next."

He hates my guts, yes. But he knows what keeps me going.

Halsey swallowed. Her throat was thick and salty with unshed tears. "Yes. Let's do that, Chief."

And she's gone. Miranda's gone. And John. And even Jacob too.

She looked at her hands, palms up, and didn't recognize them for a moment. She didn't recognize *herself.* The whole world had shifted slightly and become an alien place, and it wasn't anything to do with slipspace.

But she couldn't afford to fall apart now. She did what she'd done so many times before, and done very well: she took her feelings and what she'd persuaded herself was her normal humanity, and sealed them far away from her rational mind.

It was a prudent thing to do. But it was also the only way she could manage to draw her next breath.

When she turned around, the rest of the Spartans had gone but Fred was still there, arms at his side as if he suddenly didn't know what to do with them.

"Are you okay, ma'am?"

Halsey nodded back. Her Spartans genuinely cared about her. She wanted to think that was because she had some redeeming features, but perhaps it was all part of that relentless indoctrination that made her the center of their world by default. Either way, she was going to finish what she'd set out to do—to protect them all, whether they were hers or Ackerson's, and repair what was left of their lives regardless of what fate awaited her.

"Are *you* okay?" she asked.

Fred sounded as if it was an effort to talk. "I just never thought it would be him. I thought he'd always be there."

Olivia appeared again from a side entrance. "The Engineers want to talk to you, Doctor."

Prone drifted past Olivia and floated in front of Halsey. He started gesturing, but there was no voice translation. She realized she'd switched off the datapad. She fumbled with it, not really seeing it, and the voice came to life.

"You require us to help those who arrive," Prone said. "We can do this."

Halsey grabbed the diversion of dealing with something urgent. "Yes . . . yes, we do. We also need your help to transfer this technology to our own fleet. We want you to come back to Earth with us."

"Impossible." Prone to Drift had a stubborn streak that Halsey hadn't expected to find in a Huragok. "We were created to remain with the shield world and to maintain it."

Halsey didn't have any energy left for argument. "But we have to remove some of the Forerunner technology," she said carefully. "Some of you are going to want to come with it to make sure it's safe, aren't you?"

Prone backed away and conferred with the other Huragok in a flurry of tentacles. He edged back to her as if he had a deal.

"We will create new ones among us for that duty," he said.

"You're going to build some more Engineers, do you mean?"

"That is what we do."

"Our colleagues will be here soon. Are you convinced now that there's no threat outside?"

"We are."

"Good. Then all we need to know is when this world can be safely moved back into normal space, and where my colleagues can land to get in here."

"We will inform you," Prone said, and drifted away like a union convener who had to sell the deal to his members again. Mendez was still standing at the communications console, leaning on one arm, staring down at his boots. He'd run out of venom. He looked up for a moment but he wasn't looking at Halsey.

"Onyx to ONI control, this is Chief Mendez," he said. "Admiral, seeing as Onyx no longer exists, can we name this sphere instead of just giving it a number?"

Parangosky must have heard all the chatter in the background while she waited. "What did you have in mind, Chief?"

"If you're willing, ma'am, I think we should call it Ambrose. If Lieutenant Commander Ambrose hadn't sacrificed himself, we'd all be dead now and we'd know nothing about this sphere."

"No," Halsey interrupted. There was one thing she could still do for Kurt, and it was long overdue. "Call it Trevelyan. That was his surname before I took him from his family. The least we can do for a hero is to give him the dignity of his real name."

There was a brief silence. "I'll see that's done," Parangosky said. "And one day I'll make sure that name is declassified."

It was no more than a single grain of sand from the mountain of sins that Halsey had to atone for. It didn't change a thing for Kurt.

But she had to start somewhere.

UNSC *PORT STANLEY*, Onyx sector: February 2553.

"Well, that's something you don't see every day."

It really wasn't. Mal pressed right up to the viewscreen but all he could see was another ONI corvette much like *Port Stanley*—UNSC *Glamorgan*—that had been patiently searching the sector for months, trying to find the near-invisible source of the weird EM readings. Standing off by a few kilometers were two fleet auxiliaries, *Belleisle* and *Dunedin*. It was hard to believe there was a star out there somewhere with an artificial world wrapped around it, like a kid's surprise toy rattling around in a giant Easter egg.

"How far back do we have to stand?" Vaz asked. "It's not like they know how that thing works."

"Yeah, and they better mind that sun." Zeta Doradus was still there, minding its own business and probably wondering what had happened to the nice little planet it used to have spinning around it. "Don't want to expand right into that, do they?"

Mal had visions of the planet, or whatever he was supposed to call it now, suddenly inflating and spreading everywhere like those ill-advised times when he'd activated flotation jackets in confined spaces for a laugh. Everyone did it at boot camp when they were training to ditch over water, but this was going to be a prank on a much bigger scale.

"That's why we've got the smartest woman in the universe and all the Engineers working on this," Vaz said. "They get the decimal point in the right place."

"Is it really only fifteen centimeters across? I just can't get my head around dimensional physics."

Naomi wandered up behind them. Mal could see her reflection in the pressure-proofed glass, helmet tucked under one arm.

"Most of the scientists can't see it in their mind's eye either," she said. "But they can do the numbers. I always found that very disappointing. Dr. Halsey always said she could visualize it conceptually, though."

BB popped up beside them. "So can I. But then I'm just all pure brilliant thought."

"And modest with it."

"Are we going to feel a bump or what?" Mal kept his eyes on the imagined point in space where the sphere was going to expand into a solar system. "And we go in via the basement, right?"

He looked at Vaz and Devereaux to see if there was that same sense of wonder. Vaz just kept checking his watch as if there was somewhere else he needed to be.

"That's it," Naomi said, seeming equally disinterested in the universe's miracles. "Inside out."

"Are you okay about all this?"

"Why shouldn't I be?"

"Seeing Halsey again. Knowing what we know now." Mal meant what happened to Naomi's family, not that they were going to cuff Halsey and haul her off, but that was going to be an awkward moment too. "Osman won't make you do this if you don't want to."

"I'm a Spartan." Naomi rammed her helmet into place with some force. "I'll do my duty."

"You better leave it to me and Vaz."

"You think I can't face arresting her?"

"No, I'm sure you can. But if your mates need someone to hate for doing it, it's probably easier if it's us."

Naomi shrugged. "Let's see how things go."

That pretty well finished the conversation. Mal was worried that she now saw it as a test of her professionalism rather than an option to take the easiest path. Mal wanted to do it for her, and also for Osman: she'd been abducted too, and that kind of thing was bound to have messed her up at some level. They were both big, strapping girls well able to take care of themselves, but all Mal could see right then was little kids screaming for their mothers.

He went back to staring at nothing until his vision started to swim with wobbling points of light that weren't there, and the kids faded away. Osman arrived on deck a few minutes later and walked up to the viewscreen. She stared out, arms folded and jaw set, and suddenly he couldn't imagine her ever being a helpless kid at all.

"Doesn't look much like a momentous moment in the history of space exploration, does it?" she said. "BB, any word from the sphere? Have we got docking instructions yet?"

"Patience, Captain, our clock's running up to twenty times faster than theirs," BB said. "They're communicating with Adj at the moment. Or at least the Huragok are. . . . Oh, apparently we don't have to worry about docking. Provided we land at the right coordinates, the surface of the sphere's designed to restructure itself around the ship and create a secure airlock."

Devereaux gave BB a thumbs-up. "Now that sounds pretty damn useful. I hope we're going to make good use of all this tech."

"We are," Osman said. "Parangosky's promised a briefing on what we might do with it. Adj is going to be a busy boy."

"Ma'am, if they've got Engineers down there, can we find him a friend to play with?"

"I think we'll have to, if only to make sure there's someone to maintain him."

Mal looked at Vaz, and then at Devereaux, and both of them were still watching with arms folded as if they wanted to get it over with.

"Oh, come on," Mal said. "This is going to be something to tell your kids about."

It was the kind of harmless thing that people said, but as soon as he did, he realized it was peculiarly painful for a crew who didn't have a single regular human being on the books. The nearest they had to a normal family man on board was that bloody hinge-head. *Well, sod it.* Mal was determined to savor the moment anyway. The other ships shrunk rapidly from blobs of light to pinpricks and then vanished as *Port Stanley* withdrew at top speed.

"Are we going to get a countdown on this?" Vaz asked.

"I don't think that Huragok do countdowns."

"Here we go," BB said. "Stand by."

Mal was still trying not to blink and miss it when the stars suddenly vanished and he felt a weird tugging at his boots as if the deck beneath him was sprung. The trampoline sensation stopped as quickly as it started, but the stars didn't reappear.

"Oh my, that was spectacular," BB said. "No, seriously. It was. You should see what that looked like in the microwave spectrum. And the magnetic field. Extraordinary. But it's not *really* a Dyson sphere, not as Dyson hypothesized, because a solid shell wouldn't—"

"Go on, rub it in." Mal felt cheated. "So why can't we see it? Or any stars?"

And then it dawned on him. He *was* looking at the sphere. It was pretty well all he *could* see. His view of space was completely obscured by a vast, matte black sphere, and he could only tell what he was looking at because there was a dim arc like a crescent moon, the curve of the sphere picked out by the distant light of Onyx's sun. That sphere was as big as Earth's orbit. The expansion was both a massive anticlimax and the most amazing thing he'd ever—never—seen.

"Y'know, I don't think the Forerunners had any sense of theater," Devereaux said. "They could at least have painted it an interesting color. Or stuck navigation lights on it or something."

Osman put on her helmet, a standard infantry model with a ten-minute rating in hard vacuum. She obviously didn't think the Forerunners' technology was infallible. "Okay, people, let's get in there. You're navigating, BB."

As they piled into the dropship, Mal's adrenaline was pumping as hard as if he was about to do a drop behind enemy lines, not strolling in to arrest a sixty-year-old woman. He tested the vacuum integrity on his bodysuit, checking the display in his HUD more often than he needed to.

Just one little old lady. Okay, she hijacks ships and experiments on kids. But come on. How hard can it be to drop her? On the other hand, she kidnapped a Spartan . . .

Vaz sat opposite him, completely motionless apart from the fact that he was drumming the heel of his right boot on the deck; nothing obvious, not even enough to really move his knee. ODSTs were trained for police actions but that was all theory. Mal had only ever subdued Covenant aliens, and the general idea wasn't to take them alive and unharmed.

"I wonder what Venezia's getting up to now." Devereaux's voice came over the broadcast system. It was only a short flight to the sphere's surface, just enough time to encourage idle chat. "It's all gone quiet, hasn't it?"

"Well, I've not forgotten about them." Osman said it in that same deceptively calm, neutral way that Parangosky did. "They're still on my list."

Mal interpreted *on my list* as glassing with extreme prejudice before she *really* got down to expressing how seriously pissed off she was. There was something both comforting and inspirational about working for a ruthless bastard. He was certain she was. Letting the Muir guy live when it would have been easier to shoot him hadn't fooled Mal one bit.

So . . . what do I say to Halsey? "You're nicked"?

He did a few mental rehearsals. This would be like detaining Rasputin. "How are we doing this, ma'am?" he asked. "Do you caution her while I put the cuffs on?" He fidgeted with a couple of microfilament cuffs strong enough to hold a Brute. "If she's capable of abducting a bloody Spartan, then we better not take any chances."

"We do this by the book," Osman said. "If she doesn't cooperate, you have full authorization to use whatever force you see fit. Just remember that Parangosky wants her in one piece and capable of answering questions."

"Shame," Vaz murmured.

The good thing about having a full-face helmet was that you could take a sneaky look around as long as you didn't move your head. Mal glanced in Naomi's direction. The feed from her helmet cam said she was staring straight ahead. There was no way of telling where she was actually looking.

"Anyone interested in the hull cam feed?" Devereaux asked. "Stand by for docking in five minutes."

One of the icon positions in Mal's HUD lit up and he could now see some of the surface details of the sphere. There were no seams visible, no solid shipyard workmanship that showed its construction, just an incredibly smooth and almost velvety surface that now looked chocolate brown. He still couldn't get the scale of it yet.

"You know, it would really help if someone inside could talk me down," Devereaux said irritably. "Just some damn *numbers,* people. Okay, I'll do it the old-fashioned way from the coordinates. . . . Oh, now *that's* what I call runway lights."

Mal picked it up in his HUD at the same time Devereaux saw it. Beneath the dropship, the sphere had suddenly come to life. A riot of colored lights zipped out below them like a carpet being unrolled at high speed, resolving into blue, yellow, and coral stripes along its length. Then it started pulsing.

"I think I'm supposed to follow that down," Devereaux said. "If I'm wrong, it's been a blast serving with you all, and Vaz still owes me ten bucks."

Judging by the camera angle, the dropship was now aligned right over the light strip. Every time Devereaux veered to port or starboard, the lights at the margins glowed bright red until she aligned with the central yellow strip again. Then cobalt blue discs began popping up at increasingly closer intervals. If that wasn't a universal language, Mal didn't know what was. If he'd been the pilot he'd have assumed the lights were telling him he was coming up on his target. Eventually pulsing coral bars appeared across the width of the strip before resolving into concentric rings. They kept pulsing until Devereaux brought the dropship to a hover vertically above them, and then they locked.

"Coordinates acquired," she said. "I think I'm going to park here. Apologies for the sloppy RT procedure, but I don't know what to call this."

"On the nail. That's what you call it." BB's voice interrupted. "Stand by for a novel experience, boys and girls."

The landing strip lights disappeared and the world outside

went pitch-black. Mal assumed the landing lights had been shut down and he was looking into the blackness of space again, but his gut did a somersault. Then the lights came on again, this time piercingly white in his HUD icon and throwing long shafts into the crew bay through the cockpit bulkhead hatch.

"We're inside now." Devereaux sounded very matter-of-fact. Mal always wondered if pilots squealed with delight when they opened birthday presents, or if they just grunted. "We've come through the shell of the sphere. This is the basement, more or less. I can see Engineers. Four of them, heading this way."

The dropship's drive whined down the scale and stopped. Osman popped her helmet's seal and took it off, tidying her hair one-handed. Mal couldn't read her expression at all.

"Okay, let's do it," she said. "She's expecting an ONI tech team. I wonder if she'll recognize me."

"I did," Naomi said. "And she will too."

Mal stepped down from the dropship and landed on pristine cream flagstones. It looked like the place had never been used. Vaz sidled up to him and switched over to their helmet-to-helmet comms link, triggering the red light in Mal's HUD.

"I hope the other Spartans are as understanding about this as Naomi," Vaz said. At the end of the long passage, Mal was sure he could see shafts of daylight. "We're arresting their mother in front of them."

"Well, if they're not," Mal said, "I'm really going to miss my head."

Forerunner Dyson sphere: February 2553.

Halsey looked at her watch, then at her datapad, and then at Prone to Drift.

"Is that it? Have we—*ohhh . . .*"

Her stomach flipped and her ears buzzed, a moment of flulike faintness. It lasted only a second. Scientist or not, she was expecting such a massive unraveling of space and time to be a little more momentous. She looked around to see where the Spartans were, but she was the only one left in the workshop now.

Prone to Drift spoke via the datapad. "The shield world is now back in the other space. Your friends have entered. Is there anything else you require from us?"

"Will you cooperate with our scientists?" Halsey asked. She wondered if there was any point leaving now. She could stay here and work, without any reminders of the world outside and the precious people she'd let slip through her fingers so carelessly. "They'll spend years exploring this place."

"We maintain this shield world. Allow us to do our duty." It was one of those persistent Huragok non sequiturs. "We must maintain this shelter."

Halsey had started to understand that these were actually precise responses, gentle warnings combined with earnest pleas. This was all they did, all they were created to do, and they would carry on doing it until someone killed them or they died by some other means. Were these sterile lives, or meaningful ones? Whatever they were, they were painfully like her own.

"I understand," she said. "I'm driven too." *So driven I can't remember the last time I spoke to my own daughter, and now she's gone.* "Have you . . . created others for us yet?"

"We have constructed three to look after the Forerunner technology you wish to transport," he said. "I will fetch them."

Prone to Drift floated away and Halsey was left with no distraction to stop the bad news flooding back into the idle spaces. *John's gone, and Miranda. Cortana too.* The world would never return to normal. She found a reflective surface and bobbed up and down in front of it, trying to see enough of herself to tidy up before the ONI crew arrived. She was raking her hair with her fingers when Prone returned, sailing like a galleon ahead of three new Huragok, line astern.

"Perfect Density, Tends to List, and Leaks Repaired," he said. "They are willing to accompany the artifacts."

Halsey decided they weren't so much concerned with helping humans as focused on looking after the technology that they'd been created to care about more than life itself. She should have been able to understand that perfectly. She wondered if that was exactly how she looked to people like Mendez.

And three of them means we can keep building our own if need be. I can't help myself thinking like that. I really am a cold bitch, aren't I?

"Thank you," she said. "Your knowledge and skill are priceless. I respect that."

Prone to Drift didn't seem to know how to react. It took him a few moments to gather himself and reply. "We are here to serve," he said at last.

"And you've served well."

Halsey walked back down the passage to find the others, brushing through the inner slipspace barrier and emerging into the present day—the UNSC's present, anyway—with the new Huragok following her. It hadn't been a long exile. She hadn't even been forced to eat the rest of the ration bars. Outside, Mendez stood in the center of a huddle of Spartans.

Kelly and Linda had taken off their helmets and their expressions were completely transparent. Like Fred, the news about John had hit them hard. Halsey could see it from the way the two women stood with their eyes fixed on the ground. It had to be about John. If they'd known Miranda at all, it would have been no more than a passing acquaintance.

The Spartan-IIIs hovered on the margins of the gathering. It looked like those awful minutes before a funeral, when the more casual mourners milled around trying to find someone they knew as well as the right thing to say, but failed. Halsey debated whether to join them. It would only make them feel more awkward now, she was sure. She wondered what would happen to the rest of the Spartan-IIIs and how many of their comrades were also still missing.

What happens to any of them? What happens to any of us when everything that defines us is part of a war that's now over?

She glanced over her shoulder at the Engineers. They seemed to be making adjustments to each other, looking like nervous job candidates picking lint off one another's suits before the big interview. Perhaps she should have tried talking to them. But it was hard to know where to start a casual conversation, if that was possible at all with a Huragok. *We'll need simpler translation devices for the ONI technicians.* That was another project she knew she could immerse herself in so that she never needed to come up for air. She could just bury herself in research until the day she died.

For a moment, Halsey thought about the Spartans buried here. She couldn't decide if it was more appropriate to leave them in peace or to repatriate them, but they had no true home now. She wasn't sure that she did either.

So I've got more in common with the dead and with aliens now than I have with the people around me.

But the Katana personnel . . . perhaps we can save them when they come out of stasis. I can't face any more deaths. Not even people I don't know.

There was always a priority, always something more urgent

that needed doing rather than wallowing in grief and regret. Then she found her thoughts drifting to things that just didn't matter a damn—what had happened to her equipment back on Reach, what had happened to her journal, what had happened to completely meaningless possessions—until Mendez looked up, stared past her, and started a brisk walk that turned into a jog. The Spartans turned around as well and started heading for the tower. When she finally shook herself out of the fog that seemed to be drowning her, and she looked, Halsey could see what had grabbed their attention.

For a moment, she thought it was John.

A Spartan was striding across the grass toward her. Even though the gait was a woman's and she knew it couldn't possibly be John, she couldn't stop herself from reacting. She broke into a trot, then a run, and rushed to meet her.

Halsey almost didn't notice two ODSTs and a woman in captain's rig with the Spartan. She was carrying her helmet.

"Naomi?" Halsey pushed past Mendez, devastated that it wasn't John but somehow elated to know that one more of her Spartans had survived. She hadn't realized it was possible to experience both at the same time. "Naomi, is that you? Oh, thank God. I thought you were *dead.*"

Halsey realized she thanked God a lot considering that she didn't believe in him. The Spartan took her helmet off as Fred, Linda, and Kelly went to slap her on the shoulder. It was Naomi, all right. But she didn't look particularly happy to see them.

"I'm glad you made it," she said stiffly. Halsey wasn't clear who she was talking to, to her or to the other Spartans. Then Halsey started paying attention to the captain.

Halsey knew that face. She recognized the eyes. It was hard to pinpoint her age, but the woman was exceptionally tall and her expression said she recognized Halsey too. The woman stopped and looked her over, almost embarrassed.

Oh God. I know who it is.

She's come back to see me. The first one who ever has.

Mendez cocked his head on one side. "Well, I'll be damned," he said. "Serin, isn't it? I knew you'd gone to ONI, but—well, good to see you, Captain. Good to see you looking so damn *well* too."

"Good to see you, too, Chief." She didn't hold out her hand to Halsey for shaking. If anything, she seemed more curious about the Spartans. "I'm Serin Osman now. If anyone else is still trying to place the face, I used to be Spartan-Zero-One-Nine. But that was a long time ago."

Fred, Kelly, and Linda seemed to hold their breath for a second and then murmured.

"Oh . . . *Serin!*"

"We thought you were dead," Fred said. "But don't think for one minute that we ever forgot you."

"I know," she said quietly. "But now I'm back."

Halsey could see it now. The glossy black hair had some gray streaks, but it didn't take a lot of effort to roll back the clock and see a teenage girl, leggy and awkward from all those artificially induced growth spurts, huddled in a surgical gown and asking Halsey just how different she would feel when she woke up after surgery.

Halsey had told her the truth. All the children she'd chosen were emotionally robust and mature well beyond their years, and Halsey had seen no point in lying to them about how painful and how persistent the side effects of the surgical enhancements would be. It was better to frighten them with the truth than mouth platitudes and leave them feeling deceived and betrayed afterward.

Good grief. Listen to me. I worried about betraying them? I worried about deceiving them? The Chief's right. You stop noticing the stench and after a while, the sewer smells perfectly normal.

Until you step outside.

Halsey had told her that if she survived the procedure, then there would be a lot of pain, and that pain would go on for months or even years. What she hadn't told her—because she hadn't been certain herself—was that there was another possible state, a limbo between life and death, and that was surviving with a catastrophic disability or never regaining consciousness.

Serin had been unlucky, like the handful of others who lived but would never serve as Spartans. Some went to ONI.

So much for never.

Halsey had decided it was kinder to tell the others that Serin hadn't survived rather than say she'd been shipped back to Earth, in agony and unlikely to walk again. Serin Osman was walking now though. Halsey couldn't see any sign of abnormality.

"I admit it was hard knowing you were all out there and not being able to contact you." Osman clasped her hands behind her back, boots spread. "But Admiral Parangosky made sure I was cared for. Which, I suppose, is what brings me here now."

She looked Halsey in the eye. Halsey braced to hear some hurtful truths, a justified explosion of anger at a stolen childhood, but Osman seemed perfectly calm, as if Halsey was of no consequence to her and the life she'd made for herself was without regrets. To either side of her, the ODSTs, silent and anonymous behind their visors, moved slowly forward so that they were flanking her.

Naomi was now physically shut out of this conversation. It didn't look as if that was what she intended. The Spartan took an awkward sidestep as if she was going to intervene, but the realization was already dawning on Halsey.

The ODSTs took off their helmets and clipped them onto their belts. Her gaze wasn't drawn to the older, dark-haired staff sergeant but to his corporal. It wasn't his close-shaven hair or the hard, lean planes of his face that made him look intimidating, but the expression in his eyes. He seemed to have reached his verdict on her.

"There's an ONI scientific survey team waiting to enter this sphere after we've completed some formalities," Osman said. There was no tension in her voice at all, just a hint of weary resignation as she recited the litany. "Catherine Elizabeth Halsey, I have orders to detain you and take you to the nearest secure ONI facility on charges of committing acts likely to aid the enemy. You are now under military jurisdiction and do *not* have the right to an attorney. The maximum allowable period of detention before being formally charged or released does *not* apply. Come with me, please."

For a moment, nobody breathed. Nobody said a word. Halsey expected to be shocked, but all she felt was a strange, cleansing sense of relief. At first she thought that it was simple inevitability after what she'd done to get to Onyx, but then she started to taste a sense of martyrdom, that she *wanted* punishment, and that she needed it to be public so that everyone could see just how very penitent she was.

I'm glad the Chief isn't a mind reader. He'd say that I still think it's all about me, me, me.

Halsey took an uncertain step forward, datapad in one hand. The young marine held out his hand for it.

"I need to secure that, Dr. Halsey." He had a heavy Russian or Eastern European accent and looked as if he would have preferred to punch her in the face rather than just take her computer away. He glanced at her bag as if he could see right through it. "And the weapon, please."

She'd forgotten she had her sidearm in her bag. "But you'll need this to communicate with the Huragok." The translation software seemed much more critical than a weapon. "Oh. Yes. This."

She handed him the pistol on the flat of her hand so he was clear she wasn't going to do anything insane this time. But as she handed the datapad to him, the Spartans came to life behind her. Kelly stepped forward as if she was going to defend her.

"Captain, this is Catherine Halsey. You *know* her. She's not some common criminal. Do we *have* to do this?"

The older marine, the big cheerful staff sergeant who looked as if he would have been the life and soul of the party under happier circumstances, stepped to one side of Halsey, caught her left wrist, and snapped something around it. He did it so casually, so quickly, so *gently* that Halsey didn't realize he was cuffing her until it was too late.

Kelly spun around. "Whoa, *that's* not necessary—"

"It's okay, Kelly," Halsey said. "This had to happen. Nobody can be allowed to get away with what I did."

"Got it in one, Doctor." The sergeant looked up at Kelly as if he felt sorry for her, as if she was a child who had to be told as tactfully as possible that the tooth fairy had a criminal record as long as her arm. "Remember what happened the last time you turned your back on Dr. Halsey? And how you got here?"

Kelly wasn't going to let it go. "I was wounded. I'd been *sedated*. I wasn't clubbed to the ground and dragged here by my hair."

"My point exactly." The sergeant looked Halsey over. His name tab said GEFFEN M. J. and his zap badge indicated A+/NO V-CIN. "That's quite a black eye you've got there, Doctor. Vaz, put that on the DHR, will you? Preexisting injury. I don't want anyone thinking we beat up our prisoners."

The corporal nodded. Geffen gave Halsey the merest push and she went with them, because there was nothing else left to do.

For one second, one stupid second, Halsey found herself thinking: *I can get out of this. I've been in worse situations. I can hijack warships, for God's sake.* Then the reality returned, and she realized that not only had she run out of options, but this was where she deserved to be. Perhaps not for getting the Spartans to safety, or for taking a ship, but for an entire life of exploitative sins for which she would probably never be charged, because too many others knew about it, paid for it, and blessed it. And if they wanted to put her on trial, then she would name names.

No. No. That's not what this is about. Are you sorry? Real sorry *doesn't have space for this.* She knew this was a genuine thought because she'd stepped outside herself into the second person. *Two things, Halsey. This was your project, something you craved credit for, so be sorry. Suck it up. Forget who did what. You did what you did. And most importantly—are your Spartans going to be all right? Because that's what this is all about.*

"What's going to happen to my Spartans?" she asked.

"I don't know, but they'll be fine," Geffen said. "They're all grown up now."

Her legs were on autopilot. She walked where the charming sergeant led her, keeping a wary eye on the grim-looking Russian lad, and found herself going back into the tower maintenance area, through an exit she hadn't noticed before and along more endless, sterile, beautifully finished passages. She could hear voices a long way behind her, but not the arguments she'd expected. She was glad; she knew the Spartans would lay down their lives for her— and had in the recent past—but she didn't want that now, and she especially didn't want to see them abandon their discipline. They were elite troops. They put their personal feelings and fears to one side.

She was proud of them for letting her go without a fight.

The two marines were so silent that Halsey felt she was walking to her execution. Would they do that? Did they know what she'd really done?

Pounding footsteps grew louder as somebody jogged up behind her at a steady pace. For some reason she thought it was going to be Mendez, but it was Osman. The passage was wide enough for her to walk alongside Halsey and the marines.

"When we've got you secured, Doctor, we'll come back for the Spartans and Chief Mendez," Osman said. "I'll get *Glamorgan*'s medical officer to check them over. Then the survey team can move in and there's a surgical team ready to work on the patients in cryo. Anything else I can tell you?"

"I assume I'm going back to Bravo-Six," Halsey said.

"No, you won't be going back to Earth. You're honored. This time the mountain is coming to Mohammed."

There was only one person Osman could mean. Margaret Parangosky herself was coming to carry out the interrogation.

"Serin, may I ask you a question?"

Osman didn't look comfortable with the familiarity, but Halsey had never known her as Osman. "Go ahead," she said. "But you might not get an answer."

"Why now? After all that's passed between me and Parangosky, why did she decide to come for me now?"

Osman was a pace ahead of her. Halsey could see her expression in profile. She didn't smile, and she didn't seem remotely satisfied. She looked as if she'd finally put an aging, incontinent dog out of its misery as humanely as she could, but didn't want to dwell on the deed any longer.

"Because you couldn't flout the law and human decency one minute longer, Doctor," she said. "You were always on borrowed time, whether you realized it or not."

Halsey digested that as she turned the corner and saw the dropship with its stealth coating and a bristling array of ELINT masts extended from their protective housings. Her time *had* finally run out. At least she'd managed to make it coincide with the end of the war. And there were still four of her Spartans left standing.

She could face whatever came next.

CHAPTER 16

WE'VE PUT EVERYTHING WE'VE GOT INTO *INFINITY*. AND
NOW WE CAN PUT IN A LITTLE SOMETHING EXTRA.

(Rear Admiral Saeed Shafiq, UNSC Procurement)

**UNSC *PORT STANLEY*, on station at Forerunner
shield world Trevelyan.**

Jul had counted the days he'd been locked in this compartment by scratching a number into the bulkhead every time
his human captors switched on the lighting and placed food
in the service hatch.

It was a regular cycle. He assumed they brought up the ship's
lighting to correspond with Earth daylight, and that meant that he
had been here for eight days.

Raia would know by now that something was wrong and that
he hadn't simply been delayed on one of his gun-running expeditions. He wondered if 'Telcam was looking for him, or if he'd
known about the human ambush all along.

What do they want with me?

Jul had expected to be questioned. But he'd just been left to rot, cooped up in this tiny space with its ridiculous water supply and baffling toilet. The small comforts he took for granted at home, like clean clothing and space to stretch his legs, had been ripped away from him and he wondered if this was all part of their elaborate interrogation procedure. But they genuinely seemed to have lost interest in him. There was a great deal of activity in the ship, and none of it appeared to be about him.

He hadn't felt slipspace drives engage for several days now. The ship could have been anywhere. There were no viewscreens so he couldn't even look at the stars and work out which system he might be in.

Perhaps this is going to turn into a hostage game. But what am I worth, and who would they exchange me for?

His anger had now exhausted itself and he'd settled into an obsessive determination to find a way of getting word to Sanghelios. It frustrated him even more that Phillips, the only human he'd ever met who could speak Sangheili dialects with any degree of fluency, had disappeared and he was now reliant on the abomination that called itself BB.

AIs were meant to be servants. This one did *not* know its place. But it did speak Sangheili.

Jul hammered on the cell door. "What is our position?" he demanded. "Where are you taking me? I want to speak to Phillips." It was hard to say the end of the word, the *P* and the *S* together, so he had to settle for *filliss*. "Get Phillips for me."

The AI materialized in the cell. It was tempting to take a swipe at it, but it was ludicrous to vent his frustration on a hologram.

"*Phyllis* is busy," BB said, mimicking his pronunciation. "Look, you're going to be the guest of the ONI in a rather pleasant location. It'll be just you and a few hundred humans on a brand-new world. Lots of lovely countryside and unspoiled views."

"You haven't answered my question."

"Well, let's just say you're an awfully long way from home."

"I'll tell you nothing," he said. "What's the point of all this?"

"Well, they really wanted a live Sangheili prisoner, so who am I to deny them? All I know is that there are a lot of scientists and other people in white coats down there, figuratively speaking, and I'm sure you'll all get on famously."

Jul didn't understand what white coats signified. The avatar disappeared again, but then it popped back right in front of him. "Phillips is going to be a guest of the Arbiter, by the way. Is there any message you want me to pass on to your boss?"

"Thel 'Vadam is *not* my boss," Jul snarled. "He's a weakling who spends too much time worrying whether humans like him instead of exterminating them."

It just slipped out. It didn't matter what a human—or its computer—thought of his lack of allegiance to the Arbiter, but it dawned on him that the devious little AI had simply flushed out a fundamental answer: they just wanted to know if Jul was one of the Arbiter's agents. He was furious at himself for providing the answer so easily simply because he couldn't control his temper.

Or perhaps not. Humans are so twisted that they might think I'm simply saying that to deceive them.

"I'll just send your best wishes to Professor *Phyllis*, then," BB said, and vanished.

Jul roared with fury and punched his fist hard into the bulkhead. It was slightly dented now from constant pounding, but even if he ripped open the whole compartment, he was still marooned on a ship deep in space, and his chances of escape were dwindling every time more humans arrived. He sank back on his bunk and tried to calm himself.

The biggest threat he faced was that the isolation would slowly break him.

When there was nothing else to do except stare at the bulkhead and fantasize about the many varied ways to end a human life, a certain sensitivity developed to the subliminal sounds of the vessel. Jul could now tell when the ship's drives were maneuvering to hold station, and even when someone was ditching waste. There was a distinctive *clunk* overhead. He wondered how much could be heard outside the ship, because the AI had told him with insufferable smugness that this was a stealth vessel, and that nobody would know *Port Stanley* was there until they hit one of her mines.

Jul was also building up a picture of his environment from his sense of smell. On the occasions when a hatch opened, he could detect sweat, machine oil, burnt meat, and oddly floral scents. There was another smell that might have been a sterilizing agent or disinfectant, and now a new one—a sour aroma of human agitation, almost as pungent as their fear when he'd fought them—that got his attention. He tried to memorize it all, because one day this kind of intelligence might come in useful.

Sometime later, he heard the sound of boots, several pairs of them, thudding along the passage toward the cell. They might not have been specifically heading his way, because the cell was on one of the main passages running fore to aft in the ship. But he knew that sound.

Spartans. Demons.

Even without their heavy armor, they were much heavier than the average human and he could hear them stalking up and down the passage outside his cell, sometimes in silence and sometimes talking quietly among themselves as they went by. He recognized the voices. There were more females on board now, and an older male with a rasping voice who didn't seem very happy with life. The words made no sense to Jul, although he was starting to learn that the repetition of *goddamn* indicated a certain mood, and when voices were raised there were many more words with explosive consonants like *F* and sibilants like *S*. Even their anger lacked eloquence.

A conversation was now going on outside his cell door. He kept hearing a repetition of the word *halsey,* but he had no idea what a halsey was, only that the humans seemed particularly agitated about it.

"No, you can't talk to her." That was the female shipmaster, the one who'd had him imprisoned here. "Strict instructions from Admiral Parangosky."

"But what happens now?" That was a male voice he wasn't familiar with, neither the bad-tempered older male nor the two soldiers who were part of the ship's crew. "Where are they going to take her?"

"I can't tell you that," the shipmaster said. "But you're going to Sydney for debriefing."

Jul had no idea what they were talking about, but he could memorize the sounds and detect the emotion behind the words. There was a great deal of tension. He could smell their agitation again in their sweat, the acrid human scents that they pumped out when their stress levels were high.

The conversation stopped and the boots strode away. A few minutes later, the small viewscreen set in his cell door activated and he found himself looking at the female shipmaster—Osman—and an anonymous, helmeted Spartan. It was hard to tell the demons apart until they spoke.

"Okay, BB, read him his rights, if he has any," said Osman.

Jul recognized the name *BB*. "We're going to have to move him now. Parangosky wants Halsey transferred as soon as *Compton-Hall* gets here."

The AI appeared in front of Jul. "Time to go, Shipmaster," BB said. He had as good a command of the language as Phillips. "We're going to disembark you. Now you can do this in a civilized way and walk out under your own steam, or we can do it the cattle prod way. You do understand what I mean by cattle prod, don't you?"

"Where are you taking me?"

"Like I said, it's quite a pleasant location. We'll transfer you by shuttle. Now, are you going to behave yourself?"

"I'm not a child."

"If you resist, they'll simply shoot you. I know you love the idea of death before dishonor, but if you force them to shoot you, nobody will ever know how courageous you were anyway. I don't suppose that matters to you, because you'll know that you did the decent and manly thing, and perhaps that's all you want. But if you want to take revenge at some future date, surviving is a pretty essential part of that strategy. It's your choice."

BB's logic was seductive. "Very well. What must I do?"

"They'll insist that you're handcuffed. Please don't resist."

BB was absolutely correct. To die resisting the enemy, with or without an audience to witness the event, was a noble thing. But returning to defeat the enemy was smarter and infinitely more satisfying. Jul waited for the door to open and presented his outstretched wrists without comment as the Spartan moved in to put restraints on his arms.

"You have a very persuasive way with you, BB," Osman said. "What did you do, threaten to tell his family that he cried like a girl?"

"You have to admit it's very effective," BB said. "A little trick that Phillips taught me, which I believe he dredged up from World War Two. That's anthropologists for you."

"Sometimes I think honor is vastly overrated," Osman said. She nodded at the Spartan. "See him off, Naomi."

It was the female Spartan again. She had the cattle prod hanging from her belt. Jul kept his word and walked beside her down the passage toward the hangar, where a group of six troops were waiting. Four other humans who looked like technicians were waiting there too, all clutching datapads and all far too frail or fat to be soldiers. The hangar was as crowded as a Kig-Yar bazaar with two dropships berthed and every available space behind the safety barrier filled with crates.

One of the technicians, a female with long pale hair scraped back from her face, looked up and smiled at him as if she'd never seen a live Sangheili before and didn't know how much damage he could do her. He suspected it was delighted curiosity rather than goodwill. She said nothing.

"Jul, I've instructed Dr. Magnusson's AI in the Sangheili language, so you should be able to communicate adequately," BB said. "Don't forget to send a postcard."

"Who is this Dr. Magnusson?" Jul demanded.

"You'll find out."

"Wait—"

Jul was slammed flat on the deck in the small shuttle, face-down, secured by clamps. He wanted to show them that the Sangheili didn't take this sort of treatment without protest, but it was pointless trying to educate humans, and there was nobody he cared about who could see him compound his shame by surrendering again. He would bide his time. Once he was on the surface of this planet, wherever it was, he would find a way home.

And he would also find a way to inflict great damage on these vermin.

But first he had to learn to think like them, and he realized that escaping from his new prison wouldn't require physical strength and daring, but learning to play the humans' games of lies and deceit.

It's shameful. But I can do it. There is a greater need that it serves.

He was expecting the journey to be much longer. It seemed that the shuttle's drives had only just run up to speed and left the ship behind when they powered down again and the ship settled on its dampers. He was certain he hadn't felt the vessel enter slipspace, and he was also sure from the distinctive sound of the drive that the ship wasn't slipspace-capable anyway.

The pressure lifted from his back as the securing straps were removed. Light flooded in behind him as a hatch opened.

"This is your stop, buddy." The troops hauled him to his feet. "Come on. Just be a good hinge-head and nobody gets hurt."

Individual words jumped out at him in the noise that made up the human language. He'd heard the word *hinge-head* a lot. He put it on his mental list of words to learn and understand. He walked down the shuttle's ramp with his wrists still secured, and into a bright, sunny day rich with the smell of green things on the air, the landscape all trees and rolling grassland with no buildings in sight.

A man and a woman in a uniform that he hadn't seen before were waiting for him. They smiled in that confusing human way as if he was welcome here.

"Shipmaster Jul 'Mdama," the woman said, nodding at him politely. He could hear her speaking her own language, but he could also hear a simultaneous translation in Sangheili. "I'm Dr. Magnusson. I hope you enjoy your stay here. Please don't think of it as extraordinary rendition. Think of it instead as helping to ensure that we never have to go to war again."

The man with her—hairless and unsmiling in the same dark gray fabric coveralls as the woman—looked Jul up and down and didn't seem impressed.

"Yes, welcome to ONI Research Facility Trevelyan, Shipmaster," his translation said. "This is where we gather intelligence to protect Earth. And this is where you disappear from the galaxy."

Jul understood him too. It lifted his mood no end.

If he could understand what the humans said, then he was one step closer to working out how to get home.

"Temporarily, human," he said. "Just temporarily."

UNSC *PORT STANLEY*, in orbit around ONI RF Trevelyan, Onyx Sector.

Vaz took his life in his hands and stepped into Naomi's path as she came thundering down the passage.

"You can't see her," he said. "Captain's orders. *Parangosky's* orders. Just leave it, Naomi. Please."

It took a lot of balls to try to intercept a Spartan who didn't want to be intercepted. Vaz expected her to roll right over him and break a few bones in her determination to talk to Halsey before she was transferred to *Compton-Hall*. Those were his orders, but that wasn't the only reason he was doing it.

He tried to imagine what it would feel like to live and fight under that kind of unnatural stress for more than thirty-five years, and then find the only person you thought of as a mother was in fact a monster who'd ripped your family apart. Spartans weren't machines. It had to hurt like hell.

Naomi hadn't known what had gone on back home while she

was being whisked away to Reach with dozens of other unlucky kids whose only mistake had been to be born strong, smart, and a long way from Earth. Vaz could see her imagination was now working overtime picturing the misery that Halsey had left in her wake.

Halsey was a genetics expert. She should have known those cloned kids would stand a high risk of dying. What kind of a bitch would do that to another human being after kidnapping their real child?

"Vaz, I need to talk to her," Naomi said quietly. "I might not get another chance. I just want to know why she kept all that from us."

Vaz still blocked the passage, boots planted firmly and shoulders squared, although if a Spartan wanted to get past him there would have been nothing he could do about it. He had a pretty good idea why Halsey hadn't bothered to explain to her adoring trainees exactly what she'd done, but it would only make things worse if he said so.

"She didn't want to hurt you," Vaz lied.

"Nice try, but I want to hear it from her."

Now he could hear the stampede sound of the other Spartans heading his way. He wasn't going to let them past either. He wondered if the brutal truth might actually be kinder than letting them think that ONI was extraditing some kind of saint.

The guy in front was a lieutenant, which made things doubly awkward: Frederic. Even that offended Vaz—that Halsey had given them just first names, as if they'd always be children. They had a right to their *surnames*. Okay, they didn't remember them, but they had lineage, and they had ancestors, and they *came* from somewhere.

"Corporal, we just want to talk to Dr. Halsey," Frederic said.

What was Vaz supposed to call him, *Lieutenant Frederic*? What kind of a name was that for a grown man, let alone an officer? "I don't see what harm it can do."

"Admiral's orders, sir," Vaz said. "Please don't make me disobey my captain. She might be the next head of ONI and I value my nuts."

Frederic looked uneasy. "I'll make my representations to Admiral Parangosky, then."

Frederic turned back up the passage with the other two female Spartans. Naomi looked at Vaz and did a slow headshake that was more confusion than disagreement. She'd obey orders, but that didn't mean she wasn't having a hard time with it.

"Come on," he said. He decided to try another tack. "You're a Spartan. You don't need to hear her excuses. She doesn't control you."

"Okay, but can I ask a favor, Vasya?" She used the Russian short form. Nobody else did that. "Osman says I can see my records if I want to. She thinks I ought to see the whole thing, like there's worse to come."

"And do you want to?"

"I don't know. I wish I did. I don't have the courage to look."

But she had the guts to take on a hinge-head with her bare hands, and any number of crazy things that could get even a Spartan killed. Vaz understood why it was too much for her though. Once she read the detail, she could never forget it. Most of her childhood memories were too deeply buried to plague her consciously. But she was almost certainly speculating what her parents had been like, and how the events had devastated them, and she could have been imagining a lot worse than the reality. His automatic response was to do it, like he'd do the same for Mal. Looking out for your buddies didn't just mean giving them covering fire.

"What do you want me to do?" Vaz asked. "Just say."

"Would you read my files and decide whether I should know or not?"

Damn. How the hell will I know?

It was a massive responsibility. If he told her, it might be too painful, and if he didn't, she'd know it was because the details were too awful and maybe imagine worse anyway. Even for a Spartan, there was such a thing as the final straw.

But an ODST didn't let his buddies down.

"Okay," he said. "You trust me to do that, do you?"

"Of course I do. Thanks, Vasya. I'll let the Captain know you'll need the file."

She looked past him at the door to the compartment where Halsey was being held, and for a stupid moment he was tempted to let her in and face the consequences. But he could see Halsey making hand-wringing excuses for what she'd done, and then he'd be sorely tempted to punch the shit out of her, sixty years old or not.

The other Spartans—the ones they called the Spartan-IIIs—were huddled in the senior rates' mess with Devereaux, who was plying them with coffee and a mountain of snacks. So these were the expendable suicide troops, the colonial cannon fodder. Damn, they were *teenagers:* none of them could have been older than eighteen. If they'd been pumped full of growth hormones and ceramics like Naomi, then it hadn't worked. They were just regular-sized kids. One of the girls was so small and fresh-faced that she didn't look old enough to be out of school, let alone given firearms. She stared at Vaz like a malevolent ferret and didn't say a word.

And we're the good guys, are we?

"Everyone okay?" he asked, looking from face to face. They stared back at him. Edgy was an understatement. "We're going to cross deck you to *Glamorgan* in an hour. She's got a proper doctor."

"We're okay," said one of the lads. His name tab said ASH. "Just peckish. Are we going to Earth?"

"Yes, you're getting a debrief at HIGHCOM in Sydney. Bravo-Six. Are you old enough to drink? There's still some good bars in Sydney."

Ash stared at Vaz as if he was senile. "I'm thirteen," he said. "And we've never been to Earth."

That brought Vaz up short. "Jesus. What about the rest of you?"

"I'm twenty," Tom said. "So's Lucy here." He patted the mad ferret kid's shoulder. "But the other guys are about Ash's age, yes."

It was just making Vaz angrier by the second. For a moment, he got a glimpse of why so many of the colonies hated Earth. He'd had enough of all this Spartan crap.

"We'll make sure the UNSC shows you some gratitude," he said at last. "We'll talk to your CO about it."

Vaz walked off. Devereaux came trotting down the passage after him.

"Wow," she said. "You saw that little girlie? She decked Halsey. She's the one who blacked her eye. They're all psychos."

"You'd be crazy as well if they gave you a rifle when you were six."

"Chief Mendez must have a magic touch to cope with all that."

"Either that," Vaz said, "or he's a complete bastard."

Devereaux held her hands up in her I'm-just-saying gesture and returned to mind the delinquent Spartans. Vaz went in search of Mal and found him in the galley with Mendez.

They were talking quietly in the corner, arms folded, with that seen-it-all-no-shit expression peculiar to senior NCOs. Two cans of beer sat on the counter. Mendez was in his late fifties or early sixties, a real thug of a guy with whipcord forearms and a broken nose. So this was the man who trained all the Spartans. What the hell was *he* doing while Halsey was doing the Frankenstein stuff on the kids? Vaz couldn't work out why Mal was sharing a beer with him, but he nodded at him anyway. Maybe Mal needed to hear Mendez's side of the story first.

"Everything quiet out there?" Mal asked.

Vaz shrugged. "The lieutenant wanted to talk to Halsey, but I told them she was off-limits. When's *Compton-Hall* taking her off our hands?"

Mal checked his watch. "Six hours. Then we head back home."

Mendez wasn't saying much. He retrieved his beer and took a cigar stub out of his top pocket, staring at the frayed tip. "At least I get to replenish my supply of these."

"So you and Dr. Halsey." Vaz just couldn't make small talk with him. Something had to be said. "You've worked together a long time, yes?"

Mendez might have been born looking suspicious. He certainly looked suspicious now. "I worked with her a long time ago, if that's what you mean."

"Well, we've spent the last few weeks working with a couple of Spartans. It's hard to know what to say about a project like that."

"Then it's probably best to say nothing."

Vaz bristled. Okay, so Mendez trained the Master Chief and was some kind of legend, but Vaz couldn't let that intimidate him. He wanted to know how all this Spartan stuff could possibly fit alongside the Navy's sense of decency. He'd always despised people who wouldn't stand up and be counted. And here he was now, dithering like some gutless little clerk about whether to say something that might upset a man who'd stood by while Halsey played Dr. Mengele.

Okay, they can stick me on a charge for disrespect to a superior. But I've got to live with myself.

"One question, Chief," Vaz said. "If you knew what was happening to those kids, why didn't you do something? Any of you? I mean, how many people does it take to create dozens of flash clones and run a program that size? There must've been a whole army of technicians and doctors and military personnel working on it. Just tell me *why*. For Naomi if nothing else."

Mendez took so long putting his cigar away and moving his can of beer across the counter that Vaz thought he was preparing to swing a punch. *Yeah, why don't you try that, grandad? Go on. See what you get.* But the punch didn't come, and Vaz found himself disappointed.

"And you'd like to think that you would have handled things differently," Mendez said.

Vaz stared into his face, searching for any loss of nerve. "There's some things that you can't do and still call yourself a man."

He waited for an explosion or a punch. He didn't dare look at Mal. What he'd said didn't change a damn thing, and it wouldn't stop it happening again with other people and other kids, but he'd said it. That was better than *not* saying it.

I don't care if he's the biggest damn hero in the UNSC and rescues blind kittens in his spare time. It's still wrong and it's always going to be wrong.

"Yeah, I think I reached that conclusion a few years ago," Mendez said at last. He didn't seem to be avoiding Vaz's gaze so much as staring past him at something on the bulkhead that only he could see. "Next time I'll try to find my conscience *before* the event, not after it."

He drained his beer in one pull, tossed the can in the trash, and left.

Mal turned to Vaz, arms still folded. "Feel better now?"

"Actually, yes." Vaz didn't plan to apologize. "I do. A sense of right and wrong is all we are."

Mal rolled his eyes. "If I knew the names of any Russian philosophers, I'd probably have a really good line to shoot back at you, but I don't, and I haven't," he said. "So come on, what do you think should happen to Mendez? Okay, Halsey—it was her project. But what are you going to do about people like Mendez and everyone else? How far down are you going to drill?"

"As far as it takes. Because it's ordinary people who let it happen." Vaz busied himself refilling the coffee machine. He didn't want a fight with Mal, and he didn't want to discover anything about the guy that he didn't respect. Mal was his best friend. They'd been through a lot together. But it was a lot easier helljumping than wrestling with this kind of stuff. "The monsters don't run the gulags and the death camps and the reeducation centers. Regular people do. If they all had the balls to say no, the likes of Halsey, Zhou, or Stalin could never do it all on their own. Could they?"

"I'm not saying forgive and forget. But you know bloody well that ninety-nine percent of humans do exactly what everyone else around them is doing, even if they know it's evil or plain stupid, because that's the way humans *are*."

Like keeping my mouth shut about this. "That's not a defense."

"No, but would *you* tell ONI to shove it in the middle of a war? Look at what *we're* doing right now."

"It *wasn't* the middle of a war. This was before the Covenant showed up. It was about counterinsurgency, not genocide."

"So being killed by the Covenant is worse than being killed by some colonial tosser? You hate it when civvies second-guess us with the luxury of hindsight."

"This wasn't some split-second decision under fire. It was deliberate, it went on for twenty-odd years, and it involved kids. How hard is it to work out that was *wrong*? Seriously, Mal, how hard?"

Sometimes Mal argued for the hell of it. Vaz wasn't sure if he was arguing now or just trying to make sense of a bad situation, but this was suddenly personal, not a high school ethics debate. Whatever Halsey—and Mendez—had done, they'd done it to Naomi and Osman too.

"This coffee's taking forever," Vaz said. "I've got stuff to do."

He needed to go before he said something he'd regret. And he had a promise to keep to Naomi. He went to Osman's day cabin and peered around the open door.

She was in there with the Chief, so she was either about to repaint the bulkheads with his innards or she didn't feel too badly about his involvement. But that was her business—the individual Spartans were the only ones who had the right to forgive anyone.

"I said I'd take a look at a file for Naomi, ma'am," Vaz said, avoiding eye contact with Mendez.

Osman nodded. "Probably best done in your cabin. BB can display it for you."

He had to ask. "Have you read it, ma'am?"

"Yes."

"Would you read your own now?"

She always looked him straight in the eye, but her gaze flickered for a moment. "No."

That told him all he needed to know. He took the long route back to his cabin to avoid everyone and flopped down on his bunk. BB needed to be summoned. He made a point of not crossing the threshold, except for keeping his dumb processing eye on the environmental and safety controls. It was a thoughtful gesture.

"Come in, BB," Vaz said. "Let's get this over with."

BB's avatar popped up and the screen on the bulkhead switched from its portal to a file with more security warnings on the cover than he'd ever seen in his life.

"You're doing a very kind thing, Vasily."

Vaz tried to mimic Mal's accent, embarrassed. *"She's me mate."*

"I know you well enough by now to realize this is going to make you angry."

"Most things do."

"Call me when you need me."

"Hang on." A thought crossed Vaz's mind as the first page filled the screen. "You must have read all the files. Osman's too."

"Of course I have. I *am* the files."

"But you don't snoop in the cabins. I just wondered where you draw the line."

"I'm required to know personnel details. But it also helps me understand the Captain better. And Admiral Parangosky."

BB vanished, which in this case meant he really had withdrawn from the room. Vaz forced himself to look at the file, guts knotted. Naomi's family name was Sentzke, she came from a colony world he'd never even heard of—Sansar—and she was an only child. There were pages of reports signed by Halsey, detailing her exceptional genetic profile and so full of jargon that he started skimming over the detail, but the next page that flashed up hit him right between the eyes.

It was a weekly psychological assessment form, detailing how this six-year-old kid was coping after being snatched by ONI agents on the way home from school; whether she was eating, how much she was crying, how often she asked for her mom, and how aggressive or withdrawn she was on any given day. It would have been bad enough reading that about a total stranger, but it was all too close to home now.

Vaz found himself drowning in questions, like why people hadn't noticed all these kids disappearing for a few weeks and then miraculously being found alive, but the colonies were a long way from Earth, and a long way from one another.

There were only seventy-odd kids involved. Kids went missing all the time. They were spread across so many planets that no cop would ever have spotted a pattern in all that.

So like Devereaux said—why bother with the clones? Why the hell go to all that trouble? Halsey didn't need to.

The reports were written in disturbingly neutral clinical terminology, but they all boiled down to one thing. Naomi, like all the other Spartan kids, was terrified and wanted to go home.

Vaz read the names of the psychologists and medical officers at the bottom of those reports carefully. He wanted to remember who the monsters really were. The one currently imprisoned on the deck below him couldn't have done it without them.

You rotten bastards. You took an oath to do no harm.

He wasn't sure if he grasped half of the medical stuff in front of him, but he understood enough to realize that he didn't want to go on reading about the drugs and surgery, the brutal training, or the assessments of the kids' pain and stress levels. It would surface in nightmares one day. He was sure of it. He didn't want to know how Halsey changed them out of all recognition.

He had to though. If the people he served with had gone through this, the least he could do was read it. He stuck at it for half an hour, getting every bit as angry as BB had warned him he would, until he had to take a breather or explode. He flicked forward to the end of the file, knowing there would be no happy ending, and found he was looking at a subfile of social workers' reports about Naomi's parents.

Even in a situation like that, with outrage piled on outrage without a thought for how far the ripples of misery would spread, it was still a shock to see what had happened to the Sentzkes.

Their daughter had been returned to them, or so they thought, and for a while they'd been relieved to have her back. Then she fell ill and spent eighteen months dying. The Sentzkes were told it was a genetic illness. The social reports tossed in the consequences of that lie as if it was just a footnote:

> Mrs. Sentzke is concerned that the genetic abnormality will affect any other children she might bear. She has asked to be sterilized and the decision is putting considerable strain on the marriage.

The next page was a coroner's report, an inquest, dated six months later. Naomi's mother had finally slashed her wrists. There was a comment from the coroner about her inability to deal with her bereavement.

Vaz read it a few times, unable to get past that paragraph. Had Osman actually told Naomi all that? He'd have no idea until he asked, but if she hadn't, the worst news of all would fall to him. Part of him resented Osman for not giving Naomi the full story right away.

God Almighty. How do I tell Naomi that?

Her father, Staffan, seemed to be made of more obstinate stuff though. The social worker had included a number of police reports detailing how he insisted that the girl who'd come back wasn't his daughter, and that it was all a dirty government conspiracy. There was no genetic abnormality like that in his family, he said.

Vaz was now riveted. This factory worker, this ordinary guy, hadn't realized just how right he was. Vaz scrolled through the pages as fast as he could, but then he found himself reading

Naomi's service record. The trail went cold. There was no more mention of Staffan Sentzke.

"BB," he said. "Quick question. Sitrep on Sansar, Outer Colonies."

"Glassed," BB said, not even materializing.

Vaz thought of that Staffan, screwed by his own kind and then glassed by the Covenant, and wondered if there was any justice left in the world. He lay on his bunk for a long time, staring up at the deckhead in chaotic, numb anger. More than seventy families had been through something like that, and the only thing that had put an end to their misery was the Covenant. How many of them had been as tragic as Naomi's parents? How the hell was he going to tell her *any* of this?

He swung his legs off the bunk, determined to come back later and finish reading every last damn word. One thought wouldn't go away though. Halsey was still down there, one deck below. She'd led a charmed life, paid and praised and given nice big budgets, while all the time she was no better than any of the other war criminals throughout history who'd been tried and hanged, or who'd never faced justice at all.

Vaz knew a little about World War II because it was still compulsory history in the school he'd attended. Russia didn't forget her wars. If he'd run into Dr. Josef Mengele five hundred years ago and known what the man had done, or would do, and if he'd shot him, then he'd have been hailed as a patriot. Everyone would have said he'd done humanity a favor.

Now he had a modern-day Mengele right here.

Vaz was halfway down the passage before the thought started crystallizing. By the time he got to the ladder that would take him to the deck below, he'd already kissed good-bye to his service career and his freedom. He found himself outside Halsey's temporary cell with one hand on the door and the other resting on his sidearm. He thought of all the scientists responsible for wartime atrocities and how many of them made themselves too useful to hang, and died fat and rich and respected at a ripe old age. That was when he decided that the world could probably get by just fine without another Spartan program.

He put one finger on the lock override.

"Vasily," said the voice behind him. No, it wasn't behind him; it was somewhere overhead, in one of the ship's broadcast speakers, like the voice of God. "Vaz, I told you it would make you angry, didn't I? Come on. Walk away from it."

"Nobody ever stops monsters until it's too late," he said. "We can't claim we didn't know about this one."

"But there's always another one to take their place, Vaz," BB said. "And I think Naomi would be happier if you weren't serving life for blowing Halsey's brains out."

Vaz paused for a good ten seconds, hating himself for hesitating when he knew this woman was probably never going to face real justice. What did he have to lose? No kids, no family. Not half as much as the colonists whose lives she'd wrecked.

"Vaz—*leave her to Parangosky*." BB's tone was firmer now. "She's much more proficient than you at making people suffer. Go find Naomi. *Go on*."

Vaz felt as if he'd suddenly sobered up. It didn't stop the anger or the seething hatred, but he felt both stupid and justified, which was hard to handle.

BB was looking out for him though. That was what friends were for.

"Thanks, BB." He rubbed his face with both hands and started walking away. *Coward,* a voice said inside him. *Coward.* "Yeah, I'll do that. I hope I never have to regret this."

"You know you already do," BB said. "Now go press your best pants. We hand over Halsey, and then we go home for the memorial ceremony."

Vaz had plenty of people to commemorate. It still seemed pretty lavish to slip back to Earth in the middle of a mission. "They really need us there?"

"Yes. The Arbiter's attending."

Old enemies normally left it a decent few years before they showed up expressing respect. This was just months. It was still all way too raw, but then today was a very raw kind of day all around.

"Great," Vaz said, realizing that every step he took away from that door was proof that he was just like everyone else, compliant and gutless, unable to do what his conscience demanded. "Let's forgive every evil bastard in the galaxy."

Voi Memorial, Kenya, Earth: March 2553.

"No Army?" Margaret Parangosky, leaning on her cane, watched Hood taking his leave of the Arbiter. "He didn't invite any brass from the *Army*? Well, that's goddamn rude, even by my standards."

She turned to Osman and did that little nod that always accompanied a tip on handling interservice politics. "Even if you think that the Navy and Marines were the only ones fighting the war, then you still treat the rest as if they were right there at the front. And an awful lot of them *were*."

The coral-pink dawn had given way to a bright, crisp morning, and the memorial, the wing of a Pelican dropship inscribed with the names of the fallen, had lost its stark, monolithic look as the sun climbed higher. Osman hoped that the media had managed to get the best dramatic images of the lonely black shape silhouetted against a sky that was a convenient metaphor for shed blood. She wondered how anyone could possibly have inscribed all the names that should have been there in such a limited space, but that was the way history tended to play these things.

Something to address one day when I'm stuck at Bravo-6.

The ceremony was like any other social gathering. There were those who came for the main business of the day, which was grieving, and there were those who had come because it was a requirement. Chief Mendez looked immaculate in his dress uniform and also very pissed off. Osman could see why. She noticed the crowd part as the Arbiter took his leave of Hood—with a handshake again—and walked away to where his guards were waiting.

Parangosky watched with narrowed eyes, leaning on her cane. Osman couldn't tell if her mind was on Hood or Halsey.

"So you think Phillips is ready to be inserted," she said at last.

"Ready or not, ma'am, he's the only person who can get into Sanghelios right now. And we really need intel."

" 'Vadam's not an idiot. He'll *expect* us to send a spy."

"But he probably won't expect that spy to have contacts on the ground."

"Indeed. And if the worst happens?"

"BB can deal with it."

The intelligence business was full of euphemism. BB would give Phillips a lethal dose of nerve agent if he was captured and interrogated. It was easier for the AI to decide when things had gone too far than for Phillips to make the call himself. Osman stood back from herself and watched her spook side not getting upset about the idea. It was sobering.

"I've sent Spenser to mooch around Venezia," Parangosky said, gaze still fixed on the Sangheili shuttle. Its drives were powering up. "He was getting bored. Bad sign."

"They're still number two on our bugger-about list."

"Glad they're not forgotten. We need to focus resources on the Sangheili, so that means stopping the colonies complicating the issue. Keep an eye on that and give him a hand if need be, will you?"

"My pleasure, ma'am."

"A Sangheili attack on them wouldn't upset us at all."

"I'll do my best."

Parangosky pushed herself upright and flexed her hands. "Now for dessert. I've got a conversation to have with my favorite scientist." She'd waited a damned long time to get Halsey but she seemed more resigned than triumphant. "I wouldn't call it an interrogation because there aren't many answers I want from her. I just want to tell her a few things. And then she can make herself useful. But BB will brief you on that when *Stanley*'s under way."

Osman knew something big was looming but had learned long ago that Parangosky would tell her what she needed to know when the time was right. She'd never left her in the dark without a good reason. "Have you spoken to her at all, ma'am?"

"Not yet. Just trying to locate my own moral high ground at the moment."

"You've never actually said that you regret the Spartan program."

"Regret's an insultingly useless thing so long after the event, but I think it's better than claiming you did what you thought was right at the time. *Good faith.* Ah, I can't be doing with that nonsense—it's a politician's defense. I knew it was wrong and I still did it. So I'll stand up and admit it."

Osman wondered if Parangosky was getting ready to die. If the woman was ill, BB probably wouldn't tell Osman. But there was a great finality about the admiral, a tidying up of loose ends, and it panicked Osman every time she noticed it. But no other admiral had served so long past their active service date, and she might just have decided to retire at last.

"You're going to give a statement to the Defense Committee, then."

"When my resignation won't compromise security, yes." Parangosky smiled. She did that more often than people imagined, but rarely outside her office. "You'll be appointed rear admiral in the April list, by the way, and then the path's clear."

The news didn't sound quite as good to Osman as she'd once thought it would. "What if I'm not ready for it, ma'am?"

"Then I'll just have to stay alive until you are." She glanced past Osman at her driver. "Good team, Kilo-Five."

Osman nodded. "They've really gelled. A bit baffled and impatient without real fighting to do, but they're adapting to intelligence work very well. Even Phillips. Good call, ma'am."

"I'm glad that's worked out." Parangosky began walking back to the memorial. "You always need a core team who'll do anything for you and *you alone*. Loyalty's everything, Serin. But you know that."

Osman followed her back to the memorial, more out of concern than to see what she would do. Parangosky contemplated one of the plaques in silence for a while. It was Halsey's. It was almost as if she wanted to lock it in her memory to convince herself that something had finally come to pass. Then she moved along to the plaque commemorating the Spartans and laid her hand on it for just a moment, chin lowered.

"Sorry," she whispered.

She looked back over her shoulder at Osman, half shrugged, then turned to where her driver was waiting. Everyone paused for a moment to watch her go. It was rare for her to appear in public.

Osman saluted and wondered if she would hold ONI together for as long as Parangosky had.

As if the Admiral's exit was his cue, Mendez broke away from a conversation with the Spartan-IIs and Mal, Vaz, and Devereaux. Maybe Osman was reading too much into it, but there seemed to be a gap in the group, and Naomi was definitely standing with the ODSTs. Mendez headed her way.

"Looking good, Chief," she said.

He patted his gut, self-conscious. "It still fits after all these years, ma'am. You're back on patrol now?"

"No rest for the wicked. I expect we'll see one another again fairly soon though."

"If it's okay with you, Kelly, Linda, and Fred aren't going to take you up on your offer of access to their files for the time being, but they're grateful for the opportunity." He slipped a white-gloved finger inside his collar as if to loosen it a little. Maybe it didn't quite fit after all. "I think it's too much too soon. And maybe thirty-five years too late anyway."

"That's okay," Osman said. "They've always got the option." She reached out for his hand and shook it. "Look after yourself, Chief."

Mendez gave her one of his tight, regretful smiles. "And you stay out of trouble, ma'am."

An event like this would normally have broken down into spotting old shipmates and sinking further into reminiscence, and then, once a few suitably bracing drinks had been taken in the wardroom, she would make her excuses for an early getaway before it all got too emotional and messy for her. But she had a very good excuse for absence today. She had a coup to support.

She jerked her head in the direction of the waiting transport and gave the ODSTs and Naomi a get-moving gesture, just a discreet tilt of her thumb. They'd made a lot of effort with the spit and polish. Vaz looked especially well turned out. Osman wondered if his feckless ex-girlfriend had bothered to contact him again, and hoped that he'd had the sense to tell her to sling her hook.

"Does it offend you, all this focus on the Spartans?" she asked. The pool driver couldn't hear them in the front compartment, and Naomi had turned to gaze out of the window as if to indicate she wasn't taking part in this conversation. "I know the Master Chief played a pivotal role, but I wonder if the other side of all this adulation is almost dismissing the role of the ordinary guys who were killed and maimed to stop the Covenant."

Mal looked as if he wanted to loosen his high collar too. They'd been stuck in those uniforms for more than seven hours. "At least it's not all tea and medals for the senior command, ma'am. The Spartans were NCOs. No offense."

"None taken, Staff."

Port Stanley was close to an Earth orbit for a fast slip. Osman wondered if the detour had been worth it in lost time, because the Arbiter's visit had been uneventful and she could have hung around Sanghelios after all. But she looked at the faces around her, and decided it had been no bad thing to give her ODSTs and Naomi a chance to grieve and remember.

She couldn't think of it as closure. It was all very far from over, and there would be more names to engrave on plaques, both on Earth and on distant worlds.

CHAPTER 17

FOR US, THE STORM HAS PASSED, THE WAR IS OVER. BUT
LET US NEVER FORGET THOSE WHO JOURNEYED INTO THE
HOWLING DARK AND DID NOT RETURN. FOR THEIR DECISION
REQUIRED COURAGE BEYOND MEASURE—SACRIFICE, AND
UNSHAKABLE CONVICTION THAT THEIR FIGHT, OUR FIGHT,
WAS ELSEWHERE. AS WE START TO REBUILD, THIS HILLSIDE
WILL REMAIN BARREN, A MEMORIAL TO HEROES FALLEN. THEY
ENNOBLED ALL OF US, AND THEY SHALL NOT BE FORGOTTEN.

(Admiral Lord Hood, dedicating the UNSC memorial to
the dead of the Covenant War, Voi, Kenya, March 2553)

UNSC *PORT STANLEY,* en route for the Sanghelios sector.

"Are you seriously going through with this?" Devereaux
asked.

"How can I say no?" Phillips was fiddling with the
arum and trying to look nonchalant, but BB knew better. He suspected that Devereaux did too. "It needs doing. And it's an incredible opportunity."

"It will be, if you survive to write the paper."

"Come on, I'm a guest of the Arbiter. I'll be as safe as houses. It's only for a few weeks."

"And he's *really* safe, of course. Because people like us aren't trying to foment civil war all around him."

"Most people say *ferment,*" Phillips said, winking at her. "Correct usage always impresses us academics."

"Well, you better leave that toy behind or they'll know something's not quite right." She took the *arum* from him. "Are you *really* okay about this?"

"I don't know enough to be dangerous."

Actually, he did. That was partly why BB was going along for the ride in fragment form, with just enough of his program installed in Phillips's personal comms kit to be useful and to flag problems to *Port Stanley,* but with none of the core matrix accessible to those busy Sangheili fingers—or Huragok, if he was unlucky—if anything went badly wrong.

And if the worst happened, he would silence Phillips permanently if he couldn't be extracted. He wasn't sure if Phillips had fully grasped what a lethal injection did, because he'd hardly reacted to the news. But the man had a pretty good imagination, and he'd now settled into this dirty business with a speed and enthusiasm that made BB wonder whether he'd actually been planted within ONI by a rival agency.

But there are *no rival agencies. We castrated them all. Left them cowering in our shadow. What am I thinking?*

The natural state of paranoia affected even AIs, BB reflected. But it was a lot healthier than being a trusting soul. It certainly made for a longer lifespan.

Devereaux and Phillips hung around the dropship, waiting for Osman to show up and see him off. The captain came thundering down the gantry a few minutes later.

"All ready, then?" she asked. "Now remember what I said. However tempting it is, don't get too clever. Just observe. Concentrate on the cultural stuff, not data gathering. Just be what you really are."

"It's okay, Captain, I've got my suicide pill."

BB tried to make light of it. "It's just a sharp ejected from your personal radio, and you won't feel a thing," he said. "I'll be gentle."

"It's *so* good to have friends like you, BB."

Osman didn't seem to find it funny. Her lips compressed in a tight line for a moment. "We'll be back to extract you in a week. And you don't go *anywhere* without that radio—not even the shower. Got it? I don't care which body cavity you have to insert it in. They'll expect you to have personal comms anyway, but there's no sense in making them too interested in it."

"Yes, Mom."

"Okay. Good luck."

Osman half turned to go, then seemed to change her mind and turned back to give him an awkward pat on the back. It was the kind of stiff exchange that suggested she was convinced he wouldn't make it back. BB hoped Phillips didn't notice.

Devereaux raised an eyebrow as Osman walked off. "You're well in there, Prof."

"I'm not even going to ask what that means, but I think it scares me. Shall we go?"

They were interrupted by a cacophony of off-key singing from the gantry above. Mal and Vaz were watching from up top, arms folded on the rail and singing the theme tune from *Undercover.* It was a popular spy drama, although not with BB. Phillips laughed.

"I may be back sooner than you think, Control," he said, doing a pretty good impression of the actor's catchphrase.

"Don't get yourself killed," Mal called. "And don't let BB stick that needle in you. Nobody else can do that stupid puzzle."

"Phyllis," Vaz called. "Is it true the hinge-head calls you *Phyllis*?"

"BB, you're a bastard," Phillips muttered. "Yes, Vaz, he does, because he can't pronounce my name."

"Okay, Phyllis. We believe you."

They roared with laughter. Phillips seemed to understand the oblique language of *slagging* now, and take it for what it was—the ODSTs' way of telling him that he was one of their own and that they were seriously concerned for his welfare. A nickname was a sure sign of comradeship. He gave them a Girl Scout salute and climbed into the dropship.

This was the point where BB was more conscious of his many fragments. One aspect of him was now clipped on Phillips's top pocket, and another was still light-years away in Sydney, walking through electronic corridors to gossip, argue, peer into filing cabinets, slam doors, rap knuckles, and play pranks in the invisible and politically tangled community of AIs. At the same time, his matrix occupied *Port Stanley* and oversaw every aspect of the corvette and her crew, both consciously and subliminally. He'd tried to explain this multitasking to Mal and Vaz, and finally achieved it by comparing himself with a human being watching TV while having a conversation with the person sitting next to them, holding a datapad on their lap, and keeping an ear on a conversation taking place in the kitchen. It could all be done, even by humans. It was just done on a far broader, more complex scale by an AI.

Phillips made the journey to Sanghelios in the cockpit, sitting in the copilot's seat and chatting to Devereaux. BB was both there and not there as far as they were concerned. They seemed to have reached the stage where they could talk freely without embarrassment. He could hear how their voices and language had changed since the end of January, from the hesitation and carefully chosen words of the first days to complete informality now. In a few weeks, a group of complete strangers from unpromisingly different backgrounds had not only welded themselves into a cohesive team, but had grown comfortable with a permanent and intrusive presence like himself. He didn't judge them like a human, and they knew it

BB was happy. He could define it now. It made him feel thoroughly satisfied with his existence. He turned his attention back to *Port Stanley* while the dropship approached Sanghelios and picked up its fighter escorts.

"Do you have five minutes, Captain?"

Osman swung her chair away from the console. "Shoot."

"The Admiral's instructed me to brief you on a project that's been withheld from you until now. And don't take offense at that, by the way."

"None taken," Osman said. "I've been in ONI for too long. She said you'd brief me."

Ah, Osman was a little gem. She fully accepted there were things she was better off not knowing for the time being. It made her easy to work for. Damian Hogarth didn't have that subtle judgment, though, and expended far too much energy in pointless fishing expeditions. There was a time for trawling, BB decided, and there was a time for hauling in your nets and conserving your fuel. Osman trusted Parangosky as much as she seemed to trust anyone. There weren't many people who felt that way about the Admiral, but however Machiavellian she could be—and Machiavelli was an uncomplicated soul by comparison—she wasn't untrustworthy. What you saw was what you got; provided you saw it coming, of course.

Many hadn't.

"It's a project called *Infinity*," BB said. "To be exact, *Infinity* is a warship—a very, very expensive prototype, because she's been fitted with every scrap of Forerunner technology we've picked apart during the course of the war, and now she'll benefit from the tech Halsey found in the sphere. Unfortunately, the Woodentop Navy needed to know about her because even ONI couldn't hide anything that big in the budget, but it's still known to only a handful of very senior officers."

He got a smile out of Osman with *Woodentop Navy*. It was what he called any branch of the senior service that wasn't ONI. "So how about all those yappy shipyard workers and technicians, then?" she asked.

"There's not much yapping they can do when they've been permanently deployed in the Oort Cloud with full comms lockdown for the past few years," BB said. "Would you like to see the schematics?"

He flashed up the deck-by-deck blueprint on the screen to her left. She rested her elbows on the console and leaned forward, lips slowly parting as the full wonder of *Infinity* began to sink in.

"Ooh." She hovered on the edge of a smile. "And all that wonderful kit that Halsey's found." Then the smile iced over again. "Is that really why she went to Onyx, then? Did we misjudge her?"

"Oh, good grief, no. She really didn't know anything about *Infinity,* believe me. She would only have tried to take over the project. No, the crazy hijacker act was just that. Crazy. Not a cover for anything."

Osman's gaze went back to the blueprints again. "Who's going to have command?"

"Andrew Del Rio's been driving her for a few years. It's not easy to find competent commanders who can drop off the grid unnoticed for that long. And we've had some Spartan-Fours out there for a while too. But with the slipspace navigation refinement, I think *Infinity*'s going to be ready for trials a lot sooner than planned."

"I don't suppose I get to do any working-up in her."

"You're the heir to the ONI throne, my dear. I imagine you can do anything you like when the time comes. We might even get you on a Thursday War."

"Just tell me Hogarth isn't going to pip me at the post now my back's turned."

BB coughed. "I *am* your back. I have contingency plans to make sure that doesn't happen in the event that the Admiral's wishes aren't immediately honored."

"Bless you, BB."

"Bless the Admiral, Captain."

BB left Osman to pore over the blueprints. If he'd had physical hands, he'd have brought her a nice strong coffee so she could fully enjoy browsing through the fine detail of the ship. Where other women read magazines, Osman liked nothing better than to while away the time with a dense pile of data. There was still a lot of the Spartan in her. BB sometimes wondered what kind of operational Spartan she would have made, just the averagely terrifying kind or a full-blown angel of death.

He turned his attention back to the dropship, where Phillips was landing at the Arbiter's keep in Vadam. If Phillips had had a neural implant, BB would have known exactly how nervous he was. But in the absence of monitoring hormone levels, he could still make an educated guess from the pitch of Phillips's voice and the physical pounding of his heart. There was a lot BB could glean from riding a comms unit in contact with the man's chest. Phillips had had the sense to leave the unit clipped to his jacket pocket— conspicuous, so that the Sangheili wouldn't think he was doing any covert recording—and that also gave BB a good view of the environment.

Almost like being there, as Mal would say. Actually, I am there.

Phillips walked down a long, highly polished corridor toward huge double doors at the far end, then stopped for a moment to look back at Devereaux. She was silhouetted by the light, waiting at the open door to the landing pad, and gave him a quick wave before turning and heading back to the dropship. The outer doors closed.

Phillips was on his own now. When he walked through the imposing entrance, it wasn't the Arbiter who came to meet him but one of his staff, a particularly huge Sangheili festooned with weapons. Phillips did seem to understand them even better than BB had realized. He knew how to appear so harmless and curious that it was probably an affront to their masculinity to harm him. He was a child to them.

"I'm very grateful for the opportunity to visit Sanghelios," he said. BB could tell from the involuntary compression of the hinge-head's jaws that he wasn't expecting a human to speak so fluently to him in his own language. "Thank you for your hospitality."

There was just the tiniest hint of sly humor in that, but the Sangheili didn't spot it. Phillips followed him across the vast hall that was proof of that Sangheili taste for big, echoing, empty rooms. There wasn't a comfy chair in sight. Poor old Phillips was going to be glad to get back to *Port Stanley,* whatever enthusiastic noises he made about unprecedented access. They wound through a maze of passages until the Sangheili stopped and flung open a door.

"A child's room," the Sangheili said grimly. "Small furniture for your little human legs."

The room contained a functional mattress on a dais and what looked at first glance like a fountain. No, it was the local plumbing. *The bathroom. Oh dear. Good luck with that, Evan.* It was very Spartan, and not in the reassuringly armored and heroic sense.

"Thank you," Phillips said. "That's very thoughtful."

The Sangheili left him there and closed the door. Actually, it really was rather kind by Sangheili standards. Phillips sat on the edge of the bed and braced his elbows on his knees.

"Just the right size, Goldilocks. . . ."

"Sit up," BB hissed. "I can't see a damn thing."

"Sorry." Phillips was trying to keep his voice down. "I'm not going to think about the food. I swear I'm not going to worry about that. I'll just stick to the roast meat."

"Very wise."

They sat there for a long time in silence, wondering if anyone was ever going to come back. It was a good twenty minutes—a geological age to BB—before heavy, plodding steps echoed in the corridor outside and the door opened. This time it really was the Arbiter.

"My apologies for not receiving you, Scholar," he said. "You profess an interest in our culture. What can we show you?"

Phillips sounded genuinely taken aback. "That's most kind of you, sir. It would mean a great deal to me to see something of your ancient history." He was a little breathless. Odd: the higher gravity couldn't have been taking a toll on him yet. "If you don't regard it as sacrilegious, I'd like to see your most ancient cities. I'd like to study the evolution of your language."

The Arbiter's head jerked back a fraction. If a Sangheili's eyes could glaze over, then his just had. But it took even a prodigious intellect like BB's a second to see what was going on here. Where would Phillips be able to see the earliest examples of Sangheili language?

Almost certainly at Forerunner relic sites. Oh, very clever. Very clever indeed.

"Then I shall have a pilot show you some of the less contentious shrines," the Arbiter said. "Since the San'Shyuum were overthrown, the more pious of my brothers regard me as an atheist and a heretic."

"That's very generous, sir. May I make one more request? Do any of your youngsters have an *arum* that they would be willing to lend to me?"

The Arbiter drew his head back even farther. It was definitely either a sign of wariness or amusement. "You understand what this thing is? A very challenging puzzle."

"I know," Phillips said. "I'd like to examine one."

The Arbiter inclined his head. "Very well. As a favor to the Shipmaster of Shipmasters. The nursery analogy is complete, then."

The Arbiter left. So he had a sense of humor after all. Phillips held his breath for a few moments.

"Remind me what you're looking for," BB whispered.

"Ah, this predates our meeting, my little cubist friend. The mad monk we do business with claims to have ancient Forerunner relics from their first contact, remember. If there's a trace of that in other locations, then perhaps I can find some clues to original Forerunner data—like Halo locations."

"Gosh, I think I want your autograph."

"I have my moments. I would have asked 'Telcam himself, but something tells me he wouldn't have volunteered the information. And I really don't want to run into him on this trip."

Phillips put his finger to his lips. They waited for another half hour until another Sangheili opened the door, slapped an *arum* into Phillips's hand, and jerked his head at him to follow.

There was little useful intelligence to glean from the two-seater transport they boarded, but when the vessel lifted clear of the keep walls and headed south to the coast, a very different Sanghelios was spread below them. Phillips leaned close to the viewscreen and adjusted his jacket discreetly so that BB could get a good shot.

The glare of the sun wasn't reflecting off the sea. Fifteen

minutes outside Vadam, an area of vitrified soil covering at least ten square kilometers gleamed like an ice floe. It looked like the Sangheili had unleashed their own weapons on their neighbors and glassed them during the recent civil war.

Phillips did his idiot child act again, playing with the *arum*. "So there's been fighting here," he said. "Was it the Prophets?"

"No," the pilot grunted. "It was the war between the keeps. And the war continues." He glanced at Phillips as if he couldn't believe he was messing around with an *arum*. "Fool. You'll never release the stone like *that*."

Phillips twisted the *arum* a few more times and then shook the small gemstone from its heart. "Oh . . . beginners luck, perhaps."

The pilot stared at him. It was just as well the vessel appeared to be on autohelm.

"You have great discipline," the pilot said at last, with just the slightest hint of awe. "Can all humans do that?"

"I can only judge by similar puzzles we have . . . but no, they can't."

"Good," the pilot muttered. "Then you would be a much more dangerous species."

Phillips had a new fan. *Brilliant.* BB made a note to sweet-talk him into donating his brain to the AI program when he was done with it.

He hoped that time wouldn't have to come too soon.

CHAPTER 18

OZ, BIG MAGGIE SAYS YOU MIGHT SWING BY VENEZIA SOME
TIME SOON. I THINK YOU'LL FIND IT AN INTERESTING DAY OUT.

(Signal from Agent Mike Spenser to Captain Serin Osman,
via GC monitoring node BACCHANTE)

**UNSC *IVANOFF* research station,
orbiting Installation 03: March 2553.**

"Are you familiar with Dante's *Inferno,* Catherine?"

Parangosky placed a folder on the table opposite Halsey and pulled a datapad out of it before sitting down. The room was a windowless compartment in a UNSC orbital research station that Halsey had never known existed. If there was anything that told her she'd been out of favor for a very long time, it was finding that the chief scientist of the ONI had been kept in the dark about an awful lot of research.

But what did I expect? I kept others out of my pet projects. Now it's payback.

"It's been a long time since I read it," Halsey said.

"In English, or Italian?"

"English."

"Then you won't be familiar with a particularly exquisite Italian word. *Contrapasso*." Parangosky took an assortment of pens and styli out of her regulation black leather purse and lined them up neatly next to the folder. She was either going to make a lot of notes or sign a death warrant. "Poetic justice falls woefully short. English may be the language of Shakespeare, but when it comes to economy and elegance, you can't beat Italian."

"You're going to have to prompt me, I'm afraid."

"*Contrapasso*—the fortune-teller spends eternity in Hell with his head facing backward. The lovers obsessed by their lust are condemned to be locked in permanent coitus, longing for separation. Ironic and precise."

Parangosky got up and walked around to the other side of the table to stand over her, so close that Halsey could smell her faint perfume of jasmine and orange blossom. Halsey was rarely scared by anything that couldn't break bones or kill her, and although she was absolutely certain that Parangosky could arrange for both to happen, it was the sheer presence of the woman that made her bowels cramp.

"This is your *contrapasso*, Catherine," she said. "You've been *kidnapped*. You've been snatched away from all you know and hold dear. You've *vanished*. Only a handful of loyal and very secretive people know that you're here. And as far as the grieving world is concerned, Catherine Halsey, you are *dead*."

Halsey understood *contrapasso* perfectly now.

Parangosky was effectively the most powerful woman on Earth or off it, whatever power the UEG or Terrence Hood thought they possessed. Halsey wasn't sure if she resented that or not. She'd only ever sought to do whatever she pleased, but it was sobering to see true power exercised and realize that she could do nothing to save herself in the face of it.

But if I could walk out here now, would I? I want my martyr-dom, don't I? I've done appalling things. I shouldn't be allowed to get away with it. But it suited Parangosky for decades that I did. What's changed now?

It took Halsey a couple of moments to break off from that predator's gaze and analyze the words. She'd always thought she'd spit defiance in Parangosky's face, buoyed up by the certainty that she always escaped punishment for her misdemeanors, but it wasn't like that at all. She was a helpless, scared child. And she was scared because she had no idea what was coming next or what would happen to her tomorrow, the tactic that torturers had exploited successfully since time immemorial.

And I did that too, didn't I?

Parangosky just waited. Halsey knew she deserved whatever was coming but still felt the reflex to be defiant. She recognized this as the unlikable part of her, the self that she tried to dress up as necessary, daring, and unsentimental, but that was just a streak of selfish indifference.

"So now you know how it feels when your life is utterly at someone else's disposal." Parangosky's tone was incongruously soothing. "Like I said, you're *dead,* Catherine, and you'll remain dead for as long as it pleases me or my successor. And in the end, you may well face the actual death penalty if I decide to try you, although it's rather unsatisfying that the charges won't relate to your worst excesses."

Halsey still felt a little indignation that she wasn't entitled to. Her guilt was becoming time-worn, familiar, something she woke with every morning; but the only reason she was sitting here was because she'd done the right thing for once in her life. And Parangosky had approved everything she'd done in the Spartan program.

More or less.

"How do *you* live with it, Margaret?" Halsey asked. "Do you sleep any more soundly than I do?"

Parangosky seemed to take it as a normal conversation. She looked off to one side in the way that people did when they were considering things they didn't fully remember, and shrugged.

"I spend every day ending people's lives and manipulating them, doing things that most people in uniform would consider unconscionable. I'm not going to pretend that there's some higher morality at work here, but I'm prepared to do the dirty work to spare the consciences of others, and my barbarous acts mean fewer people die than would have done if I'd played by the rules. I think that's as near as I can come to tolerating my reflection in the mirror."

"So why am I so much worse than you?"

"Oh, I'm not sure that you are. I'm a different kind of guilty. But you *lied* to me, Catherine."

She could have said that years ago. "About what in particular?"

"Cloning."

"You knew about that."

"Not until years later."

"Oh, so this is about massaging the budget. You got your results, though, didn't you? You got Spartans, and they ended the war."

"My, there's a lot to unravel there. A little mythology, a little fudging of the dates and objectives . . . just tell me one thing. Why the clones? What was the point of that? It was totally unnecessary."

"I think the cost was justified."

"I didn't ask you for a budget analysis. I asked why you cloned those children."

Halsey found herself focused on the pens lined up on the table. For some reason she couldn't look away from them.

I thought I was trying to put things right. I told myself I went to all that trouble to spare their parents. But I should have accepted the small odds of the clones surviving. It was just a stupid, pointless token to make myself feel less of a monster.

But it made me even more of one. And now I finally know how it feels to lose a child.

"To atone," Halsey said at last. She could hear how hollow and pathetic it sounded, a spoilt brat's excuse for killing a pet. "I didn't know those clones would die."

"You're the world's foremost expert on genetics. *Why* didn't you know?"

"Because it's not that simple, and you know it."

Parangosky suddenly brought her fist down on the table with a thundering crack that no ninety-year-old should have had the strength to manage. Halsey flinched. She felt the table shudder. Parangosky leaned right over her, nose to nose, and Halsey now understood why grown men feared her more than the Covenant.

"If you genuinely believed cloning would produce a healthy child identical to the one you'd abducted, then why the hell didn't you use the clones for the Spartan program instead?"

Halsey had never asked herself that question. She realized she'd made sure she hadn't. She felt herself going under.

"*Answer me,* Doctor. You will damn well answer me."

"It's no more or less moral than—"

"You *knew.* I refuse to believe you didn't. If you didn't, then you were incompetent. And that's one excuse you can never use."

Halsey had no answer, but there were worse things than being incompetent. She hadn't felt that way before. "And you knew I'd done it, eventually, so spare me the outrage."

"Think of it as late onset retribution," Parangosky rasped. Halsey had never known her to raise her voice. "We're not dependent on your skills now, so I don't have to stomach your sense of entitlement one second longer. I've had my use of you. I think you used those clone replacements to comfort yourself, not the families. Oh, don't blame me, I made new children for them, it's not my fault that it all went wrong . . ."

Halsey could feel her breath struggling in her throat. She wasn't going to take this. It wasn't like that at all.

She went to stand up but Parangosky pushed her down again by the shoulder. "No, damn it, you'll sit and *listen* for once in your life."

"Don't you *dare* unload all this on me." Halsey had lost control of the situation, but then she realized she'd never had any in the first place. That was the most frightening thing of all. "You approved the program. You knew it was extreme. And now you've got the gall to moralize?"

"Those families had to watch their child *die*."

"They didn't lie awake every night wondering if their child had been raped or murdered or was being held captive by some pervert. They had closure."

Parangosky's voice was just a hiss. "Some of those parents are still alive."

"No." Halsey shook her head. "You can't possibly know that. I kept the only set of records. And those are a pile of ash along with everything else on Reach."

"I'm the head of ONI, for God's sake. I've had copies of all your records for many years, because you're not quite as smart as you think you are." Parangosky paused. "And you'd be surprised what survived on Reach. Your journal, for example."

Out of all the things that Parangosky could have said or done, reading that journal upset Halsey more than anything. It was a child's reaction, outrage at a parent for violating her privacy, and yet she'd always written it with that subconscious eye on posterity.

"Then I don't imagine there were that many surprises for you," she said stiffly.

"You're quite a competent artist." Parangosky straightened up, all ice again without a trace of the afterburn of anger. Halsey couldn't tell if it was a careful act or just the way the woman handled her rare displays of emotion. "I've had a team of psychologists crawling over it, but I hardly needed them."

Halsey had sketched people and diagrams as well as pouring out her thoughts. "The more people who see that, the more it compromises security."

"Whose? Yours?" Parangosky walked back to her side of the table and sat down. "State secrets are to protect society. They should conceal information like jamming frequencies, troop strengths, code words. They shouldn't be used to cover up our most bestial acts or save us from embarrassment. I've drafted a statement about my role in the Spartan program and I'll be handing it to the UEG's defense committee in due course. I'm going to die sooner rather than later, and I will *not* take this to the grave with me."

"You realize the damage that could do to restarting the Spartan program."

"There won't *be* any program—not like the Spartan-Twos, anyway. Or the Spartan-Threes, if I can help it. We're back to using consenting adults now, like we did in Project Orion."

"Now?"

"Yes, another project you were never told about. The fourth-phase Spartans. And you know why nobody told you? Because you sabotage as much as you create, Catherine. You're not a team player. But if you think you're going to spend whatever time remains to you writing your memoirs, think again. I have work for you, work that doesn't involve manipulating people, and you'll report to someone else and do as you're told. Because if you don't, I can do whatever the hell I want with you, and nobody will lift a finger to help you. How does that sound?"

Parangosky put her pens back in her purse with slow care. She hadn't written anything after all. And she hadn't asked Halsey a single question, not really, because she already knew all the answers. Detectives always said that was the best kind of interrogation.

But it left Halsey with a lot of unanswered questions. The one that was troubling her most was still the most personal and embarrassing one.

"Who else has seen my journal?"

"At least two of your Spartans," Parangosky said, heading for the door. "I'm giving the survivors the opportunity to look at their family records if they wish. But I admit I'm not sure how to square the requirement for transparency with reopening old wounds for the surviving parents whose children really *are* dead now."

Parangosky slung the strap of her purse over her shoulder and opened the door. As it swung back, Halsey caught sight of an armed marine standing outside.

She was happy to accept a life sentence—damn, even a death sentence—if they'd just gave her one chance to talk to her remaining Spartans again and apologize, perhaps even try to explain.

"Admiral? *Admiral!*" Halsey called out before the doors swung shut. "What's going to happen to them now? The war's over. What are you going to do with them?"

Footsteps came back to the door again, and Parangosky stood in the entrance.

"That depends on what they want to do," she said. "We'll probably offer them the opportunity of pulling together the remaining Spartan-Threes and integrating them into the Spartan-Four program." Halsey had to hand it to Parangosky. She really knew how to drop the full payload on someone. "Oh, and you might want to keep this. I hope you feel it's appropriate."

Parangosky reached into the folder tucked under her arm, pulled out a photograph, and held it out to Halsey.

"I thought you'd like to see the memorial they gave you." Parangosky stared into her face with evident satisfaction. It was a picture of a plaque with its neat inscription. "Ackerson has one too. Galling as it must be for you, he died a hero. Welcome to your afterlife, Dr. Halsey."

Halsey studied the photograph as the door closed again. It took her a few seconds to work out what she was looking at, but then she understood. It was a plaque on a memorial, as Parangosky had said, and it was her epitaph.

Under her carefully engraved name, service number, date of birth, and a summary of her career, the inscription read: "Dr. Halsey was on Reach at the time of its attack by the Covenant and though no body was recovered, she is presumed dead."

As memorials went, it was rather long and not at all poetic.

She wondered how much they'd found to say about John-117.

UNSC *PORT STANLEY*, Venezia Sector: March 2553.

Mike Spenser hadn't called for assistance on Venezia, but then he wasn't the kind of man to send out casual invites for no reason either. Osman checked on Phillips one last time before jumping to slipspace.

"How's he doing, BB?"

An image of a gray ceramic bowl full of something brown and lumpy flashed up on the screen in front of her. It took her a few moments to work out that she was looking at Phillips's breakfast from the perspective of his breast pocket. She was careful not to start a conversation that would attract any Sangheili attention, but it was hard to resist.

"Yum," she said quietly. "Who ate that before you did?"

Phillips let out a sigh. "Don't. Please."

"Everything okay?"

"Except the food, yes." The view shifted. Phillips had stood up and was moving toward an open window. The cityscape that Osman could see was a lot prettier than whatever he'd been trying to eat. The architecture was massive, ancient, and impressive, all billowing curves and vast arches in multicolored stone. "That's Ontom. And somewhere down there is our mad monk's HQ."

"How long are you going to be there?"

"A few days."

"Okay, we've got to slip and check out Venezia, but we'll drop out regularly to sync up BB's fragment. Don't take any risks trying to find the temple."

"I won't. I promise. Phillips out."

Osman was sure he was having the time of his life despite the occasional peaks in his heart rate. BB drifted across to the comms console and settled in front of her.

"I'm having second thoughts," she said.

"We couldn't have turned down that chance. The Arbiter would have thought it was suspicious too."

"Maybe. Has Vaz told Naomi what's in her file yet?"

"Finally. He's been very diplomatic though. He might be ninety kilos of surly muscle, but he's fundamentally kind to people he's not been instructed to kill."

There was no finer compliment, Osman decided. "He's okay, our Vaz. Although I had Mal down for ship's agony aunt."

Well, that was one boil lanced, except it wouldn't now heal cleanly. Osman made a conscious effort to put her own forgotten family out of her mind and focused on Venezia and *Infinity* until it was time to drop out of slip again and check on Phillips.

BB rotated, loitering. "Are you sure *you* don't want to know?"

"About my family?"

"Yes."

"Ever wondered why I haven't looked for myself? You must have."

"Well, motivation makes me curious. But humans ... sometimes you can step back when you know you're not going to be able to handle knowledge. That's one thing I can never do."

"Nothing more important than knowledge, right? Awareness is all we are."

"I can't hold hands or enjoy a coffee. I'm sure you can understand why my priorities aren't the same as yours."

"Okay, BB, I'll tell you. I don't want to know because I'm ashamed of myself. As long as I don't know who my folks were, I can avoid thinking what I could have done to spare them whatever misery they went through. *I was a Spartan.* Even as a kid, I could have hacked the system to find them, or even tried to escape— some kids managed that, but not me. I could have let them know I wasn't dead and that the child they'd buried wasn't me. I could have saved them from all that."

"In theory. So why didn't you?"

"I'd love to blame Halsey for brainwashing me into accepting the need for total secrecy. But looking back on it I wonder if I was just too incapable or too cowardly. Why didn't I even try?"

"You were just a child. That's why. You were a victim."

"You sure you're an AI, BB? That's a very human reaction."

"Hmm. Perhaps I need to reboot. . . ."

"Thanks for trying to make me feel better."

"I'm not. Just telling it like it is. Children don't have the power or awareness that their adult conscience tells them they had at the time. You were a child, held against your will."

Awareness is all we are. Yes, that was true. She thought of Vaz, struggling to find words for all that terrible stuff from Naomi's file, stuff that would make any human being want to throttle the life out of whoever plunged their parents into that hell, and almost weakened.

"What would you say to your parents now?" BB asked. "Purely hypothetical. If you found them now, what would you say?"

Osman had no idea. She'd shut it out of her mind a long time ago. Maybe Naomi had too, but she got the feeling that Halsey hadn't quite erased her as thoroughly as she'd wiped the other kids clean of their pasts.

"I couldn't make up for all that lost time," she said. "If they were still alive, then they'd have reached some kind of acceptance of it. What would be the point of giving them more shocks and unhappiness?"

"People have late reunions all the time. They say any time together is better than none."

"BB, are you trying to break something to me?"

"No. I said *hypothetical*. But when the Admiral finally gives her evidence to the Select Committee, we might well find parents coming out of the woodwork. There'll be no avoiding it then. We'll get every parent who ever lost a child between the ages of six and nine grasping at that straw. And that's going to be a *lot* of bereaved people."

Osman's business was intelligence, thinking through every

angle before she acted. The one thing she hadn't analyzed was what would be unleashed in the colonies when Parangosky cleared her yardarm. Part of her wanted to ignore it, and the other part saw things in terms of the impact on the UNSC.

She was going to have to get used to those gray areas.

"I'll worry about that later," she said, walking onto the bridge. The ODSTs looked up at her as if she'd said *walkies* to a dog. "Prepare to slip. Let's see how Spenser's getting on."

"Does that mean we get to stretch our legs, ma'am?" Mal asked. "Vaz wants a souvenir of Venezia."

"Why not?" That was what ODSTs were for: operating behind enemy lines. "Want to check out some covert insertion sites, Devereaux?"

"Yes *ma'am*."

Osman could have relied on burst transmissions via the Bacchante node to stay in touch with Spenser, but it was time to assess how easily she could infiltrate the colony and maybe do a few discreet checks to see if any more tagged weapons had found their way there.

And Spenser had asked. He wasn't the asking kind.

Port Stanley dropped out of slipspace a couple of hours from Venezia and took up station at a hundred thousand kilometers. Venezia might have had good tracking systems for a backwater colony, but a stealth corvette was still far beyond its detection capabilities. They wouldn't know she was there until it was too late, or maybe never, depending on what Osman decided to do if the colony pissed her off again.

CINCONI. That'll be me before too long. Damn, all this is my decision now, isn't it? Welcome to ONI command.

"Kilo-Three-Nine, this is *Port Stanley*." BB established a link with Spenser while checking on Phillips and projecting the stored feed from Ontom onto a bulkhead screen. "There, I feel better for getting all my bits back together again. Phillips looks like he's having fun."

Osman, one ear on the radio, tried to make sense of the Phillips-view of Sanghelios. She'd review the footage later, but she seemed to have lost a day of his activities in slipspace and he was now bouncing around a huge tower that gave him a thirty-kilometer view in all directions. Maybe he liked the spectacular scenery, but maybe he'd also absorbed all those tips on how to make the most of surveillance and his occasional excited comments under his breath to BB were all part of the show. Osman decided not to distract him. She could see he'd never be satisfied with a quiet life in academia now.

Got him. Let's hope it's a long career.

"*Port Stanley,* this is Kilo-Three-Nine." Spenser sounded chirpy for a change. "I've put the kettle on. Want some coordinates?"

Venezia: thirty kilometers outside New Tyne.

It was dress-down Friday as far as Mal was concerned. He held out his arms and stood in front of Devereaux in the crew bay of the dropship, waiting for an opinion.

"Do I look like an ODST on his day off?" he asked. "Because I'm not removing any more body armor."

Vaz squeezed through the hatch and inspected him as well. Devereaux cocked her head on one side.

"It's not your color," she said, tugging at the sleeve of the battered jacket. "But you've got the failed militia look down to a T. Half of them are wearing warry-looking stuff like that."

With a day's stubble, Vaz looked like a gangland enforcer. It was mainly his expression, but the scar helped a lot.

"You'll do." He leaned forward and straightened the back of Mal's collar. "Can you see this, Naomi?"

Her voice drifted over the intercom. "I still say you need me down there."

"You're a two-meter blonde, and then some," Mal said. "It'll take more than a scruffy pair of pants to disguise *that* in town."

Spartans were great assets, but they weren't made for plainclothes work. But Mal had never worked undercover before either, and neither had Vaz, so there was a certain amount of anxiety about how out of place they'd look.

"They used to say that a good SAS man could speak twenty languages while disguised as a bottle of Guinness," Vaz said. "And don't ask me what Guinness was, Devereaux. I think it was beer."

"I love your little history lessons." She took a carbine out of the locker. There was now a handwritten sign on the bulkhead that said UNSC TART-CART. "They're always so incomplete. Now if you'll excuse me, gents, I'm going to do my nails while you're gone."

She loaded the carbine and went back into the cockpit. *Tart-Cart,* as she'd named the dropship, was hidden in a deep gorge lined with pines, and even if nobody was going to stroll by casually this was still Venezia. The risks were high. But Devereaux could look after herself.

Mal and Vaz sat in the shadow of the port wing, staring down the river toward New Tyne. Spenser had said he'd be approaching from that direction and would appreciate not being shot at.

"Remind me, is he supposed to know now that we're arming hinge-heads or not?" Mal asked.

Vaz patted the canvas kitbag on his lap, full of odd bits of kit that Spenser needed. "He has to, or we can't get him to check for tagged weapons."

"Hope we don't run into our Kig-Yar fans."

"It's a big galaxy. And we all look the same to them."

"Yeah." The sound of a vehicle engine wafted in and out on the breeze. Mal pressed his earpiece. "Dev, can you see what that is?"

There was a few seconds' pause. "Looks like Spenser's pickup on the scan," she said. "Wait one . . . yes, here he comes."

Mal still had his rifle ready just in case. It was easier dealing with the Covenant, because everything that wasn't human had been out to kill him and probably still was. In the colonies, though, the enemy looked, spoke, and thought just like he did. They even carried the same weapons.

A wispy plume of dust marked the pickup's progress. Then its dull red roof broke the line of the bushes and it bounced over a few boulders to come to a halt in the cover of some trees. It was a very old civilian variant of the Warthog, heavily patched and modified. Spenser climbed down from the front seat and beckoned.

"Well, don't you two look the part," Spenser said as they clambered in. He looked Vaz over. "And you, Ivan—no getting into fights with the local Kig-Yar, hear? We can't afford to draw attention."

"I'll be good," Vaz murmured.

Mal checked out the vehicle pass taped to the windshield, surprised that Venezia had rules and regulations, but he supposed that even a bunch of terrorist scumbags had to keep a town running smoothly. The name said AMBERLEY, MIKE and the next line said SITE CONTRACTOR.

"I'm an electrician," Spenser said. "Great cover. You should see my brand-new criminal record."

"You've been telling fibs to these good people."

"Not entirely." Spenser aimed the Warthog at the road, trundling over rocks and logs to drop a meter onto the smooth black surface. It wasn't a backwater road at all, but a proper highway. "I can do basic electrical stuff. Real repairs. The bit about my being anxious to avoid contact with the CAA et al. because I skipped town with some cash from the defense forces—that's mainly embroidery."

"They check your references?"

"Of course. This is *organized* crime, not anarchic crime. Although we've got some of them too."

Mal noted the use of *we* and put it down to the spookish requirement to fit in. New Tyne loomed ahead of them, looking like a smaller-scale, low-rise version of Sydney, only in a much better state of repair. Why had he expected it to look like a shanty out of the *GlobeWar* doomsday movies that Vaz insisted on watching over and over again? These tossers had a thriving business, they hadn't had a visit from the Covenant, and they'd been here a very long time. No wonder they had a proper infrastructure.

They were a couple of kilometers out of town now. A vehicle passed them heading the other way with a Kig-Yar driving. He didn't even glance at them.

"Very cosmopolitan," Vaz said.

"You've had my last sitrep, yes?"

"No, we're a little behind with the paperwork. We've been busy."

"Ah, yes, you busted Halsey. We're going to need an awfully big carpet to sweep *her* under."

Mal's natural reaction would have been to ask Spenser if he'd heard about *Infinity* and mutter about the injustice of Halsey just being whisked away instead of being shoved out the airlock. But then he remembered that he didn't know what Spenser needed to know, what he needed *not* to know, and what he actually knew. It all went beyond opsec into a world where Mal never knew which word or syllable would be the fatal one. It was starting to permeate everything he said.

But that's the idea, right?

Vaz, who'd been slouching on the backseat with his hands deep in his pockets, came to life and leaned forward to prod Mal in the shoulder.

"Look at that," he said. "A Scythe."

New Tyne's skyline didn't just have a couple of modest sky-scrapers and a fancy spire. To the west, perched on one of the slopes, it had a gun battery. No, it had four nestled among the trees: two were recognizably M-71s, but the other two were Cove-nant kit, one of them a T-38. That was what they'd used to take a pop at *Monte Cassino*.

"You really haven't read my sitrep thoroughly, have you?" Spenser said. "This place is like a bazaar. They've got every con-ceivable kind of hardware you can imagine, and more comes in every day. We've got a Kig-Yar enclave here, Brutes, Grunts, every damn thing, and even I haven't worked out whose side each is on yet. It's Dissident Central."

"This is a joke, right?"

"I wish. You know when Earth-based terrorists used to all hang out together, and arm and train one another? Well, here we go again. It won't be long before some chancer shows up with a Sangheili capital ship and hires it out for glassing runs."

Mal turned slowly in his seat and gave Vaz a look, but he had his head down, keeping an eye on a small scanner. Mal had no idea where he could take this conversation and where it would shift from exchanging intel to talking out of turn. He'd go back and talk to Osman about that so that he had better ground rules next time out.

"You know what we're here for, don't you, Mike?" he asked.

"I know what *I'm* here for," Spenser said, not taking his eyes off the road. They were in pretty busy traffic now, crossing a bridge with toll booths. It was so *normal.* "And that's to head these bastards off at the pass. I realize you've got other bastards on your list."

"Okay, so we both know what we're talking about."

"I think so. And if we manage to kill both bastards with one stone, that would be terrific."

Mel just nodded. On the right, to one side of a grocery store— normal, normal, *normal*—there was a long road where the buildings gradually thinned out and he could see a big, wire-fenced, forbidding place like a military installation.

Spenser took one hand off the steering wheel and gestured toward it, eyes not leaving the road ahead for a second. The traffic was at a standstill. "That's where I work at the moment. The Home Guard, you could call it. Handy, isn't it?"

What a way to spend your life. Always being someone else, always among the enemy, never among your mates. Mal could see how spook personalities got bent out of shape. *I'll settle for being a tourist in this game.*

Vaz grunted. Mal looked back at him again. His gaze was fixed on the tag scanner, a small palm-sized handset that could have passed for any kind of personal comms. Vaz caught Mal looking and held it out so that he could see it.

A discreet green trace blipped rhythmically on the screen. Vaz angled the device this way and that, doing a good impersonation of casually checking his comms signal rather than what he was actually doing—picking up microtransponders embedded in ONI-supplied Sangheili weapons.

"What setting have you got that on?" Mal murmured.

"Short range." Vaz turned very slowly and ran his gaze over the vehicles around them as if he was just bored with the traffic jam. "My bet's on the truck."

"What is?" Spenser asked.

"Just checking." Mal couldn't believe that an old spook like Spenser would be troubled by gun running. "Is there some armaments clearing house here?"

"What, like Death Mart or something? Of course not. This place is porous in trade terms, shall we say, but they don't exactly have an ordnance supermarket."

"Oh well. Maybe you can take us on a guided tour of the hot spots."

"Oh, I see."

"Yeah."

"You just tracking stuff, or have you lost something important?"

So he knew. Mal breathed again. "Tracking now."

"See, it's always easier if we pool intel, but I understand."

Mal decided that Vaz's strategy was probably the wisest: silence. He sat back and just took in the rest of the ride. Spenser's Hog pickup blended into the workday traffic and as it wound its way through town, the sight of assorted ex-Covenant species going about their business started to become as routine as a mixed neighborhood anywhere on Earth.

There was no guaranteeing that any of them had ever been loyal to the Covenant, of course, least of all the Kig-Yar. There were a lot of them here.

"Okay, this is Chateau Spenser," Spenser said, turning left down a ramp and into what looked like a derelict industrial estate. "I'll bring you up to speed with what I've been monitoring since I got here. And stick the carbine under your jacket before you get out, will you? Neighbors."

He turned into the short concrete driveway of a single-story house that looked like every other one in the road. Mal glanced over his shoulder as he got out of the vehicle, but there were no lace curtains twitching. Inside, a long dimly lit passage led through to a back door with a single glass panel, with rooms to either side. Spenser led them into the kitchen.

"Down here," he said, opening the pantry door. "Long winters here, apparently. Everyone's got a store cellar."

But not everyone had ONI's latest surveillance kit stored where their pickles should have been. Spenser threw off his coat and motioned them to sit down.

"I'll get the coffee on," he said. "You can amuse yourselves looking through these. They're all congenitally paranoid about outsiders here, but that doesn't mean I haven't been able to build up profiles pretty fast." Spenser took out an old chip from his pocket, forced it into an adapter, and inserted it into his datapad. "I've been around a long time, so I've still got files from the colonial insurgency. Still a few old faces around too. And some new ones. Look." Pictures began scrolling across the small screen, some clearly from recent surveillance, others old mug shots. "Moritz . . . Lanto . . . damn, I remember shooting this jerk's dad. I should have done that before the bastard bred. That'd be before your time though."

Vaz took the pad, sat on the water-stained sofa, and began thumbing through the files. While Spenser rattled mugs and poured coffee, Mal leaned over the back of the sofa to see what kind of rogues' gallery the agent had assembled. The names meant nothing to him: it really had been long before his time, mostly while he was in short pants. There was a whole world of hostility out here that he'd never really known about.

So this was why they needed Spartans, was it?

All the files had names on them, sometimes incomplete, but that seemed to be what Spenser was doing for the time being: observing, collating, working out who associated with whom and what that association was with off-planet activity.

The Covenant was gone. These tossers could move around as they pleased now.

"Yes, it's a real models' portfolio, isn't it?" Spenser said, slapping the coffee down on an upturned crate. "Stunned you into silence with their beauty, obviously."

"We're on receive," Mal said. "Teach us, spook-master."

Spenser chuckled. "Okay, think of this bunch as divided into two species," he said. "The career terrorist, who's in it for the money, and the ideologue, who has a political mission."

He joined Mal leaning over Vaz. If there was anything Vaz hated, it was having someone reading over his shoulder, but he seemed oblivious right then. He didn't even hunch his shoulders in protest. His gaze was glued to the datapad. He'd ground to a halt at one particular file.

"Oh, yeah," Spenser said. "Now, if you saw that guy on the bus, you'd move to another seat, wouldn't you? He's got nutter written all over him. The eyes don't help. Boiled. Know what I mean?"

"I'm guessing that he's political, judging by the technical term *nutter*," Mal said.

Vaz didn't seem to be paying attention to the conversation. Spenser leaned right over him and magnified the image, and still got no reaction.

"This guy's been around awhile. Just hates Earth. If the Sangheili hadn't shot humans on sight, I swear he would have enlisted with the Arbiter. He's definitely in the market for nukes, maybe as dirty bombs, maybe as ordnance, and he's not going to be using them to rob banks."

"But he needs transport if he wants to pull a Mamore-type bombing on Earth."

"He'll get it. The Kig-Yar are getting all kinds of craft from the Brutes in exchange for arms." Spenser flicked the screen again.

"Lots of hardware floating around postwar, nobody keeping tabs on it, and suddenly our terrorists are back with more firepower than they had during the Insurrection. Weird bastard, isn't he?"

The picture looked like it was cropped from a wedding snap or something, with the man in question in a relatively tidy jacket. Mal couldn't work out from the fragment of shoulder to one side of him whether it was a bride or just a woman in a light dress, but it was a moment from a normal life. He was white-haired, maybe blond. No, Mal wouldn't have started a casual conversation him. It was those eyes.

"You still awake, Vaz?" Mal asked.

Vaz didn't move for a moment, and Mal dipped down to check he really was conscious. His eyes were shut. Then he opened them and stared at the pad for a while, not happy at all.

"I know him," Vaz said. "Or at least I know who he is."

"Shit, don't tell me you owe him money."

Vaz held the pad up for Mal, not looking at it. "We know his daughter. Check the name."

Mal tilted his head. He didn't know anyone by that name, least of all a woman. "Is she hot? Give me a clue."

Vaz turned around and even for a bloke who didn't smile much at the best of times, he looked devastated. Mal decided to cut the jokes. Spenser just straightened up and watched in silence.

"Sentzke," Vaz said quietly. "The file says Staffan Sentzke. His daughter's called Naomi."

Ontom, Sanghelios: March 2553.

BB was still undecided whether Phillips was a brilliant actor or genuinely thrilled to be allowed to wander around the ruins of Ontom.

"I think this is their equivalent of *bella Firenze*," Phillips said breathlessly. "There'll be wonderful galleries somewhere. Maybe a nice trattoria."

"Check your blood sugar, there's a good lad."

"Come on, get into the spirit of things, BB." Beneath all that excitement, he was scared. BB could detect the tremor in his voice. "Nobody gets to visit this place. Except *me*."

Phillips was sitting on the broad rail of a low balustrade next to the river that cut through the city, looking somehow less conspicuous by talking openly into his comms unit with his datapad clutched in front of him like a guidebook. Each time he moved, BB—locked into that narrow perspective from his comms cam— caught a glimpse of the audience that now gathered wherever he went. A huge four-jawed mouth with huge canine teeth suddenly filled far too much of the frame as a Sangheili leaned over to peer into Phillips's face.

"Is it true?" the Sangheili asked. "Can you speak?"

"Of course I can speak." Phillips started laughing to himself as if it was some in-joke. "I hold the Arkell Chair of Anthropology at Wheatley."

"Ah. Scholar. Yes, we thought you were too small even for a *soldier*."

Dear God, and he's still wandering around without his minder. He's going to get himself ripped apart.

BB debated whether to tell him to move on. But the locals simply seemed stunned by him. He'd collected a small crowd now, blocking out the sun and throwing deep shadows across his lap. BB decided that the locals thought he was recording copious notes. They couldn't have failed to notice him sketching furiously on his datapad like some demented tourist. Did they have any concept of human tourism? Nobody had bothered to record that in the database. They certainly understood pilgrimage, though, and BB got the feeling there was a lot of that in Phillips.

A huge four-fingered hand filled the screen. It was clutching an *arum,* this time made from pale polished wood instead of the usual ebony or mahogany type.

"Now let's see you crack *this* one."

BB had no idea how Phillips's reputation for *arum* wrangling had spread, but it had, and every time he was offered an *arum* to solve he did so in record time, and left them baffled. Now they were bringing him ever more complex ones.

There seemed to be a wide range of mechanisms, and so far Phillips had unlocked them all in less than half an hour. BB wondered whether to warn him that in the end, nobody really liked a smart-ass. He knew that better than anybody.

Phillips whistled tunelessly to himself. At one point he shook the *arum* and it made no noise. "Ah, this one's already empty," he said.

"I'd try a little humble incompetence if I were you," BB whispered in his earpiece.

While Phillips was taking an AI's eternity unlocking the *arum,* BB kept a careful eye on *Port Stanley.* Vaz and Mal were off-comms on Venezia, lurking somewhere with Mike Spenser and due to call in in an hour or so. Back at the *Tart-Cart,* Devereaux had her boots up on the console, carbine resting on her knees as she studied a service manual on her datapad. Osman was in her day cabin, poring over the schematics of *Infinity* with Naomi.

The arrest of Halsey and whatever followed would be a side-show, BB decided. The real business of coming to terms with the old Spartan program was taking place here among the few sur-vivors. It would be a footnote in the history books, like all the unsavory parts of Earth's wars, of interest only to students of medical ethics, and forgotten until the next time someone repeated it because it seemed like a really good idea this time.

"Wow," Phillips said. "Wow, will you take a look at *this*. . . ."

BB was aware of everything that was perceived by each of his fragments, but some of his multiple viewpoints got his attention more than others at any given moment. Phillips had just grabbed the top slot.

He wasn't actually talking into his radio. He'd just made a comment to himself. BB could hear the whispering noise of wood surfaces sliding against each other like a jar being opened, and then Phillips straightened up a little so that the light fell on the *arum* he was grappling with. Eventually something tumbled into his lap.

It wasn't a polished gemstone. Phillips grabbed it, and the whole angle of the image tipped as if he'd suddenly stood up.

"Hey," Phillips called. "Tell me about this one. Hang on— where did he go?"

He was facing into a forest of Sangheili at weapon-belt height. BB could only assume that whoever had handed Phillips the *arum* had disappeared. BB's first thought was that it was booby-trapped, which would have been almost reasonable given the circumstances, but even Phillips would have reacted by now if he'd found an explosive device inside.

"Who was that?" Phillips asked. His official minder, Cadan, appeared in view. The surly pilot definitely wasn't cut out for hospitality work. BB could see him now, striding toward Phillips with his huge head rolling slightly as if to say that he hadn't realized where Phillips was and he was somewhat pissed off about it.

"Who was what?" Cadan demanded.

The audience was thinning out now. BB heard something rustle in Phillips's hand. "Never mind. Somebody gave me this *arum* and walked off before I could give it back."

Cadan examined it. "The monks make that type. They make them *very hard* to open, too, so are you cheating?"

"I'll show you how I do it," Phillips promised, "but can you show me where they sell them?"

Cadan let out a long, exasperated growl. "I swear I'll kill you before this duty is over. Our children are less trouble than this."

"Indulge me. Please."

BB could now see Cadan's back as he lumbered ahead of Phillips, heading toward the old market. Phillips trailed after him. Then he started unfolding a scrap of paper, holding it close to the lens.

"BB," he whispered. "You need to take a look at this. This is what came out of the *arum.*"

It wasn't written in Sangheili. It was written in English, in awkward letters as if the shapes were unfamiliar even if the language wasn't. Few if any Sangheili could read English even if they understood some of the spoken word.

Stay off the streets. You were unwise to come here at a time like this. Wait for contact from the sanctuary of the Abiding Truth and we will shelter you.

It had to be from 'Telcam. Nobody else here would be sending Phillips notes in English. Ontom might have been too risky a lead to follow after all.

"Oh, *shit.*" Phillips's voice shook a little. "How am I going to do that with Cheerful Charlie following me everywhere?"

"Just stay calm and stall," BB said. "If 'Telcam knows you're there, he knows you've got company too."

Osman needed to be told right away. BB popped up between

her and Naomi while he hived off a fragment to place a signal to 'Telcam.

"Apologies, Captain, but I need to brief you. It won't take long. Phillips has just had a message from 'Telcam that suggests they might make a move against the Arbiter soon. He's been told to wait for further contact in case they need to shelter him in the monastery."

Osman shut her eyes for a moment. "I should have seen that coming." She stopped in her tracks. "I ought to pull Phillips out now, but that's going to raise all kinds of awkward questions. I need to talk to 'Telcam."

"I'm getting him for you."

"Okay, give me Phillips's cam feed too."

Osman stood up and started doing that slow pacing—one, two, three, turn—that was as near as she came to showing agitation. An ODST or a Spartan was a known quantity in a tight spot, but not an untested civilian like Phillips.

"Worse comes to worst, ma'am, I'll go and extract him myself," Naomi said.

The fact that Sanghelios was effectively impenetrable wasn't too much of a deterrent for a Spartan, but BB knew it was a stunt they could only pull once, and then the whole delicate relationship between the Arbiter, UNSC, ONI, and 'Telcam might come unraveled in an especially ugly way. Reigniting the war right after a peace deal wasn't quite how BB thought Osman should enter the history books.

And 'Telcam wasn't responding.

"That might not be an option," Osman said. "That's what BB's standing by for, I'm afraid."

"It won't come to that, Captain," he promised. "Although a plan B is always comforting."

BB projected the shaky, oddly angled footage onto the battle bridge monitor and Osman watched with her arms folded tightly across her chest. The view showed a street ahead, a wide boulevard lined with trees with quite a few Sangheili milling around. It was the kind of angle beloved of TV reporters who thought that kind of camera work made their undercover stuff look edgy when they'd had gyro-mounted, self-directing minicams for centuries.

Then BB recognized one Sangheili approaching Phillips on a collision course.

"Professor," 'Telcam said. "You've put yourself at great risk."

"I was invited by the Arbiter. Seemed difficult to refuse."

"But why here? Where's your pilot?"

"I left him at the inn with half the solution to an *arum*. He's quite engrossed."

The two of them started walking in another direction. There was an entrance ahead, a very old building that had to be the temple. Phillips walked through the gates and the camera went into sudden gloom.

"This is wonderful," Phillips said, swallowing hard. *Keep going, Professor,* BB thought. *That's it. Steady.* "This must date from before your first contact with the San'Shyuum."

"Correct, Professor," 'Telcam said. Figures scuttled around them in the gloom. They didn't seem to be in the building yet, just standing in the dappled shade of trees. "I'm glad you respect its antiquity and significance. Now . . . tell me what you know about Jul 'Mdama."

For a terrible moment, Phillips's heart rate went haywire. BB confirmed that the radio unit was in close enough contact with the man's chest to eject the needle, and hated himself for his instant efficiency.

"Should I know him?" Phillips managed at last.

The two of them were walking slowly toward the temple. BB could see the entrance, but there seemed to be some crowd movement streaming past them, not the usual audience Phillips now gathered. Something else had seized their attention.

"What's that?" Osman asked.

Naomi didn't blink. "I think—"

Then the cam flared, pure white, as if Phillips had turned straight into the sun and the lens was struggling for a moment, followed by a split second of silence before a dull *whoomp* registered on BB's analytical audio as an explosion. The camera tipped: maybe Phillips had fallen or dived for cover, or perhaps 'Telcam had pushed him to the ground.

"Christ, what's going on?" Osman snapped. "BB, anything you can do with that image?"

"I'll try, but—"

He could hear 'Telcam's voice, a little distant but definitely shaken. "It's not us," he said in Sangheili. "It's not *us*. What in the name of the gods is happening?"

There was no sound from Phillips, but his heart was still pounding. That was something. Then there was another booming explosion, this time without light, and the cam feed dissolved in static. BB felt as if his arm had been torn off, a real physical pain. He thought he had no concept of himself as a corporeal entity, let alone one with limbs, until that moment.

The silence was sudden and complete. And he *hurt*.

Osman reached for the comms console faster than BB imagined a human could, even a Spartan. She didn't look at Naomi.

"Kilo-Five, this is *Port Stanley*," she said. "Devereaux, get everyone back here right now. We're heading back to Sanghelios immediately. Phillips is in trouble."

And if he was, there was nothing that BB, so used to being

ubiquitous and all-seeing, could now do to help him or spare him, and he couldn't even assess the threat that faced him. He didn't even know if his fragment was still functioning. For the first time, the AI fully understood what a terrifying, uncertain world his human colleagues had to exist in.

"Let's move it, BB," Osman said. "Stand by to slip."

ACKNOWLEDGMENTS

None of this would have been possible without Microsoft staffers Jacob Benton, Nicolas "Sparth" Bouvier, Alicia Brattin, Gabriel "Robogabo" Garza, Jon Goff, Kevin Grace, Tyler Jeffers, Frank O'Connor, Jeremy Patenaude, Kenneth Scott, and Kiki Wolfkill.

Nor without the efforts of the staff at Tor Books: Tom Doherty, Eric Raab, Whitney Ross, Seth Lerner, Megan Barnard, Theresa DeLucci, Jim Kapp, Lauren Hougen, Heather Saunders, Nathan Weaver, Justin Golenbock, and Patty Garcia.

343 Industries would like to thank Bungie Studios, Scott Dell'Osso, Nick Dimitrov, David Figatner, Nancy Figatner, Josh Kerwin, Bryan Koski, William C. Dietz, Bonnie Ross-Ziegler, Phil Spencer, and Carla Woo.

ABOUT THE AUTHOR

#1 *New York Times* bestselling novelist, screenwriter, and comic book author Karen Traviss has received critical acclaim for her award-nominated Wess'har series and Ringer series, as well as regularly hitting the bestseller lists with her *Star Wars*, *Gears of War*, and *Halo* work. She was also the lead writer on the blockbuster *Gears of War 3* video game from Epic Games. A former defense correspondent and television and newspaper journalist, she lives in England.

Build Beyond™

MEGACONSTRUX.COM